Murder & Mayhem

In

Goose Pimple Junction

by Amy Metz

iconic publishing

Iconic Publishing
1050 E Piedmont Rd
Suite E-119
Marietta, GA 30062

Iconic Publishing Subsidiary Rights Department
1050 E Piedmont Rd, Suite E-119, Marietta, GA 30062

First Iconic U. S. trade paperback edition - 2012

Iconic Publishing and colophon are registered trademarks of:
Iconic Publishing, LLC.

Cover design by Karen Schmidt

Edited by Jano Donnachaidh

Dedication

Dedicated to my father for giving me the love of a good southern phrase. And to my great aunt and grandfather, whose pain and loss chronicled in this book I do not take lightly.

Acknowledgments

In acknowledging the people who contributed to this book, I must first honor the memory of the people who actually lived the tragedies of the 1930s portion of this book. While my novel is intended to be humorous, I in no way mean to diminish the tragedy of their lives. I grew up hearing the stories of the murders, and I remember thinking long ago that someone should write a book about them. It should be noted that while the story is based on real events, the characters in this book are figments of my imagination, the real murder was never solved, and the outcome depicted in this book is purely fictional.

I am forever grateful to my friends and fellow writers who offered critique, advice, and encouragement, and who supported me on the road to publishing. Thank you, Robert Hoffman, Dennis Hart, Jeni Decker, Tim Mallory, J. D. Ferrara, R. M. Keegan, Cathy Jones, Jennifer Comeaux, Nicholas Anderson, Ann Everett, Ashley Wilde, Joss Landry, Cate Carpenter, John DeBoer, Cristina Jean, and Dags, for helping me iron out the bugs and for telling me what worked . . . and what didn't. Each of these people improved my writing and kept me going. I wouldn't trade them for a farm in Georgia.

Thanks to my family—David, Jake, and Michael for letting me spend so much time in Goose Pimple Junction.

Thank you also to Karen Mathison Schmidt, for her fantastic work on the cover art. I am in awe of her talent.

Last but not least, thank you to my publisher and editor, Jano Donnachaidh, to whom I am truly grateful for his expertise and for believing in this book.

AN OLD MYSTERY

In 1932, John Hobb, father of four, is a witness to a bank robbery. He identifies the robbers and testifies against them. They are later pardoned by the governor.

In 1935, John Hobb is found in his idling car by the side of the road, dead from a gunshot wound to the head. The circumstances surrounding his death are a mystery, and the killer is unknown.

In 2010, John Hobb's murder is still unsolved when Tess Tremaine moves into his former house. She finds a job at the local bookstore, which is owned by Louetta Stafford, the youngest daughter of John Hobb. During renovations to the old house, Tess finds a mysterious old key, labeled "trunk." Mayhem ensues when she attempts to find the owner of the key: Her house is broken into twice, but nothing is taken; she finds cigarette butts and footprints outside a bedroom window; she gets threatening phone calls and ominous messages in the mail; she and a friend are attacked on the street. All of this has the opposite reaction than was intended—it doesn't scare her away, it strengthens her resolve to find John Hobb's murderer.

Murder & Mayhem

In

Goose Pimple Junction

by Amy Metz

Prologue

[1935]

Exhaust billowed into the air as the black 1934 Ford Tudor idled by the side of the road on a bitterly cold December evening. Snowflakes danced in the car's headlights as it sat just past Goose Creek Bridge, four miles south of Goose Pimple Junction, Tennessee.

Preoccupied with the cold night air, passersby were intent on getting to their destinations. While everyone who passed the Ford that night would later remember seeing it sitting on the side of the road with its headlights burning aimlessly into the cold night, none noticed the three bullet holes in the windows or the dead man slumped over the steering wheel, a bullet through his head, and a pistol in his hand.

WE'VE HOWDIED
BUT WE AIN'T SHOOK YET

swan: verb \swon\ to swear, deritive of swannee
I swan—raisin' kids is like bein' pecked to death by a chicken.

[May 2010]

"You are dumber 'n a soup sandwich, Earl."

"Oh yeah? Well, you're a hole in search of a doughnut, Clive."

Tess Tremaine walked into Slick & Junebug's Diner, past the two gentlemen arguing at the counter, and slid into one of the red vinyl booths. The old men were arguing good-naturedly, and she imagined they were probably lifelong friends, passing the time of day.

Tess smiled as she looked around the diner. She was happy with her decision to move to this friendly town. Everyone greeted her cheerfully and went out of their way to be nice. It was a pretty place to live, too. Every street in the small town was lined with decades-old trees in front of old, well-kept homes full of character, just like the citizens. She was confident she'd made the right choice. This was a good place to heal from her divorce and start a new life.

A raised voice at the counter brought Tess out of her thoughts. One of the old men spoke loud enough for the whole diner to hear.

"If I had a dog as ugly as you, I'd shave his butt and make him walk backwards," he said, jabbing his index finger at the other man.

A waitress appeared at the table. Tess hadn't seen a beehive hairdo in person until she saw this waitress. With her pink uniform dress and white apron, she looked like she jumped out of a page from the sixties. Her name tag said, "Willa Jean."

"Don't mind those two old coots." Willa Jean hitched her head in their direction. "They're about as dumb as a box a hair, but they're gentle souls underneath. Their problem is one of 'em's always tryin' to one-up the other."

She got her pad and pencil out of her front apron pocket, ready to take Tess's order, but she stopped and cocked her head, staring hard at Tess, and smacking her gum.

"Anybody ever tell you, you look like Princess Di? I just loved her, didn't you?" She bent her head slightly to the side to look at Tess's legs under the table. "Cept you look a might shorter 'n Di was. How tall are you?"

"Five-five." Tess couldn't help smiling at the compliment.

"Yep. What we have here is a mini Diana. And your hair color is a reddish-blond instead of a blonde-blonde like my girl Di. Other 'n that, honey, you could be her clone."

"Thank you. You just earned a big tip." Tess's smile lit up her face.

The waitress winked at Tess. "What can I gitcha?"

"I think I'll just have a Coke and a ham sandwich, please."

"Anything on that? Wanna run it through the garden?"

"Run it through the . . . " Tess's brow furrowed.

"Yeah, you know . . . lettuce, tomato, and onion. The works."

"Oh! Just mustard, please."

Willa Jean nodded and hollered the order to the cook as she went towards the kitchen. "Walkin' in! A Co'Cola and Noah's boy on bread with Mississippi mud."

Tess smiled and looked around the diner. The front counter was lined with cake plates full of pies covered in meringue piled six-inches high, cakes three and four layers tall, and two-inch thick brownies. Six chrome stools with red leather seats sat under the counter. The walls were packed with framed snapshots from as far back as the fifties. From the looks of it, they started taking pictures when poodle skirts were popular and never stopped. They were running out of wall space. The top half of the big picture window was covered with a "Henry Clay Price For Governor" banner. Tess spotted similar signs throughout the restaurant, and she'd noticed the waitress was wearing a campaign button.

The diner was only half full with about twenty people at various tables and booths. A few tables away, a mother was having trouble with her child. Tess heard the mother say, "I'm fixin' to show you what a whoopin' is all about!" When the little boy whined some more the mother added, "I mean it son, right now, I'd just as soon whoop ya as hug ya." She looked up to see Tess watching them and said, "I'll swan—raisin' kids is like bein' pecked to death by a chicken."

Tess laughed. "I know what you mean. But you just wait. In ten years time, you'll be wishing he were five again. The time goes by so fast."

"How many you got?"

"Just one. My son's twenty-five now, but it doesn't seem possible."

"You married?" the woman asked boldly.

"Divorced," Tess answered.

"Here's yer Co'cola, hon," Willa Jean said. "It'll be just a minute more on the sandwich. You visitin' or are ya new in town?" She propped a hand on her waist.

"Brand new as of a week ago. I've been unpacking boxes for days. I guess you could say this is my debut in Goose Pimple Junction."

"Well, all Southern Belles have to have a debut. And we're mighty glad to have ya, sugar. Lessee . . . did you buy the old Hobb house on Walnut?"

"My house is on Walnut, but I believe the previous owner's name was York."

"Yep, that's the one I'm thinkin' of. Houses 'roundcheer are known for the families that lived in 'em the longest. Them Hobbs had the house for over seventy years, up until old Maye Hobb Carter died a few years back. It was her late huband's family home and then hers, even when she remarried. She was a sweet old soul, bless her heart. We all hated to lose her, but it was her time. She had a hard life, and I reckon she was ready to meet her maker. Her daughter still lives in town, but she and an older sister are all that's left of the Hobbs 'round here. Mmm-mmm—the things that family went through."

"Willa!" the cook behind the counter yelled. "Order up!"

"Hold yer pants on, Slick," she yelled and then turned to Tess. "Be right back." Willa hurried off to get the order and came bustling back with Tess's sandwich. "It was nice talkin' with ya, hon. I'll leave ya to eat in peace. Holler if ya need anything else."

A few minutes later the door to the diner opened, and almost every head turned to see who came in. Tess noticed everybody, except for her, raised a hand up in greeting, and a few said, "Hidee, Jackson." The man's eyes caught Tess's and held them a little longer than normal. He sat down at the counter with his back to her and ordered iced tea. Willa waited on him, and Tess heard her say, "You don't need ta be any sweeter than ya already are, Jackson. I'ma give *you* unsweetened tea." She leaned across the counter looking up at him adoringly.

"Don't you dare Willa Jean or I will take my bidness elsewhere!" he said with a big smile.

Big flirt, Tess thought.

He was a good-looking man who looked to be in his early to mid-fifties, Tess guessed, but she wasn't in the market. Being newly divorced, the last thing she needed was to get involved with another man.

As far as I'm concerned, they're all Martians and are to be avoided at all cost. "Men Are From Mars, And Women Are From Venus" wasn't a best seller for nothing, she thought.

The door to the diner opened and a middle-aged man of medium height, dressed in a conservative suit and tie stuck his head in. "Vote for Henry Clay Price for governor, folks," he said, with a wide politician's smile.

"You know it, Henry Clay. You're our man. We're proud as punch to have you runnin'," Willa Jean said.

Other than the smile, Henry Clay didn't look like a politician. He had thinning auburn hair that was almost brown, and he wore round wire-rimmed eyeglasses on a round face. He reminded Tess a little of an absentminded professor.

"You gonna let out all the bought air?" Slick grumped, and Henry Clay waved and closed the door, then ambled on down the sidewalk.

Tess finished eating and walked to the counter to pay her bill. Willa gave her change and said, "Nice meetin' ya, hon. Don't be a stranger, now!"

As she closed the door she heard one of the men at the counter tell the other, "Yer so slow, it would take you two hours to watch *60 Minutes!*"

"I love this town," she whispered to herself.

* * *

A few weeks later, Tess was sitting in The Muffin Man coffee shop, laptop open, fingers flying over the keys, when she sensed someone sitting down at the table across from her. She glanced up. It was *him*. The Martian she'd been exchanging glances with for over two weeks. With her concentration broken, her fingers came to a rest. They made eye contact, and she looked away, following their pattern of the last few weeks.

Oh yeah, it was him alright. Talk about Mr. Muffin—stud muffin. She'd seen him at the post office, the grocery store, the hardware store . . . everywhere she went, it seemed Mr. Martian-Muffin was there. They'd only spoken to each other with their eyes, and she was always the one to look away first. Their silent flirting game was fun, and always did funny things to the pit of her stomach, but flirting was as far as she wanted it to go. Whenever she ran into him, she made sure to leave quickly in order to squelch any chance of conversation.

She looked back down at her computer but could still feel his eyes on her. Putting her fingers back in place on the keyboard, she couldn't think of a thing to write. Her mind was blank. She couldn't concentrate. His stare was unnerving.

Tess felt very self-conscious and couldn't help but look back at him a few minutes later. He, too, had opened a laptop, but just as she chanced another glance, he looked up and caught her eye again. He smiled.

She took a sip from her drink and tried to look nonchalantly around the store, but her eyes wandered back to Mr. Muffin. *Mr. Martian*, the scorned woman's voice in her head corrected. He was dressed casually, in jeans and a crisp light pink button-down shirt with a hint of white t-shirt underneath. He had on topsiders, no socks. She looked at her computer screen and tried to think about her book.

Focus, she told herself. *Good-looking man at eleven o'clock*, herself replied, like a bratty toddler. She took another sip of her raspberry lemonade, and eyed him over the rim of the cup.

He was tall and slim, with broad shoulders, and long legs. His wavy, sun-bleached blond hair grazed the back of his long neck. A dimple formed in his cheek when he smiled. *Of course he has a dimple*, she thought. He was hard to ignore. She looked up, and he was smiling at her again. *Dang that dimple.*

Tess put her cup down on the table, and for the benefit of anyone who might be noticing, she typed random keys just so it looked like she was working. She picked up her phone on the table, and pretended to check for messages. His table was diagonal to hers, and he was sitting facing her, so she had an ample view of him without turning her head. She peered at him from over the top of the cup as she took another sip. He was finally looking at his laptop instead of her. *No wedding ring*, she thought. *Not that it matters*, that other voice said. After a few minutes of stealth ogling, she forced herself to resume working.

She put her fingers on the keys again, but her mind remained blank. She couldn't even remember what her train of thought had been when he first sat down. Her fingers drummed on the table impatiently goading her brain. How could she be thinking this way after what she'd just been through? The cheating, the betrayal, the divorce . . . but just look at the man in front of her.

Okay, he's good looking, but he's probably a son of a gun who is indifferent, grumpy, and thoughtless. I mean, look at him. Something has to be wrong with him.

As she had this inner conversation with herself, she began to feel conspicuous just sitting there, so she started typing again, just to look busy.

She typed: *Yes, he's adorable. But he probably kicks his dog, or he's a slob, or collects his toenail clippings in a jar, or has a quick temper. Somebody who looks like that is probably very self-centered. He's probably a terrible, terrible person.*

As she typed, she began to think of more things that could possibly be wrong with this man, so she compiled a list:

He's a misogynist.
He's gay.
He's a cheapskate.
He's an axe murderer.
His idea of a good date is having you cook dinner.
He's a burping, farting Neanderthal.
He slurps his food.
He's duck footed, pigeon-toed, or flat-footed—pick one.

She giggled a little as her imaginary faults for him grew wilder and wilder. She glanced up, and found him looking at her again with that incessant grin on his face.

He gave a mock show of looking all around himself and then asked, "Do I have toilet paper stuck to my shoe?" His fingers felt around his nose, "A booger on the end of my nose?"

"What? Oh, sorry! No...I'm just...working on a book and . . ."

"Oh really? You're a writer?" He sat forward and leaned his arms on the table.

"Kind of . . . "

"Hey! I'm an author, too. There aren't many of us around these parts." He smiled that killer smile again.

She stared at him, grasping for something intelligent to say. There was no way she would tell him she was writing a romance novel.

"I'd love to read some of your work. If you'd be interested in some feedback, that is."

"Oh, that's very kind of you. I'll keep that in mind."

"As the locals would say, I believe we've howdied, but we ain't shook yet. My name's Jackson Wright. Most folks just call me Jack." He got up to offer his hand.

Ha! He's Mr. Right, she said to herself. *Mr. Right the writer.* She cleared her throat to stifle a giggle and said to him, "Hi, I'm Tess Tremaine. What kind of books do you write?" Her voice came out a little higher than she would have liked. She cleared her throat again.

"Mystery novels. I have nine published, and I'm in the process of writin' my tenth," he told her.

"A nine-times published author, wow, I'm impressed."

"Oh, don't be. I got lucky. There are plenty of writers out there who should be published and aren't. 'Course, there are also plenty who have been published and shouldn't be. But I'd be glad to help you with your book any way I can." He looked sincere.

She smiled and looked down at the table, feeling awkward and not knowing what to say. She couldn't say what she was thinking—that he could help her work on the love scenes for her book. *Oh no he couldn't*, came a sharp reprimand from the common sense half of her brain.

He broke the silence. "I'll be doin' a reading at the bookstore down the street next Saturday, and I'd love it if you came."

"I'll try to stop by."

"Let me give you my e-mail address," he said, writing on a scrap of paper.

"Writers need the support of other writers. E-mail a chapter to me whenever you're ready."

Oh, I'm ready, she thought and then mentally slapped herself.

"Do you come here often?" He laughed at himself, shaking his head. "That sounds like a lousy pick up line. I'm sorry. And considerin' my vocation you'd think I could come up with somethin' better."

"No, don't be silly," she said quickly. *Especially if it truly is a pick up line.* She took a sip to hide her smile. *You have got to get a grip, girl.*

"I do like to come here to write. Which is kind of crazy, because I don't drink coffee and it's a . . . coffee shop . . . " she felt like she was blabbering, but she couldn't stop herself. "Thank goodness they make tea and hot chocolate too. But I like to come here to write. It helps me focus. If I stay at home for too long I end up surfing the net, and I don't get any writing done at all."

"Oh, you live alone? I know what you mean, I live alone too, and sometimes the quiet is just too . . . well . . . too dern *quiet.*"

And there's one question answered—no wife. Yep, probably gay. Aren't all the good ones gay?

"So you come here to write, too?"

"Yep. I guess you could call this my office. I write here by day, and at home by night."

She nodded, not knowing what else to say. There was no way she was going to be able to write anything halfway decent with him sitting just a few feet away, and she didn't really want to continue the conversation. The look in his eye scared her. She was not going to get involved with another man. She needed to put a stop to this right away. So as she started packing up her things, she told him she was done for the day.

He cocked his head to the side and smiled, showing that dimple, as he said, "It has been a pleasure talkin' to you, Tess Tremaine. I'll be lookin' for your e-mail."

Leave now, Tess. Leave now. She smiled back at him and mumbled, "Nice meeting you. See ya."

She stood up and tried to grab her cup of lemonade, purse, and tote bag, too, but the strap of her purse slipped down her arm, causing her to spill lemonade all over the table. She felt like an idiot. She set her tote bag down, went for napkins, and frantically wiped up the spill. Waving weakly at Jack, she headed out. *I need air,* she thought as she quickly walked away, trying to get out of the shop as fast as possible.

"Tess!"

She heard him call after her. She turned around and saw him holding her tote bag, which held her laptop. He had a sparkle in his eye and was trying to suppress a smile. She had taken her purse but left the tote bag on the floor.

Feeling humiliated, she walked back to him and took the bag. When their eyes met, and their fingers touched briefly as he handed her the bag, she repeated in her head, *Martian Man, Martian Man.*

Trying to hide her embarrassment, she gave him a look that said, "Don't say a word or you're a dead man."

She turned, trying to make a graceful exit once again, but walked straight into a table. She cleared her throat, sidestepped the table, and without turning around, raised her hand up in the air as she walked out of the shop, indicating that she knew she was an idiot, and he really didn't have to point it out.

On her way out, she noticed a man in blue jeans and pointy-toe cowboy boots staring at her. She breezed past him, with the niggling feeling she'd seen him before.

How rude of him to stare.

IT AIN'T CHINESE MATH

Despurt: adjective \des-purt\ desperate
It was an act only a despurt man would commit.

[1932]

March 9, 1932 was a beautiful day in the town of Goose Pimple Junction. The sun was a welcome change from the blustery cold day before, when it snowed three inches.

There were no customers in the First National Bank shortly after two o'clock in the afternoon. The two tellers yawned and paced, waiting for the clock to chime four times, signaling they could lock up for the night. Cashier Nate Hunter walked to the front window to pull down the shade.

"What'ja do that for?" Tallulah, the other teller, asked.

"The glare of the sun was gettin' to me," he said. She shot him a confused look, and was about to say something else when her face froze and she gulped noticeably, as three men walked through the door with guns. Two of them walked to the counter, guns drawn, while a third stood watch at the bank door, a sub-machine gun propped on his hip.

"This is a holdup. We want all the money," a tall, skinny man wearing a cowboy hat boldly proclaimed to the tellers. "C'mon, c'mon, put it all in these here sacks," the stocky man in overalls and a plaid shirt said. He and the other man held out pillowcases. Tallulah froze, her eyes wide and her mouth opening and closing without anything coming out.

"What are you waitin' on," bellowed Overalls. "This ain't Chinese math, for Pete's sake. Put the money in the sack. Git movin'. And hurry it up." Looking petrified, she went to the money drawer.

"She looks as nervous as a cat in a room full of rockin' chairs," laughed Cowboy Hat.

"You," said Overalls to Nate, "git the money from the vault, too."

In a matter of minutes, the tellers, with shaking hands and rubbery legs, managed to stuff the pillowcases with forty-seven thousand dollars in cash.

"C'mon, you," the short, round man stationed at the door said, motioning with his gun to Nate, "you're comin' with us as a little insurance policy." They fled the bank, running lickety-split down the street as fast as they could while trying to lug the loaded sacks of money.

As soon as the men left, bookkeeper and auditor John Hobb came out of his office. Unbeknownst to the bandits or the tellers, he had witnessed the entire robbery. He raced out of the building, hoping to see which direction the men had gone. He saw them go south on Third Street and quickly ran back inside.

"Are you all right?" John asked, out of breath, helping Tallulah into a chair. "Did you recognize them?"

She shook her head. "I thought you were gone."

"We should call the sheriff." John quickly locked the front doors and picked up the phone.

"Sheriff! The bank just got hit. There were three of them, and they're armed. They went south on Third Street with the money and, they have teller Nate Hunter . . . "

[1979]

The young man sat at his grandfather's bedside, his head resting on his hands, which were clasped over one of his grandfather's. The room was silent except for the sound of labored breathing and the ticking of the wall clock. He sat up straight when his grandfather began speaking.

"I've done some things in my life that I ain't a proud of, boy," the old man said, lifting his head to look at the young man.

"Shhh, Papa, it's okay, it's okay," he whispered, patting his grandfather's hand gently.

"No! It ain't okay. Murder and robbery ain't okay, they're horrible, rotten acts only a despurt man would commit. But that's what I was—despurt. I want ya ta know that I only did what I had to do." He was breathless and stopped a moment, coughing, his chest heaving, as his lungs struggled for air. His grandson held a cup to his lips so he could take a sip of water before continuing.

"I wanna get this off my conscience before I die. The bank robbery of '32. I's in on it." He laid his head back on the pillows and squeezed his eyes shut. "It pains me to say that ain't all, Squirt." The young man smiled faintly at the sound of the pet name his grandfather had always used for him. Hearing it was bittersweet. He wondered if it would be the last time his grandfather said it.

"I killed a man, too. I had ta do it to protect my reputation. I *had* ta do it," the old man continued. A tear escaped his eye, falling softly down his weathered cheek; his hand gripped his grandson's tighter. "I hate havin' to admit the horrible things I done, but I want to protect my kin."

"It's all right, Papa—"

"It ain't all right, Squirt. The man had ev'dence. He told me so, right before I killed him. I laughed at him at the time. Laughed right in his face; thought he was bluffin'." He stopped again, trying to breathe, as well as keep his emotions in check.

"He said he took precautions, and one day the world was goin' ta know what a yellow-bellied coward I was. It weren't 'til after I killed him that I found the note in his pocket. It said, 'Maye, if you're reading this I must be dead. Look in the chest, Maye. It's all there.' 'Course I threw the note away, and his woman never knew about it." He sighed and then looked directly at his grandson.

"But I know he was tellin' the truth. He had somethin', some kind of proof. I'm afraid it's gonna surface some day and ruin y'alls lives. Look in his house. Promise me, Squirt, that you'll find and destroy the ev'dence before it destroys our family. I don't want ya saddled with my dirty deeds for the rest a your life. Promise me . . . " he took a deep, raspy breath.

" . . . find the ev'dence John Hobb hid, and promise me you'll destroy it."

"I promise, Papa," the young man said as a sob escaped from his throat.

THE JIG IS UP

<u>fumeer:</u> adverb \fum-eer\ from here
Where do we go fumeer?

[March 9, 1932]

"Yeehaw boys! We done it," Rod in the backseat hollered, waving his cowboy hat in the air.

"Pipe down, will ya?" said the driver.

"I'll pipe down if you'll slow down."

"Both a you knock it off, ya bunch a numbskulls. Yeah, we did it. We done pulled it off. Now we gotta git while the gittin's good. We need to dump this old heap a junk and find us a new one to take us far and wide, boys."

"Where do we go fumeer?" asked Rod.

"After we finds us a new ride, we need to split up fer a few days. Lay low. Don't do nuthin' s'picious. And YOU . . . " the front passenger, Brick, turned to Rod behind him. "Don't be drinkin' none. You get stupid when you's drunk."

"Yeah, well, I'm dry as dirt," said Rod. "'Sides, I still say we shoulda oughta taken care a the Hunter boy, 'stead a turnin' him a loose on Main."

"Yer such an ornery old cuss. Hunter won't talk. We got him jest where we wont 'im," Junior said, keeping his eyes on the road.

"Yeah, but we gotta give him some a the take," whined Rod.

"Not nessarily. Whas he gonna do—go to the PO-leece?" sneered the driver, Junior Wells. "He's in deep as we are."

"We give him his cut. We don't need no more trubba," Brick said flatly.

The other two men kept arguing, and it wasn't long before Brick had had enough. He snapped, "What in tarnation are you knuckle-heads jibber jawin' 'bout? You two nitwits shut yer pie holes. Y'all sound like a bunch of old biddies." Brick stared out the window.

"Hey. Genius, looka thar," Brick said, pointing. "Look over yonder at that Oldsie. Pull over."

"Whatta you thinkin' Brick?'

"Whatta you think I'm thinkin'? Ah swear, if yer brains were dynamite, you couldn't blow your nose." He shook his head. "I don't rightly know fer sure if our car was spotted, but I ain't a gonna chance it."

"Have you lost all of your mind? We can't just walk up and take that car," cried Rod.

"Why not?" Junior asked.

"Somebody's bound to see us, that's why not."

"Then we wait," said Brick. "We sit and watch the house, if'n nobody's around after an hour or so, we hep ourselves to that there Oldsmobile."

An hour later, Brick pushed on Rod's arm to wake him. "Hey Roddy. Wake up, ya old slug." Rod's head bobbled, and his eyes opened halfway. Brick snapped his fingers two-inches in front of Rod's face.

"Gad night a livin'. Would you get offa my back." Rod squinted as he woke up, and pushed Brick's hand away from his face.

"Roddy, listen up—you sidle up over thar and get that car. We'll gwon up the road a fer piece and you come pick us up. We'll leave this heap on the side a the road."

"How come I gotta do it?"

"'Cause this is yer first rodeo."

Stealing the car wasn't a problem since the keys were already in it. Nobody in the country bothered with taking the keys inside the house. Rod started it up and drove two miles and picked up the other two men. He dropped Brick off in Flat Rock and Junior in Greasy Creek. Then he drove on to get lost in the big city. He was going to have a vacation. He figured he'd earned it.

[June 2010]

The man had cold eyes. He looked out of his office window at the hustle and bustle of downtown Goose Pimple Junction, lost in thought. He wasn't sure if he had a problem brewing or not, but he was intent on finding out. The evidence was in that house. He was sure of it. This was the second time the sale of that house had caused him angst; the second time he had to be sure the new owner was settled in and done nosing around their new digs. Not that this new owner would find anything. He'd already turned the house upside down and came up empty, and she seemed too ditzy, anyway. There was even a chance it was gone by now, if it had ever really been there. Whatever 'it' was. He just had a bad feeling. He promised to find whatever it was and destroy it, and by golly, he was going to keep that promise to his dying day. He picked up the phone.

"Willy?" he said. "Yeah, it's me. Ya got anything new for me on that project we discussed?"

"Naw, not yet." Willy yawned into the phone. "I've been followin' her around just like you said, but I ain't seen or heard nothin' to be concerned about. I think you're overreactin'. Fact is, I think this'll be an easy, *and* fun, little project." He snickered into the phone.

"Well, as long as I'm payin' you, do what I tell ya. Keep an eye and ear on that ditz, ya hear?"

* * *

Tess had been married for twenty-six years and divorced for ten months. She'd only been living in Goose Pimple Junction for a month, but was feeling very content for the first time in ages. She'd been put through the wringer in the last few years; first, suspecting, and then finding out for sure that her husband was not only having an affair, but had several over the course of their marriage. She was glad for this fresh start.

Tess walked into Stafford's, the town's bookstore, and immediately felt a sense of tranquility. She looked around at the exposed brick walls and bookshelves packed to the rafters with books, excited to find it wasn't one of those cookie-cutter mega-bookstores. This bookstore had character. It made her want to grab a book, sit down in one of the store's big, cushy chairs and settle down for an afternoon of reading. All was quiet in the bookstore except for the hum of traffic from the street. The sights, sounds, and smells of the bookstore wrapped their collective arms around her, giving her a peaceful feeling. The aroma of the coffee shop next door made her inhale with pleasure. Tess didn't care for coffee, but she loved the smell of it. She could picture herself seeking the cozy confines of the store often.

So many books, so little time, she thought.

She walked past cute knick-knacks for sale in the cooking section. She stopped briefly in the section that held upscale journals and greeting cards, before noticing a huge black and white plaster of Paris cow jumping over a moon, hanging from the ceiling in the children's section.

I wonder if they have my book.

She found it quickly: "Brown Dog," by Tess Tremaine. It always gave her a thrill to find *her book* in a bookstore. She picked it up, running her hand lovingly over the cover. She wondered if she was doing the right thing in switching genres. She'd never written romance before.

"You can't do it," her ex-husband had said. "It was a fluke you've even had a children's book published. *You* write a novel? Ha. That's laughable."

She so wanted to prove him wrong.

Tess finally ended up in the huge section designated for fiction. *It wouldn't hurt to take a look.* She walked down the row until she was in the W's, brushing her finger over the book spines, stopping when she found the name "Jackson Wright."

She pulled the book out and turned it to the back cover. *Gosh, that man's got looks to spare.*

She gave a self-conscious glance around to see if anybody was watching and then took five of the books to the cashier, exchanging smiles with the man wearing cowboy boots sitting in a chair by the fireplace.

The clerk was an older woman, looked to be in her mid-to-late-seventies, with big hair and bright makeup. She greeted her with a "Hidee," and looked down at Tess's purchases. "Did you know the author is a res'dent of this town?"

Tess played it cool. "I think I did hear something about that."

"Oooohh, I hafta say, that Jackson is a dream." She patted her brassy-red teased and sprayed-stiff helmet-hair. "Wish we had more like 'im. I'z born 'n raised here, matter fact, my kin have always lived here, goin' back to my great great-granddaddy. Yes ma'am, I'z born here, and I'll die here. And I make it my bidness ta know everbody in town. Most everbody's a right neighborly sort, but we get all kinds ya know; and some are about as welcome as a skunk at a lawn party."

"Is he a native of Goose Pimple Junction?" Tess broke in.

"Who?" The woman looked puzzled. She glanced down at the books she was holding and slapped her head.

"Well lands sakes, you mean Jackson Wright, don't you? Nemmine me, I shouldenoughta get off on tangents. Nope, I reckon he's been here for . . . law . . . 'bout five years now. Jack lives in one a the big ole Victorian houses on Maple Street all by his lonesome, right next door to me actually." Tess nodded politely, trying to keep up with the accent.

"A course the house where I'z raised is over on Walnut. It was up for sale not too far back. I thought a buyin' it, but that house holds too many mem'ries for me. I haven't met the new buyer yet—I hear she's a divorcee from up north—but I 'spect I'll stop by sometime soon to say howdy-do and welcome her to town. Just as soon as I get some of this dad-gum work outta the way. I swan, I've been busier 'n a stump full of ants. Are you new in town or just passin' through, honey?" The woman behind the counter finally took a breath.

What a talker. "I only moved in a few weeks ago. Actually, the house I bought is on Walnut. I live at 117 Walnut—that wouldn't be your old house would it?"

"For law's sake child, it sure is." She clapped her hands together. "Well I'm just pleased as punch to find out that it has such a nice new owner. Frankly," she lowered her voice and leaned in toward Tess, "I don't think the people you bought it from had a lick a sense. They were about half a bubble off plumb, if ya know what I mean. And Lordy, they up and sold the house and moved outta town faster 'n green grass through a goose. Great day in the mornin'. Where are my manners? I'm Louetta Stafford, but folks call me Lou." She reached out to shake Tess's hand. "So tell me—how you likin' the house, honey?"

"Oh, I love it. I really do. I want to do some redecorating, but the house has great bones."

"Oooh law sugar, tell me about it. It broke my heart to see what those people did to that house. They just did it up on a lick and a promise . . . " she stopped talking when she saw Tess's quizzical expression. " . . . they didn't take their time, is what I mean. They only had the house for 'bout six years—jest long enough to make a mess of it."

"Well don't you worry, I intend to bring it back to its full glory.

I love the little house. I'm looking forward to working on it all on my own."

"Sounds like a lot of work for one girl."

"Well, now that I don't have to meet someone else's needs all the time, I'm going to concentrate on my own for a change. I'm going to fix up the house and write a book."

"Book. Oh, my. I forgot all about ringing the books up for ya." She picked them up from the counter. "Here I am flappin' my gums, and I should be checkin' you out. Say . . . did you get a gander at his picture on the sign here? Look. Ain't he the best eye candy around?" She pointed to a sign next to the counter.

"Mmm hmm," Tess mumbled, nodding her head and thinking, *absolutely*. The sign was an advertisement for Jack's book reading on Saturday. *Yep, something has to be wrong with that man. He's too perfect.*

"He'll be here on Satudee night, ya know." Lou had the thickest southern accent Tess had ever heard.

"No, I hadn't heard. But that sounds interesting." She tried to sound nonchalant.

Lou seemed more than willing to gossip, and wanting to pump the woman for dirt on Jack, Tess took a stab at bluffing. "So, um . . . I heard a rumor. Someone said he's gay. Do you think it's true?"

Lou looked at her as if she had just told her she'd seen Elvis in the non-fiction section. "Honey, I can spot a three-dollar bill a mile away, and if that man's gay, then I'm Aunt Jemima."

"Well, if he's not . . . ahem, a three-dollar bill . . . and he's not married, then something must be wrong with him—right?" She wondered if she was sounding cool and detached.

Lou pushed her big bosom over the counter towards Tess, and said in a hushed voice, "Well, if you want to know what I heard . . . ." She leaned in towards Tess. "I heard that he'd gotten a divorce right before he moved here because he was steppin' out on his wife."

She nodded her head once in punctuation to this statement, then straightened up and added, "But I'd let him eat crackers in my bed anytime, baby." And then she broke out laughing.

Both women were giggling like a couple of schoolgirls and hadn't noticed the ringing of the tiny bell over the door that signaled someone had entered or left the store. Tess took the bag of books, said thank you, and was putting the change in her purse as she turned and headed for the door.

Whump. Something hard stopped her in her tracks. That something grabbed both of her forearms to keep her steady. She looked up into none other than Mr. Jack Wright's baby blue eyes.

"You're like a one-woman wreckin' ball, Tess Tremaine. Where in tarnation are you goin' so fast, and what's so funny?"

"Oh! Hi! Jack!" she sputtered. *I do a lot of babbling around him. That and running into things.*

Lou peered over the counter and slammed her hand down on it.

"Well I'll be doggone—speak a the devil."

Quiet, you silly woman, don't say another word, Tess silently willed her. *Don't you dare tell him about the . . .*

"Is that right?" He looked from woman to woman, amusement showing on his face.

"Yessirree, Ms. Tess here just bought five 'a your books, and I was tellin' her 'bout your book readin' here on *Satudee night."*

. . . books. Don't say a word about the books. Oh, she said it. Crap and double crap. Tess's face turned bright red.

"Oh reeeeeeeally," he said, cocking his head and raising one eyebrow. There was a sparkle in his eye, and a dimple in his cheek. "Ya don't say."

"Oh, well, yes . . . I thought if I was going to have you help me at all with *my* book, then I should at least be familiar with your work . . . " she trailed off, not even believing that line herself. "But I'm afraid I have a paint brush calling my name, so I have to run." What she really had to do was get out of there fast, before she said or did anything else to humiliate herself even more.

Tess headed for the door, embarrassed to the core, not daring to look anyone in the eyes. She knew the jig was up; she just didn't want to admit they knew, that she knew the jig was up. But she glanced at him as she closed the door, and the look on his face told her—the Jig. Was. Up.

She walked out onto the sidewalk and stopped to take a deep breath. *Stupid, stupid, stupid.*

The door opened, and, afraid it was Jack, she started walking.

"'Scuse me, ma'am," she heard a deep voice call behind her.

She turned to see if he was talking to her. The voice belonged to Mr. Cowboy Boots.

"Sorry to bother you, and I hope you'll forgive me, but I couldn't help but overhear your conversation in there. I wanted to offer you my services. I'm Willy Clayton."

She looked at him, confused, not knowing what services he was talking about.

"I'm a house painter and handy man," he explained. "And all-around good guy," he flashed her a smile that she thought was probably an attempt at charm, but made him look creepy.

She couldn't help but notice in his faded Levi's and dirty cowboy boots he looked nothing like a handy man.

And the verdict was still out on all-around good guy.

A MESSAGE
FROM THE MARBLE ORCHARD

gwon: verb \gwon\ go on
Gwon over there and search the room.

[1932]

Ten days after the bank robbery, Rod Pierce was found drunk and unconscious in a motel room four hours away from Goose Pimple Junction. A deputy filled the sheriff in after he brought Pierce to the city jail.

"Coots, whatta ya got?" the sheriff asked.

"A one 'Rod Pierce,' who's been over to the No-tell Mo-tel for 'bout six days. Man'ger said he ain't paid fer his room in over three days, so he went in to check on him. Found him drunk as a skunk and called us. His I-dentification says he's from Goose Pimple Junction. Considerin' there was a hold up at the First National a week or two back, I thought you might want to know 'bout him."

"That was good thinkin', Coots. Do some checkin'. See if he's got a record."

Coots started to walk away, and the chief called him back. "There were three of 'em that did that job at the bank. Any idea if Pierce was alone at that motel?"

"I'll check that out too."

"And gwon over there and search the room. See if anything incriminatin' turns up."

"Sure thing, Sheriff."

Coots returned to the sheriff's office a short while later, with a grin a mile wide.

"Bull's-eye, Sheriff. Pierce is a former convict. Served time for petty theft and a gasoline station robbery," Coots proudly announced.

"Well if that don't put pepper in the gumbo." Sheriff Bone was pleased.

"I'll bet the police chief of Goose Pimple Junction will want to talk to this Pierce fella."

"Find anythin' else out?"

"Naw, motel owner says he was alone, far as he knows. I didn't find nothin' in the room but a bunch of empty bottles and some false teeth."

"Awright. I'ma give the chief over in Goose Pimple Junction a call. Ya never know. We may of nabbed one of their bandits."

The sheriff dialed the phone with one hand, while he took a big gulp of coffee with the other. As he waited for someone to answer, he lit a cigarette.

"Goose Pimple Junction Police Department, how may I hep ye?"

"This is Sheriff Ezra Bone from the Helechawa Po-leece Department. I need to speak to the chief, please."

"Hold one moment." Seconds later, the chief got on the line.

"This is Bug Preston."

"Chief Preston, this is Sheriff Ezra Bone, over in Helechawa. I got a man whose ID says he's from down your way. Name's Pierce. Rod Pierce. Ever heard of him?"

"Yep, I've heard of Rodney Pierce. Be glad to not hear from or about him ever again."

"Zat right?"

"We've had him for a bunch of robberies. When he's not stealin' from somebody he's drinkin' the town dry. Which is hard to do, considerin' we got a dry country already." Chief Preston laughed at his own joke.

"Considerin' your recent bank robbery, I thought you might be interested to talk to him. I got him locked up on intoxication. I can hold him here for ya if ya want."

The chief sighed into the phone. "I got three witnesses to the bank job who I could bring up. See if they can finger him. Might take me a few days to round 'em up and get over there."

"No problem. He ain't goin' nowhere. We'll dry him out and hold onto him."

[June 2010]

Tess changed clothes six times, finally settling on white slacks, a black top, and black sandals with a one-inch heel. She applied too much makeup, washed it off and applied it again, this time using a lighter hand to outline her green eyes with charcoal liner and to accentuate her heart-shaped face with 'Cedar Rose' blush. Scrutinizing her wavy, shoulder-length reddish-blond hair, she fixed and unfixed it until finally satisfied. Well, almost satisfied. After putting on dangly earrings and a charm bracelet, she sprayed perfume into the air and walked into it for just the right amount but not too much. *Well old girl, that's about as good as it's gonna get. You might as well get your butt on out of here.* Taking a deep breath, she started out.

She decided to walk. It was a nice night, and Stafford's was only five blocks away. The store was already crowded when she arrived. It appeared that Mr. Jack Wright had a following, aged anywhere from fifteen to eighty. Trying to look blasé as she scanned the room for Jack's dirty-blond head, she felt a hand on her back and turned to look directly into Jack's blue eyes.

"I'm glad you came." He smiled at her, flashing that sparkle in his eye, and dimple in his cheek.

"Oh! Yes—hi!" Nonchalantly, she straightened the books that she almost knocked off the shelf when she'd wheeled around, startled. She was thankful Jack pretended not to notice.

"You're just in time. I'm getting ready to start." Walking backward to the front of the room, he added, "Don't disappear on me when it's over—okay?"

Almost everyone had taken a seat, and the room quieted as he approached the front of the store. Tess nodded to him, feeling self-conscious that everyone was watching them with interest.

She sat down next to an older couple in the back who introduced themselves as Slick and Junebug Calloway and said they owned the diner down the street.

"Oh, yes, I've been there. I love your place."

Lou stood at the front of the room resplendent in her hot pink dress, big hair, and bright makeup. She cleared her throat until everyone stopped talking. "I wanna thank y'all for comin' out tonight. As I'm sure you're aware," she said with a huge smile, "we have a celebrity in our midst. Jackson Wright is an accomplished author who hails from our fine town. His books have consistently hit the New York Times Bestseller's list, and his ninth and newest book, "Wyatt's Revenge," has just come out. We have the decidedly special honor of bein' the first ones to get a peek at it, as well as to hear a bit of it read to us by Goose Pimple Junction's favorite citizen, Mr. Jack Wright himself."

Everyone clapped as Jack stepped forward, hugged Lou, and thanked everybody for coming.

Telling the audience he appreciated the turn out, he looked at Tess, locking eyes with her before sitting down in the big overstuffed chair and launching into reading. Firm, confident and funny, Tess liked his style of writing. His voice was strong and smooth—very masculine and powerful. With the intent to hook everyone and leave them desperate to find out the outcome of the book, he purposely ended with a suspenseful chapter.

Afterward, Tess browsed the new fiction section, while Jack signed books and charmed the socks off everyone who came to meet him.

"Well hidee, sugar. I'm so glad you came." Tess looked up to see Louetta rushing up to her. "Whadja think a the new book? I think it's gonna be the best one yay-et," Lou said, turning a one-syllable word into two.

"You may be right. And this is a great turn-out tonight."

"Idnit somethin'?" She looked around the store. "There must be fitty people here tonight. I sure am glad you made it out. I know Jackson will 'preshade it."

Tess's mind was working overtime to keep up with the Southern speak.

"Well, didja read the books? Which one didja like best?"

"The books? Oh, the books I bought—yes, I did like them. Well, it. I've only had a chance to read one of them so far. I've been working on the house a little, painting, scraping—"

Lou interrupted, "Oh honey, tell me 'bout it. If it's not one thing, it's another. This place just about runs me ragged. 'Course it's gotten a lot worse since Betty Jane had to quit. She had to have surgery—female problems, don't ya know."

"So . . . you own the bookstore?" Tess asked.

"Sure. Didn't I tell you that?"

Something clicked into place, and Tess impulsively decided to ask for a job. "Did you say you're short of help here, Lou? Are you hiring? I would love to have a part-time job."

"And I can vouch for her, Lou, she's good people," Jack drawled, coming up behind her.

"Well honey, you must be heaven sent. I've been prayin' for someone reliable to come along. I knew it would be all right. Just gotta have a little faith and a lot of patience. But God is good, and I knew he'd send me somebody special and here you are." She gave Tess a big hug, and then gave Jack one too. Beaming, she said to Tess, "I always take any chance I get to hug that man." She giggled. "Now when can you start, Tess?"

"Well, I...I suppose any time," she stammered, taken aback at how fast she had landed a job and at how forward Lou was with Jack.

"Now don't go bein' too pushy, Lou. You don't wanna scare her off, do ya?"

"Pushy, smushy, Tessie here will get used to me."

"Tess, you have to speak your mind around Lou. Don't let her work you too hard," Jack warned, putting an affectionate arm around Lou.

"Well, I'm not afraid of a little hard work, and I'm sure we can come up with a schedule that will suit us both."

"That's the spirit. Now come on back here, and we'll get some paperwork done and iron out the details." Lou headed for the back of the store, and Tess started to follow.

"Actually, Lou," Jack called after her; she stopped and turned. "I was hopin' to talk Tess into goin' for a drink with me." He looked questioningly at Tess.

"Well bless your heart, of course you were. Don't let me stop you! Y'all run along and we'll talk tomorrow, Tessie. Jest come on by in the mornin' and we'll get everythin' smoothed out."

Tess laughed nervously. She didn't want to go anywhere alone with Jack, the Martian man. The cheating Martian man. She'd sworn off men. Especially lying, cheating men.

"Lou, why don't you join us?" Tess asked, hopefully, silently saying, *Pleasepleaseplease.*

"Well, I'd love to," she said, clapping her hands together. "It looks like everybody's clearin' out of here. Jest let me get my purse and close up. I'll meet you two kids outside in two shakes of a rat's tail."

"I think I love that woman. Nobody's called me a kid in ages," Tess said, as they walked outside.

"Lou's a honey. Salt of the earth. Just be careful of what you tell her. Her tongue's tied in the middle and loose at both ends."

"Is there a thesaurus for Southern speak I could buy? A dictionary for colloquialisms?"

Jack laughed. "I mean if you don't want anyone to know it, don't tell Lou."

Tess and Jack stepped out onto the sidewalk and stood under the bookstore's big green awning. It was dark out, but the street lamps lit up the sidewalk. The trees lining the sidewalk were strung with little white lights year-round, and they gave a magical look to the town square.

"Jack —"

"You really—"

They both stopped, and he said, "Ladies first."

"I was just going to say I want to thank you for vouching for me. You don't even know me—I could end up making you look bad."

"Or you could end up cursing me for getting you involved with Lou." She looked at him funny and he said, "I'm only kidding, she's a dear, sweet, old woman, and I can tell you are, too."

Tess's expression changed from questioning to a hard stare, and he quickly corrected himself.

"I mean the sweet part. Not the old lady part. Seriously, you two will hit it off. Just don't tell her I said she was old. I'm happy to help, but I wanted to warn you not to let her bulldoze you into working more than you want. She has a way of talking people into things before they know what they're doing."

Just what has she talked you into, Jack? No, that's ridiculous. Lou must be close to eighty years old. I'm getting ridiculously paranoid. Maybe that's a side effect of being married to an unfaithful man.

"She has a way of talking, period, if you know what I mean," he added.

"Oh, I see." She was looking everywhere but at him.

"What'll it be tonight? A drink or a cup of coffee? I'm buyin'."

"Make it a sweet tea and you're on," Tess said, hoping Lou would hurry up.

* * *

Tess couldn't sleep. It was two in the morning when she finally gave in and looked at the clock. After reading another of Jack's books until well after midnight, she tossed and turned for more than an hour. Maybe it was the sweet tea that was keeping her up. Or maybe it was thoughts of Jack. He'd done some pretty heavy flirting, and she was glad Lou had been along as a buffer. Jack was good-looking, intelligent, charming, and interesting. He made her laugh—the one trait that she found sexiest in a man. But she didn't want to get involved with Jackson Wright. She needed a break from men. And she wasn't going to fall for a cheating man again. Jack was off limits. He had to be.

Not wanting to think any more about Jack, she put a light sweater on over her camisole, grabbed her laptop and headed out to the covered porch—one of her favorite things about the house.

She settled into the overstuffed cushions of the big wicker chair. It was a beautiful summer night; quiet except for the crickets' song. She took a deep breath to catch the faint scent of honeysuckle in the air. Opening the laptop, she brought up the page where she'd stopped writing.

She drew a blank. Relaxing into the chair, she tried to get her writer's head back on, wracking her brain for what she wanted to say. Nothing. For over thirty minutes she couldn't think of a thing to write.

I can't sleep, I can't write, I might as well tackle the bedroom.

Tess headed back inside and turned on a light in her bedroom. The wallpaper in the room was a big, gaudy print that hurt Tess's eyes to look at. It had big purple and red flowers on a deep burgundy background that made her feel like it was screaming at her.

"It's either you or me, wallpaper. And I like this house, so guess what?"

She took off her sweater, changed into her old grubby jeans, and gathered up all of the necessary tools. With a scraper in her back pocket, a spray bottle filled with water, and her iPod set to shuffle, Tess began spraying, scraping, and peeling off the offensive wallpaper layer after layer off the top half of one section of the wall, all the while singing along with the music.

Tess sat down on the floor to work on the bottom half of the wall, tossing the paper onto the floor, intending to scrape continuously and clean up later. Some of it came off in long strips, but most of it came off in small, thin pieces.

After working for an hour, she began to feel the effects of lack of sleep. She started cleaning up the scraps littering the floor and noticed some of the smaller pieces had fallen into the floor register under where she'd been working. Retrieving a screwdriver, Tess opened it up.

Sticking her hand in, she not only grabbed a handful of paper scraps, but also a whole warren of dust bunnies. "Ew. Yuck!" she said aloud.

Kneeling down to get better access to the register and squeezing her eyes closed in repulsion, she swept her hand along the bottom of the vent to grab as much as possible. Her fingers grazed something hard and cold, and she heard it slide across the bottom—definitely not a dust bunny. She scooped up the foreign object, a couple of crayons, and a handful of scraps, and dropped it all on the floor.

Klunk.

Brushing the dust balls away, she saw a little copper key with a small label attached by a string of yarn. It didn't look like an ordinary house key. She picked it up and turned the label over. In faded pencil it said simply, "trunk."

"That's odd," she said aloud.

Her thoughts immediately flew to Lou at the bookstore. This was her family's old house. Maybe she would know what the key belonged to. It did look very old. She'd have to remember to ask her about it tomorrow.

Tess put the key on her bedside table and finished cleaning up her mess. Back in bed, as she drifted off, she lay there thinking about how working at Stafford's would be a good way to get out of the house and meet people, while also allowing her to pick up some extra cash.

Just before she fell asleep completely, her thoughts turned to her discovery. She wondered who the trunk belonged to, how long the key had been lost in the register, and whether anyone had missed it.

YOU KEEP DRINKIN'
AND I'LL KEEP THINKIN'

hireyew: salutation \ hahy^{uh}r-yoo\ how are you
Good morning, hireyew?

[1932]

Police Chief Bug Preston took three witnesses, John Hobb, Nate Hunter, and Tallulah Maggard, to the big city of Helechawa eleven days after the bank robbery, to identify Rod Pierce as one of the bandits.

The chief and the witnesses arrived at the jail and were led to Pierce's cell. Rod Pierce was disheveled, wearing clothes that looked like he'd slept in them for a week. It had been even longer since he'd shaved, and he didn't have his false teeth in. Red-rimmed grey eyes sat under dirty, matted brown hair. Staring at them blankly through the bars, he decided he needed a drink. The others thought he needed a bath.

"Well?" asked the sheriff. "The man's a drunk and a bum. Question is, is this yer man?"

John Hobb said, "That's the man I saw pointing a gun at our teller and demanding money."

Tallulah agreed. "Yessir. That's the man who done stole our money and nearly scared the fire outta me."

Nate Hunter studied Pierce for several minutes before saying, "I *s'pose* he could be one of the men I saw in the bank that day."

"What do you mean '*you s'pose*'? Is he or id'n he?" Bug Preston asked. Hunter nodded his head.

"We'll need one a you boys to transport him to Goose Pimple if ya don't mind," Preston drawled to the sheriff.

"Chief, do you know how our town got its name?" Sheriff Bone asked, out of the blue.

Everyone looked at him blankly.

"Helechawa. It's short for 'It's hell each way'," he laughed. "But the town itself ain't no bed a roses neither. Old Coots here'll be glad to oblige, just ta git outta town."

[June 2010]

Tess slept for only six hours before she got up, got dressed, and made a batch of muffins to take to Lou. She walked into the bookstore shortly after it opened. There were already several customers in the store plus one who followed her in. She noticed his cowboy boots right before she noticed the red Chuck Taylor sneakers on a pair of skinny, hairy legs inside the store.

The tennis shoes belonged to the skinniest teenager Tess had ever seen. She thought, *He's so skinny he probably has to run around in the shower just to get wet.*

When they'd gone out for tea after the book reading, Lou had told her there was another part-time employee who mostly kept the shelves stocked and in order and carted around the heavy boxes for her.

He was dressed in khaki cargo shorts and a t-shirt imprinted with the words, "I put ketchup on my ketchup." Tess tried to suppress her smile at his t-shirt but failed. She wasn't sure which was funnier: his name, the way he looked, or his t-shirt.

"You must be . . . Pickle." She'd never forget his name, that was for sure, but she'd have a hard time calling someone "Pickle," even though Lou assured her everyone called him by his nickname.

"Yes'm. Can I hep you?" He had a thick southern accent and a friendly smile.

"I'm Tess Tremaine, I think we're co-workers now. Lou hired me yesterday."

Comprehension rose on his face. He wiped his hands on the side of his shorts and stuck out a hand in greeting. Pickle looked to be fifteen or sixteen-years-old with blond, almost white, hair and a cowlick at the top of his head. He had big brown eyes and freckles across his nose. Tess shook his hand, thinking he was polite but shy. After an awkward silence she asked, "Is the boss around?"

Just then, Lou came out of the office. "Tessie!" She had on the brightest yellow blouse Tess had ever seen and lime green pants. Her hair was particularly bouffant, and her rouge and lipstick were bright and freshly applied, highlighting, instead of disguising, her many wrinkles.

She took one look at the pineapple muffins and said, "Well I'll be. You are definitely hired, honey. What a sweet thing for you to do. Now come on back and we'll have us a chat. Peekal, mind the register," she called over her shoulder.

"What's Pickle's real name?" Tess whispered, walking alongside of Lou.

"His given name is Dylan."

"How did he get the name Pickle?"

Lou looked up at the ceiling like she was pulling an answer from the air and finally said, "I think it was his daddy who first called him that on account a the name *Dylan* remindin' him of dill pickles. I think his mama liked the name Dylan, his daddy didn't, they had a coin toss, and he lost. He never took to it, though, and started callin' him 'Peekal.' I guess it just sorta stuck. He's a hard worker, but dumber 'n a bag of hammers, so I'd rather not leave him out there by himself for long. Let's go over some things right quick."

They sat in Lou's office discussing what Tess's duties would be, how much time she wanted to put in at the store, and filling out paperwork. After everything was ironed out, Lou sat back. "I didn't get a chance to ask ya last night—how're you takin' to the house?"

"Oh, I love it, Lou. I absolutely love it. I love the character of the house—the arched doors, the exposed brick walls, and the hardwood floors. And I love the covered wraparound porch. The house just needs a little redecorating, which I'll do mostly myself."

"Lands sake, child, tell me about it. Like I told you the other day, the people had it before you didn't have a lick a sense. It broke my heart to see what they did to it."

The front bell jingled, signaling that someone had come into the store. Lou leaned back in her chair so she could peer around the corner of the office door and see out into the store.

"Looks like the place is fillin' up. We best rescue Peekal. Come on, I'll give ya a crash course on the register, and then I'm puttin' you to work."

They started for the front desk. As they walked, Tess said, "I wanted to ask you about something, Lou. I've been stripping wallpaper off the master bedroom walls, and it's a real job. But last night I . . . " She turned and stopped abruptly, just in time to keep from running into a customer.

"Mornin' Buck, hireyew?" Lou asked the man. He was a tall, nice-looking man, wearing a suit and tie and a forced smile. Tess remembered seeing him around town a few times in the weeks she had been here.

"Oh, I'm fair to middlin'." He looked to be in his late forties or early fifties and was studying Tess. "Mornin', ma'am."

"Have you two met?" Lou looked from Tess to the mayor.

"We've howdied, but we ain't shook yet," Buck drawled. Tess smiled, remembering Jack introducing himself that way. *It must be the Goose Pimple equivalent of "Nice to meet you."*

"Buck, this is Tess Tremaine, she bought the house on Walnut, and I scooped her up to hep me around this old place. Tessie, this here is Buck Lyle, our esteemed may'r."

"Mare?" Tess asked.

"Ma-ar," Lou said, trying to enunciate.

"I'm the *may-or,*" Buck explained. "I am pleased to make your acquaintance, ma'am. How're you takin' to our fair town so far?"

"I'm glad to meet you, too. I love it here. The people, the town, and the house."

"The house on Walnut . . . You mean she bought your old family place, Lou?"

"Yessiree."

"That old York fella that you bought it from, Miss Tess, he was two bricks shy of a full load . . . " He looked around to see if anyone else was listening and then he added, "...and his woman was purty as a punkin, but half as smart."

"Oh, Buck, now hush. They ain't around here ta defend themselves. You mind yer p's and q's."

"I know it, I know it." He mimed zipping his lips.

"What brings you in this mornin', Buck?" Lou asked. "I mean, May'r."

"I'm on my way over to John Ed's for a meetin', but I thought I'd shoot in here real quick and get a birthday present for Aunt Olivia.

She likes that purty stationery you carry, and Lord knows she goes through it faster 'n all get out. That woman writes thank you notes for her thank you notes." He shook his head in disbelief as he headed toward the stationery section. "Nice meetin' ya, Ms. Tess," he called over his shoulder, giving her a wink.

Lou turned to Tess. "I thought he'd never quit bumpin' his gums. Now what was it you were sayin'?"

"Oh. Yes. Well, last night I was peeling the wallpaper off of the master bedroom walls, and I found a key that had fallen into the floor register. It had a label attached that said, 'trunk,' and I wondered if it might belong to your family. It's a thin, copper key, and looks pretty old."

Lou's face went white underneath her bright rouge. "Ya don't say," she mumbled, pulling Tess behind the counter. Tess noticed she suddenly wouldn't look her in the eye and began to shuffle papers around on the desk.

"Seeing that it was your family's house, I thought maybe you'd have an idea of what it belonged to . . . " Tess let her sentence taper off when she saw the strained look on Lou's face.

"Lou, is everything all right?"

"Huh? Oh, yeah, honey, everythin's just fine and dandy. There was actually an old trunk in our attic that we could never find the key to. But we were able to get another one. I 'preshade you tellin' me 'bout it, but why don't you keep it? Make it yer good luck charm or sumpthin'. I'd just as soon not think about that trunk."

* * *

Lou finished Tess's orientation of the bookstore, and Tess worked for the rest of the day. She was so tired at five-thirty when she left the store she didn't see Jack standing across the street.

"Howdy, Tess Tremaine. Lou didn't work ya too hard today, did she?" Jack broke into stride with Tess.

"Not at all, Jack. I told you I'm not afraid of a little work. I'm just a little tired."

"And did you have a good first day at the bookstore?"

"I did. Besides getting my bearings, I got quite a lesson in Southern speak. People in this town sure do use a lot of words and a lot of syllables to describe an otherwise simple notion."

"I think you'll find Lou as colorful as she is kind-hearted. She's a fixture around here. I don't know what we'd do without her. Who else did you meet?"

"Well, I met the mayor. He seemed nice." Tess gave Jack a sideways glance.

"Ah. The mayor." Jack sounded annoyed.

"What does that mean?"

"Well, just 'tween you and me... he's got the personality of a dishrag. And he's highfalutin, on account of comin' from a long line of Goose Pimple residents. Thinks he owns the town."

"Ah," Tess mimicked.

Her exhaustion caused them to walk at a slow pace. When they were a block away from her house she wondered why Jack was still walking with her.

"Um . . . Jack . . . do you mind if I ask where you're going?"

"You mean you forgot you invited me to dinner?" he said with a straight face.

Tess looked up at him, surprised, but Jack couldn't hold his smile. His face gave him away. "I'm just kiddin'." He shrugged his shoulder. "I need some exercise. You don't mind if I walk with you, do you? I promise I won't impose myself on you for dinner."

"I don't think you could call the pace we're walking 'exercise'."

"Okay, I'm out for a nice early evenin' stroll..." Jack amended, " . . . an amble . . . a mosey . . . a saunter. Any of those meet with your approval?" he teased.

As they reached 117 Walnut Avenue, a puzzled look came over her face when she looked at the front of her house.

"What's the matter?" he asked, when they stopped on the sidewalk.

"The curtains." She stared at the house, perplexed.

"What about the curtains?" Jack followed her up the front walk, confused.

"They're closed. I never close those curtains." Tess's face was full of worry.

"Are you sure?" Jack asked, as Tess unlocked the front door.

"Of course I'm sure. Don't you think I would know if I closed my curtains or not?"

"Okay, okay, simmer down. Let me go in and look around first. Stay here on the porch."

She started to follow him inside, but he held up one finger and said, "Stay."

"I am not a dog, Jack. I can go in my own house if I want to."

Jack went in first, but Tess followed him, gasping when she saw the living room. Suddenly there was a noise in the kitchen, and Jack went down the hall in a flash. By the time Tess stumbled into the kitchen it was empty with the back door wide open. She looked around the room, thinking how she had left it in perfect order. Turning in a circle, rooted to one spot, she looked in horror at the destruction. Drawers were pulled out and overturned, cabinets were wide open, papers that had been stashed in a drawer were all over the floor, along with utensils, measuring cups, ice cream scoops, tea towels . . . practically everything in her kitchen was now on the floor. Jack came in through the back door, breathing hard. He bent at the waist and rested his hands just above his knees, trying to catch his breath.

"Jack, what in the world…"

"Tess, I saw a flash of somethin', or someone, I guess, but he got away. He's long gone into the woods now. We need to call Chief Price. He doesn't have a large police force, but maybe they can fan out and try to catch the guy." While he was calling the police chief, Tess went to the other rooms of the house. Every one of them was in total destruction; even the mattresses were overturned. She stood in the doorway of her bedroom in shock at what had happened to her little haven, when Jack came up behind her.

"Is anything missin'?"

"How would I know?" she answered faintly. "How could I possibly tell in this mess?"

She bent down to pick up some of the clothes on the floor, but Jack stopped her.

"Tess, don't touch anything until John Ed Price gets here. He needs to see everything exactly the way we found it."

"Who would do this?" Tess asked weakly. "I thought Goose Pimple Junction was a quiet, crime-free town. That was one of the reasons I chose it."

"Goose Pimple Junction *is* a quiet, crime-free town. I can't remember the last time we had a robbery."

"I need air." Tess headed for the front porch. She sat—stunned—

until the police arrived. The chief came himself and sent some of his officers into the woods in search of the intruder, but an hour later they came back empty-handed.

"Sorry, Chief. We gave it our best shot. Didn't find nothin' but squirrels and birds out there. We'll go back out if y'ont us to, but I don't see much point. That cat's long gone now."

Tess leaned toward Jack and said out of the corner of her mouth, "Yont?"

Jack whispered back, "If you want."

"Ah," Tess nodded her head. "I didn't realize I'd need a translator when I moved here."

"Stick with me, kid." Jack winked at her.

Several hours later, the police had gone, and Jack had helped Tess put most everything back in order. She was sprawled in a chair; he across the couch. "I don't get it. Nothing seems to be missing. Who would do this? What were they after?"

"I wish I knew. Whatever it was, I don't think you have to worry about them comin' back. They got to every room in the house. I think we came in right at the tail-end of their spree."

"That's what's so strange. Nothing seems to be missing," she said. "And it's so scary, too." She shivered. "What if I'd have come home alone? Anything might have happened. I am so grateful to you, Jack."

"Yeah? How grateful?" He waggled his eyebrows at her.

"Want to order a pizza?" Tess asked, ignoring the innuendo.

"If that's the best you can do," he sighed, dramatically. "See? I told you that you'd be havin' me to dinner."

Later, as they ate, Tess asked, "So why isn't your speech as Southernfied as some of the other locals? I mean, you have an accent, but it's not as thick as most of the others in town. You've lived in the south all your life, haven't you?"

"Southernfied? Could I find that word in the dictionary?"

"You know what I mean," Tess said around a mouthful of pizza. She hadn't been hungry until she smelled the pizza. Then she became ravenous.

"Well I reckon..." Jack suddenly had a thick southern accent. "...ahem . . . I reckon that I can tolk Southern if I wont. But my mama wasn't from the south and she raised sand every time my brother's and my speech started slantin' too much that way."

"Raised sand?"

"You never heard of that expression? It means kickin' up a fuss. I think it comes from animals pawing at the ground, kickin' up dust or sand when they're upset about somethin'."

"So you're fluent in Southern, but you don't speak it?"

"I guess you could say that. Although I do lapse into it every now and again." Jack paused for a minute. He could still see the worry on Tess's face. "Tess, are you okay?"

She nodded her head, looking down at the glass of Coke in her hand and poking at the ice with her finger. "Yes. It's just different being on my own. I've never really worried about my safety before. Someone's always been there to take care of me. I like my independence, but it does have its downside too. It's weird thinking about some stranger's hands being all over my things. It's unsettling," she said, feeling a bit embarrassed.

"Sure it is. You don't have to feel bad about feelin' that way. I could stay tonight if you want." Tess's eyes shot up to him, and he quickly added, "On the couch, of course. On the couch." He pushed his palms out toward her, in a gesture meant to stop her from thinking the worst.

"Thanks, it's nice of you to offer, but I need to stand on my own two feet. I need to be able to take care of myself. I'll be fine. I'll turn on the television for company."

"There's nothin' wrong with askin' friends for a little help now and then. You don't have to do this alone."

"But I need to, Jack," she said firmly.

"Maybe you should get a dog."

"I'll think about it."

"Can I ask you a question?"

"That depends on the question."

"Why don't you close your curtains? When we got home tonight you knew somethin' was wrong because the curtains were closed. You never close them?"

"I won't say never, but practically never. I like bright, natural sunlight. I can't stand dark rooms, especially in the daytime. And even at night I feel closed in with the curtains drawn."

"Tess, if you had come home alone, tell me you wouldn't have gone into the house alone."

"I wouldn't have gone into the house alone," she recited.

"Do you mean that?"

"Probably. I'm not that crazy."

"Just promise me if anything like this ever happens again you'll call me or John Ed and wait for us. Don't do anything stupid in the name of bein' brave and independent."

Later, as Tess got ready for bed, the key fell out of her pocket. She had taken it with her, intending to show it to Lou and maybe Jack, but Lou didn't seem interested, and then she forgot all about it. She put it on her key ring, hoping Lou was right about it being a good luck charm. She went to bed with her television and a light turned on in every room.

* * *

"I told you to do some SNOOPIN', not destructin'," a voice boomed over the receiver. "Shoot . . . if you had bird brains you'd fly backwards."

"Well shucks, boss, I thought you wanted to find somethin', not diddle around."

"If I wanna diddle around, I'll diddle AROUND," he yelled into the phone. "It's my gallderned money. All you did was draw attention. You didn't find a thing *or* accomplish anything. Slow and steady, do you hear me?"

"Yeah, I hear ya. You wanna diddle around. But like ya said, it's yer money. I just thought you wanted that key she found."

"You know what? I do want that key. Find it, galldernit. I want you to stay on Ms. Tess Tremaine like mud on a pig. I wanna know about every new little home improvement she makes, even if it's only a new toilet paper hanger. But listen and listen good. You can't make it look like we want the key. It has to look like she lost it. Gad night a livin' you're ignert. From now on, you keep drinkin', and I'll keep thinkin'."

GET YOUR STRAW
OUT OF MY KOOL-AID

over to: preposition \oh-ver too\ at
She was over to the diner.

[1932]

One week after three witnesses identified Rod Pierce as one of the bank robbers, he was in court. Unlike the last time Nate Hunter, John Hobb, and Mrs. Maggard had seen Pierce, he was now dressed neatly in a suit and tie in the courtroom. His hair was clean and combed, face soft as a baby's bottom, and false teeth in place.

John Hobb did a double take as he stepped up to be sworn in for testimony. He was asked, "Is this one of the men you saw rob the First National Bank of Goose Pimple Junction, on March 9, 1932?"

Hobb stared at Pierce. He didn't look exactly like the man he'd seen twice before, but even with his improved looks and seated behind a table, John was absolutely positive. "Yes, it is," he replied.

"Can you tell the court what happened that day?"

John's voice was clear and strong. "Mr. Pierce and two associates entered the bank. While one of them stayed as a lookout at the door, Mr. Pierce and another man brandished firearms, and demanded the clerks fill their pillow cases with the money from the cash drawers and the vault. Then they forced our clerk, Nate Hunter, to go with them, and they went runnin' down the street like scalded cats."

As John left the witness stand, he recognized a face in the back row. He went straight to Chief Preston, seated in the third row, sat down next to him, and whispered in his ear.

Next on the stand was Nate Hunter. After being asked if the defendant was one of the men who robbed the bank on March ninth, he replied, "Yes, it is." He went on to corroborate John Hobb's account of the robbery.

When Tallulah took the stand, she was nervous but sure of herself.

"Is this the man you saw brandish a gun on March ninth and rob the First National Bank?"

"It shore is."

"How can you be so sure?"

"He stood right in front of me and said they were robbin' us. I remember Mr. Pierce said I looked as nervous as a sinner in a cyclone." A tittering went through the courtroom from a few of the people in the audience. "As God is my witness, he's the one," she said, pointing at Pierce.

"Thank you, Mrs. Maggard."

The defense attorney stood and said, "Your honor, I have one witness today."

"Call 'em," the judge said.

"I call Calista Castle to the stand."

While the gaudily-dressed woman sashayed her way to the front of the courtroom, Chief Preston made his way to the back of the room.

When the witness was sworn in and seated, she was asked her address.

"I reside at 511 North Peachtree Way." She started to sit back in her chair, then leaned forward again, and added, "That's in Henclip."

"Your Honor, for the record, let me state that Henclip is approximately 129 miles from Goose Pimple Junction," the attorney said.

"So noted," the judge replied.

"And were you in Henclip on March ninth of this year?" he asked her.

"Yes, I was," she answered, smacking her gum loudly.

"Who were you with on that day in Henclip?"

"I was with Roddy Pierce." Whispers spread through the courtroom.

"All day?"

"Why, yes."

The county attorney took over questioning and asked the witness, "What time were you with Rod Pierce on March ninth, Miss Castle?"

She looked confused. "I disremember."

"Well, do you remember what you and Rod Pierce did on that day?"

Her eyes shot to Pierce, who stared back blankly. She nervously touched her neck, then smoothed her dress down on her lap. Finally, she said, "We went on a picnic."

"Miss Castle, let me refresh your memory," the attorney said, stepping out from behind the table and walking toward her. "On March eighth of this year, we had a snowstorm here in Goose Pimple Junction. Do you expect us to believe the very next day, only 129 miles away, you *went on a picnic?*"

She looked nervously from Pierce to the county attorney. "Well . . . well, I think so."

As soon as it was announced that Pierce would be held over for trial, court was adjourned, and Bug Preston stepped forward and approached Brick Lynch, who was seated in the back of the courtroom.

"Brick Lynch, you're under arrest for armed robbery."

"Jest couldn't mind your own bidness, could ya, Hobb? Yew gonna believe his lies?" Brick spit out as he was being handcuffed. The deadly cold look Brick shot at John sent a shiver up his spine.

The chief led Lynch past Hobb and whispered, "Don't worry, John. You have a reputation around town as being an honest, fine upstanding member of the community. Everyone knows you are as good as your word, and would not wrongly accuse an innocent man. Stick to yer guns, buddy."

[June 2010]

The day after the break-in, Tess woke up early again, got dressed, forced down a muffin and juice, and went outside to cut some of her hydrangeas to take to the bookstore. She bent over, trying to cut one last stem from the bottom of the bush.

"Wow. Now that's a view," she heard someone say.

Startled, she shot up, whirled around, and saw Jack. "Excuse me?"

"The flowers . . . they're beautiful," Jack said, grinning like a possum in a persimmon tree, and motioning to the flower-laden bush.

"Oh . . . thanks." She recovered from the surprise and noticed he was holding a bunch of sunflowers in his hand.

"Yours are lovely, as well."

He held them out to her. "Special delivery."

"What's this for?" A big smile spread across her face.

"Well, you had quite a scare yesterday. I wanted to give you some cheer."

"Oh, thank you, Jack. They look like a bouquet of smiles. That's very kind of you. Would you like to come in?" She motioned toward the house as she started toward it. "I'm heading over to report for my second day of work, but you can help me put these in water first," she said, leading him to the kitchen.

"How 'bout you put them in water, and I'll watch. Then I'd be pleased to walk you to work, Ms. Tess." He and his exaggerated southern accent followed her into the house. She shook her head at him and his dialect and got a vase from the cabinet.

He leaned against the doorjamb, his arms crossed over his chest, watching as she cut the stems under water and put the flowers in the vase.

Feeling self-conscious, she said the first thing that came to mind. "You know, my ex-husband used to quote, somebody—I can't remember who. He said he 'liked children too, but he didn't go around chopping their heads off and sticking them in vases around his house.' I, for one, think flowers belong in and outside of the house. Thank you, again, Jack."

He watched her for a moment and finally said, "What a desolate place would be a world without a flower. It would be a face without a smile, a feast without a welcome. Are not flowers the stars of the earth, and are not our stars the flowers of the heavens?'"

"Wow. I love that. Who said it?"

"A.J. Balfour. Don't ask me who he is or how I remember it, I just do," he laughed, giving her a smile that rattled her.

She set the vase down a little too forcefully in the center of her small kitchen table and stood back to admire the flowers, telling herself she was immune to Jack's smile.

"I love sunflowers. They're one of my favorite flowers. That was so nice of you. And totally unnecessary."

"Are you doing all right this morning?" His expression changed to one of concern.

"Yes, I'm fine. I slept like a baby." She made an attempt at a confident smile. "Well . . . " she said, clearing her throat. " . . . are you ready?"

As she locked the front door, he said, "I thought you weren't goin' to let Lou work you too hard. Here you are heading off to work again, first thing in the morning, two days in a row."

"Lou's trying to catch up with all the work that's backed up since her former employee left, so I offered to help out. I don't mind. Yesterday was fun. I met a lot of people." They stepped out onto the tree-lined sidewalk and started toward town in an amiable silence.

Finally Jack spoke. "So, Tess Tremaine, what's your story?"

"Mister, my story is longer and stronger than you have time for," she said lightly, although she was totally serious.

"Oooooh, a mystery, I like mysteries."

"Yes, I know. After all, you *are* a mystery writer. Unfortunately, my story isn't a mystery, it's just a mess." She made a show of looking at the flower garden in the yard they were passing. She was uncomfortable talking about herself.

"Ah, a woman with baggage."

"Baggage out the wazoo, mister."

"Wazoo. Define that term please."

"Oh, don't get cute with me. You tell me *your* story."

"You tell me yours, I'll tell you mine," he said in a Grocho Marx imitation.

"Uh, I believe the saying is *show. Show* me yours and I'll *show* you mine."

"Okay, we can do that too, if you want." Their eyes met, and he held them, giving her a challenging smile.

He was embarrassing her. She couldn't hold his gaze. She gave him a wry smile, shook her head, and kept walking.

"All right. I'll quit teasing you. You're just so much fun to tease." His voice got serious and he said quietly, "I worried about you last night. Is there anything I can do for you?"

"You worried about me? Aw, Jack, it was only a break-in. And I told you—I'm fine. Do you visit all of the home invasion victims in town?"

He laughed. "The easy answer is no, because we rarely have home invasions in Goose Pimple Junction. The totally honest answer is no, because you're a special case, Tess Tremaine."

When she blushed, he added kiddingly, "You're new in town. I just want you to feel welcome."

"Of course. That's very nice of you, Jack." She tried to suppress a wide smile.

"I noticed some photographs in your house yesterday but never got a chance to ask—you have a son?"

"Yes, he's twenty-five."

"You're not old enough to have a grown kid."

"Unfortunately, I am."

"Where does he live?"

"Alabama. How about you? Kids?"

"I have a daughter. She's twenty-five."

"Isn't that coincidental. Should we introduce them?"

"Maybe," Jack said, with the accent on be.

"And how's your book comin' along?"

"Oh, it's coming I guess."

"And you still have my e-mail address, right?"

"That I do."

"Well, I hope you'll use it and won't let it languish in the bottom of that purse."

When they reached the bookstore several minutes later, Tess thanked him again for the flowers, and Jack walked off down the sidewalk, as she went into the store.

Pickle was just inside the entryway, wearing a T-shirt with a bowl of cereal and spoon on the front. The shirt said, "Cereal Killer."

"Morning, Pickle," she said, very aware she was going to have to get used to dropping her 'g's' at the end of words. She was beginning to feel like a foreigner. "I see you're hard at work again putting books on the shelf. Is Lou around?" Walking over to the register desk, she put the vase of hydrangeas down.

"Oh, she's over to the diner, but she'll be right back . . . oap . . . here she is now."

Lou came in bustling with energy, in a bright, hot pink dress and big hair perfectly in place. "I'm so mad I could chew up nails and spit out a barbed wire fence."

Pickle stooped down and picked up several books out of a box. "Im'a workin', Miss Lou, I ain't a lolligaggin'," he said in an apologetic tone.

"Oh, Peekal, I ain't mad at you, honey." She made a face to Tess and said in a whisper, "If brains were leather, he wouldn't have enough to saddle a June bug, bless his heart." Louder, so Pickle could hear, she said, "You go on about yer work and keep an eye out for customers at the reg'ster. Tessie and I have some jawin' to do."

She led Tess back to the office by the arm and immediately started throwing questions at her. "Are you awright honey? I was just up to the diner and heard about yesterday, but John Ed wouldn't tell me a goll-dern thing. That man's as full of wind as a corn-eatin' horse. I don't give two hoots and a holler if it's '*Official bidness*,' I wanna know what happened. You had an intruder last night?" Her voice rose to a fever pitch. "I'll bet you were just about frightened out a your skivvies. And you bein' alone and all . . . that's no way to treat somebody, let alone our town's newbie."

"Lou, I'm fine . . . " when Lou's eyebrows went up in question, Tess added, " . . . really. I was a little shook up last night, I'll admit. But Jack helped me put everything back together reasonably well, and I don't think anything was taken."

"Oh Jack did, did he?" Lou leaned forward, eager to hear some gossip.

"It's nothing like that, Lou."

"Well, shoot." She went back to the subject at hand. "I just can't believe it happened. Some people's got grits for brains. I'm so glad you're awright. John Ed wouldn't tell me much, the old coot, but it didn't sound like there was gonna be much of an investigation. Makes me embarrassed on account a the whole town."

"Why don't we put it behind us and get to work?" Tess opened the door to find Pickle stepping back quickly, then busying himself straightening some books nearby.

Lou saw him, too. "Peekal, get your straw out of my Kool-Aid."

Tess turned with a puzzled expression, and Lou whispered, "It means mind your own bidness." She punctuated the sentence with a firm nod of her head.

"Peekal, I'm gonna be on you like white on rice if I ever see your ear up to my door again," she hollered.

Pickle turned scarlet all the way to the tips of his ears and mumbled, "Yes ma'am," before loping off across the store, obviously trying to put as much distance between Lou and himself as he could.

The rest of the morning was quiet with not many customers. Around mid-day the mayor came into the store. His short, dark hair was just beginning to grey at the edge of his face, making him distinguished looking. Every time Tess saw him he was in a coat and tie. He stood about five feet ten, and was extremely thin. He wore tortoise shell preppy glasses, and when he smiled, his bright, white teeth were prominent on his face.

"Hello, Mayor, nice to see you again. How are you?" Tess asked.

"Well, I'm fine as frog hair, but twice as jumpy. Although comin' in here always has a calmin' effect on me. But how 'bout you? I heard what transpired over't your house yesterday. I came by to see if you're all right." He oozed southern charm.

"That's really not necessary. I'm just fine."

"Oh, honey, you're better 'n fine, you're lookin' purty as a speckled pup." He leaned a little too close to Tess, leering slightly at her.

Lou came to the rescue. "Mare! What in the Sam Hill are you doin'?" She rounded the counter and came at him like a mama bear protecting her cub.

"What do you mean, Lou? I'm just jawin' with Ms. Tremaine," Buck said innocently, taking a few steps back.

"Yeah, well, with all due respect, take yer jaw somewhere else. I'll not have you makin' inappropriate comments to my employees." She folded her arms in front of her and glared at him.

"Whoa, Nelly. Keep yer big hair on." He turned to Tess with his hand over his heart. "Ms. Tremaine, I most sincerely apologize if I've offended you in any way. I just think if a man sees a beautiful woman, he has an obligation to tell her. Would you allow me to tell you over dinner, maybe?" His smile filled his face.

He looks respectable, and besides the leer he seems like a nice man. But his charm is a little over the top. And he's still of the male persuasion, and I have sworn off getting mixed up with any more of his kind.

"Thank you, Mayor . . . but I can't. I appreciate the offer, though."

He looked at his watch. "It's comin' up on lunchtime. Lou, you do give your employees time off for lunch, dontcha?"

"A course I do, but I brought lunch for us all, and we're gonna eat in the office today." She gave Tess a quick wink. "Now Tess, would you mind startin' on that new display over in the cookin' section? Tell ya what, I'll go with ya and getcha started. You have a good day, Mare."

"And you as well, ladies," he chuckled.

The day went by quickly. Tess met more of the townspeople and continued her lesson on Southern speak. She was beginning to think if she just shoved her fingers in her mouth while she talked, she'd be half-way there.

When she got home shortly after three o'clock, she changed into her work clothes, grabbed her iPod, and started removing the rest of the wallpaper in her bedroom. Working until late into the evening, she only stopped once for a quick sandwich. Finally she came to a stopping point, cleaned up the mess, and got ready for bed, exhausted.

As she crawled into bed, she heard a dog barking outside, and a faint creak that sounded like her back door when it opened and closed. Her hand reacted on its own, reaching under the bed for the Louisville Slugger she'd stashed underneath for protection. She sat straight up and listened hard. Nothing.

She swung her feet to the floor and stopped to listen again. Still nothing. Gripping the bat until her knuckles were white, she walked out her bedroom door and stood at the top of the steps for several minutes, straining to hear the slightest sound. The house was silent.

She went back to bed but kept the bat in her hand. She lay there, looking at the shadows in the room, worrying and wondering.

The house was too quiet. She grabbed the remote to the small television that was housed in the top part of her armoire. With one click David Letterman came on. She turned over on her stomach, bat still in hand, and listened to Dave while she drifted off.

She was sound asleep within minutes, and her hand relaxed, dropping the bat with a clunk to the floor. She never heard the clunk or the creaking of the floorboards.

A HISSY FIT WITH A TAIL ON IT

preshade: verb \ pree-sheyt\ appreciate
I don't 'preshade your innuendoes!

[1932]

The kitchen smelled like bacon and coffee.

"I can't believe my eyes," John Hobb said to his wife, as he read the morning newspaper. "You won't believe this. *I* can't believe this! What's wrong with that baboon?" John slapped his hand down hard on the table.

"What's wrong, John?" Maye frowned at him while pouring two cups of coffee.

"They really are getting out. I thought it was only talk. Even though they were sentenced to twenty years, after only serving *three months*, they're getting out," he said in disbelief. "Says here they were granted full and free pardons by Governor Shelby who, quote, 'concluded they were the victims of mistaken identity' end of quote."

"I can't believe they never gave up the name of the third man. He's out there, scot-free," Maye said, as she whipped together eggs and milk, preparing to make scrambled eggs.

"Nope. Never did. Now there's three of them who are out free and clear. I didn't tell you yet, but I hear tell there may even be a fourth man involved."

"Why didn't you tell me?" Maye asked, propping her hands on her hips.

"Because it may only be the rumor mill workin' overtime."

"But you only saw three men in the bank that day." Steam billowed and the skillet sizzled as she poured the egg mixture in.

"Yes, but some people are saying maybe there was a fourth man waiting in the getaway car, or maybe someone helped them get the guns, or . . . well, you know how people talk. Probably nothing to it. But it doesn't matter. They're all getting off scot-free! It just isn't right."

* * *

When Brick Lynch got home from his three-month stint in prison he was bitter and full of resentment. His wife, Maisey, was sympathetic.

"That John Hobb's the kind a man who thinks the sun come up just ta hear 'im crow," Maisey grumbled.

"Maisey, if it weren't for that do-gooder, I wouldna had to miss outta three months a my life," he whined. "Not to mention having to live in that rat hole."

"I know, Brick darlin', but you're home now, try to put all that unpleasantness behind you."

"I cain't. He shoulda kept his cotton-pickin' blabbermouth shut. Me and Roddy are gonna have ta teach him a lesson in civility." He stared coldly out at the trees rustling in the slight breeze.

* * *

The next day Rod Pierce and Brick Lynch met with a third man at Humdinger's, a hole-in-the-wall bar on the outskirts of town. The man was wearing a fine suit, a silk tie, and wingtip shoes. He stuck out like a sore thumb. They sat down at a dark table at the back of the room, out of earshot of others.

"Thanks for takin' care 'a the governor for us. Three months in that joint *seemed* like twenty years," Lynch said.

"Keep it down! You want somebody to hear?" Sore Thumb asked.

Lynch snorted. "Ain't nobody in here conscious enough ta hear." He scanned the room. "Look at ol' Slew Foot over thar. He's three sheets to the wind."

"What's Hobb know 'bout the robbery?" Pierce asked the man, taking out a pack of cigarettes.

"Not sure yet. I think he suspects there was a fourth party involved, but he's keepin' things purty close to the vest."

"He ain't said nuthin' yet. What makes you think he will?" Pierce lit his cigarette and offered the pack to each man.

"Cause he's Danny Do-gooder, that's why. The world oughtta give him a medal for bein' so dad-burned good." Lynch struck a match with his thumbnail and lit his cigarette. "Nominate him for sainthood or somethin'."

"Whatta ya wontta do about 'im, Brick?" Pierce took a deep drag on his cigarette.

"Pardon or no pardon, he's still a rat. I wontta give 'im my own brand a medal," Brick said, eyes dark with hatred.

"Just simmer down," Sore Thumb said. "We can't go off half-cocked. We have to bide our time. If we do anything now, it'll be obvious who did it. The man doesn't have enemies. Except for you, Brick. Let some time go by. See what develops. He ain't got nuthin'. Chances are, he'll let it drop."

"Ain't gonna change the fact that he squealed on me. You give 'im more time, and he may squeal on you, too," Lynch said, pointing his finger at Sore Thumb.

[June 2010]

Tess got out of bed, stepped on the Louisville Slugger that had slipped out of her hand the night before, kicked it back under her bed, and limped to the shower. When she finished dressing, she headed to the kitchen but stopped dead in her tracks two steps out in the hall.

Footprints.

She looked closer at the hardwood floor. The prints weren't muddy, but looked as if whoever they belonged to had walked through something wet, making their shoes just damp enough to leave a faint imprint on the floor. Tess was sure they had not been there when she went to bed.

She remembered leaving her own shoes by the back door the night before. And the footprints were obviously much bigger than her size seven feet. Heart pounding, she ran back to her bedroom where she pulled the bat from underneath her bed. Then she started back down the hall, ready to hit a homer if someone stepped into her strike zone. She tracked the shoes to the kitchen and back up the steps in the middle of the house. The prints led down the upstairs hall and into each bedroom.

Tess peeked into each room but saw nothing out of place. In her mind she could hear Jack asking her to promise to call him or Chief Price if anything else ever happened. She grabbed her cell phone and took it outside, calling the police department and sitting down on the porch to wait for them.

Ten minutes later, John Ed was standing in her den. "You mean that's all the ev'dence you have? *Shoe prints?* Wudda you want me ta do? Put out an APB for ever'body in town who wears a size ten?"

"Chief, someone's been in my house! I can assure you I'm not making this up."

"That ain't somethin' I can hang my hat on, missy."

"Why don't you quit patronizin' the lady and start tryin' to figure out why somebody keeps breakin' into her house, John Ed?" Jack's voice came through the front screen door. He opened it and let himself in.

"You ain't got no dawg in this fight," John Ed said, glaring at Jack. "Or do you?" He turned to Tess and then back to Jack with a suggestive expression.

"One . . . " Jack ticked off points on his fingers, " . . . it's my *business* because this lady's a friend of mine. And two . . . " Jack said exaggerating his southern accent, "I don't 'preshade your innuendoes!"

"Aw, Jack, don't go gittin' yer knickers all in a bunch. She had a hissy fit with a tail on it. I was only tryin' to calm her down, that's all."

"Well wouldn't you have a *hissy fit* if someone kept breakin' into *your* house?"

"And just how did you know that's what the call was for this mornin'?" Chief Price asked, looking suspiciously at Jack.

"You know you can't keep anything quiet in this town, John Ed. Now quit arguin' and take the woman seriously. What are you gonna do about this?"

Too nervous to just stand around, and wanting something to do, Tess went into the kitchen to make some tea while the men continued to argue. The thought that someone had been in her house while she was sleeping sent shivers down her spine, made her sick to her stomach, and she could feel the hair on her arms standing on end. The men continued to argue in low voices, but she couldn't hear what was said. She no longer cared. It was obvious the chief thought she was just a hysterical female.

She filled the teakettle with water and put it on the stove. She wasn't hungry but thought maybe eating something would calm her roiling stomach. While waiting for the kettle to boil, she absent-mindedly grabbed a box of Banana Nut Cheerios out of the cabinet and stood over the sink, eating from the box.

"Are you okay?" Jack stood leaning against the kitchen doorway, his legs crossed and one foot propped on a toe.

Tess jumped and whirled around at the sound of his voice, spraying Cheerios across the room.

"No thanks, I've had breakfast," he laughed. "You a little bit on edge?"

She let out a heavy sigh and sat the box on the counter with a thud. He bent down to help her pick up the cereal.

"Tess, I think it's safe to say that for whatever reason they keep comin' back, they're not gonna hurt you. If they'd wanted to do that, they would have done it last night."

"That's a pleasant thought." Tess was on her hands and knees, sweeping the Cheerios with her hands, and scooping them up to throw in the garbage. "But you're probably right." She wondered if he noticed her hands shaking.

He stood, putting his hands on his hips. "Tess, don't be offended by this question, but . . . do you . . . have any drugs in the house?"

"*What?* Jack, no, of course I don't have any drugs in this house. How could you even think such a thing?"

"I don't. I just had to ask it. Drugs, firearms, and high-end loot. That's usually what people are after when they break into a place. Since your high-end loot is still here, and I don't peg you for the gun-totin' type," his eyes wandered to the Louisville Slugger baseball bat in the corner of the kitchen, "drugs are all that's left."

Tess sat down at the table and put her head in her hands. "I think back to a little over a year ago, when I had a quiet, ordinary, mundane life. Then my world exploded. I thought moving here would let me get back on an even keel. Now I'm having to learn a new language, I have wallpaper stuck to the walls, and I have a stalker. So much for my good luck charm!"

"Hold it! Hold it just one minute! Number one, I think you're slightly exaggeratin' on the foreign language thing. Number two, I'd be happy to help you strip . . . the wallpaper." She shot him a look. "Number three, I'm sure you don't have a stalker, unless you want to count me. And number four, what good luck charm?"

For the next few minutes Tess filled Jack in on what she had found and told him about her talk with Lou.

"So it's not a good luck charm." Jack shrugged. "It's just an interesting antiquity. Put it on your key ring and forget about it."

"And what about the repeated break-ins?" Tess asked. "This is really freaking me out."

"Well . . . I could stay over . . . " Jack quickly changed course when she gave him yet another pointed look.

"In that case, are you workin' today?"

"Not until two o'clock, why?"

"What say you and I take your mind off everything by goin' to lunch at Slick and Junebug's?"

"Well . . . " Tess hemmed, "I should get some things done around here before I go into work."

"Come on, it's only a quick bite to eat. We'll be in public. And if you insist, I'll even refrain from biting."

The way he was looking at her made her nervous. *I could so easily fall into his arms, where I'd feel safe again.* He was sitting so close, she could smell his aftershave lotion, feel his body heat, and when she looked at him all she could think about was running her hands through his hair and kissing him silly. *NO, I have to stand on my own two feet. I have to get a grip. And not a grip on Jack!*

"Hell, no!"

"Pardon?" Jack asked, one eyebrow raised questioningly.

Did I say that out loud? Crap.

"I said, 'HEL-lo.' You know, like, HEL-lo, no biting." *Liar liar, pants on fire...*

"Well, then, I'll be back to pick you up in an hour. How's that?"

"That'll give me time to get those footprints off of my pretty hardwood floors," Tess said, taking her mop out of the closet and trying to feel brave.

* * *

The minute Jack opened the door to the diner, Tess smelled the wonderful aroma of freshly baked bread. Tess stiffened slightly at Jack's hand on her back directing her in, but seeing the two old men sitting at their regular perches at the counter made her smile. She realized it was the first time she'd smiled all day.

"Afternoon, Jackson," Clive said.

"Afternoon, boys. How're you two fine gentlemen doin' today?"

"Hangin' in 'ere like a hair in a biscuit," Earl said.

"Yeah, but he's about as useful as a pogo stick in quicksand," Clive stage-whispered to Jack.

"Gentlemen, have you met Tess yet?"

"We've howdied . . . " Clive started to say.

"But we ain't shook yet." Tess beat him to the punch.

"Clive Pierce, Earl Hicks, I'd like to present Ms. Tess Tremaine. Ms. Tess, this here's Clive and this is Earl." Jack motioned to each man as they were introduced. Tess noticed Earl didn't have one tooth in his whole head.

"Well ain't she a dandy!" Earl said with a toothless smile.

"Down boy." Jack playfully pushed down on the man's shoulder. "You're too old for her."

"Yeah, well . . . you wait—one day soon 'at gal is gonna drop you like a hot potato, and I'll be righcheer waitin'," Earl said, pointing his finger at Jack. Jack laughed and led Tess to a booth.

"Jack, do those men think we're seeing one another?"

"Prob'ly." Jack grinned.

"But we're not!"

Jack started patting himself all over, from his head, down his torso, saying, "I am visible, aren't I? I mean, you *can* see me, right? And I can see you . . . " Tess rolled her eyes, shook her head, and directed her attention to the chalkboard menu at the front of the diner.

Junebug arrived at the table, and with her hands on her hips she looked down at Jack. "Well lookie at what the cat dun drug in."

"Hey Junie! That's no way to talk to our newest resident," Jack teased.

"I was referrin' ta *yew*," Junebug said, smiling. "Hidy, Tess, hireyew?" She moved her smile over to Tess.

Tess looked at Jack questioningly and he mouthed, "How are you."

"Oh!" Tess laughed, "I'm fine, June . . . bug . . . how are you?"

"Right as rain and twice as nice," she joked. "And you, Jack?"

"So hungry I could eat a stink bug off a dead skunk."

"Sorry, we're fresh outta that t'day. What else can I gitcha?"

"I think I'll just have a salad with ranch dressing and sweet tea, please," Tess said.

"And I'll have a hamburger with lettuce, 'mater and onion, and a Dr. Pepper, please, pretty lady." Jack had suddenly started speaking in his exaggerated southern drawl.

"Watch him," Junebug said to Tess, pushing her pencil into her hair behind her ear and pointing at Jack. "When he puts on that southern accent, he's up ta no good!"

She headed off toward the kitchen hollering, "Burn one, take it through the garden and pin a rose on it! Cow feed! I need an MD and a tea with high octane."

"You'll get used to it." Jack smiled at her.

"I think it's great. I may not always understand it, but I think it's great." She tried to act natural, but she was wound tighter than a dime store clock. She felt like every nerve in her body was buzzing.

Jack noticed. "Hey, are you okay?"

They locked eyes for a moment, and she looked away first, taking in a deep breath. "I've never had a break-in and now I've had two in one week. Someone's been in *my house*, Jack. And once while I was in it. I'm terrified."

Junebug came back to the table with their drinks. She saw the worried look on Tess's face. "You all right, sugar plum?"

Tess nodded and took a sip of her tea, and Junebug left to take an order at another table.

"And the really weird thing is, nothing is ever taken. Why would someone break in just to look around? What are they after?"

"I don't know, Tess. It's a strange occurrence in this town. Maybe they just wanted to gaze at your lovely face while you slept."

"Jack, do you take anything seriously?"

"Honey, if it involves you, I am taking it seriously."

HE'S SO UGLY
HIS COOTIES HAVE
TO CLOSE THEIR EYES

bidness: noun \bid-nis\ business
Mind your own bidness.

[1935]

Goose Pimple Junction was a typical small town, where the hub of activity centered on the town square. On the south side of the square was the courthouse, which took up one entire block. The town filling station was on the southwest side, and next door sat The Majestic movie theatre, followed on the northwest side by Burke's bakery, whose owner, Burke Henderson made the best doughnuts in seven counties. A combination candy shop and newspaper store sat in between the bakery and The First National Bank on the northeast block. Daffodil's Home Goods Store, which sold everything from clothing to furniture, was diagonal to the bank on the east side. Completing that block was Ernestine & Hazel's, a small five-and-dime store, and next to that was a diner. In the middle of the square was a wide green expanse, scattered with trees and benches, and a raised gazebo in the center.

A typical Saturday afternoon in the heart of downtown Goose Pimple Junction would find all of the businesses humming with activity, but none more so than the Pure Oil filling station, which was always busy washing cars, checking oil, fixing tires, and pumping gas. Often, the police were parked up at the gas station, but you could count on them definitely being there on Saturdays. There was room on the side for them to park, and so many things happened in the heart of downtown, you saw it if you were at the station.

Drunks constantly got into fights in the town square. In fact, it was a regular Saturday afternoon occurrence for the filling station owner, Psalmist David, P.D. to most people, to have to get out the water hose and wash the blood off the driveway after the police tried to arrest some drunkard who didn't want to be hauled off to the drunk tank.

Since the police were almost always at the station, they began to give its phone number out as one of their own. It got so that P.D. was calling to relay messages so often, they decided to install a whistle with an air compressor on it—a loud one, like the kind used at a factory. If one of the police cars wasn't parked there when a call came in or a fight broke out, P.D. would blow the whistle, and the police would come see what was needed.

Once, a drunk named 'Hard Times,' who was built like a tank, was all fired up and itching for a fight. The police chief, Bug Preston, and his deputy had followed him from a bar around the corner. It wasn't long before he was shouting insults at the chief on the sidewalk in front of Ernestine's and Hazel's Sundries. The deputy disappeared, leaving Bug to face off with the drunk.

"Hey y'all! Come o're hare and take a lookit this cracker jack po-leece man. He's so damn ugly his cooties have to close their eyes," Hard Times yelled. He swayed a little, and got a grip on a light post to steady himself. Then he began to loudly sing insults. "He's soooo uglyyyy his mama took him everywhere she went so she didn't have to kiss him goodbyyyyyyye."

The chief shot back, "You ain't worth the powder and shot it'd take to blow you to kingdom come, Hard Times."

Swaying and having trouble getting his words out, Hard Times said, "I am . . . I am gonna skin . . . your . . . your neck and . . . rrun your . . . your lleg through it!"

"Oh yeah? Well you better give your heart to Jesus, 'cause your butt is mine," the chief said.

Everyone knew Bug Preston was trigger-happy, but the drunk apparently forgot. The chief pulled out his gun and fired between the man's legs. It didn't faze Hard Times, but it distracted him enough that a deputy was able to sneak up behind him and hit him over the head with a tire iron, knocking him out cold.

Another time, John Hobb and the other tellers watched through the bank windows as two police officers got into a disagreement that got out of hand. They both pulled their weapons, one taking shelter in the inset door of Daffodil's, and the other across the street behind the corner wall of the diner. In typical Old West fashion, they both stepped out at the same time, aimed and fired, killing each other simultaneously.

Those were occurrences that, while tragic or dramatic, weren't unusual in Goose Pimple Junction. But one Tuesday morning, something happened that was unique. P.D. was in one of the bays, working on a car, when the family of a man recently arrested, and doing time in the jail, showed up. The three brothers confronted P.D., pulled a gun on him, and said, "We know you have a whistle to call the police. So call 'em. *Now*."

P.D. was a God-fearing, decent, honest man. He knew the men wanted an ambush. He said, "That's not the way to handle your problem, boys."

One of the brothers snarled, "Mind your own bidness."

Another man pointed the gun in his face and repeated, "Now," motioning for P.D. to go into the office, "or I will walk a mud hole in you and stomp it dry," he said through gritted teeth.

But old P.D, wasn't stupid. Instead of blowing one long blast, like he normally would, he blew two short ones. The police chief heard the whistle and figured something was wrong. He and two of his men snuck around the back of the station and into one of the bays. They had a police car drive slowly down the street to get the men's attention.

P.D. had seen Bug beside the office door, and to distract the men, he pointed down the street to the police cruiser. "Well, here they come. You boys mind if I slip out back?"

The three men, cocking their weapons and taking positions in the station's office, were intent on the police car out front, giving Bug and two of his men a chance to sneak in and surprise them. While Bug went for the man who looked to be the leader, the other officers pushed guns into the backs of the other two men.

"Drop yer guns and say yer prayers, son," Bug drawled. The men were apprehended without incident.

[June 2010]

Tess was exhausted. She'd spent the day scraping more walls. Having successfully completed her work in the master bedroom, she went to bed tired, but not sleepy. She tossed. She turned. She needed sleep. Why wouldn't her mind cooperate?

She gave up on sleep once again and got out of bed for her laptop. She wanted to sit outside on her porch, but was afraid of what, or who, might be out there. She climbed back into bed, tucking her sheet and quilt around her, placing her computer on her lap.

Tess opened up the chapter she was currently working on, but couldn't concentrate. She thought of e-mailing Jack, but it had been a week since their lunch at the diner. She hadn't seen him since then and thought he'd probably lost interest in her. *It's just as well. Story of my life.* She decided to stop thinking about him.

Her mind wandered to her son and whether she'd received an e-mail from him. Logging on to her account, she found two e-mails waiting, one from her son, and one from a friend back home. None from Jack. Nicholas was settling into his new home, job, and town nicely. He seemed happy.

The second e-mail was from her friend Sara, wondering how she was doing in her new house. Tess was getting ready to reply when a new e-mail came in. This one from Jack. She took a deep breath and opened it.

Subject: update
From: jwright6964@yahoo.com
To: mtess@yahoo.com

Hey, Tess—I've missed seeing you. I haven't had much chance to ask around town about what we talked about. I'll try to do that tomorrow. Have you thought any more about talking to Lou? See ya soon.

J.

She drummed her fingers on the keyboard for a minute while she thought about what to write back. She hit "reply."

I'll think about talking to Lou. I'm not sure it's the way to go, just yet. What are you doing up at one a.m.?

t.

She went back to replying to Sara's e-mail but noticed a flashing tab about five minutes later. It was a chat invitation from Jack.

mysteryman: *I'm reading my latest chapter to Esmerelda. It's putting her to sleep. What are you doing up?*

Btw—what does the m stand for in mtess?

"Who's Esmerelda?" she said aloud. "Surely he doesn't have a woman at his house while he's instant messaging me. That cad! I'm not asking. I won't give him the satisfaction."

mtess: *Couldn't sleep. Writer's block. Mary Tess.*

mysteryman: *Mary Tess. I like it. Writer's block? You didn't ask, but my first suggestion would be to put down the pen, so to speak. It's about as useless to you right now as using a snow shovel to scrape wallpaper, and all you're gonna do is frustrate yourself.*

mtess: *Pen and snow shovel have been put away for the evening. Thanks.*

mysteryman: *The next thing I'd do is find something to relax your mind awhile. Let's see, what'd do the trick? How about a nice quiet homemade dinner for two? It's too bad you don't know of someone who shares in your craft to invite over.*

Oh, no he's not, she thought. He wouldn't be inviting me to dinner at the same time he's entertaining another woman. He wouldn't do that. But Lou did say . . .

Another IM came in.

mysteryman: *Yep, I think what you need is to have some fella put dinner together for you tomorrow night . . . well, I guess that would be tonight. If you don't mind me saying, I think I know just the right guy. I'll tell him to expect you for 8:00. I hope I'm not being too presumptuous. Bye Tess.*

"Oh good grief!" she shrieked aloud, pounding the bed with her fists. "What am I supposed to do now? That man is unbelievable! Oh!" she banged her head against the headboard. *If I call him to decline, he'll just insist I come. I am not going. I refuse to be one of his conquests.*

Since Jack had logged off of Yahoo, she decided to send him an e-mail.

Subject: Dinner
From: mtess@yahoo.com
To: jwright6964@yahoo.com

Jack, thanks very much for the dinner invitation, but I'm afraid I have to decline. I already have plans.

She sat back and looked at her message. He couldn't argue with that. She hit send.

* * *

The next morning, Tess went into the yard. She worked her way around the side of the house to the back, pulling weeds and deadheading blooms as she went. It was early morning, but it was starting to heat up. She sat down on the brick walk to rest, looking around her backyard. Her eyes swept around the perimeter of the yard, and she compiled a wish list in her head, mentally planning what she'd like to plant in the fall.

Deciding she could stand the heat for a little while longer, she scooted herself down the path, shifting from sitting to kneeling. The first thing that caught her attention was the small flowerbed under her office window, where small patches of purple, white, and yellow coneflowers were planted. Noticing some of the normally upright stems of the flowers were lying horizontally, she edged closer and saw that a portion of them had been trampled. She immediately thought of her dog, since he used to get into her previous garden almost daily. *But I don't have a dog now.*

Tess tenderly picked up the trampled stems, looking to see if they were salvageable and noticed two fresh cigarette butts in the dirt.

Standing up to take a better look, she froze. Rain the previous night had made the garden slightly muddy, which made the footprints planted directly beneath the window particularly noticeable.

She stepped back as if she had seen a snake. Cold chills ran up her body. Someone had been watching her.

THEY ATE SUPPER
BEFORE THEY SAID GRACE

nemmine: interjection \nem-mahyn\ never mind
Aw, nemmine. I don't have any proof.

[1935]

It just seems s'picious," John Hobb whispered to his brother Trevor,
three years after the bank robbery. They'd met for coffee at the local
diner, and John couldn't help using his brother as a sounding board.
"I know what Nate Hunter makes, and it's not enough to support the
fancy new suits of his and the new Desoto. How's he swingin' all that?"

"Beats the heck outta me, John. I don't know the man."

"I've been thinkin' more about the day of the robbery." John leaned
forward conspiratorially, even though there was no one around them to
hear. "Know what seems strange to me? About a minute before the
bandits came into the bank, I remember seein' Nate goin' over to the
window and lowerin' the shade."

"So? Maybe the sun was too bright," Trevor said, shrugging. He
pulled a flask out of his pocket, looked around to make sure no one was
watching, and poured an amber liquid into his coffee.

"See, the thing is, nobody's ever pulled that shade down before or
since. So why then?" John was deep in thought and didn't notice the
flask.

"Hmmm . . . I see what you're gettin' at. He was givin' 'em the green
light to go ahead with the robbery."

"And another thing: why would they take *him* as a hostage? It
woulda been much easier to control a little lady like Tallulah than a man

as big as Nate."

"Now there might be somethin' to that—" Trevor tried to interject, but his brother was on a roll.

"There are too many red flags. I don't want to think poorly a Nate, but it just doesn't add up." John shook his head and looked out the window.

"That's 'cause you're a bookkeeper," Trevor teased. "Why's everythin' gotta add up? Maybe some things ya just cain't explain." He narrowed his eyes and looked closely at his brother. "I know that look a yours, though. Whatta you thinkin'?" He took a sip of coffee and winced.

"You know what I'm thinkin'," John replied. "Aw, nemmine. I don't have any proof. I can't accuse a fella worker of wrong doin' just 'cause he's got some new duds, and he pulled a shade down. Long as I've known him, he's been straight as string. He couldn't do somethin' like that now, could he?"

"I don't know him, John. But it sounds like you ain't got no call ta accuse 'im of anything."

"Yeah, you're right. But I think I have to put these questions to him, just to clear my mind. Thanks for listenin', Trevor. You comin' over'ta house tonight? Maye's fixin' pot roast and coconut pound cake."

"Shoot, John, pot roast or no pot roast, if you're invitin', and Maye's gonna be there, I will be too, sure as a cat's got climbin' gear."

"Trevor! That's my wife you're talkin' 'bout."

"Yeah, well, if anything ever happens ta you, I'm first in line." Trevor brought his coffee cup into the air, in a mock toasting gesture.

* * *

"He's getting' wise to me, Brick. What am I gonna do?" Sore Thumb hissed. The two men were again at Humdinger's, their favorite meeting place. There were only three other people in the bar, and they were too drunk to think, let alone listen in on a conversation. The men were far enough away from the bartender, too, but still they kept their voices low.

"I say it's time ta start spinnin' some yarn about one Mr. John Hobb," Lynch answered.

"Whatta ya mean?"

"What I mean is, you spread the word, that you think durin' the hold up, *he* hepped hisself ta the till. And you say maybe *he* was in on it from the beginnin'. We spread enough out there 'bout his *possible* guilt, and we let the waggin' tongues take it fumm'air." Lynch took a swig of his beer and licked the foam from his mustache.

"Have you taken leave a your senses? Who's gonna believe that about John? He's salt a the earth kind of people. Not ta mention that he's tighter 'n bark on a tree. Who'd believe he was in on a robbery or that he had money to spend?" Hunter said, skeptical of Jenning's plan.

"Man's gotta put shoes on four kids. Maybe he needed the money." Lynch belched, then his thin mouth curled into an evil smile.

"Hmmm . . . "

"And ain't you ever heard the expression, 'Cold as a banker's heart'? All we gotta do is plant the seed." Lynch scratched the back of his neck. "You can lie like a dirty cur dog, so I know you can pull it off."

"All right, I guess we can try it your way." Sore Thumb was still skeptical.

"And after the hens get a cluckin', you and me's gotta have us a private meetin' with ole Johnny boy," Lynch said, before letting out a huge belch.

[June 2010]

"Of course I'm sure they're not my footprints," Tess insisted into her cell phone. "There are two clear footprints underneath my window that look like someone was standing there, looking in my office, and there were cigarette butts next to them. Plus they trampled my flowers. I'm telling you, this is getting weirder every day. I'm starting to get scared."

Tess needed to confide in someone, and she didn't dare call John Ed again, so she'd called her son as she walked to work. She knew John Ed would just laugh at her. Lou would overreact. And she didn't want to call Jack. He was trouble.

"I'm almost at Stafford's, sweetie. I have to go. Yes, I'll keep you posted. No, you don't need to come. I'd love to see you, but I know it's hard for you to get away. I'm fine . . . really. Okay, sweetie, bye-bye."

Holding a plate of chocolate chip cookies she'd made for her co-workers, Tess slipped her phone into her purse and walked into the bookstore a few minutes before ten o'clock. Pickle was already hard at work. Unfortunately, he was standing right behind the door, and she didn't see him until she stepped inside and closed it. At that point, she jumped a mile, and in trying to hold on to the cookies, fell backward into a table of books.

"Oh Good Lord, Pickle, you scared me half to death," Tess said, trying to stand up straight again.

"Sorry, Mizz Tess, all I did was stand here," Pickle said feebly. He stood there in baggie shorts, a black t-shirt, and black Chuck Taylor's, looking completely confused.

"It's all right. I'm just on edge lately. Here, have a cookie." She pulled aside part of the plastic wrap and held out the plate of cookies to him.

"Good save, Miss Tess. You may have knocked the books off the table, but you saved the important thing—that plate a cookies."

"I'm glad you like them," she said, reading his shirt, which said in large letters, "FEDERAL WITNESS PROTECTION PROGRAM" and underneath that, in smaller lettering, said, "You Don't Know Me."

"So is that how you got the name 'Pickle'? It's your Witness Protection name?" she said jokingly.

"Uh . . . no ma'am," he said in all seriousness, grabbing another cookie. "This is just a t-shirt. I'm not really in the Witness Protection Program."

He's either really clueless or really good at acting. Tess patted his arm and took the cookies to the back room, where she also put her purse away. After a quick chat with Lou, she went out to fix the table of books on which she'd wreaked havoc.

The morning went by quickly, due to the steady flow of traffic in the store. Lou had been on the phone in her office for most of the morning; when she came out she was not her usual jovial self.

"Is everything all right, Lou?" Tess could see the worry lines on her face. They didn't match the cheerful hot pink dress she had on.

"What?" she said, distractedly.

"Is everything all right?"

"Oh, yeah, honey, everythin's all right. I've been talkin' to my daughter. She gave me a little bad news."

"Oh." Tess didn't want to pry, but didn't want to appear apathetic, either.

"She's gettin' a divorce, so she and my granddaughter are gonna come live with me. Least fer awhile."

"Oh Lou, I'm so sorry. How old is your granddaughter?"

"She's nine. Ya know, selfishly, I think it might be nice ta have them around the house. I mean, I wish she weren't gettin' a divorce— that's just awful—but it'll be nice ta see 'em everyday. Nothin's more important than family. Martha Maye knew all she'd have ta do was ask, and I'd say come on."

"Lou, do you mind me asking how long you've been a widow?"

"Course not, honey. It's been eleven years now since Vince has been gone, bless his soul. He was a keeper, and I miss 'im everyday."

Lou drifted off into the store as another customer came up to the register.

Tess was arranging a book display in the store's big picture window later that morning, when she glanced outside and did a double take. A very striking woman was walking down the sidewalk *with Jack*. She watched as they stopped to talk to someone.

"She's his ex-wife." Lou sidled up next to her.

"Esmerelda?"

"Ezzie? Lord, that's funny!" Lou laughed, smacking her hand down on the table. Tess looked back out the window. She wondered what was so funny. "No, her name is Corrine."

The woman was tall and slim, with jet-black hair that she'd combed back into a chignon. She was dressed in a beautiful knee-length yellow linen dress and two-inch mules. Her legs were tanned and toned. Every man who passed by took a second look.

"She's a knock-out," Tess said.

"Oh . . . she's hotter than the sun, but not as bright." Lou was still standing next to Tess, with her arms crossed in front of her. They both stared out the window.

Tess moved to get back to work when she realized she'd been staring, but when she turned she sent two stacks of books flying to the floor. She and Lou picked them up and Tess quickly got back to work, saying, "I didn't mean to stare . . . she's just so . . . so . . . sleek and beautiful."

Tess tried to inconspicuously look out at Jack and his ex-wife, who were still standing across the street, chatting. She wondered if Corrine was the reason she hadn't seen Jack lately.

Another man joined them on the sidewalk. Finally, Lou spoke, and Tess realized that Lou had probably been watching her, while she'd been watching Jack.

"Don't worry. That's her boyfriend. Them two ate supper before they said grace," Lou whispered.

Tess didn't have the foggiest idea what she was talking about, since it was only mid-day. "I'm not worried. Um . . . supper? Are you talking about last night, or—"

"Living in sin, a course," Lou broke in. "Them two ate supper before they said grace. Ain't you ever heard that expression bafore?"

Tess laughed. "I've heard a lot since moving here, but that one I have not heard before."

"Ya know, I don't see why Jack ever married her in the first place. They're like two cheeks on a big butt . . . " Tess furrowed her eyebrows in an, 'No, I don't know' expression, and Lou finished her thought. " . . . the only thing they have in common is a fart."

Tess laughed and playfully hit Lou's arm. "Oh, *you* . . . "

"What's so funny?" Pickle came up behind them. His hair was sticking up from the cowlick at the back of his head, and he had chocolate on the side of his mouth.

"Oh, Peekal, never you mind!" Lou took him by the arm and led him away. "You better go and get yerself some more a Tess's cookies for fortification. I'm expectin' a delivery any minute, and I'll need your help. With any luck, we'll get ten big boxes today."

They walked off toward the back room, and Tess turned back to the window. Jack and Corrine had moved on. She looked down at the table and then quickly back out the window. How long had *he* been there? The would-be handy man. She didn't remember seeing him when Jack was standing there, but there he was—sitting on a bench across the street and looking directly at the bookstore, one denim-clad leg propped on the other knee while he drew on a cigarette. He saw her through the window and slowly raised a hand to tip his hat in greeting. She waved quickly and finished up her work at the table. She was arranging a display; she had no intention of *being* the display.

* * *

Tess didn't realize the time until she overheard Pickle ask if it was all right if he went home for the day. She left for the day too, but stopped in the diner for a quick bite to eat before going home. She'd just sat down in the red vinyl booth at the front window when Buck slid in across from her.

"Evenin' Mizz Tess. Would you allow me to join you?"

"Oh. Hello, Mayor . . . I suppose so. How are you?"

"I'm exemplary, thank you! I saw you come in the restrunt, and thought it would be a good time to stop and catch my breath." He squinted his eyes at the chalkboard list of daily specials. "What looks good today?" Buck looked back at Tess for a brief moment, giving her a leer, and added, "Besides the obvious." He winked at her before returning his attention to the menu board. Tess cringed.

"The lemon meringue pie looks good to me, but I suppose I can't have that for dinner," she said, trying to fill the silence but not babble, too.

Just then, Junebug appeared at the table. She was a pretty woman, even in her seventies, with long white hair that she always kept up in a bun. Thin, and genteel, she always wore just the right amount of make-up, and she wore casual, stylish clothes underneath her apron. The only deviation in her appearance was whether the bun was on top of her head or at the back of it. Slick liked to joke that she was feeling frisky when she put it on top.

"Hireya'll?" She plopped her order pad on the table so she could use both hands to fix the knot on the back of her head.

"Junie, if I was doin' any better, I'd have ta hire somebody to help me enjoy it!"

"Aw, gwon, Buck, nobody can be doin' *that* good." Junebug lightly pushed his shoulder. "'Specially in this weather. It was hotter'n blazes all day, and now it's comin' up a bad cloud out there."

"We shore do need the rain," Buck said. "It's sa dry, the trees are startin' to bribe the dogs."

"That it is." She ducked her head down for a better look outside, then stood up straight. "Okay, enough chit-chat, Chet. I got other customers to wait on. What kin I gitch y'all?"

Tess said, "I'll have the tomato soup, a corn muffin, and sweet tea with lemon, please."

"And I'll have some a Slick's liver'n onions, please, ma'am," Buck said, adding, "Oh, and some coffee, too, please, Junie."

"Okeedokee," Junebug said, writing on her pad. She looked up at him over her reading glasses. "You don't usually order coffee, Buck. By gonnies, the whole town's turnin' upside down. Would you like a little cream with your coffee, or do you want it unadulterated?"

"Unadulterated," Buck said, decisively, without a hint of a smile. Tess propped her elbow on the table, and her chin on her fist, partially covering her mouth to mask her smile. She worked some multiplication problems in her head to keep from giggling at the southern vocabulary. A boom of thunder directed her attention outside, and she noticed the rain coming down hard.

Junebug started off toward the kitchen, and Buck started to talk, but Tess didn't hear him; she was listening to Junebug give the order to Slick.

"Walkin' in! Gimme a splash a red noise. Put the lights out and cry. Mud and a sweetie, and sour it. The sweetie, not the mud."

"Sorry." She realized Buck had said something to her. "Say that again?"

"I asked how the renovatin's comin' along." Buck sat back, folding his hands on the table.

"Slow but sure. It'll take me a while to do everything I want to do. But I'm enjoying it."

"Good, good. Do ya need any hep?"

"Oh gosh, no . . . thanks, I'm doing fine."

"I used to play in that house as a boy. My mama was friends with Lou's mama and she'd go over thar for coffee and take me along. It's some house."

"I hear you've lived here all your life, and your family's been here for how long?"

"Ya know, I don't rightly know exactly when my kin first came here, but I know they at least go back to my great great-grandparents."

"This is certainly an interesting town."

Junebug came over with the coffee and iced tea and set them on the table. She pointed out the window. "There goes Peekal, bless his heart. He dudn't have the sense ta get outta the rain. My stars and garters, he couldn't find his rear with his hands in his back pockets."

It was still pouring down rain, but Pickle didn't seem to be in a hurry; he was sauntering down the sidewalk, hands in his front pockets, rain pelting his red baseball cap. Junebug shook her head. "That boy's just like his daddy. Neither one of 'em have the good sense God gave 'em."

"That kid's a good'un, Junie, you know that," Buck said, watching Pickle.

"Yeah, you're right. Food'll be out in a New York minute." Junebug walked back toward the kitchen.

"All right. Back to the subject at hand," Buck said. "Your house."

"What about it?"

"I used to love to play down in the basement. And the backyard. Man alive, you've got a great backyard. Of course, I never could bring myself to play on the back porch. In the eighties they glassed it in and made it the pretty sun room that it is today, but back when I was a boy, there were so many wild stories floatin' 'round, I was convinced there were ghosts back there."

"Ghosts?"

"Oh yeah, if those walls could talk. Mmm, mmm. That house has seen some tragedy."

"Oh. I had no idea."

"Well, I reckon you should know, it bein' part of the history of your house, and you bein' Lou's employee and all. She dudn't like ta talk 'bout her family much, but . . . her grandmama was murdered on that back porch, only two short years after her daddy had been murdered . . . "

ALL HAT AND NO CATTLE

<u>mill</u>: noun \mil\ meal
Enjoy your mill.

[1935]

Maye Hobb called up the stairs, "Samuel! Johnny! Y'all stay out of that bedroom and away from the wallpaper mess. I don't want that wallpaper glue traipsed all through the house or in your hair or on your clothes!"

Hearing her husband John's low, patient voice upstairs talking to their sons, she felt confident he would keep the boys away from their bedroom. She went back to fixing dinner.

John came downstairs a short while later looking worried and pre-occupied. He'd been busy up there for a while, first in the bedroom, then up in the attic. Maye asked him what he'd been doing, and he said, "Maye, I need to tell you somethin'. You know the big trunk up in the attic . . . "

She put her hand up to momentarily silence John, listening toward the stairs. "I mean it boys!" she hollered. "You stay away from that wallpaper mess!"

She stirred the spaghetti sauce and said, "You look worried, John. What's the matter?"

John took a deep breath. "Maye . . . "

She glanced at the wall clock. "Oh, will you look at the time. We've got to eat supper and get to church." Going to the bottom of the steps, she called up, "C'mon boys! Ima Jean! Louetta! Supper's ready!"

* * *

The wallpaper stuff was tempting. Johnny and Sam had been playing around it almost all day. Their fingers were itching to get at that paste. They were playing in the hallway outside their parents' bedroom door, tantalizingly close to wet, gooey fun.

Sam "accidentally' sent a toy car flying into the room their mother had just warned them away from. Johnny chased after it. The car bounced off the bottom of the Victorian dresser, and rolled backward, striking his shoe before careening into white mopboard. It bounced back and forth from the wall to the door until it finally stopped behind the pine door.

Johnny picked it up and said, "We need something to weigh it down a little." He looked around his parents' room and then walked over to their dresser. He saw a thin copper key, with a tag attached by yarn. "This'll be perfect!"

Johnny got down on his hands and knees to put the key on top of his car.

"Sam! Lookit this!"

Sam watched as the car shot across the room, straight as an arrow, the tag trailing along in the air, mimicking the exhaust in a car's wake.

"Nifty!" Sam readied his car. "On the count of three, we'll race 'em, okay?"

They barely heard their mother yell up the stairs, "I mean it boys! You stay away from that wallpaper mess!"

They both sat at one end of the room, cars side by side.

"One . . . Two . . . Three!"

The cars shot all the way across the room, only stopping when they reached the finish line—the wall. Johnny's car got there first and bounced backward, hitting Sam's car as it careened toward the wood-work. Sam's car skidded sideways, bounced off the wall, and back into Johnny's car, knocking the key off, and sending it into the floor register.

Clink. Clink. Clink.

"Uh-oh—the key!" The boys went over to the register, knelt down, and peered in. It was deep and dark, and they couldn't see anything. "Holy cannoli! What'll we do now? How are we gonna get the key back?"

"C'mon, boys! Ima Jean! Louetta! Supper's ready!" their mother called up the steps.

"We'll get it later. Come on, we gotta get downstairs for supper," Sam said.

They grabbed their cars and ran from the room.

* * *

John helped Louetta, his youngest child, up into her chair and sat her on top of some books that boosted her high enough for the table. The family ate quickly and noisily.

Several times John started to say, "Upstairs in the attic—" but each time he was interrupted by one of the kids. Maye finally excused everyone, instructing them to get ready to leave for church.

He sat quietly at the dinner table while Maye and Ima Jean cleaned up the dishes, talking and laughing together. He was deep in thought, with a serious expression on his face, until Louetta tugged on his arm. Then his face lit up with love. She climbed up onto her daddy's lap, nuzzling her nose into his neck. He wrapped his big bear arms around her and squeezed her tight, closing his eyes and breathing in her sweet smell.

"I wish you could go ta church with us too, Daddy."

"Me too, Butterbean. But I have to go to a meetin'." He gave her another big squeeze and kissed her forehead. "Now go get yer shoes, and I'll help you put 'em on."

"Why'd he say ya had to go all the way up there tonight?" Maye asked her husband, as she dried her hands on the dishtowel.

"I don't know why. The message only said he needed to see me and it couldn't wait," John explained for the second time. He wanted to spend time with his family as much as they wanted him to, but he'd gotten an urgent message that he couldn't put off. "But Maye . . . "

Louetta came back into the room and climbed back onto his lap, handing him her shoes. He didn't finish his sentence.

"I'll drive you and the kids up to church. You can attend the service and fellowship time, and I'll be back to pick you up with time to come in, visit a spell, eat some of that mouth waterin' chocolate cake you're takin', and drink some bad coffee."

Maye let out a long sigh, but there really was no use in arguing about it. She walked to the bottom of the stairs. "Come on kids, time to go!"

"Maye, I need to tell you about the attic trunk . . . " John began but was again interrupted when the three other Hobb children came lumbering down the steps and began pulling out coats, scarves, and gloves, all talking over each other.

"Daddy, can we play in the snow when we get home?"

"Dad, have you seen my Bible?"

"Daddy, tie this shoe, please."

"Mama! Daddy! Look at my loose tooth!"

Maye handed out hats and mittens, insisting they all wear them.

Ima Jean, the oldest, whined, "Do I have to wear a hat? It messes up my hair."

Her brother, Sam, piped up, "She wants to look her best for *Walter!*"

She swatted him on the arm, and he jumped back out of her reach, laughing.

"That's enough, you two," their father warned from the kitchen chair where he was scrawling something on a piece of paper and stuffing it into his pocket. "And yes, you have to wear a hat." He helped Louetta put on her hat and mittens, then held Maye's coat open, while she slipped her arms inside. He gently tugged on the bill of Johnny's hat in a gesture of affection.

"Come on crew, off we go."

It was an unusually cold December night with a light snow flitting through the air. Outside, the children breathed heavily to see their breath in the air. They loaded up and headed over to the First Methodist Church where they had been members for twelve years. John was a deacon and Maye was the secretary of her ladies circle. They were there every Sunday morning and evening and every Wednesday night.

John pulled up to the side door of the church. Imitating a train conductor's voice he said, "All out! First Methodist Church, stop one!"

They piled out of the car, with a quick "Bye, Dad" or "See ya!"

Maye said, "No, keep that hat on until we get inside . . . " as John tried to say, "Maye, the trunk in the attic..."

Louetta pulled on her arm. "Come on, Mommy!"

Maye turned back to look at John, leaning down, peering back into the car. Deciding he couldn't say what he wanted to in only a few seconds, and not wanting to worry her needlessly, he simply gave a weak smile and said, "Save a piece of cake for me."

She stood up to close the door and said, "Okay, darlin'. Hurry back."

"I'll be back before you know it," he called after them. They waved, and he watched them disappear through the church door.

[June 2010]

Tess listened in horror as Buck told her about Lou's father being murdered two years before her grandmother was murdered. She gasped and covered her mouth with her hand. "Oh my goodness. I had no idea."

"Yep, Lou doesn't like to talk about it at all. It was a horrible tragedy. Seems like Lou's mama had one tragedy befall her after another. And she was left with four youngins to raise. Mizz Maye did a good job with 'em youngins though, as you can witness through Louetta."

"Mercy goodness. That would make a good novel, wouldn't it? Was either murderer ever caught?"

"Nellie's was. There whadn't ever any doubt about who killed her. Poor Maye witnessed it herself, God love her. But, Lou's daddy? Naw, some said her father's death was suicide, some said murder. It wasn't ever solved. Matter fact, I guess it's still on the books. What they call a *cold case*. Hey, I heard you're a writer. You write true crime?"

"Oh no." Tess shook her head. "I was thinking it would be something Jack could sink his teeth into."

"Hey—you know what would make a good story?"

"What's that?" Tess asked, just as Junebug appeared at the table with their food.

She served the meals and then asked, "Can I gitch y'all anything else?"

"That'll do it, Junie," Buck said.

"Alrighty, enjoy your mill."

Tess's confused expression as she watched Junebug walk away prompted Buck to say, "Your *meal*. Enjoy your meal."

"Ah! Thank you for the translation."

After taking a bite, Buck continued. "Okay, I think you'll like this one. Goose Pimple Junction used to have some real scoundrels. Around World War II, I hear tell there was a fight on Main Street just about every Saturday afternoon . . . "

Tess listened to Buck's story of Goose Pimple Junction lore. He was nearing the end of his story when she saw Jack walking toward the diner. She immediately felt guilty because she'd told him she had plans for the evening. Starting to wave as he entered the diner, she quickly dropped her hand when he sat down at the counter and didn't look her way.

"But ole' P.D. had his thinkin' cap on that day. He blew the whistle, but he blew it in a different manner than was the usual signal, see. The sheriff heard it, and figured somethin' waddent right. So he hoofed it on over to the station, but he went the back way. He and his deputies snuck in through the back door, and they subdued the louts and hauled 'em off to the pokey."

"That's some tale. And that was some fast thinking."

"True story," Buck said proudly, finishing off his dinner. He glanced over his shoulder, following Tess's eyes, and saw Jack sitting at the counter. "Well thar's Jack, now. Hey Jack! We was just talkin' 'bout you!"

Jack looked over his shoulder indifferently, but didn't get off the stool. "Zat right?"

"Yep. Tess said you might could use some 'a Goose Pimple Junction's true crime to write about. But she'll hafta tell ya all 'bout it some other time. We gotta git goin'." He looked out the window. "Tess, it's pourin' down bullfrogs out there. You have t'allow me to deliver you home. You walked to work, didn't ya?"

"Oh, well . . . yes, I did walk, but I was going to stay and have a piece of that lemon pie. Thank you for the offer though."

"Now what kind a gentleman would I be if I let you walk home in this weather? I insist. How 'bout you get that pie to take home?"

"Yeah, Tess, how 'bout gettin' take away? You must have other plans," Jack said sarcastically.

Tess didn't like being told what to do. She was not about to go any-where until she was darn good and ready. She'd rather get soaked to the bone than be manipulated. She signaled Junebug. "One piece of your lemon pie for *here*, please." Then she pasted on her most charming smile and said firmly to Buck, "Thank you anyway for the offer, but I'll be fine."

Buck shot an annoyed look Jack's way, but quickly recovered. "Well, thank ya for the favor of your kumpny tonight, Tess. I will be seein' you around." With that, he gave Junebug some dollar bills, said, "Keep the change," and disappeared out the door and into the rain.

Jack got off of his stool and walked over to Tess's table.

"You were ignoring me," she accused, smiling up at him.

"Looked like you didn't want to be disturbed. Didn't know your *plans* included dinner with Buck."

"Please sit down, Jack. I have two interesting things to tell you about," she took a deep breath, "plus an apology."

"Are you sure your dance card isn't full? Sure you don't have *plans?*"

"What is your major malfunction?" Tess said in an exaggerated southern drawl.

"Woohoo! Tessie's been takin' lessons in Southern speak! Well done, lady, I'm impressed." He gave a show of tipping his imaginary hat. He was teasing her, but the chill of a moment ago seemed to have thawed a bit.

"I got that one from Lou. Now I did say I have an apology to make. Are you going to sit down?"

Jack smiled, his eyes softening, and dimple showing. "Since you asked so nicely."

"Not that I should have to explain to you, but Buck joined me unexpectedly tonight."

"It wadn't a date?" Jack shot back. "Then what were your *plans?*"

"No, it was not a date." She took another deep breath and let it out. "Okay, I'm sorry. I may have exaggerated when I said I had plans. I apologize . . . " She was groping for words and feeling embarrassed at the discovery of her little white lie. She didn't feel like she had to explain anyway. It wasn't like he had a claim on her. Finally, she said, "Can we move on now? Do you want to hear what I found out, or not?"

"Not. I want to hear why you made up an excuse to decline my dinner invitation."

Tess looked out the window, searching for the right words. How do you tell someone you don't want to get involved with him because you heard he cheated on his wife? She really didn't want to discuss it with him, and she didn't want his excuses or lies, either. She'd had enough of that with her ex-husband. Finally she looked right at him and quietly said, "I just divorced a ladies' man. I don't want to go down that road again."

"And you think I'm a ladies' man?" His voice was almost a screech. In a more normal tone he said, "I guess I'll just have to prove to you

I'm not."

She smiled shyly at him. "I guess you will."

Jack's grin was lopsided. "Okay, apology accepted. Discussion to be continued at a later time. Now lay it on me. What did Buck have to say?"

Just then, Willy the would-be handyman entered the diner and shook off the rain like a wet dog. "Shewee! It's rainin' so hard the animals are startin' ta pair up." He was loud enough for everyone in the diner to hear. He saw Tess and Jack and walked over to their table.

"Hey, y'all. How's the renovatin' comin' along, sweet cheeks? Need me yet?" Willy's creepy grin spread across his face.

"It's . . . uh . . . coming along just fine, uh . . . Willy, right?"

"I knew you'd remember me." He stood there smiling down at her, his hands in his denim jean pockets. "How 'bout you and me go for a drink some time?" He winked at her.

The bluntness of his invitation caught Tess by total surprise. She sputtered and stammered and was trying to think of a polite way to say 'no' when Jack answered for her.

"No," he said bluntly.

"Well, mister, you're kind a cute, but I ain't no homo sapien. I was askin' the lady."

"I'll agree with you there, but I believe you mean *homosexual*, and I'm not either. I'm answerin' for *the lady*, and I said, *no*," Jack said more forcefully this time.

Junebug came bustling up to the table with Tess's pie and a sweet tea for Jack. "Willy? What's the matta with you? I know your mama taught you better manners than that."

Slick sidled up to the table too, and joined in. "Willy, I'll give you a shiny new quarter if you'll park yer ornery butt over yonder on one a them stools."

"Shoot," Willy muttered. "I feel like a banjo. Everybody's pickin' on me. Okay, okay, I'll go. But I will see you later, darlin'." Enunciating his words, he nodded his head, pointed his finger, and winked at Tess, before starting toward the stools at the counter.

Jack started to get up, but Tess reached across the table to grab his arm. Fortunately, he was partially standing, because unfortunately, she knocked over his tea, spilling it all over the table and onto the spot where he'd just been sitting. The accident lightened the mood, and everybody laughed, making her face blush red with embarrassment.

Slick started off after Willy. "Nemmine him, Jack. I'll give him a tutorial on politeness."

After Junebug had cleaned up the mess and brought a new glass of tea for Jack, Tess took a bite of her pie and watched a rain drop slowly make its way down the outside of the window.

They were both quiet for a minute until Jack said, "How'd he know you're workin' on your house?"

Tess blew out an exasperated sigh. "He said he overheard me talkin' in the bookstore. He followed me out the door the other day and said he's a handyman and wanted to offer his services."

Jack snorted. "He's about as handy as a back pocket on a shirt."

Tess laughed, and Jack softened but not completely.

"And I'll tell you another thing, he's all hat and no cattle."

"What does that mean?"

"Means he's one who pretends to be what he's not. He's all talk and no substance. He's a fake, a braggart. He talks big, but he can't follow through."

"Do you think I just fell off the turnip truck?" She was a little offended. "I can spot a fake when I see one."

"Okay, Tess, I didn't mean to insult your intelligence." He took a deep breath. "I don't know why I'm all riled up tonight. Guess I just got my feelin's hurt."

"Well, drink some of your sweet tea before I manage to spill it again. Maybe it will make you sweeter."

"What did you have to tell me?" Jack sat back, taking a long gulp of his tea.

Tess filled him in on what Buck told her about Lou's father and grandmother. She thought the filling station story was interesting, so she told him about that, too, in case he really might want to include it in one of his books.

"Well, that's interesting news. Why don't ya ask Lou about it?"

"Well . . . I can't get that look on her face out of my mind when I told her about finding the key. Not to mention Buck said she doesn't like to talk about the murders. Jack, her face spoke volumes."

"Yeah, well that is unusual, she usually lets her mouth speak volumes." Jack saw the look of reprimand on Tess's face and got serious. "Could be it's just too painful." He looked at his watch. "Got any plans for the evening? I mean *real plans*?"

"Not really, why?"

"Just for fun, wanna do some research at the library?"

"Sure . . . I guess so."

Tess and Jack paid their bills, said their goodbyes, and left the diner. As they passed the big picture window she saw Willy pick up his cell phone.

Weird duck, she thought, and a shiver passed through her.

MURDER
IN
GOOSE PIMPLE JUNCTION

scurtt: verb \skurt\ scared
You're a skurtt a me!

[1935]

After the Sunday evening service, Maye took her place at the refreshment table in the basement of the church to serve her famous chocolate cake. Her four children were the last in line, and she joined them at another table where they ate cake, drank punch, and listened to the men swap tall tales. She looked at her watch. Seven-thirty. *John should be back any time.*

Her sister-in-law, Denise, sat down next to her with a questioning look on her face.

"You all right?"

"Hmm? Oh, yeah honey, I'm fine, why?"

"You look worried . . . preoccupied."

Maye had a niggling feeling that was making her uneasy. A sense of foreboding. She had thought she was successfully hiding her feelings.

"Is it your daddy? This'll be the first Christmas without him. And last Christmas couldn't have been an easy one—he was so sick then. It'll be hard for you this year."

"I do miss him," Maye admitted. "Maybe that's it. I don't know. I just feel edgy."

Eight o'clock.

They would be locking up the church before long. Her brother, P.D., joined them at the table.

"John not back yet?"

"Naw, he must've gotten held up. He'd best hurry though, or the kids and I'll be sleepin' in the church." She manufactured a smile. The niggling grew.

Eight-o-five.

As people said their goodbyes and departed from the fellowship hall, Maye went to help clean up, while her brother entertained the kids with magic tricks. Time seemed to be crawling.

Eight-twenty-two.

Maye looked from the clock to her brother. He pulled a quarter from behind Louetta's ear as she sat on his lap, wide-eyed. Maye wrapped up her cake. It was almost the children's bedtime. The hall was just about empty. She wondered how much longer they should wait for John. Another glance at the clock.

Eight-twenty-five.

"How you do that, Uncle P.D.?" Johnny asked.

"How do I do what?" P.D. smiled. "Hey, boy, is that a loose tooth?" He put his fingers up to Johnny's mouth and pulled them back with a quarter between his two fingers. "Naw, it was just this quarter. Never know where it's gonna pop up." Johnny looked at him skeptically, with one eye squinted.

P.D. glanced at Maye, and their eyes went from the clock back to each other.

Eight-thirty.

"One more time," Louetta begged. "Doo't again."

Maye said her goodbyes to the pastor and his wife, and then walked over to her family, glancing at the clock one more time.

Eight thirty-five.

She looked at her brother. He nodded in silent understanding.

"C'mon kids. Uncle P.D.'s gonna take y'all home."

*　*　*

Ten-thirty, the kitchen clock said. Maye poured some hot water from the teakettle into a mug and then impatiently poured it into the sink. *Where could he be?*

The kids had gotten baths and were snug in bed. John still wasn't home. She walked to the front window. The driveway was empty. Something was wrong. Maye could feel it. She'd sent her brother home and wouldn't be able to reach him at this late hour. She couldn't sit around any longer waiting and wondering. She put on her coat and went next door to the pastor's house.

Maye noticed the alarmed looks on the reverend and his wife's face as she told them John hadn't come home. Nearly beside herself with worry, she pleaded with them.

"I know it's late, and I hate to put you out, but can you drive me up toward Goose Creek Bridge to look for him?"

"Of course we can, Maye. Helen's mama's visitin', and she can stay with the kids while we're gone." The reverend, his wife, and mother-in-law quickly got coats on, all the while reassuring Maye everything would be all right.

Once in the car they rode in strained silence, with Maye sitting straight-backed on the edge of her seat, straining her neck in every direction along the way, searching for John's car.

Ten minutes later, as they crossed Goose Creek Bridge, Maye saw a car parked just beyond the bridge. Exhaust billowed into the air, and snowflakes danced in the headlights of the black 1934 Ford Tudor as it sat idling off to the side of the road. "That's him!" Maye cried, gripping the door handle tightly.

"Now, Maye, you stay here, and let me go investigate," Reverend Baker said, slowing the car to a stop.

But Maye had already jerked the handle up and jumped from the car, stumbling as she landed.

"John!" she yelled as she ran toward her husband's black Ford.

[June 2010]

"This is it!" Jack said. He and Tess were seated in the back of the library with stacks of six-inch thick, twelve-inch tall hardbound books on the table. They both had a book open in front of them.

"Finally!"

"This is a December 20, 1935 Goose Pimple Gazette article about

Lou's daddy." Jack's eyes went from the article to Tess. "Tess, Buck was right. He *was* murdered."

"Oh my gosh."

Jack scanned the article. "This one was written right after the murder, so it doesn't sound like they had a clue of who did it, at that point, at least. It only says he died from a gunshot wound to the head, fired at close range."

"How horrible."

Jack continued scanning the old newspaper article, slowly shaking his head. "This is awful. It says, ' . . . on the night of the murder he took his family to church and said he'd be back to get them after he went to a meeting. When he didn't return, his wife and the pastor went looking for him. Maye Hobb found him, dead behind the wheel, with his car still running and three bullet holes in the windows of the car. There was one bullet hole behind his right ear, and an exit wound in his left temple.'"

Tess got up to read over Jack's shoulder. "And they had no suspects. How strange."

"You know, this might be a good premise for a book. I'd like to find out more about this case. We need to do an Internet search," Jack said.

"For what?"

"To see if there's anything else through the years that was discovered. See if we can get more of the full picture."

Tess gathered her things. "The library's about to close, though. Come on, we can do it at my house."

In a low voice, Jack said, "Honey, I thought you'd never ask."

"Do an *Internet search*, Jack." She shot him a chastising look. As they walked out, she glanced at him, and he flashed her a big smile.

"You're impossible, you know that?" But she couldn't help returning his smile.

Her smile fell, and she swallowed hard when they reached the door, and she thought back to their arrival at the library. Jack had driven them in the pouring rain, and Tess remembered having to squeeze in close to him under the umbrella, as they walked from the car to the library door. She remembered the rain pounding on the umbrella, his arm around her, their bodies touching, as they both crouched together trying to stay dry. The smell of his aftershave lotion, the feel of his hand on her waist, the heat of his body . . . *Oh, crap*. She shook her head, telling herself to stop thinking about it.

She immediately started working multiplication tables in her head, her favorite form of distraction. She was working so hard on not thinking about Jack, she tripped on the sidewalk. He caught her, holding her close for a moment, and all she could think was, *oh crap, oh crap, oh crap. Oh holy crap.*

"I believe you could trip over a cordless phone, Tess."

"Just call me Grace."

The rain had stopped, but it was pitch-black outside, hot and steamy. Jack steered Tess to his car, with his hand again at the small of her back. A scene from the television show *Lost In Space* flashed in her mind. Danger! Danger Will Robinson!

He opened the car door for her, and as she got in, she glimpsed something in the back seat. While he went around to get in on the driver's side, she reached back and picked it up. He got in and saw her holding his spare umbrella.

"Oops?" he said, smiling guiltily. Her accusatory glare turned to laughter at his smile. She just shook her head, but as they drove to her house she once again turned to mathematics.

Thirty-two times sixty-nine equals . . . two thousand, two hundred and eight. Seventy-five times twenty-six equals . . . one thousand, nine hundred and fifty . . .

"What are you thinkin' about so hard over there, Tess?" Jack asked after a few minutes.

She stopped multiplying, and lied, "Just thinking about Lou's father."

It didn't take them long to get to her house. They went in the side door, which opened to a hallway that was narrow, made even narrower due to a table sitting against the wall just a few steps in. Tess walked into the house first and stopped to turn on the lamp sitting on the table. The darkness made the expectant air between them more electric. Jack's nearness rattled her.

She groped for the lamp, accidentally knocking over a picture frame. Jack squeezed past her to pick it up, putting his hands on her waist, his body brushing hers as he passed.

Oh, for all that is good and holy.

He stood to hand her the frame, as she turned on the light. He was so close. She began to babble. "Can I get you something to drink? Eat? Come on into the den, where my laptop is," she said in rapid-fire succession, pushing past him.

He followed her into the den, where she immediately turned on the lamps on each end table, the lamp on the desk, and the built-in lights over the bookcase. He chuckled, but didn't say anything.

"Would you like anything to drink? Sweet tea?" she asked again, realizing she hadn't given him a chance to answer before.

"I'm fine thanks, sweetie," he said, suppressing a smile. She stood there staring at him, and he laughed and added, "Oh! You said *sweet tea,* not *sweetie.* My mistake."

"Mister, you are such trouble."

They sat on the couch, and Tess logged on to the Internet with her laptop. It only took about thirty minutes to find what they were looking for.

"Click on this, Tess." Jack pointed to a link on the screen. As the page came up, he moved closer to her. She moved the computer to his lap, and they read silently for several moments. "This says Louetta's father was a witness to a bank robbery. He was the only witness who could identify a man named Lynch and place him at the scene of the crime. Looks like Lynch was convicted, then pardoned by the governor."

"Pardoned? Why?" Tess stared at the computer screen.

"He and another man, Rod Pierce, both only served three months of a twenty-year sentence. The governor pardoned them on grounds of mistaken identity."

"Oh my heavens."

Jack read part of another article out loud:

> *Eighteen months after the murder, a Mallard County Grand Jury indicted Brick Lynch, one of the two men convicted of the First National Bank robbery, and his former wife, Maisey Lynch, for the murder of John Hobb. Mollie Hall, a woman employed by Maisey's family, testified she'd overheard the Lynch couple talking about the murder.*

> *Hall testified that Maisey Lynch had led a colorful life starting at the age of sixteen, when she married C. C. Testerman, the Mayor of Helechewa. After Testerman died, Maisey married Helechewa Police Chief, Sid Hatfield, who also died mysteriously, as Testerman had. Lynch was Maisey's sixth husband.*
> *The trial of Brick and Maisey Lynch was postponed twice, but*

eventually held, and a jury found them not guilty in less than five minutes after Judge J. F. Bailey ruled that Mollie Hall's testimony was incompetent. Both Brick and Maisey Lynch were set free. Rumors and stories abounded concerning the murder of John Hobb, but no one was ever convicted of the crime.

"What rumors?" Tess wondered aloud.

Jack tapped a few keys. Opening another online page, he read it silently and then pointed to the screen."This was written in 1979, as part of an effort to document the history of the city. It looks like some people insinuated he killed himself.

"It says here:

Some people saw a connection between the killing and identifying the bank robber, but some also thought there might have been a connection with money that was still missing from the bank, and a mysterious meeting he went to that night, that could never be corroborated.

It hints that he might have taken some of the bank's money. It also says his murder was never solved."

"How horrible. To know that some people thought your father died because he was involved in something shady, others believing it was murder to avenge his testimony against a bank robber, and still others thinking it was suicide. But that's absurd. If it were suicide, why would there be bullet holes in the car windows?" She scooted away from him slightly.

"And why would the car still be running?"

"I don't know . . . I just don't know, Jack. I'll look online some more tomorrow. See what else I can find."

"Without me? Your partner in true crime?" he said sarcastically, putting the laptop on the coffee table and sitting back against the couch.

"It's been a long day, and I have to work tomorrow," she explained, her fingers playing with her necklace.

"Mmm hmmm . . . "

"What do you mean, 'mmm hmmm'?"

"I think you're a scurtt 'a me!" His exaggerated southern drawl was back.

"Don't be silly." Tess said to his chest, avoiding his eyes. "I am not scared of you, it's just getting late, that's all."

He leaned towards her, and she leaned back.

"See! You flinched! You *are* a scurtt of me!"

"Don't bother using that Southern speak on me." *Don't rise to his bait, Tess.*

Jack slowly moved closer to her, reaching his hand out to play with her hair. "One question. Do you really think I'm a ladies' man?"

She took a deep breath and let it out. "I don't know. But I don't want to be one of a string of many, Jack."

"What makes you think you would be?"

Tess looked away, trying to think how to answer him.

Looking back at him, she felt an invisible pull. *Oh, Lord, help me*, she thought, right before he kissed her. His hands gently cupped her face, and she sank into him and kissed him back in a long, hard kiss before pulling away.

"What is it, Tess? What are you afraid of?" he asked softly, their faces still close. "Is it me, or were you just burned that badly in your divorce?"

She moved out of his arms, looking away from him. "In the marriage . . . in the divorce . . . " she trailed off.

"How can I convince you to give me a try?" he asked, standing to go.

"Jack, just about the time you 'convince me,' you'll be ready to move on."

"Why would you think that?"

"It's called experience." She followed him to the door.

He turned to look at her. "One of these days, Tess Tremaine, you are gonna like me! Mark my words!"

Watching him walk down the walkway, she whispered, "That's the problem, Jack. I *already* like you."

WHO LICKED THE RED OFF YOUR CANDY CANE?

<u>forty-eleven</u>: adjective \ fawr-tee ih-lev-uhn\ a long time
I've known him for forty-eleven years.

[December 15, 1935]

The lights of John Hobb's car were still on, and the engine was running when the reverend, his wife, and Maye Hobb found it. Maye ran, stumbling several times along the way, to her husband's car, her whole body sick with dread and panic. She jerked open the door to find him slumped against the wheel, lifeless eyes staring at her, with dark, sticky blood coming from his left temple and nose. Maye couldn't process what she was seeing. Her hand went up to her mouth as a cry escaped. The blood in her body plummeted to the ground. Her knees buckled; the reverend got there just in time to catch her before her legs collapsed.

He wanted to help her back to his car, but she refused. On shaky legs she paced back and forth next to her husband's car, while Mrs. Baker ran to a nearby home to call the police. Bug Preston was on the scene within twenty minutes.

This couldn't be happening, Maye thought. Her husband couldn't be dead. He wouldn't leave her alone to raise their four children. Her boys needed a father. He was the love of her life. He wasn't dead. He just wasn't. She couldn't stop pacing. Her hands, feet, nose, and ears were so cold they were hurting, yet her feet wouldn't stop. The pain was a sign she was still alive. She couldn't feel anything else. The reverend finally got her to stand still, and they prayed together, the car's lights illuminating them along with the snowflakes. After the prayer, she slowly sank to her knees, and then to a sitting position on the ground, tears streaming down her face.

Bug found three bullet holes in the front and driver's side windows of the car, but discovered only one had struck Hobb.

"It looks like he was hit rightchere." Bug pointed behind Hobb's right ear to his deputy, "with the bullet emerging rightchere." He indicated the wound right behind John's left temple. "I want fingerprints taken and bloodhounds out here right now. And that means ten minutes ago! And let's do a spiral sweep."

John's revolver was in his right hand and somebody suggested suicide. But that was quickly ruled out because the gun did not appear to have been fired.

"This may not be the scene of the crime. He might have been murdered somewheres else, and his body was driven back here and left. I'd say they put his gun in his hand to make it look like suicide, but the dimwits forgot to fire it. Or he knew he was in danger and got his gun out but never got a chance to use it."

"Why'd they leave the car runnin'?" a deputy wondered aloud.

"I reckon they'uz in a hurry," Bug told him . "I want men goin' door-ta-door. Let's find out if anyone saw anything. I want prints, bloodhounds, and witnesses. And I want it fast as greased lightnin'."

The bloodhounds arrived and took off, with men following. Someone had found P.D., and he arrived to take Maye home. She sat in his car like a statue on the way back. She was cold. So cold. She didn't think she'd ever be warm again. Inside or out.

[June 2010]

The rain had stopped completely, and the sun was bright once again when Tess started out for work. After locking her door, she looked at the keys, specifically the one she'd found. It was still on the key ring, and she ran her fingers over it, as if it were a rabbit's foot, before putting the keys in her purse. She walked, preoccupied, for about a block, until she noticed a jogger coming toward her. As he got closer she realized it was the mayor.

Just wave and pass on by please. But he didn't make it that easy for her.

He slowed and came toward her with a huge smile.

"Mornin' Tess," he said, doing a U-turn around her, and falling into step. "I see you got home last night without meltin'."

"Good morning, Mayor. Yes, thank you, I got home just fine."

"Aw, now you don't have to be sa formal. Call me Buck, long's I'm not on official bidness."

"Do you jog often . . . Buck?" she asked, wishing she could just call him Mayor.

"At least five times a week. But I'm in trainin' now for the Fourth a July mini that's comin' up. Have you heard about our town fair on the fourth? It's a real shindig, let me tell you!"

"I did hear something about it. It sounds like a lot of fun."

"Lou told me you're a baker. You oughtta enter somethin' in the bakin' contest. They have purt near everything . . . pies, cakes, cookies . . . long as it's homemade, you can enter it."

"Well, I just might do that. Don't let me keep you from your run, now."

"Oh, you can keep me," he said, looking sideways at her and smiling. "Shoot, I can run any ole time, but it ain't often that I can accompany a purty lady to town."

Tess glanced in the window of the hardware store as they walked past, and saw Jack inside talking to Art, the owner. She waved, and he raised his chin in a nod, his eyes going to Buck.

When they reached the bookstore Tess said, "Thank you for the escort, Mayor..." He gave her a look, so she said, " . . . Buck. This is my stop. Have a good day."

She took a deep breath and let it out as she disappeared inside her safe haven. In the back room, she found Pickle eating a jelly donut. A blob of jelly oozed out onto his shirt, right above the writing: "Runs With Scissors."

"Mornin' Ms. Tess! Hireyew?"

"I'm just fine, Pickle. How are you?" she said, reading his white t-shirt. "Do you really?" Her lips slowly curved at the corners.

"Do I really what?" He gave her a blank look.

"Run with scissors." She pointed to his shirt.

"Aw, ya got me! Good'un, Mizz Tess!"

"You ought not to do that you know, it's not safe," she kidded him.

"No, Mizz Tess, I don't really run with scissors. It's just a t-shirt."

* * *

Tess didn't know Willy had come into the bookstore until he sidled up a little too close to her and leaned over her shoulder saying, "What doin', doll?"

Tess jumped to her right, out of Willy's personal space.

"I'm working, and I'd appreciate it if you didn't sneak up on me like that," she said, hand over her heart.

"Aw shucks, darlin', don't get cross on me. I's only bein' friendly."

"Can I help you, Willy?" Tess demanded.

He looked her up and down and purred, "You're lookin' fine today, Ms. Tess. Do you by any chance have any raisins?"

Confused, she said, "No. Why . . . "

"Well then, how 'bout a date?" He gave her a Cheshire grin.

Tess briefly closed her eyes, then turned to walk away from him. "Excuse me, I need to do some things in the back room."

Willy called out, "Wait!" She stopped and turned, hands on her hips. "My apologies. I was blinded by your beauty. So, I'm going to need your name and number for insurance purposes!" He came too close again, into her personal space.

"Willy, please stop." Tess backed up, feeling uneasy. She didn't want to be rude but couldn't get over the audacity of the guy.

"I know I don't have a chance, but I just wanted to hear an angel talk," Willy tried yet again, continuing to move toward her.

She tried to catch Lou's eye, but she was busy talking to Chief Price and his son, the candidate for governor, who had come into the store just before Willy.

When Tess looked back at Willy, he startled her by being so close their clothes touched. She jumped again, knocking over a stack of books, along with a sign. Lou and the men looked over at the commotion. Tess gave her a pleading look before she bent down to gather the books, and Lou made a beeline for them.

"My stars and garters, Willy! How'd you sneak in here 'thout me knowin' 'bout it?"

"Mornin' Mizz Lou. I didn't do no such thing. I walked in through the front door, big as daylight," Willy defended himself. "Mornin' Chief. Henry Clay," he said, as they walked up.

"Mo'nin' Willy. Whatchew doin' in here? You wouldn't know a book if it hit you in the face." John Ed laughed and turned back to share his joke with his son.

"Hey now! I like ta read. You just don't know me well 'nuff."

"Don't go givin' him no store credit, Lou," John Ed warned. "He doesn't have a pot to pee in or a window to throw it out of."

Willy shot the chief an angry look. "Who licked the red off yer candy cane?"

Lou said out of the side of her mouth, "He don't cotton to your sarcasm, John Ed." More loudly she said, "Are you sayin' yer in here to do some bidness?"

"I'd like to look around, if you don't mind," Willy said indignantly.

"Hep yourself. Just keep yer lookin' ta the books and not my employees! You ain't in a grocery, but I can see what you're checkin' out."

"Yeah, well, I feel like I'm in a grocery. There's somthin' in here I wanta bag," Willy mumbled as he walked away.

Henry Clay smirked at the remark. He turned toward Tess, held out his hand, and introduced himself. "'Scuse my manners, ma'am, I'm Henry Clay Price."

Tess shook his hand, saying, "I'm Tess Tremaine. I've seen your campaign signs, but I didn't know you're the chief's son."

"Well, ever now and then he claims me."

"Find any more mysterious footprints lately, Ms. Tess?" John Ed looked smug.

"Actually, Chief, I did. Under my bedroom window." Tess glared at him.

"Well lands sakes, that coulda been anyone. I sure am glad you didn't call me over for that one."

"Don't mind him, Tessie," Lou said of John Ed. "He'd gripe with a ham under each arm. But he has a good heart. He's takin' your case more seriously than he's lettin' on. I've known this man for forty-eleven years. He's good people."

Lou pulled Tess with her toward the register desk, adding in a low voice, "But Willy? I suwan-ee, child. Jesus loves him, but he's the only one. You best watch that booger."

* * *

Tess walked home slowly, deep in thought. She enjoyed working at the bookstore but hadn't planned on putting in as many hours as Lou was asking for. When she volunteered to lock up for her, she never realized how long of a day it would end up being. But with Lou's daughter going through a divorce, she needed to be at home to help her daughter and granddaughter move in, and Tess was happy to help. Things would settle down again soon, she told herself.

Her body was tired, her mind was preoccupied with thoughts of Lou's family, and her eyes were enthralled with the streaks of red, pink, and blue in the early evening sky. Walking past Ernestine & Hazel's Sundries, she waved at Ernestine, who was locking up for the night. She'd heard the woman's name wasn't really Ernestine, but they just called her that ever since she bought the store. *Funny town*, Tess thought. Next was Rhubarb's, the fruit market named for its owner, Barbara Ruther; her store was already dark inside and locked up tight. As she crossed the street, her eyes went to the beautiful sky again.

She stepped up on the curb and started toward The Silly Goose, an upscale bar and grill. Totally entranced by the unusual red color of the setting sun peeking through the buildings, she was caught completely by surprise when someone suddenly reached out and pulled her into the bar and grill's dark doorway.

WHATEVER BLOWS YOUR DRESS UP

<u>hare</u>: adverb \hair\ here
What's he doing hare?

[1937]

"Trevor Hobb is the black sheep of the family," Bug Preston told his deputy. "Always has been. I remember old Mrs. Cox in fifth grade sayin' to him, 'You certainly are *not* like your brother.'"

"I know what you mean, Chief. Trevor ain't smart, or charming, or particularly handsome like his brother was. John had it all, and poor Trevor barely had any."

"He wadn't known for his honesty, neither," Bug said.

"Say . . . how come some people call him Blister?"

The chief chuckled. "On account a him bein' so lazy. Folks started callin' him "Blister" because he never showed up until the work was finished."

"Whatta you make a him pointin' fingers at Nate Hunter?"

"He told me that, and I laughed in his face. Told him he was lyin' like a no-legged dog. Told him to git on outta here and stop spoutin' nonsense like that. Said not to breathe a word of it to Maye. Poor old widow woman, left to raise them kids all on her own. She don't need that worry."

"I heard he's been hangin' 'round her house a lot lately."

Bug tucked his chin and looked at the deputy over his glasses. "Well he is the kids' uncle, ya know."

"But, Chief, you know Trevor's always had a crush on Maye."

"That's 'zactly why I don't think he'll say no more 'bout it. He don't want her questionin' his sanity. He knows it sounds like crazy talk."

* * *

"Maye, you've always tolerated his flirtin', and it seemed harmless since you were both married, and everybody knew you loved John more than life itself. But you ought not to encourage him now." Maye and her sister-in-law talked while they did the dishes.

"Oh, don't be silly, Denise. Everybody knows I'm still in mourning."

"That may be, and don't take this the wrong way, but I know you like the attention. It's just that you're unknowingly encouragin' him. He seems to get bolder every time he comes over."

"Oh, it's only harmless fun."

"Honey, you and I may know it's all in fun, but does he?"

[June 2010]

A hand reached out from the dark doorway of the Silly Goose, grabbed Tess by the wrist, and pulled her off the sidewalk. She froze, her whole body rigid.

Then she screamed, even as she saw Jack standing in front of her, his right hand in the air as a sign of surrender, his left hand still wrapped around her wrist. Her self-defense reflexes hadn't yet gotten the memo to cease and desist. Her knee became a groin-seeking missile as she wrenched her arm free. Fortunately, he anticipated her reaction and leapt out of kicking range.

"It's just me, for pity's sake!" Jack said. "It's just me! It's just me!" He repeated, hands out in front of him, until she dropped her knee and slumped back against the brick wall.

Glaring at him, with one hand on her chest and the other on her forehead, she tried to catch her breath. She was furious with him for scaring her like that. She took her purse off of her shoulder and whacked him on the arm with it.

"Hey!" he yelped.

Another whack.

"Hey!"

Whack.

"HEY!"

"Jack! How could you?" she screamed.

"I'm sorry! I really am—I saw you comin' and thought it would be fun to surprise you. I didn't think that it would scare you like that. I'msorryI'msorryI'msorry!" She glared at him. "Let me make it up to you by buying your dinner." He tried to reach out and touch her arm.

Putting her purse straps back over her shoulder, she stepped out of the darkened doorway, onto the sidewalk, and out of his reach. Her heart was still doing the rumba, and her adrenaline was doing push-ups. She sat on a bench in front of the restaurant to try to calm down. Jack cautiously sat next to her.

"Please, Tess. I really am sorry I scared you. I was only playing around. Have dinner with me. Please?" He looked at her as if *she'd* hurt *his* feelings. She sat glaring at him, trying to return her stomach to its rightful place. He touched her hand and added another "Please?"

She acquiesced. Tucking her hair behind her ears, she eyed him suspiciously. At the end of a deep sigh, she grumpily said, "Oh . . . all right. But don't you dare *ever* pull a stupid stunt like that on me again!"

"Never ever. I promise." Jack held up his scout's honor fingers.

Once they were seated at a table on the patio, Jack said, "Let's start with a drink to calm your nerves."

"Jack, did you do that on purpose?" Tess asked, narrowing her eyes at him for the second time that night.

"Do what on purpose?"

"You wouldn't have scared me in order to offer me a drink and try to get me drunk, would you?" She looked at him suspiciously.

"Well, I have to admit this is working out better than planned."

"Aha! You admit you planned this!"

"Now don't go putting words in my mouth!" He sat up straight and leaned forward. "I don't think you could define *planning* as the fleeting thought I had between the time I first saw you walking toward me, to when I grabbed you. But if you insist, then okay, you're right. In that short span of time, I hatched the diabolical plan to make you have dinner with me. But I did not plan to get you drunk. That would just be a bonus."

"After you all but attacked me?"

"I did not attack you! I merely tugged on your arm."

"Mmm hmmm." Tess looked up at the waiter who had arrived at their table. She pasted on a smile and said, "I'll have a martini, please."

After Jack ordered a Newcastle Brown Ale, and the waiter had gone, he said, "So you decided to get drunk with me, after all!"

"One drink. *One drink*, Jack. That will not make me drunk. What is with you?"

"You're just so darn fun to mess with, Mary T." Jack's eyes sparkled mischievously.

He was spared a retort because Tess spied Willy entering the restaurant. "Oh no," she groaned.

Jack followed the direction of her eyes, through the big glass windows, inside to the bar, where he spotted Willy, resplendent in full cowboy regalia. He was sporting a black western shirt with pearl snaps and a skull embroidered on each side of his chest. Each skull held a rose stem in its mouth, with the embroidered rose snaking its way up the shoulder. He had on a bolo tie with black leather cords that held a large silver arrowhead slide. His denim jeans looked painted on, and the cowboy boots and a black cowboy hat completed the ensemble.

"He's dressed to impress. In his own mind," Tess said.

"What in the world?" Jack gaped, as Willy settled into a seat at the bar. "If he weren't so ridiculous lookin', I'd say he was tryin' to catch the eye of a certain pretty lady."

"Well he certainly looks like a fish out of water in this place. I mean, he looks nice enough with his bolo tie and all, but . . . skulls and roses?"

"I'd venture a guess he's trying to show his badass side with the skulls, and his softer, tender side with the roses. You know, with those two qualities, he could be quite the catch," Jack said dryly.

"If it weren't for his lack of brains, his perpetual sneer, and his crude personality."

"I'm surprised he can sit. His pants are so tight, if he farted, he'd blow his boots off."

"Jack!" Tess covered a laugh with her hand over her mouth.

The waiter reappeared with their drinks. After he took their dinner orders and left again, Jack decided to shift gears.

"Are you planning on goin' to the Fourth of July shindig?"

"Yes, I thought I'd go for a while," she answered, warily.

"Good. How 'bout I pick you up and we go together?" He didn't wait for an answer but just bulldozed on. "Look, I've gone for the past few years, and I always get hit on by all the blue hairs. You'd be doing me a favor by going with me. It would help keep them at bay."

"Oh, so I'd be kind of like your bodyguard," she said, more as a statement than a question.

"You say taters, I say maters." Jack grinned, dimple appearing.

"I think that's 'you say tomatoes, I say tomahtoes.'"

"Idn't that what I said?" he asked facetiously. He sat back, and took a long drink of his beer. He finally returned the glass to the table and said, "I'll be by to pick you up at one o'clock. We'll make a day of it. Okay?"

She eyed him guardedly. "I don't know, Jack."

"Tess, let me prove to you I'm not a bad guy. I want to get to know you better. I want to spend time with you." He pleaded with his eyes.

Sixty-four times twenty-eight equals . . .

"Well lookie hare!" Willy suddenly stood at their table, with a fake grin on his face. "Just the woh-man I was hopin' ta see. I've purt' near busted two sets of knee caps lookin' for you."

"Well, now you've found her, and you can see she's busy. So scram," Jack growled.

"Now, you ain't got no call ta act mean like that. I'us only bein' friendly, is all." Willy held his hat up to his chest, trying his best to look hurt. "I even happened by yer house, but ya weren't thar."

"No shit, Sherlock . . . " Jack began, but faltered under Tess's glare. "We were havin' a nice civilized dinner until you came by."

"I wadn't talkin' ta you, ya old coot."

"Well, you know what they say about age . . . "

"No, but I know what *I* say. And I say, you're old."

"Age and treachery will always overcome youth and skill," Jack said through slitted eyes.

"Willy, is there something I can do for you?" Tess asked, putting her hand on Jack's arm.

"Why yes, as a matta fact there is. You can say you'll go ta the Fourth a July town hoo-ha with me." Willy shot a sneer at Jack.

"Oh." Tess sat back, surprised. "I'm sorry, Willy, but I just told Jack I'd go with him."

Jack gave a surprised look at Tess before folding his arms and shining a satisfied grin at Willy.

"Well. Whatever blows your dress up," Willy said coldly. He turned and disappeared as fast as he had appeared a few moments before.

"So now who's whose bodyguard?" He saw a worried expression on

Tess's face; he sighed and said, "You weren't tellin' Willy a tall tale, were ya? You *did* just agree to go with me to the town celebration—right?"

"Hmmm?" Tess's gaze moved from the door Willy had walked through to Jack. "Yes, I meant it. I just don't understand Willy's interest in me. I'm only five years younger than you are. He's got to see me as old, too."

"That man is trouble. He hasn't done anything other than be a pest, has he?"

"There's just a certain edge to him, and there's something that happened the other day that I haven't told you about."

His face got serious and he said quietly, "Tell me, now."

"I think someone may be stalking me." He raised his eyebrows and she continued. "I found two footprints and some cigarette butts beneath my office window the other day."

"You *what?*" he exploded. Tess shushed him and he lowered his voice. "Why didn't you tell me? Did you call John Ed? Tell me you called John Ed."

"I didn't call John Ed," she said quietly, guiltily.

"Mary Tess Tremaine . . . "

"Jack, I wasn't about to give that man another opportunity to say I was having a . . . a . . . a hissy fit with wings . . . "

"A hissy fit with a tail," he corrected her.

"You know he would have just laughed at me. Actually, I did tell him later, when I saw him at the bookstore. He couldn't have cared less."

"But that was solid evidence. Cigarette butts would have fingerprints on them."

"I didn't think about that."

"You think Willy might be involved in this?" He leaned toward her.

"I don't know. I just find his behavior odd."

"You're a beautiful woman, Tess. It's not that I'm threatened by old Willy, I just don't like him around you."

"Okay, can we talk about something else now? How's your book coming along?"

Later that night, as Jack drove her home, Tess thought about what a nice evening she'd had, despite its beginnings. The martini, the food, the atmosphere at the restaurant, talking and laughing with Jack . . . she let out a sigh as she looked up at the sliver of the moon.

"What?" Jack asked.

"Nothing. It was a wonderful evening. Even if it started off rocky." It had been a long time since she remembered feeling so good.

He pulled into her driveway, and for the first time since she'd met Jack, Tess knew what she wanted. When he stopped the car and turned to her, she didn't look away. When he leaned toward her, she moved to him. He took her face between his hands and brought their foreheads together. She pushed her hands into his hair. They both closed their eyes and reveled in the moment.

Slowly, Jack pulled back and kissed his way down Tess's face until he reached her mouth. She returned the kiss, soft and tentative at first. After a few minutes, the kisses were no longer soft, or tentative.

BEAUTY'S ONLY SKIN DEEP, BUT UGLY GOES ALL THE WAY TO THE BONE

dreckly: conjunction \ drek-lee\ directly
I'll catch up dreckly.

[1937]

It was a hot summer day, and every window in the house was open.

WUMP! A loud noise carried from the upstairs window of the Hobb house.

"Ow! Johnny! Stop it!"

WUMP! Came the noise again, the sound of something hard landing on something soft.

"No Johnny! Stop! I won't do it again! I promise!" a little girl's voice cried out.

WUMP! WUMP! "I'm gonna jerk a knot through your head!" Johnny yelled.

"Stop beating me! Stop beating me! Help!" Louetta's little voice screamed.

Maye was in the side yard gardening and heard it all. She continued picking beans, as if nothing was wrong. She even started softly humming to herself.

WUMP! "That'll teach ya!" Johnny yelled. WUMP!

"AHHHH! Johnny! Stop beating me!" Louetta yelled again.

"I'ma knock you into next week!" he hollered.

Maye finished picking her beans and went to stand underneath the window. "Okay, you two, that's enough. Ain't nobody out here 'cept me and the beans, and they don't cotton to yer hijinks. Now you two c'mon down and help me set the table for supper."

Louetta appeared at the window. "Aw, Mama, I thought Uncle Trevor was comin' down the street . . . "

Johnny's head popped up. "Did we scare old Mrs. Happenay? Did she hear us?"

"No, she did not. I told you, nobody's out here. Now quit all that foolishness and come down and make yourselves useful."

An hour later, Trevor arrived. He was becoming a regular at the house. "You sure are lookin' fine, Maye," he drawled, looking her up and down.

Giggling, she briefly allowed him to kiss her cheek, and then she skittered on back to the kitchen. "Trevor, would you put the bread on the table, please?"

"Sure, anything for you, sugar."

"Kids! Supper's on!" Maye called, and the four Hobb children came running.

"Uncle Trevor, Johnny's been beating me," Louetta baited her uncle.

"Again?" Trevor said with a straight face.

"Uncle Trevor, I got an A on my arithmetic test today. Wanna see?" Ima Jean asked.

"After supper, sugarplum," Trevor said, absentmindedly.

"Uncle Trevor, can you take me up to town tomorrow," a voice came from the end of the table. Trevor wasn't sure to whom the voice belonged. It didn't matter. He just wanted to eat Maye's delicious chicken and feast on her beauty.

"I 'spect so," he said, looking at Maye.

"Trevor, you're too good to us."

"You know I'd do anything for you, Mayepie."

After supper, Trevor was helping dry the dishes when there was a knock at the door. Maye went to answer it, and in a moment he heard a deep, male voice. Walking around the corner, he saw Louie Crane, the widower farmer down the road, standing in the doorway.

"Whatta you doin' here?" Trevor grunted.

"Evenin', Trevor. I just came by to bring Maye some 'a my prize maters. I know how she likes them so." The tall gentleman was looking lovingly at Maye, who was holding three huge bright red tomatoes.

"Louie, that's mighty nice 'a you. C'mon in and let me send some cake home with you."

Louie stepped inside, while Maye disappeared into the kitchen. Trevor glared at him in silence. Louie returned the sentiment. Maye came bustling back out of the kitchen with a huge chunk of pound cake dripping with vanilla icing.

"I hope you enjoy it, Louie." She patted his arm.

"Aw, I'm sure I will Mizz Maye. Ever since Julia died, I haven't had homemade baked goods. Thank ye. I'd best be off now." He waved. "Bye y'all."

Trevor didn't utter a word until the man was well down the sidewalk.

"You lead him on," Trevor accused.

"I do no such thing. I'm only bein' neighborly."

"Well, why'ont you be neighborly with me?" He reached out to grab her around the waist.

"Trevor, I done told you, I'm not gettin' involved with a married man!" Maye maneuvered tantalizingly just out of his reach.

[July 2010]

Tess and Jack walked the few blocks to town for the town's Fourth of July celebration, commenting on all the homes' patriotic decorations.

"The town does the Fourth of July up right," Jack commented.

Every home leading in or out of town had a big American flag posted either on the house or lawn.

"I've never seen so many decorations in all my life." Tess looked first one way, then the other, trying to take it all in.

"The women's club sponsors a contest, and people really get into it, decorating houses in any way imaginable, ranging from tasteful to downright tacky."

To prove his point, they passed a house where window boxes with red, white, and blue flowers spilled out over the sides, and mini American flags sprouted among the foliage. Several houses had red, white, and blue bunting hanging from covered porches. Small flags lined the sidewalks leading up to some of the houses. Streamers decorated trees in one yard; in another, mini versions of the stars and stripes were attached to tree limbs, making them look like leaves. Tess was so engrossed in a lawn's solid sea of mini Old Glories, she wasn't watching where she was going and almost tripped over a dog. Jack caught her arm. She glanced up at him with a look that said, 'don't say a word.'

"Do the businesses have a contest, too?" Tess asked once they reached town.

"Oh, yeah, each one has to outdo the other."

Every business was in full regalia, with streamers, bunting, flags, or balloons decorating their storefronts. Some had red, white, and blue lights surrounding the doors. Almost all had a sign in their window wishing America a happy birthday.

Tess smelled the mingling scents of hot grease, barbecue, and pop-corn. Looking around, she saw five men dressed as Abe Lincoln and two as George Washington. Jack pointed out two people dressed as the Statue of Liberty wandering around. Crazy, creative homemade patriotic hats and glasses were on more heads than not. How someone could wear glasses with little flashing light bulbs, and walk straight, Tess couldn't understand. She had never seen so much red, white, and blue in such a condensed space. No one dared wear any other color that day. Even Pickle sported a red t-shirt, this one with words that said, "Lock Up Your Daughters!"

Jack saw Pickle's shirt and said, "I'm not even gonna touch that one."

At one-thirty, the annual bike parade began. Children of all ages paraded down Main Street on decorated bikes, strollers, and wagons with patriotic colors. Several dog owners had decorated their canine friends in Fourth of July style, and they followed the children down Main Street with the dogs soaking in the attention, oblivious to the embarrassment they should be feeling. The local high school's marching band led the way for cars carrying Miss Goose Pimple Junction candi-dates and the mayor's car. A bright red fire engine, with its lights flash-ing, brought up the rear.

After waving to all of the parade participants, Tess and Jack mean-dered through the various booths, sampling barbecue, hot dogs, potato salad, and fried apple pies.

"Tess, I'm full as a tick on a fat dog," Jack said. "Let's go find a seat. I think the winner of the Miss Goose Pimple Junction Contest is about to be announced."

Tess was too full to walk another step when they took seats next to Lou, who was dressed in red, white, and blue, and wore a headband with glittery red and blue stars on springs that looked like antennae.

"Well hi, y'all!" Lou said, reaching out to pat each of them. "Hireyew?"

"Lou, if I was any happier I'd be twins," Jack said.

"Well, set yourselves down and get ready to feast your eyes, Jack," Lou said with a wink. Looking at Tess she added, "And you?"

"I'm too pooped to pop," Tess complained. "How are you?"

"Aw, honey, I'm having a good face day!"

"Yes, you are, Lou," Tess laughed, "yes, you are!"

"What are you talkin' 'bout woman? You always have a good face day!" Jack said.

Lou took a break in the joking to lean toward Tess's ear, whispering seriously, "You know what yer doin', right?" Tess gave her a questioning look.

Their conversation was interrupted when a thirty-something brunette and a young girl, who looked to be about nine years old, sat down on the other side of Lou. The woman had brown hair and eyes that were so brown they were almost black. She had a pretty face, but her body was shaped a little bit like a pear. The little girl looked just like her mother, minus the pear shape.

"Aw, here are my babies now. Tessie, meet my new roommates. This is Martha Maye, my daughter, and this here is Buttabean, my granddaughter," Lou proudly said. "Girls, this is Tess and Jack."

Martha Maye leaned over her mother to shake hands and said, "Don't worry, I didn't actually name my child 'Butterbean!' That's just our special name for her. Feel free to call her Carrie!" She smoothed Butterbean's hair back. "I'm so glad to meet you both! I've heard so much about you."

"I'm happy to meet you, too, Martha Maye . . . and . . . " Lou looked expectantly at Tess, and Tess said, " . . . Butterbean." Lou gave a head nod and flashed a satisfied smile.

"May I ask why you call your beautiful granddaughter 'Butterbean?'" asked Jack.

Lou and her daughter looked at each other, exchanging a meaningful glance. Finally, Martha said, "It's a special name because it's what Mama was called as a child."

"And this little Buttabean is a special child." Lou's eyes suddenly glistened with tears.

"Even though any grandmother would say that, I have to agree with her." Martha Maye combed her fingers through the little girl's long brown hair.

"Lou are you gonna do your usual commentary on the contest?" asked Jack, changing the subject.

"Well, honey, I don't know if I should. Tessie here'll think poorly of me if I go shootin' my mouth off as usual."

Tess looked to Jack for an explanation.

"See, Miss Goose Pimple Junction is not chosen on talent, looks, or brains, but more or less on popularity," Jack explained. "Of course, whichever contestant's father glad-handed the most voters might have somethin' to do with the outcome, too. The contest is a parliamentarian's nightmare. You saw the voting over at the Piggly Wiggly grocery store all last week, right?" Tess nodded. "Well, did you know anyone could vote each and every time they visited the store, if they wanted?" Tess shook her head. "It's true," Jack continued. "And the best seat in the house for the announcin' of the new Miss Goose Pimple Junction is right next to Lou. She won't sugar coat anything, she'll give you the unvarnished truth on each contestant, and she'll entertain you while she's at it."

"In that case, Lou, please don't censure yourself on my account."

"Well, all right, if you're sure . . . " Lou looked like she might need some more prodding, but the music started, and the mayor appeared on the makeshift stage. "Afternoon, everyone! And Happy Birthday, America!" The crowd applauded enthusiastically.

"Let's warmly welcome the lovely ladies, our fine contestants for Miss Goose Pimple Junction." Buck swung his arm out toward the women, who were walking on stage to applause and whistles.

"These beautiful young women don't need an introduction, but it's protocol, so I gotta do it," he continued. "Our first fine contestant is Araminta Lehigh."

Araminta stepped forward, twirled around, in model fashion, and stepped back.

Lou put her hand up to the side of her mouth and whispered to Tess, "She looks like she made an ugly pie and ate every slice!" Jack leaned in, and Tess whispered Lou's line to him.

"Cornelia Crump," the mayor said into the microphone. Cornelia proceeded to step up and twirl.

"Land sakes, she can't help that she's ugly, but she could've stayed home," Lou whispered.

"Julia Cole," was the next contestant called. She stumbled a bit as she stepped forward.

"Bless her heart," Lou said, "She's so tall if she falls down she'll be halfway home."

By now, Jack was leaning over Tess's lap so he could hear Lou's commentary straight from her, since Tess had her hand over her mouth, trying not to laugh out loud.

"Nellie Baker."

"Mmm mmm, look at her." Lou shook her head. "She's so buck-toothed she could eat an apple through a picket fence."

"And last but not least, Frona Walker."

"Aw, it's not right to say what I thank a poor Frona, bless her heart."

"Lou, you can't stop now! This is the last one!" Tess begged.

Lou took a deep breath, put her hand up to partially cover her mouth, and whispered, "She's so ugly they had to tie a pork chop around her neck to get the dog to play with her."

"And the winner is . . . Julia Cole!"

Lou leaned over Tess's lap and whispered, "I know Julia's mama is happy. That child was so ugly when she was born, her mama used to borrow a baby to take to church on Sunday."

"Lou, you outdid yourself this year. Excellent commentary." Jack patted her on the back, as the audience dispersed.

"I don't understand," Tess said, confused. "Why aren't these women more . . . 'beauty queen-like?'"

"Well, now see, there's your problem. You're thinkin' Miss Goose Pimple Junction's a beauty contest. No, honey. This contest idn't about how you look, it's about who you know. Social prestige and power. That's why I don't mind makin' fun of the girls. There's not a one was in it on account of their beauty or brains or talent. It's all just a crock a . . . "

"Mama!" Martha Maye interrupted. "Little pitchers have big ears." She hitched her head toward Butterbean.

"Oh yeah, sorry, honey. Anyway, it's all in good fun. Well," she said, looking behind Martha Maye. "Hidee, Henry Clay. I figured you'd be around."

Henry Clay Price had quietly walked up to the group and was standing right behind Martha Maye. He had a wide smile on his face and a campaign button on his shirt that said, "Henry Clay Price for Governor." Martha Maye turned, saw him, and promptly wrapped him in a friendly hug.

"Henry Clay! How long's it been? It's so great to see you!"

His face turned bright red, but he looked extremely pleased to see Martha Maye, too. "What are you doin' here, Martha?"

Lou jumped in and said, "It's nice to see you Henry, but we'us just headed up to the watermelon seed spittin' contest. Martha Maye, you and Butterbean, are comin', too, ain'tcha?"

"Mama, y'all take Butterbean and gwon ahead, I'll catch up dreckly. I wanna talk ta Henry Clay a minute."

They all strolled off, leaving Martha Maye and Henry Clay behind. As they walked, Lou brought Tess and Jack up to date on her daughter and Henry.

"Martha Maye and Henry Clay—idn't that cute how that rhymes!" She shook her head. "Anyway, they grew up together. He's been sweet on her, long's I can recollect. They even dated, against my better judgment, the summer she was home before her last year in college. But it was right about then that she met Lenny, and he swept her off her feet and away from Henry Clay."

"Did Henry Clay ever marry?" Tess asked.

"Oh, yeah. But his wife ran off with the mailman. Or somethin' like that. I think it broke his heart when Martha Maye got married, and he married on the rebound. You wanna hear a funny story about your mama?" She looked down at Butterbean, who nodded her head. "When they were in junior high skule, Henry Clay came up to her one day, out on our driveway. He handed her a note that said, "Will you be my girlfriend?" Well, she didn't know what to do, so she said, 'Wait a minute, I gotta go ask my mama.' And in the house she ran. She asked me what she should do. I told her to tell him she already had a boyfriend. So she went runnin' back out and told poor ol' Henry Clay, 'My mama said I'm already seein' somebody and I can't see two boys at once.'"

Everyone laughed at Lou's story, and Tess said, "He seems like a nice enough fellow."

"Henry Clay's a banker, aspirin' to be the gov'nor. He's made a good livin' for hisself. He just worries me a little about gettin' on with Mart. He's a nice boy, but he don't have the sense God gave a chigger. He's got too much book-smarts, and not enough common sense. And he's a typical politician." She stopped and looked at her granddaughter. "Buttabean, you wont a sno-cone? Here," she gave the girl some money, "go gitcherself one. It's hotter 'n a fritter out here."

Just as Butterbean skipped away, Buck strode up to their group. "And a marvelous fourth of Joo-lye to y'all."

After a brief chat, Buck moved on, but Tess was surprised at Lou's comment: "Beauty's only skin deep, but ugly goes all the way to the bone." She sounded meaner than Tess thought was possible of Lou. "I don't have much use for him. He don't have a lick a sense either."

Then, just as soon as the cloud had come on her face, she brightened again, as Butterbean rejoined them, sipping on a blueberry sno-cone. "Let's stop by and take a look-see at the bakin' contest. They shoul-doughtta have the winners by now."

They went to look at the myriad display of baked goods. Lou didn't know that Tess had entered her apple pie. When she saw Tess's name next to the blue ribbon she exclaimed, "Well butter my butt, and call me a biscuit!"

"I won?" Tess asked, a bit shocked. A big smile came over her face, reality sinking in. "I won!"

"And look here, Granny, your peanut butter cookies won, too!" Butterbean said, with a blue mouth.

"And your fudge," Jack said, moving down the line, "*And* your coconut cake, Lou. You two gals cleaned up!"

After reveling in their victories, they watched Clive and Earl battle it out in the watermelon seed spitting contest, with Earl being the victor. The next event was one for fathers and daughters.

"Whatta ya say, Butterbean? Wanna sneak in with me?" Jack asked.

They watched as all of the fathers in town, and Jack as a substitute father, donned goggles and had their faces lathered with shaving cream. The children were given squirt guns, and at the count of three, the race was on to see who would be the first to squirt their daddy's face clean. Jack and Butterbean didn't win, but they had a ball.

Just as Jack predicted, as they made their way through the crowd that day, all of the ladies fawned over him. Tess was introduced over and over again to some women who were clearly jealous and others who were glad to see him "with such a nice girl."

At dusk, Jack grabbed Tess's hand and led her away from the heart of town and the crowd of people, to a grassy hill where they'd be able to watch the fireworks alone. Tess protested, but Jack was persistent. She wasn't sure the other night had been a good idea. Maybe she'd let her guard down because of the martini, but she wanted to keep her distance from Jack now. There was still that matter of him cheating on his wife.

"Jack! What are you doing?" Tess towered over him, as he settled onto the cool grass at the very top of the hill. Lying down, he put his hands behind his head and scowled up at her.

"I do believe you could start an argument in an empty house, Mary Tess!"

"Jack, what are we doing up here? People will think we're being anti-social."

"You wanted to spend time alone with me," he said, grinning and looking up at the sky.

"What?" she screeched.

"Well that's what you said . . . "

"I said no such thing and you know it!"

"Oh, maybe it was me who wanted to spend time alone with you," then he grinned, reaching out to pat the grass beside him. "Come on in. The water's fine."

"Jackson Wright! I can't believe . . . "

"Shh, shh . . . now just simmer down. Stop arguin' and relax." He looked up at her. "Please?"

Nothing was said as she sat down next to him, bringing her legs up to her chest and wrapping her arms around her knees.

"How's the book comin'?" He sat up on one elbow and looked at her.

"I haven't had much time to work on it lately. Between working at the bookstore and researching Lou's family . . . "

"Hey! I meant to ask. Did you look any further online? Did you find anything?"

"Yes and no."

"Yes and no?"

"Yes, I looked, and no, I didn't find anything," she explained.

"Dang."

"Yeah."

"So what's our next move?"

"I don't know. I haven't figured that out yet."

"Well, do you still think we shouldn't approach Lou about it?"

"Yes, I have a hunch it's still too painful for her even all these years later."

"Okay, maybe we could discreetly talk to Martha Maye. She might know somethin'."

"That's a good idea," she said, genuinely enthused.

"Yep, I'm full of good ideas." He moved closer to her.

DOES A FAT KID LIKE CAKE?

<u>lilac</u>: verb \lahy-lak\ lie like
You lilac a dirty cur dog!

[1937]

The mosquitoes and fireflies were thick on the hot July evening when Trevor Hobb sauntered up his sister-in-law's front walk. She sat on her porch swing, trying to stay cool, breathing in the sweet scent of honeysuckle and watching her children. The sun had set long ago, and all was quiet except for the cadence of the crickets and the squeals of her children in the yard as they tried to catch lightning bugs. Maye watched the tiny spurts of light flash throughout the pitch-black yard and was in such a reverie she wasn't aware of Trevor's presence until he'd been there for several minutes. Hearing him swat a mosquito, she turned her head and found him leaning against the porch column, silently watching her.

"Trevor!" she said, startled. "I didn't know you were there."

"Sorry to scare you, Maye." He came up on the porch and sat down beside her. "The kids sound like they're havin' fun."

"The simple joys of life. A summer evenin', catchin' fireflies," she said wistfully.

Trevor reached out for her hand. She pulled it away from him and asked, "Would you like a refreshment? I have some lemonade and cookies in the kitchen. Are you hungry? I can get somethin' out of the ice box."

"You're my simple pleasure, Mayepie. But I don't get you. You run hot and cold on me. Why are you fightin' me now? You know I'm crazy 'bout you."

"Trevor, you and I can't be. We just can't. Please get that through your head."

"You don't mean that, Maye. I know ya don't. I know I didn't have a chance when John was alive, but now that he's gone, let me take care of you and the kids. Let me make you happy again. I want ta marry you."

"That's impossible, Trevor. Don't talk like that." Maye got up and walked across the porch.

"It's not impossible. I know you want me. I've been comin' to your house for over a year now, and you haven't discouraged me one iota. You know how I feel 'bout you. I have always loved you. I always will."

"Trevor! Don't talk that way! You're a married man!"

"I'll get a divorce. Say you'll marry me, and I'll divorce Billie Jane, and you and I will be together. Say yes, Maye. Say yes. Be mine." He was down on his knees in front of her, all but begging. "Marry me." He clutched her hand.

"Trevor, stand up, the children will see you!" She pulled away.

"I don't care who sees me. I don't care who knows I love you, Maye. Do you hear me? I love you."

"I cannot marry you, Trevor. I cannot."

Trevor stood up. In the dim light, Maye couldn't see the hurt and anger in his eyes. He ran his hands through his hair and looked out at the carefree scene in the yard. The children sounded so happy. And he was so miserable.

"Is it someone else? Is that it?" Maye didn't answer.

"I won't let you marry someone else, Maye," he said in almost a whisper.

"Don't talk like that! You don't have any say in who I marry."

"I do, and I won't allow it, Maye. I'll kill both you and the man before I'll allow you to marry anyone else."

[July 2010]

A few days after the Fourth of July celebration, Tess and Jack had arranged to meet Martha Maye at Slick & Junebug's Diner. Tess walked over after work and arrived first. Clive and Earl, who seemed to have grown roots from their butts into the stools at the diner, greeted her.

"Is it hot enough for you, gentlemen?"

"I don't know about the weather, but you, missy, are definitely hot enough for me!" Clive said, with a sparkle in his eye.

"Forget it, Clive, she likes me better, don't ya, Tess?" Earl flashed a toothless smile.

"Oh, you two! You sure know how to make a girl's day!" Tess patted them both on the back as she slid past them. "Hey, Slick!" She waved at Slick behind the window, working in the kitchen.

"Hey, Mizz Tess! Junebug'll be right out in a jiffy."

Tess heard Clive say, "You're nuttier 'n a squirrel turd if you think that purty lady would be interested in you."

She laughed to herself and headed for a table, settling into a booth in the back. She sat back and looked around the room. A couple of teenagers sat at a booth sipping milk shakes. An older gentleman sat by himself, reading the newspaper and drinking coffee. And Clive and Earl cackled at the counter. It was late afternoon; the dinnertime rush would start soon. Through the window, she saw Jack crossing the street, and she quickly checked her compact mirror to make sure she had on enough lipstick. Jack stopped for some good-natured ribbing with Clive and Earl and then he headed to Tess's table.

"'Scuse me, madam, is anyone sitting here?" He flashed that dazzling smile of his.

"Well, actually, I was hoping a handsome man would fill that seat, but you can sit there while I wait." She smiled innocently.

Jack made a show of clutching his heart. "Tess! You wound me!"

"Somehow, I think you'll survive." Her eyes went to the door where Martha Maye had just entered. She managed to get past Clive and Earl without too much commotion.

Pickle came in right behind her, and the men were busy teasing him about his shirt that said, "Ninja Cleverly Disguised As A Physicist."

"Hey, y'all!" Martha Maye said, coming toward them. Ever the gentleman, Jack got up to greet her and moved to sit next to Tess, allowing Martha Maye to take his place. They all settled in. Jack's thigh nudged Tess's. She pretended not to notice.

"It was so nice of y'all to invite me out. I left Butterbean with Mama at the shop, so I cain't stay long, but it's nice to be out with grownups for a change!"

Junebug appeared from the back, wiping her hands on her apron. Taking the pencil from behind her ear, she said, "Here's all my little chickies, home to roost!"

Jack hollered toward the kitchen, "Slick! Watch out! Junie's bun is on top of her head today!"

Junebug pointed her pencil at Jack. "That's gonna cost ya, mister. Whatever you're gonna order—we're out of it." She turned to Tess. "Let's see . . . I'll bet you want sweet tea with a lemon."

"And lots of ice, please."

"Check," Junebug said. "We're gonna turn you into GRITS, yet."

"Pardon me?"

"Girl Raised In the South," Martha explained. "Sweet tea for me too, please, Junebug, and no lemon."

Junebug started to walk away, and Jack hollered, "Hey! What about me?"

"I done told ya," she called back. "We're out of it."

"Out of what?" he asked in mock disbelief.

"Whatever it is you want." She turned her head briefly to flash a cheesy grin at him. Then she hollered into the kitchen, "Two sweeties with lots of hail and sour one."

A few minutes later, Slick came out of the kitchen with an order of fried green tomatoes and a glass of sweet tea, which he sat down in front of Jack. "'S'on the house," he deadpanned, before walking away.

Jack got right to business.

"The pleasure of baskin' in your lovely company was just one of the reasons why we asked you here, Martha Maye."

"Oh?" Her eyebrows shot up.

"Tess and I heard about, and subsequently have been researching, the murder of your grandfather. We think it's a helluva story, and I'm considering using it in my next book. But there are holes all over the place. We think it's a sore subject for your mom, so we thought we'd ask you . . . " Jack didn't know how to continue.

"Oh, you're right. Mama won't talk about that." Martha Maye sat back from the table.

"Do you think she'll mind if I write about it?"

"Does a fat kid like cake?"

"Ah, criminy. What if I helped solve the murder?"

"Jack, she doesn't want it solved."

"Why on earth not?"

"She has her reasons, bless her heart."

"Well . . . how much do you know about what happened back then?" Jack asked.

"I never knew him, of course, so it's not a sensitive subject for me like it is for Mama. And I never heard much, because she was so little at the time she hardly remembers, and what she does remember is painful. What do you want to know?"

"Anything you know," Jack said. "If that's not too intrusive."

"Oh my gosh, these things are good!" Tess said, around a mouthful of fried green tomatoes.

"Well . . . lessee . . . " Martha Maye took a sip of her tea while thinking. "Mama said her daddy took the family to church on that Sunday night, and then went to a meetin'. Apparently he'd gotten a message that his uncle wanted to see him right away on an urgent matter."

"What was the meeting about?" Tess asked.

"Well that's the thing . . . nobody ever could figure out who called him. His uncle said it wasn't him. I'm not sure how my grandfather got the message, but I do know that whoever left the message, and why, remains a mystery. 'Course there were some who said he made the message up. Said he was up to no good. They suggested he was involved in somethin' shady havin' to do with the bank robbery. Do y'all know 'bout the robbery?"

"Yes, we did see a newspaper account of that," Tess said, as Junebug arrived at the table with the food.

"Alrighty then." Junebug set down a bowl of pea soup in front of Martha Maye. "I have a Frenchman's delight." She put a salad and crackers at Tess's place and said, "Cow feed and a dog biscuit for you, darlin'." And last she set down a bun pup and some cherry gelatin. "And a bun pup, and nervous puddin' for Mr. Trouble here."

"Aw, Junie, how long you gonna be mad at me? You know I love you. I just love to tease you."

"Jackson, you know I cain't stay mad at you for long."

Jack waggled his index finger at her and she bent down. He kissed her cheek, and she swatted his arm.

She tried not to grin. "Y'onta drag that dog through the garden?"

"Just ketchup will be fine, sweetie." She went off grumbling about silver-tongued devils. Jack wasted no time getting back to the subject at hand.

"So people thought your grandfather was in on the robbery?"

"Not necessarily." Martha Maye took a sip of her soup. "That was one version. But some thought he may have found out about somebody else's involvement and was bein' given some hush money."

"How horrible!" Tess moaned. "How did your grandmother get through all of that? I mean, she had the horror of finding her husband shot to death, and then she had to deal with all the wild rumors. What a horrible time it must have been for her."

"Oh, honey, you don't know the half of it."

"What else is there?"

"It was a horrible year—1935 was. My great-grandfather died in January of that year, just eleven months before my grandfather died in December."

"Oh no," moaned Tess.

"Your poor grandmother," Jack said.

"Is there anything else you can tell us about his murder?"

Martha Maye took a spoonful of soup, then said, "There's one thing that's always stuck out, the few times Mama's talked about that night."

"What?"

"Mama said *her* mama talked for years about my grandfather tryin' to tell her about somethin' that night, but she never gave him a chance."

"That is odd," Tess said.

"Yep. Grandmama said he kept sayin' he wanted to tell her about somethin' in the attic—somethin' about the trunk in the attic. Noboby knows what he . . . " Martha Maye's sentence trailed off.

At the word 'trunk' Tess froze, fork in mid-air. She turned to look at Jack, as he turned to look at her.

"What'id I say?" Martha Maye asked.

"Whoa." Jack whistled. "Tess found somethin' in the house, Martha Maye."

"What did you find?" Martha Maye looked at Tess. Tess reached into her purse and pulled the key off of her key ring. "This. There was a tag attached that said, 'trunk'."

Martha Maye took the key and looked at it. *"Trunk?"*

"Trunk," Jack and Tess said together.

Tess looked at Jack and said, "Jinx, buy me a Coke!"

"Where'd you find it?"

"It was in the floor register in the master bedroom. It must have fallen in there and no one realized it," Tess explained.

"Well, I'll see if I can broach the subject with Mama—"

Tess interrupted her. "I told her about the key right after I found it. She didn't say much, except they'd gotten a replacement key for their trunk way back when. But the look on her face was one of . . . I don't know . . . strain . . . or alarm . . . maybe just pain. I felt like I shouldn't ask her any more about it. She told me to keep the key."

Jack took the key from Martha Maye and twirled it between his fingers, as Tess filled a plate with fried green tomatoes and spooned sauce over them. "These are *so* good," she said, mostly to herself.

"I do know that the trunk in the attic was searched thoroughly after my grandfather died. My grandmother was sure there was somethin' in it that would help solve his murder. But nothin' was ever found . . . "

"I wonder why your mother reacted the way she did when I told her about the key," Tess murmured.

" . . . Then, when my great-grandma died, Grandma Maye put all her keepsakes in the trunk, and I don't think it was touched until we sold the house."

"Where is it now?" Jack asked.

"I 'spect it's in Mama's attic."

"When did your great grandmother die?" Tess asked, looking up to see Henry Clay.

"Hey, y'all. What's goin' on?" Henry Clay asked. He and a teenage girl had entered the diner and walked up to their table without any of them being aware of it. She went on past their booth and joined Pickle at the table behind them.

"Henry Clay! Hireyew?" Martha Maye reached out to touch his arm.

"Happier than a pig in slop. Hire y'all?"

They all mumbled they were fine, and then Tess asked if he'd like to join them.

"I don't want to interrupt anything." But he squeezed in next to Martha, not looking like he cared if he interrupted anything or not. "What're y'all talkin' 'bout?"

"Oh, I's just tellin' 'em some of our family history. Ya know, Henry Clay's folks are—or were—Mama's age, and they've lived here all their lives, too. Well, his mama's passed, now. They were so young in '35, I don't imagine his daddy would remember much. Do you think he would, Henry?"

"Naw, I wouldn't think so."

"Hey, Henry Clay, how's the campaign goin'?" Jack asked.

"Aw, I reckon it's goin' all right. I'm havin' trouble convincin' some parts of the state that I'm not as country as a turnip green. But even though it's early in the game, I'm as busy as a cranberry merchant most days."

"Well nobody said the road to the top would be easy. But I'd rather wear out than rust out, wouldn't you?" Jack said.

"I hear ya, Jack."

"Say . . . I've got a little free time these days, you want me to come by your headquarters and help fold and stuff or somethin'?" asked Jack.

"I'd be much obliged."

"I could come, too," Tess offered.

"Well count me in!" Martha Maye said.

"That's mighty kind of y'all. Anytime you can, I could use the help."

"Well," Tess said, "I should be going home now. It's been a long day."

Jack stood to let her out of the booth. "Why don't I walk you home?"

"Well, for one thing, it's not on your way," she said facetiously.

"Oh, did you think I was really askin'?" He smiled down at her, daring her with his eyes to challenge him. Tess's sigh signaled her surrender, and Martha Maye and Henry Clay laughed.

Jack said, "Night y'all," and followed Tess to the cash register.

"You li'lac a dirty dog!" Clive yelled.

"Oh yeah? Well you're lyin' and yer feet don't match!" Earl shot back.

"Earl! That don't even make sense," Clive told him.

"May not make sense, but it's true 'bout you." Earl jutted his chin in the air.

"Junie, how do you put up with these two old coots?" Jack laughed.

"Aw, I'm so used to 'em, they's just white noise now. I think they came with the place when Slick bought it, and I think they'll be here when Slick really buys it, if you know what I mean!"

"What does she mean?" Tess asked Jack, as he paid Junebug.

"When he buys the farm . . . you know, Goes to Adios Park . . . "

"When he goes to the Marble Orchard," Earl added.

"When he checks into the Wooden Waldorf," Jack countered.

"When he goes to the Dew Drop Dead Inn . . . " Clive interjected. "When he's no longer eligible for the census . . . "

"When he moves into upper management. Or—hey! How 'bout this one—when he goes to McCemetery!" Earl volunteered.

"When he's knock, knock, knockin' on Heaven's door . . . " from Clive again.

"When he's promoted to Subterranean Truffle Inspector . . . " from Earl.

"When he gets the ultimate tax shelter," Junebug threw in.

"Okay! Okay! I get it!" Tess laughed, holding her hands up in defeat. "They will still be here when Slick's 'out of business', so to speak." Everyone groaned.

"Why's Tess putting me out of bidness?" Slick came up behind Junebug.

"Oh, for Pete's sake!" Tess threw up her arms. "See? You all are getting me in trouble!"

"You'd better watch your back, Slick. This woman's trouble!" Jack joked.

"Good night, all!" Tess said in exasperation.

"Y'all come back," Junebug called after them.

"Count on it," Jack said, as he stepped outside.

Tess and Jack walked out into the sticky, humid night. The sun was just starting to go down, and the humidity was so thick you could almost wring out the air. After Lou asked her if she knew what she was doing with Jack, combined with her own mixed feelings, Tess had successfully avoided Jack's advances on the night of the Fourth of July, but now she was beginning to worry about him walking her home. He would want to come in, and if he came in, he would want something to drink, and if he had something to drink, he would sit down, and if he sat down, he'd want to sit close to her, and if he sat close to her . . . *Oh crap.*

She didn't know what she wanted. Before meeting Jack, she thought she wouldn't ever take a chance on being hurt again. She was just fine by herself, thank you very much. However, the more she was with Jack, the more she was losing her resolve and her self-control. But if he cheated on his wife, then he had a big stop sign on his forehead, as far as she was concerned. She was a jumble of confusion as they walked down the sidewalk.

They left the busy town square, and began walking past houses on the way to Tess's. It was a quiet night; everyone was indoors in the air conditioning seeking reprieve from the heat. Tess felt a bead of sweat trickle down her back.

"So, Mary T. What did you think of what Martha Maye told us?"

"I think Lou's mother had a tragic life. When I first came to town, Willa Jean, at Slick's, told me Maye's mother had a hard life, but I couldn't begin to fathom what she meant. It's truly . . . "

Crack!

Jack was on the ground before Tess could blink, and then someone shoved her hard, while ripping her purse from her arm, twisting it, and throwing her onto the sidewalk next to Jack.

HIS BIG MOUTH OVERLOADED HIS BUTT

ideal: noun \ ahy-dee-uhl, \ idea
Do y'all have any ideal who it was?

[1937]

July 7, 1937 was a scorcher. The thermometer was inching north of one hundred that afternoon, as Maye Hobb and her mother, Nellie Lawrence, ironed clothes. Bringing their work onto the back porch and hoping to catch whatever breeze was in the air, they talked, as they worked, about the upcoming birthday celebration for P.D.—Maye's brother and Nellie's son. He and his wife had a baby on the way, and they wanted this birthday to be special.

"Let's make ice cream," Nellie suggested.

"But P.D. is the one who usually does the cranking. Is it fair to make him work on his birthday?" Maye worked the iron over a shirt while she talked.

"It is if he wants ice cream. And Johnny and Samuel can help, too. At least until close to the end, when it gets so hard to crank."

"Aw, you know P.D. will be plumb tickled to death with whatever we do. We'll have to have fried chicken and half runner green beans. But, Ma, will you do the ringin'? John always killed the chickens for me, and now . . . well, it's just not my favorite chore."

"Sure, honey, I don't mind. I'll pluck and cut it for you, too." She wiped the sweat from her face and neck with a dishtowel. "Whew . . . It's so hot I b'lieve you could pull a baked potato right outta the ground."

"That's entirely possible." Trevor stood in the doorway, mopping his brow with a handkerchief.

"Trevor," Maye said, startled, "I wasn't expecting you this afternoon." She immediately was unnerved because of the look in his eye and the charged air around him.

"I'ma ask you one more time, Maye. Will you marry me?"

Nellie gasped and took a step back. Maye put the iron down and answered calmly, "No, Trevor. I told you no, and I meant no."

"Well if I can't have you, nobody will!"

Maye saw the gun for a brief moment before Trevor lifted his right hand, aimed, and fired. She saw a flash just before a bullet hit her in the upper chest, under her right shoulder, and she went down like a bag of flour.

"Lord have mercy!" Nellie said, staring at Trevor in shock and disbelief. Trevor aimed and fired again, this time hitting Nellie in the neck. Maye, still conscious as she lay there, felt the floor tremble as her mother fell to the ground. The sound of her mother's body hitting the floor would remain with her for the rest of her life. Maye decided to play dead, praying he would stop shooting and leave. *Lord, protect us, save us . . .*

Trevor turned and ran down the creek bank behind the house.

As soon as she heard him run, Maye began crawling to the front of the house. Her neighbor, Sam Happenay, heard the shots and ran to Maye's house, where he found her lying on the front lawn covered in blood. He carried her into her house where he found Nellie, barely alive. Maye regained consciousness briefly, uttering, "Trevor . . . it was Trevor."

While word spread about the shooting, and help raced to the Hobb house, men from all over the county were already in hot pursuit of Trevor. Some thought he was insane. Armed with guns, clubs and any other form of weapon they could find, they set out meaning to capture him dead or alive.

Daniel LeMaster raced to the filling station the minute he heard the news. P.D. was out front sweeping when he pulled up.

"Hop in, Psalmist David, I need to talk to you for a minute."

P.D. saw the serious expression on his father-in-law's face and didn't hesitate. He stepped inside to tell his employee to mind the store until he came back. As they headed out of town, they passed a group of men heading into the hills with baseball bats and guns.

"What in tarnation is goin' on?"

"There was a shootin' today." Daniel's eyes were fixed on the road, his hands gripped the steering wheel tightly.

"Who?"

"Let's drive up yonder and we'll talk."

"Why are we goin' all the way up the mountain just to talk?"

"Cause I'm afraid of what you might do when have that talk."

"Denise?" P.D. whispered.

"Denise is fine." Daniel drove up the side of the mountain, on a winding, twisting dirt road. They reached the top, and when he was satisfied they were far enough away from town, he parked. Daniel turned to look at P.D and said quietly, "Yer ma and Maye were shot this afternoon. It was Trevor."

It took a few minutes for the news to sink in. P.D. stared at his father-in-law, stunned, murmuring, "Maye...Mama?" Then he didn't say anything, he just turned, got out of the car, and with balled fists, began to walk down the mountain.

Daniel ran to P.D., pulled him back, and held on to him with both hands.

"I have to find Trevor," P.D. said through his teeth. Daniel held his son-in-law's shoulders and pushed him back toward the car, which was no easy task. The two men struggled on the dirt road, Daniel struggling to restrain P.D.

Breathing hard, Daniel said, "P.D., you're a God-fearin' man. You're a kind-hearted, decent, gentle soul. You don't want to go after Trevor. Think of Denise and the baby on the way."

Four days later, on P.D's twenty-second birthday, Nellie Lawrence was laid to rest.

[July 2010]

After Tess was pushed to the ground, she sat up and turned as quickly as she could, looking all around her. Her knees hurt, and when she rubbed them she realized her hands were scraped raw, too. She didn't see a soul around. Jack was lying face up on the grass next to the sidewalk. She hadn't been knocked out when she was shoved, but he had—either from the force of the blow to his head, or from the fall, she wasn't sure. He was out cold, blood trickling from the back of his head.

She'd gotten the wind knocked out of her when she was pushed, and she took several deep breaths as she moved over to Jack and began patting his cheeks in an effort to wake him up. She said his name several times, frantically looking up and down the quiet, empty street for help. Then she saw his cell phone attached to his belt. She pulled it off, and called 911 while simultaneously running her hand up and down his chest, feeling him breathe in and out.

At least he's breathing.

Sitting on the sidewalk, with the hot concrete burning through her skirt, Tess tried to rouse Jack, and to think of something to use to stop the steady stream of blood coming from the back of his head.

"Jack!" She leaned over his face, feeling gently around the back of his head to investigate the injury. Her hand came away covered in sticky blood. With her fingertips, she tenderly wiped away the sweat building on his forehead and on either side of his nose. She could hear the faint sounds of a siren in the distance. Turning his head to the side, she knelt to get a better look at his wound, and felt the grit and the heat biting into her knees. Pulling the tail of her blouse out, she unbuttoned the bottom two buttons so she could use her shirttail to stop the flow of blood. Gingerly turning his head, she saw that, miraculously, the wound didn't look too severe. But there was a lot of blood. When her knees couldn't stand the searing heat any longer, she tried to sit back down, but she toppled over and had to right herself. She looked around to see if anyone had seen her make that graceful move.

"Jack?" She could have sworn she saw one of his eyes open when she changed positions. Then she noticed something different about his face. It wasn't as slack as it had been. In fact, he looked like he was trying not to smile.

"Oh for Pete's sake," she said, crossing her arms. "Give it up, Jackson. I know you've come-to. I saw your eyelid open."

Slowly, he opened his eyes, still trying not to smile.

"Just what do you think you're doing?"

"Honey, I've been dreamin' about you runnin' your hands over my body and unbuttonin' your shirt for weeks. I wasn't about to stop you."

"Luckily for you, Bub, the ambulance is pulling up, and here comes a police car, too, or I might have added to your injuries." Then her tone softened, and she looked at him with concern. "Are you okay?"

"I think so. And I wasn't playing possum for that long. I just couldn't resist enjoyin' your TLC for a few minutes longer."

"You're incorrigible!" she sighed, smiling and shaking her head at him.

Police officer Skeeter Duke took her statement, while an EMS technician named Nosmo King Brown examined Jack. Tess saw the mayor talking to one of the other police officers. Buck was in running shorts and looked hot and sweaty, like he was in the midst of another one of his jogs.

"So neither of you can offer any information on the assailant?" Skeeter asked.

"I'm afraid not," Tess said. "It happened so fast, and the culprit blindsided us from behind. He was gone before I could look up. Jack was knocked out right away, so I know he couldn't have seen a thing."

Both Skeeter and Nosmo King got into their vehicles to finish writing up their reports. Tess tried to bite her tongue, but she *had* to ask.

"Nosmo King?" She leaned into Jack, whispering out of the side of her mouth.

"Yep. His mother, Zinnia, couldn't think of a name for him, and when she was in labor she looked up and saw a 'No Smoking' sign. She liked it, and the rest is history. He has a sister named Placentia. Zinnia heard the word 'placenta' in the delivery room and took to it. I suppose it could be worse."

She nodded. "News sure does travel fast around here." Tess looked at the crowd that had developed.

"Oh yeah, especially news of a crime, since it's such a rare occurrence around here," Jack said, holding a wet towel to his head.

"And here comes Louetta, Martha Maye, Butterbean, and Henry Clay. Look how fast that eighty-year-old woman can move." Tess waved to them.

"Tessie! Lands sakes, what happened, honey?" Lou ran up to Tess and Jack, who were sitting on the back of the ambulance.

"I'm not really sure—" Tess began.

"Lou, it happened faster 'n a knife fight in a phone booth. One minute I was walkin' down the sidewalk and the next I was layin' on the ground like road-kill, with an angel leanin' over me." He winked at Tess.

"Jackson, you look like you was inside the outhouse when lightnin' struck. You poor baby! Are you all right?"

"Do y'all have any ideal who it was?" Martha Maye asked.

"No idee-a," Jack said, enunciating the word. Martha Maye didn't seem to notice.

Lou looked around at the group of people who had gathered out of curiosity, to gawk, or to offer help. She saw Buck over by the police cruiser talking to Skeeter's partner and she grunted. "May'r Buck. What's he doin' hare? He's about as useful as buttons on a dishrag."

"Mama, quit bein' ugly," Martha Maye whispered. "'Y'all have ta 'scuse Mama, she's all worked up on account she thinks the Mayor's all fer the Barnes and Noble Bookstore chain to come in to the new shoppin' center over on Route 42. It'll put her outta business for sure."

"Aw, he says he's fightin' it, but did he fight the MacDonalds when they wanted in?" she said, with an emphasis on Mac. "His big mouth overloaded his butt. That's his problem."

Jack whispered to Tess, "Means he talks a lot, but doesn't do anything."

"Mama!" Butterbean said, tugging on her mother's arm.

"And if that ain't true, grits ain't groceries, eggs ain't poultry, and Mona Lisa was a man." Lou crossed her arms and glared at the mayor even though he was oblivious. He was animatedly talking to a group of people.

"Mama!" Butterbean pulled on her mother's arm again. "Granny said 'butt'!"

"I know, honey..She's sorry." She shot her mother a look. "All right. This isn't a place for youngins. I'm glad y'all are okay. I'll be takin' Butterbean home now. I'll bring y'all a cake tomorrow. Henry Clay, you comin'?"

"Thanks for coming to check on us, Martha Maye and Henry Clay," Tess said. "Lou, you should go on, too. We're about done here, and they're going to take Jack to the hospital for observation . . . "

"Oh no, they are not!" Jack was emphatic. "I'm fine. I just have a little headache. And I'm *not* goin' to any hospital."

The two women tried to convince Jack to go to the emergency room only for a little while, but his mind was made up. He signed a release, while Nosmo King stood shaking his head.

Skeeter motioned toward his car. "Come on, y'all, load up, and I'll drive ya home."

"Tess, can you get in?" Jack asked, as they approached her house.

"Yes, I keep a spare key hidden in the garage, in case I ever lock myself out. Thank you for the ride, Skeeter. Lou, take care of him, now, okay?" Tess shot a worried look at Jack.

"Honey, he's in good hands," Lou crooned.

Jack clutched the door, pleading teasingly, "Don't leave me with this woman! She'll eat me alive!"

After Skeeter dropped them off, Lou fussed over Jack until he gently, but firmly, made her go home. Then he sat on the couch with his basset hound, absentmindedly scratching her ears, as she sat next to him in near nirvana.

Suddenly, he bolted up from the couch so fast he sent the dog into a barking frenzy. He turned off all the lights, to make it appear to Lou as if he had gone to bed. He knew she'd be watching. He went to the linen closet, pulled out a fresh pillowcase and stuffed it in his back pocket, as best he could.

He attached the leash. "C'mon girl, let's go for a walk. And be quiet! We can't let Lou know we're leavin'."

YOU GOT YOUR STUPID HEAD ON TODAY?

'roundcheer: adverb \ round-cheer\ around here
We didn't have any trouble 'roundcheer till you came.

[1937]

Trevor Hobb ran down the embankment from his sister-in-law's house, splashing through the water of Duckbill Creek. He followed it for a short distance, trying to get back to his home. Breathing heavily, he started up a hill and heard the voices of several men. Startled, nervous, and sure they were looking for him, he lost his footing and fell down the incline several feet. He laid flat against the hillside, listening for the men. Sensing they weren't very near, he crawled to the hilltop and peeked over the edge and around a tree. There were at least a dozen men. Some had shotguns, others had pieces of wood, tire irons, baseball bats, or clubs. Word had spread fast. They knew what he'd done, and they were on his tail. He scrambled back down the hill, slipping and sliding to the creek, splashing through and to the other side. He ran for about a mile, and then climbed a hill to Chester Ward's home. Out of breath, wheezing, and gasping for air, he banged on the door.

"Chester, I need to use yer phone." Trevor talked around great gulps of air.

"Sure, Trevor. What's wrong?"

"I just need to use the phone."

Chester led him into the house, and Trevor put the murder weapon on a table as he passed it. He immediately called Luke Blair, an employee at the First National Bank.

"Luke, this here's Trevor. I need yer hep. The posse's after me, and they're out for blood. I don't want to die, or get beaten. I'll turn myself in if you'll call Bug and tell him I'm at Chester's, and that I'll surrender peacefully. I don't want to be harmed."

"Good Lord, Trevor, it's *you* the whole town is up in arms over?"

"I did what I had ta do. Will ya call Bug? Tell him where I'm at." He listened a moment, then said, "Yeah, Chester's house." He hung up and collapsed into a chair, head in his hands.

Chester said, "You're in a heap a trubba, huh?" Trevor didn't answer. Chester left him alone and went to the window to watch for the police car.

"Trevor, they're here," he said five minutes later. "Go peacefully, just like you said, now, ya hear?"

Trevor nodded, stood up, and walked to the door, as Bug and his deputy got out of the car. He walked outside with his hands high above his head. "It's on the table over yonder." He motioned with his head toward the house. Both men knew he was referring to the murder weapon.

The deputy went for the gun, and examined it. He came out of the house and reported, "Two of the four cartridges have been fired."

Bug patted Trevor down, put his hand in his pocket, and pulled out a handful of shells for the gun.

"You made a wise choice in comin' in peacefully, Trevor." Bug handcuffed him. "You're in a heap a trubba already. Come on, let's head fer yer new home."

[July 2010]

Tess had just gotten out of the shower and put on a camisole and pj bottoms when her doorbell rang. Frightened over who was at the door, she quickly grabbed her Louisville Slugger and crept down the stairs. She'd turned all of the downstairs lights off earlier except for the one over the kitchen sink and the front porch light. Peeking around the wall and looking through the big glass panes that were inset in the double wooden front doors, her heart beat fast. Seeing Jack standing on the front porch, she took a deep breath.

"Jack," she said, opening the door, oblivious to how little she had on. "What are you doing here? Are you all right?"

"I wanted to make sure *you're* all right."

Tess noticed Jack's Adam's apple wiggle up and down as he looked at her. Her pj bottoms hung low on her hips and her camisole clung tightly to her torso, showing every curve she had. She was briefly self-conscious, but her attention was soon diverted when she stood aside to let him come into the house, and she saw his companion.

"I'm fine. And who is this?" She was delighted to see the dog.

"Esmerelda, meet Tess. Tess, this is Esmerelda, or Ezzie, for short. I hope you don't mind that I brought her. I didn't want to leave her alone all night."

"Esmerelda!" Tess said under her breath, as she bent to pet the basset. "She's a dog!"

"Of course she's a dog. What did you think she was—a pot-bellied pig?"

She looked up at him, surprised at the sharp sarcasm in his voice.

"Sorry." He rubbed his head. "Headache."

Tess finally realized what Jack had said when he came in. "All night? What are you talking about? What's going on?"

"You didn't call a locksmith yet, did you," he stated, more than asked.

"Well . . . no . . . it's late. I thought I'd call in the morning."

"I figured as much. I can't let you stay here all night alone, knowing that someone has your keys and could easily get into your house. You *did* cancel all of your credit cards though, didn't you?"

"Of course, but Jack . . . "

"And," he held up a finger to silence her. "You'd be doing me a favor, too. Nosmo King said it would be best if someone were with me for the next eight hours, because of my head injury, so we can be of mutual benefit to each other."

"But . . . "

"*And*," he held up another finger, "I'll sleep on the couch. *And* I brought my own pillow case," he pulled it out of his back pocket, "so I won't get blood on yours."

"Jack . . . "

"*And*," he held his whole hand up this time, "I promise I'll be a total gentleman. Frankly, I'm too worn out, and my head hurts too much to make a pass tonight." He noticed the bat in her hand and added, "Besides, you're armed and dangerous."

* * *

The next morning before Tess opened her eyes, she had a vague sense of somebody on her bed. As she slowly awakened, she felt something, or someone, pressed up against her rear. Her eyes flew open. She slowly twisted her head to see who was in her room. On her bed.

Esmerelda.

Tess had been sleeping curled in an S shape, and she woke up with Esmerelda snuggled into the bottom part of the S—right behind her thighs and up against her butt.

"How'd you get up here?" She reached out to pet Ezzie's velvety ears and turned over so she could snuggle up against her. The dog rewarded her by moving to the head of the bed and planting kisses on Tess's face.

"You're a stealthy little thing, aren't you?" Ezzie's tail thumped against the bed. "Either that, or I was out cold." She snuggled up to her, realizing how much she missed having a dog. "So you're the Esmerelda Jack's been reading to." Ezzie looked back at her innocently, with sad basset hound eyes. "That's what I get for assuming, huh?"

After Tess got dressed, she went downstairs and found Jack sitting up on the edge of the couch, elbows propped on his thighs, his head in his hands. He'd already folded up the blankets and sheet and stacked them neatly on the pillow.

"Morning, Jack. How are you feeling?"

"Hmph." He gave kind of a snort. "I'd have to feel better to die."

"Do you want me to take you to the doctor?" She sat down beside him, while Ezzie sat at his feet, nudging him with her nose for attention.

"Naw, I'll be all right." He rubbed Ezzie's ears and ran his other hand over his forehead. "I could use somethin' for this headache, though."

"Coming right up." She moved quickly toward the kitchen, returning with ibuprofen tablets and some orange juice.

"Are you okay, Tess?" He popped the tablets in his mouth and took a long drink of the juice.

"I think so. My hands hurt like the devil, but I'm mostly unnerved about the attack . It was terrifying." She put her hands to her face. "That sound of your head being hit—I can't get it out of my mind. How are you?"

"I'm unnerved that all of this is happening to you. And the fact that they're amping it up to violence. I'm worried about you."

"Let's talk about it some more after breakfast. I have a four-cup coffee pot, so I could make you some coffee, or some hot tea."

"Thanks, coffee would be really great, if it's not too much trouble."

"No trouble. Would you like to take a shower? It might make you feel better. I put some fresh towels in the bathroom; you could shower while I make some breakfast."

"Maybe that would be a good idea." Holding his head, he grimaced as he stood up.

The house was filled with the aroma of bacon and coffee filling the house by the time Jack finished his shower.

"I followed the wonderful smells and the sound of your voice to the kitchen." Jack came into the room, brushing his wet hair back with his fingers.

She handed him a mug of coffee. "Breakfast is almost ready."

He took a sip, and pointed to the mug. "Honey, this is great coffee!"

She rolled her eyes but couldn't help but laugh.

"Who were you talking to?"

She blushed. "Esmerelda. She was telling me all of your secrets."

"Ezzie, you traitor!" Jack sat down, taking Ezzie's face into his hands. "You women always stick together."

"Oh, don't worry. I didn't get much out of her."

Tess set a plate of scrambled eggs, toast, and bacon down in front of Jack just as the doorbell rang. "That's probably the locksmith. I called him while you were in the shower. I didn't expect him here so soon, though."

She went to the door, but instead of the locksmith, she brought John Ed back to the kitchen with her. The chief was a big man with a beer belly hanging over his belt. Baggy pants were held up with a big buckle shaped like a pistol. His bottom teeth jutted out in front of his front teeth, and he had big ruddy cheeks and dark eyes. He reminded Tess of a bulldog.

"I's lookin' fer ya, Jack. Didn't know you two had dinner before sayin' grace." John Ed stood in the doorway looking at Jack with a smirk on his face.

Jack started to translate for Tess, but she stopped him with a hand up. "Thanks, but I've got that one."

Jack scowled at the chief. "We haven't been, John Ed. I came by to make sure Tess was all right, and she invited me for breakfast. Not that it's any of your damn business."

"Well, I wanted to talk to ya both anyway, might as well be together. I got the straight and skinny from Skeeter when I went in this mornin'. Sorry I missed all the commotion last night. You hurt bad?"

"We're fine," Jack said through clinched teeth.

"'Sides checkin' on ya both, I wonted to see if either a y'all could fill me in on why Mizz Tess here," he nodded in Tess's direction, "keeps gettin' into mayhem."

"I don't reckon we can help you, John Ed. Tess is the victim here, why aren't you out findin' who did this, instead a harrassin' her?"

"Got any enemies, Tess? Owe any money? Witness to a crime somebody dudn't wont ya rememberin'? Anythin' goin' on in yer life I shouldoughtta know 'bout? Involvement with the mob?"

"The mob, oh please," Tess looked up at the ceiling as if praying for patience. "No, Chief. Nothing. I have no idea why these things have happened."

"Seems a might strange we don't have 'ny trouble 'roundcheer till you happen into town."

"John Ed. Tess told you. I told you. We have no idea why this happened." Jack spoke slowly, with exaggerated patience, as if trying to reign in his temper. "You got your stupid head on today? Why do you want to keep on huntin' where there ain't no stink?"

"Boy, you can put your boots in the oven, but that don't make 'em biscuits."

"Just what exactly does that mean?" Tess asked.

"It *means* . . . " Jack glared at John Ed, " . . . that he thinks we're lyin'."

The phone rang, and Tess went to answer it. "You're saved by the bell, Chief. Or maybe I am. I was getting ready to say something I shouldn't."

The two men stared each other down while she talked. She hung up a minute later, saying, "That was Lou. She wanted to know if I had seen you, Jack. She went over to your place to check on you, and when you didn't answer, she got concerned."

"How long you say you been here?" John Ed asked, suspiciously.

"John Ed, you're wastin' daylight. You keep asking questions we've already answered."

"She add grumpy to your eggs, Jack?" John Ed smiled a disingenuous smile.

"No, John Ed, whoever hit me over the head gave me a dose. Now why don't you get out there and find out who did it?" Jack's voice was getting louder and angrier. His attempt to keep impatience at bay was failing. He put his palm on his forehead. Ezzie stood next to him and gave a low growl, her eyes fixed on John Ed.

"I never figured a basket hound fer a guard dog." He shook his head in disbelief. "I see everthin' in this job. Well . . . I'll let myself out." He turned to leave the kitchen.

Tess followed to see him out anyway, and as she did, she saw Jack mouth, "*Basket* hound?" She shrugged and went with John Ed to the door.

When she came back, she found Jack writing on a piece of paper from a pad she kept by the phone.

"Hope you don't mind," he said, indicating the paper he was using.

"Of course not. Did you have a sudden urge to make a grocery list?"

"No," he said absentmindedly, continuing to write. Finally he looked up. "I think I know why these things are happenin'."

She took a bite of her cold eggs. "You do?" She took Jack's plate to the microwave to reheat the eggs and then did the same with her plate.

Jack waited until she got back to the table to speak.

"Well, are you going to tell me?"

"I want your undivided attention." He set the pencil and paper aside. "What's new in the life of Mary T?"

Tess looked at him, puzzled. "Town? House? Job? There's a lot new in my life."

"Now narrow it down," he prodded, taking another mouthful of eggs. "Mmmm . . . Good eggs, by the way."

"Jack, are you going to tell me, or are we going to play twenty questions all day?"

"Okay, okay. You recently found somethin'." She stared at him blankly. "The key. Last night when we were talkin' about it bein' connected to Lou's daddy's murder . . . I think we were right. All of the stuff that's been happenin' has got to have somethin' to do with the key. Martha Maye said Lou didn't want to know who the killer was. Maybe somebody else doesn't want *anybody* to know."

"But who would know that John Hobb had tried to tell his wife about something in a trunk before he was murdered? And who knows I have, or had, a trunk key? *Had* being the operative word, because it doesn't matter anymore. Whoever took my purse took all of my keys. The trunk key, too—it was on my key ring."

"Au contraire, mon cherie." He reached into his shirt pocket and held up the key with his thumb and forefinger. "Voila!"

She sat there looking at him with her mouth open, so he added, "Remember? Last night at the diner. You showed the key to Martha Maye. Then I took it from her, and you were engrossed in talking and eating, so I stuck it in my pocket."

"Well I'll be . . . " she said, realizing what had happened. "So he didn't get the key. But who would care about it anyway? Anyone who was involved in the murder would surely be dead by now."

"That's what we have to figure out, Boo. Who would care, and why. And you know I do like a good mystery."

STILL BUYIN' GREEN BANANAS

ate up: verb \eyt uhp\ eaten up, consumed with
*He was so ate up with love he couldn't stand
the thought of any man havin' her.*

Goose Pimple Gazette
July 30, 1937
Widow Testifies In Murder Trial

There was a collective gasp in the courtroom on Thursday, July 22, when Maye Hobb was carried in on a hospital cot, accompanied by her doctor and a nurse. Only fifteen days after being shot in the chest, she was carried into Mallard Circuit Court, still too frail to walk on her own. She was allowed a brief reprieve from her hospital room to testify in the murder trial of her brother-in-law Trevor Hobb, who shot and seriously wounded Maye, and killed Maye's mother, Nellie Lawrence, on July 7. Maye is thirty-four years old and the widow of John Hobb.

Trevor Hobb was the brother of John Hobb, who was found dead in his car with a bullet to the head at the Goose Creek Bridge on December 15, 1935. Both men were sons of C.C. "Cooter" Hobb, a prosperous Duckbill Creek farmer who has thrived in the development of oil and gas in the county.

John Hobb was an upstanding member of the community, who worked at the First National Bank from 1923 until the time of his death. He was a trusted employee who served in numerous positions at the bank, including auditor, cashier, and teller. It was John who identified Brick Lynch as one of the bandits who robbed the First National Bank in March of 1932. Lynch was convicted of the robbery, but was pardoned after three months by Governor Shelby. Lynch and his former wife, Maisey, are accused of John Hobb's murder. Ironically, their trial was due to begin next week. It has been postponed.

Not much is known about Trevor Hobb, except what has been gleaned during the course of his trial for murder. He is married to Billie Jane Hobb, and has four children.

Nellie Lawrence, widow of John E. Lawrence, was visiting the home of her daughter, Maye, when Trevor Hobb entered the home and shot both women. In her testimony, Maye stated that Trevor had made numerous advances to her since her husband's death. Hobb told her he wanted to divorce his wife and marry her, but she said she turned him down flat, telling her brother-in-law that such an action was impossible, and she would not marry him. She testified that he responded that he wouldn't allow her to marry anyone else and if she tried, he would kill both her and the man. Tragically, she hadn't thought he was serious.

Maye Hobb described Trevor as calm when he came to her home on July 7. It was her testimony that he again asked her to marry him, and when she refused, he pulled out a gun and shot first her, and then her mother. Nellie Lawrence died two days later. She was fifty-nine years old. She is survived by two daughters, Araminta Daniels, and Maye Hobb, one son, P.D. Lawrence, three sisters, four brothers, and six grandchildren.

On Tuesday, July 27, 1937, Trevor Hobb was found guilty of the murder of Nellie Lawrence by a jury of seven women and five men, in spite of a plea of insanity. He was sentenced to life imprisonment with a recommendation of no pardon, and no parole.

[July 2010]

"Who have you told about the key?" Jack asked Tess, as they continued their conversation about why bad things kept happening to good people, namely Tess.

"Well . . . " Tess looked out the window, thinking. "I told Lou. And you. And Martha Maye . . . I think that's all."

"And those are three names we can safely rule out as the culprit. So we have to assume it's someone they told, or someone who overheard you. When you told me, we were sitting right here. When you told Lou, was there anyone else who could have overheard you?"

"We talked about it in the bookstore, so I suppose there might have been." Tess thought for a minute. "I remember Lou pulling me behind the counter after I initially told her about the key. I don't know if anyone in the bookstore was within earshot."

"Last night when we talked to Martha Maye, the diner was pretty crowded. It's possible someone could have overheard us. Although it doesn't seem likely. I don't remember seein' anyone out of the ordinary."

"He must have followed us from the diner, or how else would he know where we were? Unless this was just a random mugging."

"Tess, Goose Pimple Junction doesn't have random muggings. It just doesn't happen."

"I think we need to talk to Martha Maye again," Tess said.

"I think you're right."

Jack left shortly after breakfast, but he insisted she keep Ezzie. "She's no guard dog, but she'll bark if she hears somethin'. It would make me feel better if she was here with you." Tess relented. It hadn't taken much to talk her into it. She was glad to have the company.

She cleaned up the breakfast dishes and called Martha Maye to ask if they could meet the next morning for breakfast. Tess was starting to feel guilty about doing all of this behind Lou's back. She decided to talk to Martha Maye about that, as well.

Ezzie lay at Tess's feet as she opened her computer and began to work on her book. She didn't get very far before the doorbell rang.

"Mr. Mayor, what can I do for you?"

"I just wonted to check on ya, and see how you're fairin' after last night's mishap." He presented her with a bunch of bananas.

"Wonder if he brought beer, too," she said under her breath. It reminded her of on one of the worst dates she'd ever had; the man brought her bananas and beer. Some men bring flowers, or chocolate, or wine. *But bananas and beer?*

"What's that?" Buck had invited himself in, pushing his way right past Tess and Ezzie.

"Oh! . . . I said . . . bananas . . . are here!" Tess held the bananas in the air.

"I figured you needed somethin' healthy. How are you after last night? That was a terrible thing that happened, and I was worried about ya."

"I'm fine, really. Just some sore palms." She held up her scraped hands. "Jack got the worst of it. Maybe we should take these to him."

Buck looked down at Ezzie, who was eyeing him distrustfully. "Ya mean he's not here?"

"No, why—"

"I thought with his dog bein' here and all," he interrupted. "And I saw John Ed a while ago and he mentioned…"

"Ezzie's my houseguest for a while." This time she interrupted, angry that the police chief had been gossiping about her.

"Is Jack goin' out of town? You dog sittin'?"

"Something like that." She didn't want to admit that a basset hound was her guard dog.

Buck stood there awkwardly, and Tess didn't make an attempt at small talk. She just wasn't up to it.

Finally, Buck said, "Well, I'll be goin'. Just wanted to make sure you're all right."

"Thank you, Mayor."

"Buck," he corrected, as he stepped outside.

Tess had just sat back down at her computer when the phone rang. Lou's voice rang out loud and clear. "Tessie! You all right? You'd best be takin' care a yourself. Listen, the reason I called is, Martha Maye and I made you a cake. Well, actually, if ya don't mind, we're gonna give half to you and half to Jack. So's it okay if I bring it over't your house now?"

"Of course that's okay, Lou. You didn't have to do that."

"Well, we sure did. Now you sit tight, and I'll be over right quick."

Tess was inundated all day with baked goods and casseroles, starting with Lou's Lemon Raspberry cake. Someone new rang her doorbell, one after the other, all afternoon with some sort of homemade food item. She didn't get much work done, but she felt pampered and taken care of. It was a good feeling.

* * *

The next morning, Martha Maye was waiting in a booth at the diner when Tess arrived. Willa Jean was on duty, and Clive and Earl were in their regular places. As she entered, Clive said, "Tessie, Tessie, are you all right, sugar booger? We heard what happened to y'all—that's just about the most awful thing to happen 'round here in I don't know how long."

"Yes, thank you, Clive, I'm okay. It was scary when it happened, though."

"Well, I'm glad to see there's no lingerin' effects—you look prettier than a glob of butter meltin' on a stack a wheat cakes."

Across the room, Martha Maye called out, "I b'lieve they could charm the dew right off a honeysuckle. He already tried that line on me, not more than five minutes ago."

"Aw, don't mind him, ladies. He could talk the hair off a dog," Earl said.

"And you're older 'n dirt," Clive shot back.

Tess left the men to battle it out, and as she headed for the table, she noticed Pickle dash past the diner window.

"Hi, Martha Maye. Was that Pickle who just ran down the sidewalk?"

"Yes," Martha Maye nodded, looking at her watch, "if I had to guess, I'd say that the bank's about to open, which I 'spect means Charlotte Price will be walkin' up any time now. She has a summer job as a teller." Tess raised her eyebrows and Martha continued. "Mama said Pickle and Charlotte have been an item for about six months now. She said he never did have a lick a sense, but since he's been seein' Charlotte, his brain has been rattlin' around like a BB in a boxcar."

"He doesn't really seem to be all there," Tess admitted. "Although he's a sweet boy."

"Well, he's sweet on Charlotte."

"Charlotte Price. So she's the one who came in with Henry Clay the other night at the diner?"

"Yep, she's his daughter. And John Ed's granddaughter, 'a course."

There was a commotion at the front door, where Jack was making his way in.

"Hidee, Jack," Clive said.

"Z'it hot enough out thar fer ya, Jack?" Earl asked.

"Shewee, it's hotter than forty hells out there, boys." Jack clapped Earl on the back and made his way to the ladies' booth.

"How are you, Jack?" Martha Maye asked.

"I'm still buyin' green bananas." Jack slid in next to Tess.

What's with all the bananas lately? "Okay, I'll bite. What's that supposed to mean?" Tess asked.

"It means I'm doin' so good, I'm expectin' be around long enough to eat the bananas when they're ripe."

"*Oh!* I like that."

"Sorry I'm late, but Butterbean wanted to talk, and I got waylaid coming down the driveway."

"I'm *so* sorry, Jack. She hasn't made that many friends in town, and when she finds fresh meat, she tends to run off at the mouth." Martha Maye looked embarrassed.

"Aw, it's not a problem. She's a sweet girl. And after that, Pickle nearly ran me off the sidewalk."

"What did his t-shirt say today?" Tess asked.

"Jesus Is My Homeboy."

Willa Jean arrived with coffee for Jack. "Have a cup of coffee, sugar britches. It's already been saucered and blowed." She batted her eyelashes at him.

"Well, that's mighty nice a you, Willa Jean. You're too good to me."

She blushed, and said, "I was worried about ya, hon. I couldn't believe it when I heard the news of y'all's muggin'."

"Thank you, Willa Jean, but we're all right. I assume you were worried about Tess, too?"

"Hmm? Oh . . . yeah . . . of course." She took her pad and pencil out of her apron pocket. "Are y'all ready to order?"

Tess started. "I'd like two scrambled eggs with toast."

"And I'll have two fried eggs over easy with bacon," Martha Maye said.

"I believe a western omelet and an English muffin sounds good today," Jack said. "And bring us three orange juices, too, please."

"Okay, that's an Adam and Eve on a raft and wreck 'em, flop two over easy with two pigs, a cowboy, burn the British, and a sun kiss times three." They nodded hesitantly. "Comin' right up." Willa Jean walked away, yelling, "Walkin' in…"

"I reckon y'all wonta finish our conversation from the other night," Martha Maye said.

"If you wouldn't mind … " Tess hedged.

"Naw, I don't mind. I just didn't wonta get into it in front a Henry Clay … it's … it's complicated."

"You don't have to explain," Jack assured her.

"All right now, what else y'all wonta know?"

"You said your grandmother was murdered, too, but they caught her killer, right?"

Martha Maye snorted a sigh. "Yeah, they caught him. The killer was Mama's uncle." She looked up as Willa brought their juice.

"Fresh squeezed just fer you, darlin'." Willa winked at Jack.

"Well, thank you, Willa Jean. See ladies? It pays to hang around with me!" The women looked at each other and shook their heads.

Martha Maye continued, after a sip of juice. "My mama's mama and my great grandmamma were on Mama's back porch that day, on account a it bein' sa hot." She stopped talking for a moment, then slapped her hand down on the table. "Well cut my legs off and call me shorty! It was around this time a year that it happened. Lessee … yep, I b'lieve the shootin' was on July 7. I remember 'cause it was seven-seven-thirty-seven. Idn't that somethin'? Almost to the day."

"That really is a weird coincidence," Tess said, wide-eyed.

"Well, anyway," Martha Maye continued, "they were ironin' and jawin' and all of a sudden Uncle Trevor appeared. Some people said he was insane. I don't rightly know if he was or not. I guess a fella'd have to have a screw loose to shoot his sister-in-law and her mother. He was so ate up with love he couldn't stand the thought of any man havin' her."

"Ate up?"

"Eaten up, consumed with love," Jack explained.

"Yeah," Martha Maye said quietly. "Thank goodness Mama and my aunt and uncles didn't see it. The boys were down at the crik playin' around, Aunt Imy was down the street at a friend's, and Mama was sound asleep upstairs takin' a nap. She slept through it all, which was a blessin'. My great Aunt Denise and Uncle P.D. came over 'n got Mama.

P.D. was tore up about it, but he and Denise kept the kids while Grandma was in the hospital. It wadn't but a few weeks later 'n Trevor was tried and convicted, lickity-split." Martha Maye looked up when Willa Jean arrived at the table with their food.

Once the food had been served, Martha Maye's face brightened. "Actually, I might could find some newspaper clippin's if y'ont a see 'em."

"Do you think we could?" Tess asked.

"I don't see why not. But we'd best not include Mama. Why don't I try ta find 'em, and bring 'em over to your house, Tess." Martha Maye was suggesting, not asking.

"That would be great. Thank you." Tess hesitated before she said, "Martha Maye, if your mother found out about our little project . . . how do you think she would feel?"

"I cain't rightly say. I don't 'spect she'd mind us talkin' 'bout it, as long as *she* doesn't have ta talk about it, ya know?"

"I just don't want to go behind her back. I'd hate to offend her."

"So . . . you really think that key you have might pertain to my grandfather's murder?"

"We're not sure," Jack said. "But we'd like to try to find out—if you don't think it would hurt your mother."

They ate in silence for a few minutes. Tess finally said, "So, your grandfather's brother killed Lou's grandmother, and was convicted." Martha Maye nodded her head. "And that was after your grandfather was murdered, but his killer was never found. Is that right?"

"Yep. That's about the size of it."

"Did they have any suspects?" Jack took a huge forkful of omelet.

"Well . . . there were those who thought that man—Brick Lynch, I b'lieve was his name—did it outta revenge, even though he was pardoned of the robbery conviction by the governor. He was indicted and tried for the murder, but he was acquitted.

"And then 'a course some people saw it as a suicide. They said my grandfather was into some shady dealin's and was in over his head. And still others thought he knew somethin' he shoulden-oughtta know, and he was killed to shut him up."

"What did your grandmother think?" Jack asked.

Martha Maye cocked her head. "I just don't know. Hmm . . . I'll see if I can casually broach the subject with Mama. I'll wait for an opportune time."

She chewed for a bit and then added, "I'll keep our conversation under wraps fer now, how 'bout that? I'll kind a feel her out about it first. And you said she knows about the key you found?"

"Yes, I told her about it right away, because I knew it was her old house. But she wasn't interested in talking about it."

"Well, you let me do some pokin' around. I'll see what I can come up with."

LIKE THE UNDERSIDE OF A
TURNIP GREEN

<u>sweet tea</u>: noun \sweet tee\ southern wine, iced tea with
a pound of sugar in it
Would you like lemon in your sweet tea?

[July 2010]

"You will not believe what that dog of yours did!" Tess said into the
phone, feeling very stressed.

"Ezzie? Um . . . what'id she do?"

"While I was at the diner, she opened my cabinets and drug out my
cupcake keepers *that had lids on them,* and she ate an entire container of
cupcakes, including the wrappers, AND an *entire container* of brownies!"

"Uh-oh."

"*And . . .* " Tess glared at Esmerelda.

"There's an 'and'?"

"*And,* she opened every cabinet she could reach, and pulled everything out onto the floor!"

"Tess, I'm not trying to make light of this, but are you sure it was
Ezzie who did this?"

Tess froze. "You think someone came in my house again?" she
asked in a voice barely loud enough for him to hear.

"Well, Ezzie's never done anything like that here, and with all the
trouble you've been havin' . . . "

"Jack, do you keep baked goods in your cabinets?"

"Well, no . . . "

"I rest my case." Tess was sure this was havoc wreaked by a canine, and not a human. Especially when she looked at Ezzie with a guilty expression and her ears back. As she talked, she picked up the mess that was all over her kitchen floor. "Don't you feed this dog?" she practically shrieked.

"I'm so sorry, Tess. She's never done that before. Listen, let me make it up to you. Let me do somethin' special for you tonight."

"Like what?" Tess's voice softened.

"Wear somethin' casual, and I'll pick you up around seven o'clock, all right?"

"Where are we going? Casual has a wide meaning."

"It's a surprise, Mary T. Go with it." She could hear his smile over the phone, and she could picture the dimple that came with his smile. She smiled, too, and hung up the phone.

* * *

That evening Jack was right on time, but Tess wasn't ready. Since she didn't know where they were going, she didn't know how to dress. She stood at her bedroom window and watched him get out of his car.

"Red polo and khaki shorts," she said to Ezzie, who promptly let out a whine.

The doorbell rang, and Ezzie went racing to see who was there. Tess called down the stairs, "Come on in! I'll be right down."

She quickly put on hot pink shorts and a white sleeveless linen blouse. Pushing her feet into white sandals, she fluffed her hair and took a deep breath. Suddenly Lou's voice popped in her head, "You know what you're doin', right?" The times she'd been out with Jack hadn't really seemed like dates. Tonight felt like a date.

No, she looked at her reflection in the mirror, *I don't know what I'm doing.*

Jack was lavishing attention on Ezzie when Tess walked into the den. He stood up and greeted her with a huge smile. "You look beautiful."

"Thank you, Jack. How's your head?" She moved to his side, turned his head with her hand, and pushed his hair away in the area of his injury, to see for herself.

"Well, Nosmo King said I'd feel like the underside of a turnip green for a while, which I did, but I'm doin' better now, thank you. How 'bout your knees and hands?"

"Not too bad," she said, extending her leg and holding her hands palms up to show the healing cuts and scrapes. "I'm ready to go, if you are. Just let me grab my purse."

Throwing her purse over her shoulder, she came back into the room saying, "So, Mr. Mystery Man, where are you taking me?"

"Mystery Man? Who? Me? Excuse me, ma'am, but *I'm* not the mysterious one—you are!" He put a hand at the small of her back as they started for the door. Ezzie had also followed, and Jack stooped down nose-to-nose to have a word with her. "I wish I could take you, old girl, but I'm afraid you'd eat all the food. You behave now, Esmerelda. Stay out of trouble." He bopped his finger playfully on her nose.

Jack followed Tess out, and she locked the deadbolt. "Well . . . you write mystery novels, and you're being mysterious about where we're going tonight . . . hence the name, Mr. Mystery Man."

"Well then," he opened the car door for her, "that would make me Mr. Mystery *Writer* Man. Outside of my novels, I'm an open book."

Once he'd slipped into the driver's seat she said, "So that's the way you want to play it?" She looked sideways at him and he flashed a cheesy grin. "Okay, Mr. Mystery *Writer* Man, where are you taking me?"

He started the car and backed out of the driveway. "That, pretty lady, is for me to know and you to find out."

She couldn't believe he wasn't going to say where they were going. "You're really not going to tell me? What happened to the open book?"

"Okay, okay! I'm takin' you on a pic-a-nic, Boo Boo," he said, using his best imitation of Yogi Bear, which was actually pretty good.

"It's a perfect night for a pic-a-nic, Yogi."

"I want to show you a spot that I came across recently. It's beautiful, and I think you'll like it."

A Chris Isaak CD played low on the car stereo, and she looked out the window as they drove down the street, heading out to the country.

"I have some friends who own some property not far from here, and they said we were welcome to use it," he explained. "I thought it would be the perfect place for a picnic. They haven't built on it yet, and the land is totally untouched, except for the little bit of mowing I did this afternoon."

It wasn't long before they arrived at their isolated destination, and

Jack was leading her up a trail in the woods to a spot near the top of a hill. The view was breathtaking. Wildflowers and ferns were to the left and right of them. Just as Jack said, he'd cleared a spot from the trail to the edge of the hill.

Tess stood looking in awe at the field of flowers. Jack ran to a tree, reached behind it, and then came back with a vase overflowing with wildflowers. "Don't worry, not one flower was harmed in the making of this clearing!"

Tess clapped her hands together with excitement. "You didn't mow any down?" She took the vase from him.

"Not a one. I'm not a murderer, Mary T." There was that smile again. It made her stomach do the happy dance.

He put his hand out for hers. "There's more. Come here, I wanna show you somethin'."

They walked up a steady incline, between trees, fields of tall grass, and flowers, to level ground at the top of the hill. Tess gasped when she looked down at the hill they were on. It was a rocky incline, with a pronounced drop, dotted with scraggly trees and huge boulders, and ending with a beautiful lake at the base.

They stood side-by-side for a few minutes, just taking in the glory of the day. Big, billowy clouds bumped each other in the sky, and the sun was starting to make its descent. The caw of a bird brought Tess's mind from wonder at the beauty of her surroundings to wonder of how she could have allowed herself to be brought to the middle of nowhere, with a man she really didn't know all that well, to the top of a hill with a very steep drop, where one push would send her crashing into the jagged rocks, careening to her death . . .

Jack squeezed her arm. "I'll be right back." His touch made her jump. He headed back to the car and returned with a huge blanket under one arm and a picnic basket in his other hand. He spread the blanket out and disappeared once more. "Can I help?" Tess called after him. Her moment of doubt was over and she felt guilty. *What was I thinking?* Just a moment later, he was back with a cooler.

"Jack, I can't believe you've gone to so much trouble!" Tess tried to open the basket, but he swatted her hand away. "Ah, ah, ah! No peeking! And it was no trouble. I did some shopping this afternoon, a little mowing, and here we are."

Jack opened the picnic basket and pulled out two huge roast beef sandwiches on homemade buns, a container of potato salad, pretty plates, napkins, and forks. She watched, wide-eyed, as he brought out a container with big, deep red strawberries, chunks of fresh pine-apple, and bite-sized banana slices, followed by a bowl of melted milk choco-late. "For the fruit," he explained. Two bottles of sweet tea were pulled from the cooler, and he poured it into two plastic wine glasses, handing one to her. Her stomach did a little flip and she pulled her eyes from his, taking a sip to mask her nervousness.

"I remember you saying you weren't all that fond of wine, right?" He waited for approval.

"Sweet tea will do just fine, Jack."

Soon they were talking, laughing, and eating, and Tess's nervousness dissipated. Having been so engrossed in conversation, they hadn't noticed the sky getting darker, not from the setting sun, but due to the increasing clouds. The low rumble of thunder off in the distance made them look up.

"Uh-oh," Jack said, looking at the darkening skies, "I didn't think to look at the weather report, it's been so nice all day."

"Oh Jack, I saw there was a chance of rain, but I didn't think it would come on this quickly. We'd better start packing up."

Tess felt a few raindrops, and looked up at the trees as a gust of wind pushed through them, sending the branches swaying wildly and the leaves singing. More drops fell as they threw things in the basket and cooler. Tess felt and heard the wind as it surged through the trees. All of a sudden, the skies opened up, unleashing sheets of rain. They scurried to finish packing up, but decided to run for the shelter of a huge maple tree instead of getting totally drenched by going to the car. Even so, by the time they were safely under the tree, they were both soaking wet. Jack scrounged in the picnic basket for some paper napkins, handing them to Tess so she could dry some of the rain from her arms and legs. He leaned back against the tree trunk and watched as she moved the napkins over her glistening skin. She heard his breath catch and looked up to find him staring at her. She looked down. The rain had completely soaked the white linen of her blouse and lacy bra, making it practically see-through. She saw that not only had the rain made the cloth transparent, but the blouse now clung to her breasts, forming their perfect outline.

He brought his gaze up to hers, and she could see the heat in his eyes and the look of pure desire on his face. They looked at each other for what seemed like thirty minutes, but was actually only a few seconds. The rain plopped loudly on the leaves above them and poured down around them, but the tree's dense foliage kept them from getting wetter. The pounding of the rain mingled with the pounding of Tess's heart as she returned Jack's gaze, aching for him to touch her.

"Damn, Tess. I'm not going to be able to hold back for much longer. If this is too much too soon, we'd better make a run for the car. Because with you standing there looking like that, in about five seconds I'm not going to be able to keep from touching you."

Eyes locked on Jack, Tess took a small step toward him, and he reached for her, pulling her into his arms. As he kissed her, he turned her around, gently pinning her against the tree. He parted her lips and explored her mouth, running his tongue along her lower lip, and then back into her mouth. She kissed him back, arms wrapped around his broad shoulders, and widening the stance of her legs so he could fit in between them, drawing him closer to her. The kiss was electric and hot and intimate, urged on by the sound of the rain. Jack brought the kiss to a gradual halt so they could both catch their breath. She leaned back, resting her head on the tree trunk behind her. He braced his hands on either side of her head and pushed back from her a bit, looking into her eyes.

"Wow," she laughed softly, "when you plan a picnic, you really plan a picnic."

He leaned in again for another kiss. The sound of the rain, the cocooning effect of the sprawling tree, and the darkness falling around them made the moment feel very intimate. He groaned and pulled back slightly, studying her face.

"I wasn't ready for it to end." He outlined her bottom lip with his finger. "Although I have to admit I liked the special effects." He indicated her wet blouse.

"Jack, why don't we go to my house, and get out of these wet clothes . . . "

He leaned in to her and nuzzled below her ear. She said, "I mean, we can change clothes—I have a few of my son's things I think you can wear while I put your clothes in the dryer. And we can continue our picnic."

"That sounds perfect." Jack kissed her again. "Well not perfect, because perfect would have been finishing our picnic back there on that hill as the sun set, but I like your solution." The rain was letting up and had slowed to a steady stream. They picked everything up and ran to the car. She managed to slip only once on the dash back down the trail.

Jack opened Tess's door and stowed everything in the back once she was inside. He got in behind the wheel and slumped back into the seat, laying his head against the headrest, catching his breath. He sat up, put the key in the ignition, and then turned to look at Tess. He leaned over to give her another long, mind-blowing kiss. His hands began to unbutton her blouse.

"Jack . . . "

He sat back, reaching for the back of his polo shirt. He pulled it off over his head, leaving on the t-shirt underneath, and handed it to Tess. "Here. You'd better put this on if you want us to safely get to your house."

TAKE A LONG WALK OFF A
SHORT PIER

<u>allgitout</u>: adjective \awl-git-out\ all get out
I'm attracted to you as allgitout.

[July 2010]

Jack and Tess walked into her kitchen to find the freezer door wide open and an empty gallon carton of chocolate ice cream on the floor. Ezzie had somehow managed to open the freezer side of Tess's side-by-side refrigerator and helped herself to some ice cream. She'd licked the container so clean it looked as if she'd washed it. She looked up at them from under the kitchen table with guilty eyes and ears droopier than usual.

"Really, Ezzie? Again?" Tess said in exasperation.

"Oh, for cryin' out loud, Esmerelda! What did you do?" Jack bellowed. Ezzie shrunk back further under the table. "You come out here right now!" She looked at him pitifully, her tail hanging down in guilt.

"Ezzie . . . " Jack warned. She slowly made her way to him.

"You've never behaved this way at home! What's the matter with you?" He was down on the floor, looking at her eye-to-eye. Ezzie whined. Her tongue took a big, wet swipe at his nose.

"Jack, she's licked this carton clean. It was almost full! How did she do that? I'll bet her little tummy hurts. That's a lot of ice cream, not to mention chocolate's not good for dogs. Do you think we should take her to the vet?"

"No, I think we should just watch her. Tess, I'm so sorry. She really never has done anything like this at my house. I don't know what's come over her."

"Maybe she's rebelling. She doesn't want to stay here."

"Now who wouldn't want to stay here with you? She's got it made in the shade!"

"Mmm hmmm." Tess didn't sound convinced. She walked toward the door. "C'mon. Let's find you some dry clothes."

She showed Jack into the guest bedroom. "I think there are some gym shorts and t-shirts in here. Why don't you see what you can find in the dresser, and then we can stick your clothes in the dryer. I'll change, too, and meet you back in the den." The look on Jack's face said he'd rather stay in the bedroom with her, but he just nodded as she closed the door.

Tess changed into dry clothes, and went to find Jack's wet ones, but he'd already put them in the dryer. She joined him in the den. He was sitting on the floor next to the open picnic basket, his back up against the couch, Ezzie at his feet. He'd lit three large candles that were already in the room, leaving on only one small lamp. Even though the light was low, it was apparent he was larger than her son, because the t-shirt he had on was form fitting, and the gym shorts were too short.

"What are you smiling at?" Jack asked her.

"I'm just really enjoying tonight. I see we're picking up where we left off." She sat down next to him, her back leaning against the couch.

"Well . . . almost . . . " Jack said playfully, turning to her.

"Did you say something about dessert?" she asked innocently.

Jack pulled out two huge brownies and a baggie full of green M&M's from the picnic basket. "I can't take credit for these brownies. They're from Mrs. Ward—part of the outpouring of community TLC."

"Jack," she laughed, "I can't possibly eat all of that! I can't believe you went to this much trouble." She took a huge bite. "But thank you! Oh my gosh, this is delicious." She looked at the bag of green M&M's in Jack's hand and cocked her head. "Why green M&M's?"

Jack got a sly grin on his face as he opened the baggie and popped an M&M in his mouth. "A buddy of mine told me he once got lucky with green M&M's."

"Oh reeeeeally?" Tess said, looking him in the eye and tossing a few in her mouth.

"Tess, I want to say somethin'."

She swallowed hard and looked over at him, waiting for what was to come.

"I think you know that I'm attracted to you as allgitout. I think you're a beautiful, smart, sexy woman. The more I get to know you, the more I like you, and the more I want to know. But I don't want to rush you. I may not know the reasons why, but I know you're hesitant to get involved. I was beginning to think I just wasn't your type. But after that kiss . . . " Jack's voice trailed off, and he shook his head, looking down at the floor. He looked back at her and said softly, "After that kiss, I'm thinking that the attraction is mutual, but beyond that, I'm thinking that I really want to put my hands all over you." Tess gulped.

He took the brownie out of her hands and set it aside. Moving closer, he put one arm on the sofa behind her head. "What are *you* thinking?"

Tess dropped her head onto his shoulder. "I'm thinking let's put the cards on the table, Jack. No games."

"Okay . . . "

"Would you tell me why you got divorced?" Her head was still on his shoulder as she looked up at him.

"If you promise to believe me."

"I promise."

He took a deep breath, held it, and then let it out slowly. "I've heard some rumors around town, and I know some people think I cheated on my wife. The fact is—Corrine was unfaithful to *me*."

Tess was not expecting that. She sat up straight and turned so she could look at him better. "Oh Jack, I'm so sorry." She shook her head and looked down at her hands. "And here I was believing the rumors and thinking you were the unfaithful one. I'm such an idiot." Her eyes snapped back to his face. "You weren't unfaithful, too, were you?"

"Not once. Not ever."

"Well then, we share something in common, Jack. My husband cheated on me. Several times. I think I was the last to know. Talk about a girl with her head in the sand."

"Yeah, well, I think I was one fry short of a Happy Meal, myself," Jack said. "It started with her buying anything and everything. We had a Lexus and a BMW in the garage, but she went out and bought a Mercedes. She bought tons of clothes and started going weekly to the spa for facials and massages. She wanted us to join the country club; she wanted a maid; she was out of control. We stopped talking and started being roommates. It was actually kind of a relief when I found out about her affair. I was glad to have an excuse to end the marriage. We're better friends now than we were when we were married."

"I saw you with her the other day. She's beautiful."

"Yeah, she and her boyfriend came to see me about some crazy investment scheme. I told 'em to take a long walk off a short pier." Jack scooted closer to Tess again. "I said it nicely, of course," he added. She laughed.

"Jack, I just don't want to rush into anything. I was totally blindsided by my husband's secret life. I felt betrayed and stupid for being so trusting. I was just getting my sea legs back and then you came along. To tell you the truth, you were right when you said I was scared of you."

He trailed a finger down her cheek to her collarbone and back up. Their eyes locked. A burp escaped from Ezzie, who was lying a few feet away. They both laughed.

"That should have been a mood stopper," Jack said, still looking at her intently. "But even that can't distract me." His fingers played in her hair, while his thumbs caressed her face.

"I had a nice time tonight, Jack. Thank you for going to so much trouble. I can't remember the last time I felt so utterly spoiled."

"The night's not over yet, ya know." He cupped her face with his hands and brought his lips to hers.

Before she knew what she was doing, she'd moved onto his lap and was kissing him like there was no tomorrow. He wrapped his arms around her and pulled her tightly into him. She clutched his neck and pushed into him but wanted to be even closer, so she moved to straddle him, never breaking the kiss. He groaned and deepened the kiss, kissing her harder, moving his hands up and down her back. She could feel him as she pressed into him, moving slowly, making them both moan.

As Jack unbuttoned Tess's shirt, she pulled his t-shirt up, running her hands over his chest. It had been forever since she'd felt this intense desire, since she'd felt this desirable. Her shirt was untucked and unbuttoned, and Jack's hands were moving up.

Then Ezzie jumped up, barking as the phone rang, shattering the moment. Tess broke the kiss and sat with her head down for a few seconds before reluctantly pulling herself off his lap and crossing the room to answer the phone. Ezzie stealthily inched over and snatched

Tess's brownie, devouring it in seconds.

"Hello?" she said huskily, as Jack watched her. She modestly pulled her shirt together. "Martha Maye! Hi!" She looked over at Jack, who was mouthing, "Tell her you're busy."

"No, no, it's not too late," she said, shaking her head at him.

"Tomorrow. Tell her tomorrow," he whispered.

Turning her back to Jack, she said, "Sure, Jack's here, too, come on over if you want . . . Okay, see you in a few minutes." She hung up the phone and turned to Jack. He'd thrown his head back on the seat of the couch and was looking at the ceiling.

"I guess you heard . . . "

"Tess," Jack said without lifting his head. "You're killing me."

WELL, SLAP MY HEAD
AND CALL ME SILLY

<u>turrible</u>: adjective \tur-uh-buhl\ terrible
That rain kicked up the humidity somethin' turrible.

GOOSE PIMPLE GAZETTE
December 20, 1935

JOHN HOBB FOUND SHOT TO DEATH

Body Found Near Bridge On Road In Parked Auto
Death of Prominent Young Man Remains Mystery

Funeral services for John Hobb, killed Sunday night by an un-known person near the Goose Creek Bridge were held Wednesday afternoon at two o'clock at the First Methodist Church. The Rev. Otis J. Baker conducted the services. A quartet with Abe Barber, Reverend Baker, J. E. Walker, and Charles Williams sang several selections. Burial followed in the church cemetery.

No new developments have been uncovered in the case at this time, but the department is working overtime for answers to this myste-rious and tragic murder of the young banker, upstanding citizen, and family man.

John Hobb, thirty-three years old, and General Auditor for the First National Bank of Goose Pimple Junction, had been employed by the bank for the past twelve years. He was found shot to death at the wheel of his automobile Sunday night, near the Goose Creek Bridge. His wife found his body around eleven o'clock on Sunday evening, December fifteenth. It is believed he had been dead for about four hours. No motive for the murder is known, and clues as to the guilty party are scarce.

According to reports, John Hobb took his family to Sunday evening church services about six o'clock and intended to drive out to Duckbill on some business, returning to the church to take his family home. His wife was worried when he failed to come back, and late that night when he still had not returned home, she became alarmed. Reverend Baker, Mrs. Baker, and Mrs. Hobb went to search for him. His car was discovered parked on the side of the road, near the Goose Creek Bridge with the lights burning and the motor running. Mrs. Hobb discovered his body slumped over the wheel. According to witnesses, his revolver was in his hand, but it had not been fired.

The police were notified immediately and rushed to the scene of the crime. Three bullet holes were found in the glass of the car. Mr. Hobb had suffered a single gunshot to the head, with entry just behind his right ear and exiting from just below his left temple. An officer was placed at the car to preserve the integrity of the crime scene, and his body was removed to Pearson's funeral parlor. A coroner's inquest held Monday morning found that Mr. Hobb died at the hands of an unknown party. Bloodhounds were brought to the scene, but failed to pick up any trail. Fingerprints were taken as evidence, in an effort to discover the killer.

According to passersby, Mr. Hobb's car was seen parked about seven o'clock at the spot where it was found. Several people who saw the car by the side of the road earlier in the evening assumed it was preparing to turn around and thought nothing was wrong. Neighbors nearby did not hear shots fired, which leads officials to believe that the actual shooting might have occurred somewhere else and the car driven to Goose Creek Bridge where the car was found.

Family and friends have no theories as to the reason for the murder. Mr. Hobb was a young businessman of highest regard and had no enemies, as far as it is known. He was the son of the late C.C. Hobb of the Jake Creek section of Mallard County, and is survived by his widow, Mrs. Maye Lawrence Hobb; four children, Johnny, Samuel, Ima Jean and Louetta, all under twelve years old. His mother, three brothers, five sisters, and numerous relatives also survive.

[July 2010]

"Oooh Lordy! It's sa hot the hens are layin' hard-boiled eggs." Martha Maye stepped into Tess's house, wiping her face and neck with a hankie. "That rain kicked up the humidity somethin' turrible, and that's what'll getcha more 'n the sun. It's so sticky out there you can purt near wring out the air." She reached down to pet Ezzie, who'd come to the door to protect Tess.

"You mean you walked all the way here?" Tess asked.

"Oh yeah, honey, it ain't that far; besides, it quit rainin', and I needed the exercise." She patted her behind as emphasis and walked into the den where she saw Jack, the candles, and the picnic basket. "Well slap my head and call me silly! I interrupted somethin', didn't I?" She looked from Jack to Tess. "Ah, shoot. Why didn't ya tell me? Say— is there a full moon out? There must be, 'cause there's lovers everywhere I look. I passed Pickle and Charlotte on the way here. I don't know what that girl sees in him. I swan, if that boy had an idea, it would die of loneliness. A course, she's no state fair prize either; she's so conceited, if God made one better He forgot to tell her." Tess unconsciously took a deep breath, in reaction to Martha Maye talking so long and so fast without a breath.

"Whoa! Martha Maye! Slow down!" Jack stood up.

"Dj'yer clothes shrink in the rain or somethin', Jack?" She eyed the short shorts he was wearing and the shirt that was pulling tight across his chest.

"Actually, the rain got me soaked, and I borrowed some of Tess's son's clothes while mine are in the dryer."

"And you're not interrupting." Tess put her arm around Martha Maye and directed her to a seat. "Come on in and sit down. Can I get you some tea?"

"Why that would be lovely, thank you!"

Tess came back with the tea just as Martha Maye was telling Jack, "It went over like a turd in a punchbowl."

"What did?" Tess asked, handing Martha the tea.

"Talkin' ta Mama 'bout her daddy's murder. She just plain won't do it. I tried every which way to get into the subject, and she cut me off ever time. But—" She took a sip from her tea, "I did find these in the family Bible."

She pulled a book, holding a Zip-loc bag with newspaper clippings, out of her large tote purse. She opened the bag and carefully took out one of the brittle, browned clippings. The title, "John Hobb Is Found Shot To Death Near Bridge" in bold print was at the top. Tess sat next to Jack on the sofa and read the article out loud. Once she finished, the three of them sat in silence for a bit, everyone lost in their own thoughts.

Martha Maye broke the silence by taking out a second article titled, *"Two Women Wounded By Gunfire."* Tess took it from her.

"The subtitle says, *'Maye Hobb, Mother Shot, Trevor Hobb Surrenders, Details As To Cause, Events, Hard To Explain.'*" Tess read to herself for a minute. "It says your grandmother was wounded in her left breast and arm. Her mother was shot in the neck and neither was expected to live. How horrible."

"Mama must have been scared to death. There she was, a little girl who'd already lost her daddy, and it was lookin' like she was gonna lose her mama, too. And both by gunshots. Mmm, mmm." Martha Maye shook her head.

"It says your uncle surrendered voluntarily but wouldn't make a statement. And then it goes on to say, 'Maye is John Hobb's widow, the man who was found dead in his car in December 1935.' The writer tells about that incident and ends by pointing out the fact that Brick Lynch was out on bond, charged with his murder. It specifically points out that your grandfather testified against Lynch on the robbery charge. This makes it look like the town folk thought it was Lynch who killed him."

Jack reached for the pile of fragile newspaper clippings on the coffee table and looked through them. In doing so, he moved his bare foot up against Tess's under the coffee table. He picked out another article titled, *'Mrs. Lawrence Dies From Pistol Wound.'* As he read, he stroked her foot with his toes.

Tess held her leg still and looked at Jack with apologetic eyes, hoping Martha Maye didn't know what was going on under the table.

"It looks like your great grandmother died two days after the shooting. Good gracious, she was only fifty-nine years old. This article says she was shot in the neck and her spinal cord was severed. But it looks like by then they felt Maye was expected to live."

Tess picked up another article. "This one says that Trevor surrendered to the police. At least there wasn't a long, drawn out investigation. It looks like the only things the murders had in common was that they happened to the same family and both involved gunshots." Tess continued to scan the article and moved so she was sitting on her foot, causing Jack to smirk.

"Or did Trevor kill his brother to pave the way for him to move in on Maye?" Jack asked.

"They charged Brick Lynch with the murder, but he got off because the judge said the prosecution's witness couldn't be believed. Is that right?" Tess asked.

"Yep, I do remember Mama sayin' he was slipperier than snot on a doorknob. Mama thinks he got off twice because money greased the palms of a certain governor and a judge."

"Does she think Brick Lynch killed her father?"

"Tessie, I just don't rightly know for sure."

"Do you know if he still has any relatives living in town?" Jack asked.

"I don't know of any Lynch folk in town." Martha Maye ran her hand up and down Ezzie's back.

"Wouldn't necessarily have to be a Lynch. If he had a daughter, she'd have her husband's name, and the kids would have a different name, too," Jack pointed out.

"If the chest is in your mother's attic, why don't we give the key a try?" Tess asked.

"Well, I don't see what good it would do. Mama said they got a replacement key and didn't find anything unusual in that trunk."

"At least we'd know we had the right trunk." Tess put the newspaper clippings back in the Ziploc bag.

"I guess it's a possibility, if y'all are bound and determined, but it'd have to be sometime when Mama's not home, and usually when she ain't home, I'm busier than a moth in a mitten. I'll have to call ya sometime when it suits. Meantime, I'll ask around 'bout any relatives of Lynch."

Jack had slipped his hand underneath Tess's hair and was lightly massaging her neck, with his fingertips.

"Ohhh. Oh-kay, Martha, we'll just play it by ear," Tess said, trying to cover her near moan. Jack coughed and left his fist over his mouth to cover a guilty smile.

Martha Maye gathered up the clippings. "Well, I 'spect I should be goin' now."

"Jack, your clothes should be dry now. Why don't you change back into them and give Martha Maye a ride home? It would be silly for her to walk, since you're both going to practically the same place." His stare unnerved her, and she added, "And since it's so hot out there." *Because it's way too hot in here.*

Jack pursed his lips, but he reluctantly agreed.

"That'd by mighty kind a you, Jack. My daddy would turn in his grave if he knew I was out this late by myself. He used to say ain't nobody out at this time a night but burglars and bad women."

While Jack was gone to get his clothes, Martha Maye looked down at Ezzie, who'd worked herself halfway up onto her lap. "She's not much of a guard dog."

"Isn't that the truth! But Jack said it makes him feel better to know that at least she'll bark if someone should try to come into the house again. I'm sure your mother told you about the recent break-ins."

"She did. Aren't you afraid to stay here by yourself with nothin' more than a sloth on feet for protection? A sweet sloth, but still a sloth." She smiled down at the dog and rubbed her ears.

As if on cue, Ezzie lifted her head, sent her nose up in the air, and let out a big howl.

"It's just me, Ez," Jack said, coming back into the room.

"It's time we get on home, Jackson, if ya don't mind." Martha Maye got to her feet.

Tess and Ezzie walked them to the door. "Thanks for coming over, Martha Maye. We'll talk again soon."

They walked onto the porch, and Martha Maye said, "Okay, you two, I'ma gwon over't the car and let you say your goodnights."

"Oh, Martha Maye, you don't have to—"

"Speak for your cotton-pickin' self, blabbermouth," Jack interrupted, pinching a bit of Tess's shirt and pulling her back toward him.

Martha bustled down the steps, and Jack reached for Tess's waist, pulling her into him. "Next time can we pick up where we left off?"

Tess smiled and propped her arms on Jack's shoulders, her hands playing with the hair at the base of his neck. "Possibly," she said, coyly.

"I can take Martha Maye home and be right back, ya know." He kissed her cheek, about a millimeter away from her lips.

"Jack . . . "

"Don't tell me this was a mistake." He kissed just under her ear.

"I wasn't going to. And I'm not trying to be a tease. I just think we should take things slowly."

Jack finally found Tess's lips.

And then Martha Maye screamed.

SHUT THE DOOR AND CALL THE LAW

dootcher: verb \doo-tchur\ a reprimand, do what your
Dootcher mama says.

[1937]

"You've ate that chicken till it's slick as a ribbon, Psalmist David," Maye teased her little brother.

"And it's so good I can hardly keep my toes still. You make the best fried chicken in seven counties, Mayepie."

"Mama, what's slick as a ribbon mean?" asked Louetta.

"Means he ate all the meat clean off the bone, leavin' it slick—see here?" she held a bone up to show her daughter.

"Mama, kin I take baby Johnny out and walk him?" Ima Jean wanted to know.

"How 'bout you clear the table first?" Maye responded.

"But Mama . . . "

"Dootcher mama says now, Ima Jean," P.D. admonished.

"Quick! Let me hold him before she comes back to collect him," Maye said as soon as her daughter left the room with an arm full of plates. She took her nephew in her arms and crooned, "You're cuter 'n a bugs butt, little fella . . . "

"Maye, you're gonna wool that baby to death," Denise said with a smile.

"Mama, what does that mean?" Louetta asked.

"She thinks I'm gonna give him too much lovin', Buttabean. Would you like to hold him?"

"Can I?" Louetta asked, with her hands folded like she was praying.

"Sit on down here first, Bean." Once Louetta was situated, her mother put the baby in her lap.

Maye disappeared and came back with a coconut cake. She cut a big slice and put it in front of her brother. "My goodness, that's a gracious plenty!" he said, eyeing the huge piece of cake.

Maye finished serving cake to everyone before she sat back down at the table.

"P.D., I don't wanna bring up a sore subject, but . . . can I borrow the money, or cain't I?" Maye asked, impatiently.

"Aw, Maye. Why do you want ta put good money down on somethin' that oughtta be police business?"

"Because I don't trust Bug Preston any farther 'n I can throw him. Him or his deputy. One of 'em will lie, and the other'll swear to it."

"P.D., she's right. He's so crooked, when he dies they'll have to screw him into the ground," Denise said.

"You don't know that, you're just annoyed he hasn't made an arrest. He's good people, and he's tryin' his best. You listen to the old biddies too much, honey. He's workin' on it. Just give him time."

"I'll give him time. But there's a lot of ways to skin a rabbit. I wanna hire this private detective," Maye insisted. "Will ya loan me the money or not?"

"If you're sure that's what you wonta do," P.D. said, resignedly.

"Now can I walk little Johnny?" Ima Jean asked again.

"All right. But stay in front 'a the house."

"Maye, don't go gettin' yer hopes up," P.D. said seriously. "And don't insult the alligator before you cross the stream . . . and not at all if you go home that way!"

"What's that supposed ta mean?" Maye said, irritably.

"You know what it means."

Maye inclined her head.

"Means don't go rubbin' Bug's nose in the fact that yer hirin' somebody to do his job."

Maye harrumphed and crossed her arms. "I say if he can't run with the big dogs, he oughtta stay under the porch."

[July 2010]

Martha Maye ran back to Tess's front porch, screaming a blue streak through the night air.

Jack and Tess ran to her, as Ezzie shot past them and raced into the yard.

"Shut the door and call the law! There's somethin' or someone in those tall pine trees over yonder!" Martha Maye stood clutching her purse to her chest, clearly terrified.

Jack ran past her. "I'll check it out."

"Jack!" Tess tried to call him back.

"Y'all go on back inside. And lock the doors," he called as he ran toward the trees.

She went to Martha Maye, taking her hand, and leading her into the house. "What was it? Was it a person? Could it have been an animal?"

Martha Maye's breathing was deep and heavy. "I saw a big black form, not five feet away—just standin' there, real still like. It ran off soon as I got near to it, and . . . it was definitely not an animal, unless it was Squash Squash. He . . . or she . . . or it nearly scared the livin' daylights outta me."

"It's all right, Martha Maye. I don't think there have been any Sasquatch sightings around here. You're safe. I'm sure whoever it was is long gone, or else heaven help him if Jack gets a hold of him."

Martha Maye gripped Tess's arm. "We should call John Ed."

"And tell him what? That you think you saw something? He'll laugh his head off."

"Agggghhhhh. The audacity of that man. Then I'm callin' Henry Clay." Martha Maye got her cell phone out.

"What for? Jack's here . . . " Tess let her sentence drift off when she could see Martha Maye was intent on making her call.

Jack was gone for nearly five minutes. Just as Tess was starting to panic, he came walking back to the house with Ezzie in his arms. Tess watched for them out the front window and met them at the door.

"I think she had a bead on him. She ran until her little legs couldn't go any more. She may be small, but she's fast. I think she could make quick work of somebody's ankles, maybe even jump up to get a mouthful of butt." He set Ezzie down.

Tess bent to pat her. "That's my big brave Esmerelda, yes you are . . . "

"I'm gonna check around back, make sure nothing or no one is there. Be right back." Jack disappeared around the side of the house. Tess took a panting Ezzie in for some water and a dog biscuit, closing and locking the door again.

"Tessie, would you like to come 'n stay with Mama and me? We've got room and we'd be glad to have ya."

"Thank you, Martha Maye, I appreciate that, but I'll be fine."

Both women jumped when Ezzie let out a loud bark, followed by a knock at the front door.

"Boy, she's a good watch dog. She's like Radar. She barks before something happens," Tess said.

"That's prob'ly Henry Clay. I'll get the door." Martha Maye stopped and turned to Tess. "Is my hair all right?"

Tess smiled. "It looks great."

Jack knocked on the back door, as Henry Clay came in the front.

"Who wants cake and brownies?" Tess placed an overflowing plate on the table.

"Now tell me again what happened." Henry Clay grabbed a brownie off the top.

"I don't care what anybody says, I saw somethin' or someone out in the pines," Martha Maye told him. "And tell him about all the break-in episodes, Tess."

After filling Henry Clay in, he said, "I haven't heard of anything like this 'round these parts in all my born days."

"Henry Clay, you've lived here for a blue million years, but I've been gone so long, I'm outta the know. D'you know if Brick Lynch had 'ny family? Any relatives that might still be livin' 'round here?"

He pursed his lips and looked up into the air, thinking for a minute. Finally he said, "Well sure, he had a daughter who had a couple a kids. I b'lieve the son lives out on Brick's old property, matta fact. His name's Crate Marshall. He's a biker-type, even though he's so poor he'd have to borrow money to buy water to cry with. I 'spect he spends all his money on his motorcycle and his beer. Don't rightly know what he does for a livin'. He's a real character. Mean and ornery. I wouldn't wonta mess with him. Why 'ont y'all just back offa this, and let Daddy figure it out."

"Because he doesn't seem to believe there's anything to figure out.

He thinks I'm a hysterical female, prone to hissy fits with tails." Tess gestured wildly in the air.

"Wull, I'll talk to him. Let me handle it, okay?" Henry Clay raised his eyebrows and looked at the others around the table. They nodded.

"How's the campaign goin' Henry Clay?" Jack asked.

"Oh, it's comin' along all right. It'd be a whole lot better if my esteemed opponent wasn't so rich. I swear I think he buys a new car each time one gets wet. But he's got one huge strike against him."

"Only one?" Martha Maye teased.

"It's a bigun. He dudn't have the sense he was born with. The wheels are still turnin', but the hamster's dead, if ya know what I mean."

"Henry Clay, you're so soft-spoken it's funny to hear you say something like that," Tess said.

"Wull I don't go runnin' down Main Street hollerin' it big as daylight, but I can form my own private opinions, can't I? Y'all aren't gonna blabber to the media are ya?"

"No, I guess not." Tess smiled, wondering if he wasn't a bit of a dim bulb himself. "How long have you worked at the bank?"

"Right about twenty years, ever since college."

"Oh? Where did you go?"

"Duke University."

"Jack, I don't think I ever asked where you went."

"Ole Miss," he said. "And you went to UVA, is that right?"

"Yes, how'd you know?"

Before he could answer, Martha Maye interrupted with, "I went to Georgia State, that's where I met 'he who shall not be named.'"

Tess put her hand on Martha Maye's shoulder. "How are you doing with the divorce?"

"Okay, I guess. Lord only knows when the divorce will be finalized."

"Whatta you mean?" Henry Clay cocked his head.

"It's just hard gettin' everything ironed out. Custody, possessions, finances, figurin' out where my little Butterbean and I are gonna live. We can't stay at Mama's forever."

"How long have you been divorced?" Tess asked Henry Clay.

"Oh, 'bout four years now, I think," he said. "You?"

"Almost a year."

"A little over two years," said Jack of himself.

"This rightcheer's like a support group! Ever one of us is divorced."

Henry Clay slammed the table with his hand. "We oughtta have weekly meetin's or sumthin'. You know—like a support group does. Least to help Martha Maye out in this tryin' time."

"Well I don't see what it would hurt," Jack said. "I'm in."

"Me too," Tess said.

"How about our first "official" group meeting at the Silly Goose in a few days?" Jack asked.

"I think that'll be good, but let me check my schedule when I get home. I never know what my CM has planned for me."

"Is Charlotte involved in the campaign?" Jack asked.

"Naw. She helps out at headquarters, but that's about it."

The four talked for a while longer, until Tess tried to stifle a yawn. Henry Clay looked at his watch. "Shoot. It's almost midnight. I know what you're thinkin', Tess."

"You do? What's that?" Her face flushed because of what she was thinking about Jack.

"You're thinkin' the same thing my mama used to think when we used to have comp'ny who stayed and stayed."

They all looked at him, waiting for him to tell them what it was.

"Once they'd finally left, she'd say, 'We just wanted to have the neighbors over for dinner, we didn't plan on takin' 'em to raise.'" They laughed at Henry's falsetto voice, mimicking the voice of his mother.

The men made one more sweep around Tess's yard, and then Jack and Tess waved from the front porch as Martha Maye and Henry Clay left. Jack turned to Tess and said, "Well . . . "

"Jack, thank you for a wonderful evening. You went to a lot of trouble and the picnic was truly special."

"Tess, will you be all right by yourself tonight?" He stepped closer to her, taking her into his arms.

"I'll be fine. I have my guard dog, you know."

He kissed her softly at first, then deeper and harder. He pulled his lips from hers, but stood close, looking into her eyes. "There's more where that came from, anytime you're ready." He kissed her again.

I'm ready. Take me, take me now. But when he ended the kiss, she simply said goodnight.

After he left, Tess turned out the lights on the first floor, and Ezzie followed her upstairs to get ready for bed. When the phone rang she was brushing her teeth. She looked down at Ezzie, who was lying on the floor. Ezzie looked back at Tess with her head resting on her paws, her eyeballs the only movement on her body.

"That's probably just Nick. He'll be worried when I tell him what's going on, and I don't feel like getting into it right now. And if it's Lou, she'll just try to convince me to stay at her house. Let's let it ring, Ezzie." Ezzie's tail thumped on the floor twice.

The phone stopped ringing and went to voice mail, but the caller didn't leave a message.

Tess rubbed moisturizer on her face as she walked to her bed. She lay down, and Ezzie jumped up with her. "It's been one heck of a night. This attraction to your daddy is getting out of hand." Tess played with Ezzie's ears. "But gosh, can that man kiss."

Thoughts swirled in Tess's mind. Jack's searing kisses, thoughts of Lou's family tragedies, Martha Maye's screams, it all replayed in her mind.

The ringing phone startled her. "Oh, for Pete's sake," she said out loud, reaching for the phone. "Hello?"

"Yer stickin' yer nose where it does not belong," a raspy voice whispered. She couldn't tell if it was a man or a woman. She could barely hear what the person said.

"And why is that?" she asked, in a voice that sounded stronger than she felt.

"Just never you mind, missy," the voice hissed. "Just stop being Mizz Sherlock Holmes or you'll be sorry."

The line went dead.

THE ONLY THING THAT WOULD MAKE
HIM DUMBER
IS IF HE WAS BIGGER

<u>tee-nincey</u>: adjective \tee-nine-see\ very, very small
It doesn't matter if it's one litte bit, one tee-nincey bit,
or one great big bit.

[July 2010]

Tess had lay awake for hours after the ominous phone call, and she slept fitfully after that, until falling into a deep sleep sometime around dawn. When her alarm went off, she didn't hear it and overslept. She was going to be late getting to Stafford's if she didn't hurry. She quickly dressed, rubbed Ezzie's tummy, then closed her in the bedroom, grabbed her keys, and headed to the car. She yawned as she dialed the phone and listened to Jack's voice mail message.

At the beep she said, "Jack, this is Tess. I'm sorry to bother you, but I got a weird phone call late last night. I'm a little freaked out. Well, maybe a lot. I have to go to work right now, and I don't want to discuss this around Lou. She said she didn't need me for very long today, so I'll be leaving the bookstore around two o'clock. Maybe we can talk then? Okay . . . bye."

She drove to work, since it made her feel less vulnerable and also because she was exhausted. She pulled into a parking spot several spaces down from the bookstore and noticed Jack waiting out front.

"I just got your message." He rushed to meet her at the car. "Are you all right? What happened? Who called? You sounded a little tense."

She sighed. "Yeah, I'm a lot tense. Someone called last night after you all left and said I was, 'sticking my nose where it didn't belong,' or something like that. He . . . she . . . it . . . whoever it was said I should butt out or I'd be sorry. And then they hung up."

An alarmed look came over Jack's face as he listened to Tess. "Did it sound like a man or a woman?"

"Yes. No. I mean, I don't know. It was impossible to tell. It was kind of a raspy whisper. Jack, you're just as involved in this as I am. Why wouldn't they call both of us?" She studied Jack's face and added, "Or did they?"

"No. My guess is the person figured you could be scared off more than me. I don't think they know you very well." He gave her a reassuring smile. "Aw, Tess." He pulled her into a hug and then stepped back. "I hate that you're going through all of this. Why don't we just forget about it? It's not worth you getting hurt or terrorized over. Lou doesn't care, so why should we? Or why don't you let me do some digging for a while? Let's keep you out of it."

"I don't want to forget about it. I don't like the feeling that someone is watching me, but the fact that they're getting bolder says volumes. Somebody thinks I'm going to find out something; I want to know why they care. Besides Jack, you know if we don't get to the bottom of this, I'll never be able to stop looking over my shoulder, or sleep with both eyes shut at night again, as long as I live here."

"But Tess, this person is getting more menacing. I'm afraid for you. Please think about letting this go."

"Maybe . . . but there's one more person I want to talk to before we do. Are you free this afternoon? Can I pick you up when I'm done here?"

"Yeah, I have a feeling about your maybes. Are you going to tell me who it is you want to talk to?" He followed her toward the bookstore.

She smiled. "Not yet. Are you in or not?"

He let out a frustrated sigh. "Woman, you drive me crazy on so many levels . . . but . . . okay. Come and get me when you're done here." They stopped at Stafford's door. "But don't you dare go anywhere without me, you hear?" You want me to hang around the bookstore today?"

"Thank you, Jack. But I don't think that's necessary."

Lou was in the back room accepting boxes from a UPS delivery when Tess went into the store. She put her purse away, called to Lou, "I'm here," and got out to the register desk just as the phone rang.

"Stafford's, can I help you?"

Silence. But Tess could tell someone was there.

"Hello?" she said, apprehensively.

She heard a click and then the dial tone.

* * *

A few hours later, Tess was tired of talking. People had been in and out all morning, but they hadn't come in for books. Most of them wanted to hear all about the mugging. She'd told the story so many times she thought she could recite it in her sleep. And then Willy came in.

"Hey, Doll!"

"Willy—hello. How are you?"

"I'm busier than a one-legged man at a butt kickin' contest. I just stopped in to say hey." Lou came out of her office and scowled at him.

"Okay, Lou, I confess. I didn't come in to look for no book taday. I came in to see how Tess here's doin'. I done heard about the alter-cation the other night, and I wanted to check and see if there's anythin' I can do."

"Well that's mighty nice a you, Willy. But as you can see, our Tessie's doin' just fine." Lou patted Tess on the arm.

"Thanks for stopping by, Willy," Tess said, trying to scrutinize his facial expression and body language.

"Wull, I don't like thinkin' a you in harm's way. You call on me, ya know, if there's any way I can hep. You just call out my name, and you know wherever I am, I'll come runnin'."

"Winter, spring, summer, or fall?" Tess said, sarcastically.

Willy continued with the lyrics of the James Taylor song, singing off key. "All ya got ta do is call . . . "

"Okay, okay, Willy." Lou began pushing him toward the door. "That's enough. Time you get movin' on and let Tess get back to work. I'd say come back, but then, I'm afraid you would."

"Aw, Lou, why you got ta treat me that way? I never did anythin' to you."

"Willy, I b'lieve you could make a preacher cuss! You go and get a respectable job, and quit hangin' around here botherin' my employee, and I'll consider a change a heart concernin' you." Lou practically shoved Willy out onto the sidewalk and shut the door in his face.

She took three steps before the door opened behind her. Willy stuck his neck around it, and with a cold tone of voice said, "I'll have you know I'm plenty busy with work right now. I'm busy as a funeral home fan in July."

Lou pointed her finger at him. "That's luvely. Now—OUT!"

"That Willy," she said disgustedly, walking back toward Tess. "You can't get rid of him. He's like a booger you can't thump off. When will that boy take a hint? I swan, the only thing that would make him dumber is if he was bigger."

Two o'clock rolled around, and Tess was on her way out when Pickle reported for work.

"Hey, Pickle," she said greeting him, while looking at his white shirt with black lettering that said, "Do you know the muffin man?"

She pointed to his shirt and said, "Sure I do. He lives on Drury Lane."

She left him with a confused look on his face.

Tess pulled into Jack's driveway and found him, Martha Maye, and Butterbean talking in the yard.

"Miss Tess! Miss Tess! Watch this!" Butterbean took a few running steps and then cartwheeled across the yard. When she came to a stop, she turned around and cartwheeled back, landing right in front of Tess. "D'ja see me? D'ja see me?" She hopped, slightly out of breath, from foot to foot.

"I certainly did, Butterbean. That's fantastic!"

"Thank you. I'm takin' gymnastics lessons with Miss Paprika," she said, proud as punch.

Martha Maye sighed. "I used to could do cartwheels across the lawn. Those were the days. Show us some more, sweetie."

When Butterbean had cartwheeled off again, she said, "Great day in the mornin', Tess! Jack was just tellin' me 'bout your phone call last night. This is gettin' too scary for me. Do y'all really think this is all over that stupid key?"

"Is it the key? Is it your grandfather's murder? I don't know. What else could it be? But that brings me to something I wanted to ask you, Martha Maye."

"Whassat?"

"Henry Clay mentioned Brick Lynch had a grandson who lives on his old property. Crate, I think he said. Do you know where his farm is?"

"Ya know, I knew that was Lynch's old farm, but I didn't know his grandson lived there now, or even that he had a grandson, for that matter."

"Mary T . . . " Jack's voice held a warning.

"Jackson . . . " She gave him a look, matching his tone. "I just want to have a chat with the gentleman. That's all."

"Tess, Henry Clay said he's a dangerous sort. Said stay away from him," Martha Maye said.

"I don't like it, Tess. Not one little bit." Jack crossed his arms across his chest.

"One litte bit, one tee-nincey bit, or one great big bit. It doesn't matter. I'm going to talk to the man, and you can either come with me or not."

Jack acknowledged his cooperation with a big sigh. Then he did a double take. "Did you just say tee-nincey?"

"She's been hangin' round my mother for too long," Martha Maye laughed.

Tess made a shooing motion at Jack. "The farm, Martha Maye?"

"Here's what do. Go out past Mack Knob Road until ya get to Route 67. Take a right, and his place is out there a right far piece, oh . . . maybe ten miles or so. Ya cain't miss it. It's got a mailbox painted like a confederate flag. But y'all be careful."

* * *

Crate Marshall lived in a one hundred-year-old farmhouse that had seen better days. It was a weathered white two-story, clapboard-sided house, on about five acres of farmland. It had a winged-gable-roof in the center, with a covered front porch that looked ready to fall in at any moment, and two chimneys on either side of the house. There wasn't much green anywhere to be seen on the property, except for some scraggly trees and bushes here and there. Two rusty cars, one up on blocks, sat to the right side of the house, and a chicken coop with about a dozen chickens was on the left, with a few loose in the yard. A hand-painted sign saying, 'no trespassing—that means you,' was hammered into the dirt about halfway up the dirt and gravel driveway.

Tess pulled up almost to the house and parked. She looked at Jack.

"You sure you wanna do this?" he asked.

She nodded, and they got out of the car. They were halfway between the car and the house when two Rottweilers came barreling toward them from a dilapidated red barn behind the house. The ferocious bark announced their eminent arrival as well as their displeasure with guests.

JUST CUT YOUR SHAMER OFF
AND FEED IT TO THE CHICKENS

<u>zat</u>: pronoun \zat\ is that
Zat right?

GOOSE PIMPLE JUNCTION GAZETTE,
Thursday, April 6, 1939

A case against the New York Life Insurance Company, originally filed in Mallard circuit court by Mrs. Maye D. Hobb, of Goose Pimple Junction, Tennessee, was transferred last week for trial during the May term of Eastern district court at Helechewa.

A lawsuit stemming from a $10,000 death claim, in which the insurance company is named defendant, claims that John Hobb was shot and killed by an unknown person on December 15, 1935. Mrs. Hobb asks for $10,000 double indemnity benefits under a $5,000 life policy held by her husband at the time of his death.

In an answer to the petition, filed by the insurance company through Attorneys Crane and Shore, of Nashville, liability under the policy is denied by allegations that the cause of Hobb's death was suicide.

[July 2010]

Tess froze when she saw two huge dogs bounding toward them. Then she screamed. "JAAAACK!"

"Car, Mary T, CAR!"

Tess turned too fast and her right foot bobbled on her sandal. *Only I could fall off a one-inch heel.* She wobbled and then righted herself, and the heavy purse fell off her shoulder. Jack came up behind her, grabbing her purse and her arm. "Come on, Grace." He pushed her into the car. She scrambled over the console and into the passenger seat, and he followed, practically sitting on top of her so he could close the door tightly.

With both of them safely in the car, the dogs stood barking ferociously just a foot away, as Tess and Jack cowered inside.

The front door opened, and a huge man stepped out onto the porch, pushing mirrored sunglasses over his eyes. He had a confederate flag do rag on his head, and a cigarette poking out of his lips underneath a pencil-thin mustache. A grey wife beater shirt revealed tattoos on each bulging bicep, and his torn denim jeans were tucked into black biker boots. He stood with his hands on his hips and a menacing look on his face.

"Good gravy, he could be the Mr. July for a biker dude calendar." Tess stared, slack-jawed and wide-eyed.

The dogs continued their protective stance and enthusiastic greeting.

The man took the cigarette from his lips and hollered, "Cain't you folks read? Sign says no trespassin'." He paused for a beat, then added, "That means you."

Tess opened the car window two inches, and called out, "Are you Crate Marshall?"

"Folks call me Tank." He took a deep drag of his cigarette. "State your bidness."

"My name's Tess Tremaine, and this is Jackson Wright. We'd like to talk to you for a few minutes about your family history, if that's all right."

"What fer?" he called out guardedly, over the barking dogs.

Jack opened his car door and stood with it as a shield. The dogs moved forward slightly, but kept their distance, emitting a low growl. "I'm writing a book on some events in Goose Pimple Junction's history. I'd like to talk to you about your grandfather; hear his side of the story on the bank robbery of '32."

Tank stood on the bottom step of the porch, staring at them for a full minute, smoking his cigarette. He finished it, dropped it to the ground, and stomped it out with his booted foot. Jack turned to get back in the car.

"Foghorn! Leghorn! Freeze!" The dogs stopped growling and sat down, tongues hanging out as they panted.

Tess looked at Jack, not sure what to do. Finally, Tank said, "Well come on, if yer comin'. I ain't got all day."

They got out of the car, and slowly walked past the dogs, with Tess saying, "Nice doggies." The dogs didn't move an inch. Once Tess and Jack reached the porch, Tank held the door open for them. As they went into the house, he called to the dogs.

"Thaw!" The dogs ran back to the barn.

The inside of Tank's house was not what Tess expected. The furniture and décor suggested a 1950's housewife lived there. The sofa was pea green under a plastic couch cover. A worn out, but clean, brown recliner with a doily draped at the top sat between the couch and the fireplace. An antique oak rocking chair, with a cane seat sat opposite the recliner. A framed rose painting hung over the fireplace, and old family pictures decorated the walls. It looked like Tank had literally moved in and not changed a thing. The only signs of his presence in the house were the smell of cigarettes, the haze of smoke hanging in the air, and the gun magazines sitting on a long pine coffee table in front of the couch.

Tess had second thoughts about going in as she looked through the cloud of smoke, which hung thick in the room. Jack pushed gently on the small of her back, and she reluctantly moved forward. She resisted the urge to wave her hand in front of her face to dispel the cigarette smoke.

Tess and Jack sat on the couch, and Tank took the recliner. Now that they were up close, Tess could see the tattoos more clearly. His right arm featured a Goth chick, with long, flowing hair and voluptuous breasts spilling out of a skin-tight leather vest; she was wielding a large sword. The left side displayed a tattoo of, aptly enough, a tank.

"What's this 'bout a book?" Tank pulled out another cigarette from the pack.

"I write mystery novels, and I'm interested in writing about the bank robbery, for which I believe your grandfather was pardoned."

Tank put the cigarette between his lips, and Jack added, "I'm interested in learning more about the death of John Hobb, too."

Tank lit his cigarette with his Zippo lighter, then snapped the lid shut with the flip of his wrist. "Zat right." He removed his sunglasses, placed them on the coffee table, and rubbed one eye. "Sounds like you already know a good deal about it."

"We were wondering if your grandfather ever talked about the robbery or Mr. Hobb's murder," Tess explained.

"Huh. Yeah, he talked about the robbery. Felt real bad 'bout it, matter a fact. He'd get drunk and start moanin' and groanin' 'bout how he'd brought shame to the family, and so on. And Grandma would always say the same thing ever time. I can hear her now sayin', 'Jest cut your shamer off and feed it to the chickens.'"

"Your shamer off?" Tess echoed.

"You ain't from round here, are ya? Basically, she meant that guilt idn't helpful. What's done is done and ya have ta move on."

"What about the money?" Jack asked.

"What about it?"

"What happened to it?"

"He never came out and said as much, but I kinda think he had to use most of it to grease the governor's palms. Whatever else was left, he probably spent over at Humdinger's."

"Any idea how much his cut was?"

"Negative."

"Do you know what happened to the other men who were involved in the bank robbery?" Tess asked.

"Yeah, I think Rod Pierce died about five years later. And Junior ended up gettin' caught for another job he pulled. I think he spent most a his life rottin' in a cell."

"What about a fourth man?"

"What about him?"

"Did your grandfather ever talk about a fourth man being involved? John Hobb or someone else?"

"Negative. I wouldn't know anything about that."

Jack cleared his throat and asked the sixty-four thousand dollar question. "What about John Hobb's murder?"

"Sounds like you know more 'n me."

"Who do you think killed him? Did your grandfather ever talk about that?"

Tank ran his hand over his stubbly cheeks and wide nose. His eyes grew dark, and he answered, "Can't hep ya."

Cautiously, Jack said, "Is that . . . because you don't want to . . . or because you don't know?"

"What difference does it make? I ain't answerin'."

Jack got his wallet from his back pocket, pulled a hundred dollar bill out, and placed it on the coffee table.

Tank stared at it for a few silent moments. Tess couldn't tell what he was thinking. His eyes went coldly from the bill to Jack. Jack reached out to take it back, but Tank gave in.

"Shoot. Hold on a damn minute." He took several drags from his cigarette, then put it out in a bean bag ashtray on a small table to his left. "I heard my granddaddy talk about it *once*. He was there, but another man did it. I ain't sayin' who the other man was. I ain't no rat. Any other questions?"

"Do you know why he was killed?"

"Negative."

Tess looked at Jack, and he raised his eyebrows, as if to say, 'It's up to you.'

"Would you mind telling us where you were last night around eleven o'clock?" she asked.

"Why?"

"Just humor me. Please."

"Didja hear the one 'bout the duck who went into a bar?"

"I'm not talking about that kind of humor . . . Mr . . . .Tank."

"Tell me what you're accusin' me of first."

"I'm not accusing you of anything, I'm just asking."

"I was home," he answered reluctantly.

"Anyone with you?" Jack asked.

"Negative."

"Okay, Tank. We'll be on our way. Thank you for your time. If anything should come to mind, will you give me a call?" Jack handed him his card.

"Will do."

They walked to the door, and Tess turned around to look at Tank. "Do you by any chance know Willy Clayton?"

"Dudn't everbody?" he snorted.

"Have you seen him lately?"

"Seen him. Ain't talked to him. He was over to Humdinger's the other night. There were so many people in that place, you couldn't stir 'em with a stick."

"Was he with anybody?"

Tank snorted again. "Yeah, he was with Peaches McGee." He chuckled and scratched his head. "She's what you might call a loose woman."

"Okay, thank you again, Tank," Tess said quickly, opening the door. *It's definitely time to go.*

They headed for the car, with chickens squawking and scurrying out of their way. Just as they reached the car, Tank called out from the porch steps. "Watch out or you'll plow up snakes."

They got in the car, and Tess started the ignition. "Any idea what he meant by that?"

"Yeah, I've heard that expression a time or two. He means to be careful what you do or you'll stir up trouble for yourself."

"Do you think it was a veiled threat?"

"I don't know. He didn't really strike me as an evil person. Tough as nails, rough as a corn cob, and he's got about as much class as a guest on the *Jerry Springer Show*, but I don't peg him as violent."

"Why do you suppose he didn't want to say where he was last night?"

"Pride. You put him on the defensive, and he didn't want to be there."

"Well, thanks for going with me. It wasn't a complete waste of time, was it?"

"Not at all. We learned Brick Lynch was definitely one of the bank robbers, as well as, at the very least, a participant in the murder, and we learned this state has had some very crooked politicians once or twice. Not that it's any surprise."

"Do you think he was telling the truth about the money? That his grandfather spent it on hush money and booze?"

"Assuming he had to bribe a governor to beat the robbery sentence and a judge to beat the murder charge, yeah, I think it's possible."

"But you don't think he's to blame for the break-ins or for hanging around my house last night?"

"Nope. I think his hesitancy to talk is out of loyalty to his grandfather, plus his natural surly nature."

"Well, if he's not the perp, then who is? Who else would care about some stupid old key that goes to a stupid old trunk that has nothing in it but stupid old keepsakes?"

"Tess, I wish I knew. But whoever it is, he's getting bolder."

She glanced over at him and saw him smiling at her. "What? Why are you smiling?"

"Did you just say *perp*?"

HAPPIER THAN A PIG IN SLOP

Hemlock remover: noun \ hem-lok re-moo-ver\ Heimlich
maneuver
He's choking! Somebody do the Hemlock remover.

[July 2010]

Tess knelt on the grass, trying to fix the sprinkler in her front yard when
Jack arrived to take her to The Silly Goose for the first official divorce
support group meeting.

"Hi!" he called across the yard, climbing out of his truck.

Tess didn't look back but called out, "Hi, yourself! I'm trying to fix
this blasted sprinkler. It keeps getting stuck in one position. I'm almost
ready."

She fiddled with the sprinkler head, but it wouldn't budge. She
pulled on the little lever in the middle, bringing the full force of the cold
water shooting directly into her face and the side of her leg. "OH!" she
screamed, jumping up.

"Dadnamit!" She stomped around in a circle, dripping, and madder
than a wet hen in a tote sack. Her hair was plastered to her head on one
side, and one black linen pant leg was soaked, along with her face and
neck.

"Can I help you?" He tried his best to stifle a smile.

"No. Thank you." She kneeled back down, again tinkering with the
object of her wrath.

"How's my girl?" he called, standing clear of the water zone.

Tess swung her head around in surprise.

"Ezzie?" he said, reminding Tess of her houseguest.

"She's . . . I think she misses you. I was working in my office this morning and realized she wasn't around. So I went looking for her and found her in the kitchen licking her chops, with two empty bags at her feet—one of marshmallows and one of chocolate chip cookies. The funny thing is, I don't know where she got them. I didn't even know I had them."

"Well, what can I say? My girl likes her vittles."

Tess had continued working on the sprinkler as they talked; she directed it toward the hydrangea bushes and stood back several steps hoping to see it oscillate back in her direction. Still no movement. "Golldernit!" She stomped back over to the sprinkler.

She tried to get the entire middle part of the sprinkler to move, but once again, it went in the exact opposite direction, further soaking her hair and face. "Ahhhhhh!"

"Tess, don't you think you should turn the water off while you fiddle with the sprinkler?" Jack asked, no longer able to keep from laughing.

She looked up at him between strands of wet hair. Through gritted teeth, she said, "If I did that, I wouldn't know if it was oscillating again."

But she stomped over to the spigot and turned it off. Then she stormed around the side of the house, returning a minute later with a miniature replacement for the offending sprinkler. "I have to get some water on these bushes. It's as dry as the dust in a mummy's pocket out here."

Jack's eyebrows went up, and his mouth turned into a wide smile. "You're becoming more southernfied every day."

She attached the new device, turned the water on, and satisfied it was doing a reasonable job, said, "Come on in while I get dried off."

"I don't know—am I safe in there? On second thought, maybe I'd better come in and rescue Ezzie."

"I'm sorry, Jack. I wasn't fussing at you. Just venting my frustration. Sorry you had to get in the middle of it."

"It's okay. I do want to see Ezzie. Your little mishap will give me some time with her."

Tess dried off, put her hair in an 'up-do', changed into a clingy red dress, and then went to find Jack. She watched him for a minute as he talked softly to Ezzie and rubbed her belly. She was lying on the floor looking like she was in heaven, her little stubby feet sticking straight up, her back leg twitching every now and then when Jack hit the sweet spot.

"Okay, I'm ready."

He looked up. "Wow. You look great. I like that even better than the black pants," he said, unable to take his eyes off her. "And let me tell you, I liked the black pants."

She laughed self-consciously. "You don't think it's too much?"

"I think it's perfect. Where do you want Ezzie while we're gone?"

Jack closed Esmerelda in Tess's bedroom, and they headed out the door. Tess had been so engrossed with her sprinkler when Jack arrived, she hadn't noticed what he was driving. She stepped down from the porch and looked out at the driveway.

"Oh. My. Gosh." Her mouth hung wide open.

"You like it? This is Bessie."

"Bessie" was a 1954 cherry-red Chevy pickup truck.

Tess was circling the truck in awe. "Jack, she's beautiful! I *love* it! How come I didn't know you had a truck?"

"Because it's been in the shop being restored. Isn't she a beauty? I bought her a while back, and this guy who does restoration on the side has had it for what seems like forever. He's been slowly but surely working on it. I just got it back today. I hope you don't mind riding in a truck to dinner."

Jack held the door for her, his eyes following her legs into the truck. He ran around the front of it, hopped in, and held up his seatbelt. "We added these."

Tess ran her hand across the rich, brown leather upholstery. She looked through the back window behind her and saw the truck bed, made out of wide, gleaming oak slats. Every inch of the truck was shiny and clean.

"I can't believe this, Jack! This is fantastic!"

"She has all the original glass, but brand new wide, white radial tires, and new shocks." He backed out of the driveway. "The wiring looks like it's been replaced, so we left that as is, but he rebuilt the brakes, detailed the chassis, and even put a new exhaust system under it. All the gauges work. It's still six volt, as it should be. I was tooling along at fifty-five miles per hour after I picked it up, and it did wonderfully. And she only has seventy thousand *original miles* on her. The transmission shifts great, and the engine purrs." He stopped at a stop sign and revved the engine.

"Let's see . . . what else?" Jack was radiating excitement. "It has the optional external oil filter. Oh yeah—check out the compass on the dash—how cool is that?"

"Jack this is *very* cool."

He was quiet for a moment and then said with a sly smile, "Back there in the yard—did you say, 'Dadnamit? And golldernit?'"

* * *

They arrived at The Silly Goose and found Martha Maye and Henry Clay already at a table.

"Hi y'all!" Martha Maye exclaimed. "Idn't this fun?!"

"It is indeed, Martha Maye! Hi Henry Clay, how are you?" Tess asked.

"I'm finer than frog hair split four ways, thank ye. Hire y'all?"

"We're great." Jack rubbed his hands together as he sat down.

"Well, come on, spill it! Why are you smilin' like a goat in a briar patch?" Henry Clay looked from Jack to Tess.

"Because of the sweet ride out in the parking lot." Jack's eyes danced and twinkled.

"What sweet ride?"

"A 1954 Chevy 3100 pickup truck, in pristine condition. Only seventy thousand original miles on it." Jack was almost jumping up and down in his chair with excitement.

"I gotta see this! Ladies, will you 'scuse us?" The two men wound through the tables and out the door to the parking lot.

"Well?" Martha Maye asked. "Did you talk to Crate Marshall?"

"Tank. He prefers to be called Tank. And yes, we did."

"Tank? What kind of fool name is that?"

"Well, I'm just guessing, but I'd say it's because of the way he looks. The man does kind of resemble a tank. He's huge."

"So what'id he say?"

"He confirmed that his grandfather was guilty in the bank robbery, and he said Brick was there…when your grandfather was murdered."

"Oh, gracious light." Martha Maye sat back in her chair, as if the wind had been knocked out of her. "Well, I can't say I'm surprised, but it's still somethin' when you hear it out loud."

"I'm sorry, Martha Maye." She patted her arm. "He said he thinks his grandfather spent all the stolen money bribing governors and judges. What a shame—so much heartache and pain for nothing. It's so sad."

Tess looked around the restaurant and then added, "Would your mother know if either of the other two men connected with the bank robbery had family still living here?"

"She might. Or Clive, or Earl, or even Buck might know."

The men made their way back to the table with Jack looking like he had springs in his shoes, and Henry Clay beside him, gesticulating wildly.

"Well, she's a beaut. I have to say I'm jealous," Henry Clay said as they settled back down at the table. "What say we order? All's I've had all day is a RC and a moon pie. I'm starvin'!"

When the food came, everyone commented on the rareness of Henry Clay's steak. "I've seen cows hurt worse than that and get well," Martha Maye said in disbelief.

"That's just the way I like it! The only time I get real meat is at McDonald's, and it's always overcooked." Tess and Jack exchanged looks.

A few minutes later, Henry Clay started coughing, and then he held his throat with a terrified look on his face. Martha Maye was talking a blue streak about her soon-to-be ex-husband, but she noticed him first.

"Oh, m'gosh!" She stood up so fast she knocked her chair over. "He's chokin'! Somebody do somethin'! Does anyone know the Hemlock remover? Ohma gosh ohma gosh!"

Jack jumped up, shouting, "Stand up, Henry Clay." He grabbed him from behind, putting his left hand over his right fist just above his waist-line. He forcefully performed a squeeze-thrust once, upward into his stomach, but Henry Clay's face was turning beat red, and his eyes were bulging in fright. Jack repeated the action once more, this time success-fully dislodging the piece of meat, to everyone's great relief. None more so than Henry Clay, who dropped back into his chair, coughing, and wiping his face, which had broken out in a sweat. The other diners in the restaurant applauded wildly.

While Martha Maye attended to Henry Clay, Tess asked Jack, "Where'd you learn how to do that?" He just shrugged.

An embarrassed Henry Clay excused himself to the restroom, and the others resumed eating, slightly shaken. When he returned to the table, he acted sullen, pouty and quiet, refusing to eat another bite. As soon as everyone finished eating, he suggested that the first official meeting of the divorce support group end early.

"Y'all, I hate to eat and run, or not eat and run, as the case may be, but I need to be gettin' on home."

They said their goodnights, and Jack took Tess for a ride in Bessie, as the sun set and the full moon came into its glory. They got back to her house a little before nine o'clock.

"Would you like to come in?" she asked, opening the front door. Jack hesitated, and stood in the doorway looking at her. She took his hand. "Come on."

When Jack went into the den, after springing Ezzie from lock-up, he looked surprised to find Tess had lit several candles around the room. She was sitting on the couch waiting for him.

"Would you like something to drink?"

"No . . . thanks . . . I'm good." His eyes scanned the room and then settled back on Tess. "How about some music?" she asked.

"Sure."

She kicked off her shoes and walked to the bookshelves, flipping through her music on the iPod until she reached the playlist she wanted. She placed it in its dock and The Dixie Chicks' "Cowboy Take Me Away" started to play. She walked over to Jack and held out her hand. "Dance with me, Cowboy."

Ezzie sat on the carpet and watched Jack and Tess slow dance through three songs. They talked softly and held each other closely; Tess alternated laying her head on his chest to looking up into his eyes as they swayed to the music. She ran her hands through his hair, forgetting about the area at the back of his head that was still sore from the mugging. She saw him wince as her fingers brushed over the spot.

"Oh, it still hurts. How are the headaches?"

"Better. Feel free to run your fingers through my hair anytime." He smiled down at her.

Finally, she took his hand and led him to the couch. He leaned over, took the clip from her hair, and watched it tumble down around her face. He kissed her, his mouth taking hers hard, his arms pulling her into him. His kiss was all passion and hunger, and she returned it enthusiastically. In a few minutes time they were lying down, and the kisses were so hot and heavy, Tess wondered if the windows were fogging up.

Ezzie, who'd been lying on the floor sleeping, suddenly lifted her head and barked. Five seconds later, the doorbell rang. Ezzie began barking in earnest, running to the door.

They stopped kissing, but didn't move.

"No freaking way," Jack whispered against her lips. He propped himself up on his elbows on either side of Tess and looked down at her, trying to slow his breathing.

Someone knocked on the door.

"Are you expecting anyone?" Jack started to move away.

She pulled him back down to her. "No. Be quiet and maybe they'll go away."

He kissed her.

The doorbell rang again.

Tess groaned in frustration. "I'd better see who it is."

Jack moved, and Tess got up, straightening her dress and hair as she headed to the door.

Jack muttered, "You have *got* to be kidding me."

He stood up to tuck his shirt in and could hear Tess's surprised voice as she opened the door.

"Nicholas!"

SO GOOD TASTIN'
IT'LL MAKE YOUR TONGUE SLAP YOUR BRAINS OUT

<u>jaeet</u>: verb \jeet\ did you eat
Jaeet yet?

[July 2010]

Tess returned to the den with a tall, twenty-something, good-looking man.

"Nicholas, this is my friend, Jack and his girl, Ezzie. Jack, this is my son, Nicholas."

"It's really good to meet you, Nicholas." Jack stood, reaching to shake Nicholas's hand.

"Jack is the writer I told you about."

"I'm real glad to meet you, too, Jack. Is that your '54 pickup out there?"

"It is! I just got her back from the shop today."

"Man, she's sweet."

"I'd be happy to take you for a spin in her sometime."

Nicholas's eyes lit up.

"Nick, is everything all right?" Tess touched her son's arm. "What in the world are you doing here out of the blue?"

"I was worried about you. I decided to take a few days off and come check in. See for myself what's going on." He looked around the room, and the look on his face said he knew what had just been going on in the last few mintues.

Tess hugged him again, keeping her arm around his back as she led them to the kitchen.

"Come on in here, and let's see about something to eat." She looked down at Ezzie, "And of *course* you too, girl."

She took brownies out of the domed cake plate and set them on the table.

"So, what exactly *is* going on?" Nicholas reached for a brownie. "I mean with all the mayhem. I feel like I've gotten bits and pieces, but not the whole story."

Tess looked at Jack, wondering if she should tell Nick everything.

He nodded encouragingly. "Go ahead," he told her, and they spent the next hour talking about all that had happened, and what they had learned about Lou's family.

"This is wild stuff, Mom. It's like you're in the middle of a Columbo episode or something. So, what are you gonna do next?"

Tess took a deep breath and looked at Jack. "Good question."

"I've talked to your mother about letting it all go, but . . . "

"But if someone tells my mother not to do something, it just makes her dig in her heels that much more."

Jack smiled at Tess with a 'you might as well plead guilty because we both know you' kind of look. He looked at his watch. "It's getting late. I'd better go. And I'm taking you home with me, my beautiful Esmerelda." He patted Ezzie on the back. "Tess has a human to watch over her and eat her out of house and home now."

Nick looked questioningly at his mother, and she said, "Tell ya later. But he wasn't casting aspersions on you. Just poking fun at Ezzie."

"Tess, are you still workin' in the morning?"

"Yes. Ten to two. Why?"

"Why don't I swing by here about noon thirty and take you to lunch, Nick?"

"Sure, that would be great."

At the door, Jack and Tess did an awkward should-we-hug-no-lets-clasp-hands-no-let-me-kiss-your-cheek kind of dance. Nick looked at his feet and then blurted out, "I think I'll just go get my stuff out of the car."

Tess and Jack burst out laughing once Nick cleared the porch. "Come here, you." Jack reached for Tess and pulled her into his arms.

"Jack, I'm sorry about tonight. I really had no idea he was coming."

"It's all right. You have a great kid. I'm glad he's here. I think I'll sleep a lot better tonight knowing you're not alone." He gave her a tender kiss. "There will be other nights."

"I'm counting on it."

As Jack drove off, Tess and Nick waved. He looked down at his mother. "Noon thirty?"

"That's a goosepimpleism. Hang around long enough and you'll be talking like one of the locals, too."

* * *

Later that night, Tank Marshall made a phone call.

"It's me," he said, lighting a cigarette. "Hells bells, I know I'm not supposed to call you, but this is important. That woman and her *friend* were out to the house today askin' all sorts a questions."

He listened for a minute, then said, "Of course I didn't tell 'em anything. I did my best to put it all on Granddaddy. But I don't think she was convinced, and I don't think she's gonna quit. You'd best come up with a new plan, buddy."

He listened again. "I don't wanna know, nor do I care what you do. It don't concern me. I'm just sayin' come up with a new angle. Design a new plan. Change tactics. 'Cause you're T minus dumb and counting if you think your current strategery is goin' to stop *that* little lady."

* * *

Tess got up the next morning and made chocolate chip muffins, Nick's favorite. He was still sleeping when she left for Stafford's, so she left him some muffins on the table, and took the rest with her, choosing to drive to work again.

The door to the bookstore opened as she approached. "Hidee, Mizz Tess!"

"Good morning, Pickle!" She slid past him as he held the door open for her.

"Why thank you, that's very nice of you." Tess breathed in deeply as she entered the bookstore, inhaling the aroma of coffee coming from next door.

"No problem. I saw ya comin'." Pickle craned his neck trying to see what goodies Tess had brought in this time.

She looked at his green t-shirt with white lettering. She hadn't seen a repeat t-shirt yet. This one said, "Have You Met My Imaginary Friend?" and had an arrow pointing to the left.

"What's his name?" Tess asked with a wry smile. "Or is it a she?"

Pickle looked puzzled. "My name's Pickle, Mizz Tess. Is who a she? Whatchew talkin' 'bout?"

Tess studied him for a moment. "Are you pulling my leg?"

He looked down at her legs briefly. "Wull . . . no ma'am."

She held out the plate of muffins. "Pickle, have a muffin. Would your imaginary friend like one, too?"

Tess could see the light bulb go off in Pickle's head. "Ah, thank ye, ma'am. Roger would love a muffin!" He took two off the plate.

Lou came bustling out of her office with her purse on her arm. "Mornin' Tessie! Peekal, take those muffins to the back room, and don't spill crumbs all over the floor!"

Tess offered her a muffin, but Lou declined. "No thank you, sugar bear, I'm so busy, I don't have time to cuss the cat. I'm late for a meetin' with the not-so-honorable mayor. Will you hold the fort down while I'm gone?"

"Of course, take your time."

Around eleven o'clock, Taterhead, the postman, came in. "Mornin' y'all. Hot dayum, it feels good in here! It's hotter out there than two rabbits making babies in a sock."

"And it's only eleven o' five." Tess met him halfway in.

"Here ya go." He handed her the mail. "Through rain, snow, sleet or heat . . . " he trailed off, as he made his way back out of the store. "Bye y'all."

Tess flipped through the envelopes. Her brow furrowed when she saw one addressed to her. She took the rest of the mail into Lou's office and put it on the desk. Walking back to the register area, she opened the envelope and pulled out a single sheet of paper with words spelling out letters taped to the page. She might have been scared if it hadn't been so ridiculous. *Really? Letters cut out like in a ransom note? Who is this person and where did they go to crime school?*

LAsT WaRNinG. I'*m*
W*at*ChiN*G* Y*o*U.
d*ON't* MaKe m*e*
d*O* SoMeT*h*iNG
Dra*s*TiC.

"Crap a shit, Mizz Tess. What's that?"

Pickle's voice over her shoulder made her jump. "Oh! Pickle! Didn't I tell you not to sneak up on me like that?"

"Sorry, Mizz Tess, I don't mean ta sneak up, I'm just bein' me. What's that all about?"

"Oh, it's just a joke, I'm sure. Nothing to worry about."

"Okay, I'll be in the back room sweepin' up if ya need me."

Tess called Jack, but his voice mail picked up. "Hey, Jack, just wondering if you by any chance got any weird mail today. I may try to catch you and Nicholas at the diner in a while. I have something to show you."

Stafford's had a spurt of business for a while; Lou came back in and immediately began helping Tess at the cash register.

Shortly after one o'clock, there was a lull, and Tess asked Lou, "Do you mind if I step out for just a bit? "I'll work past two if you need me to. I just want to drop in on Jack and my son Nick at the diner."

"Your boy's here? That's wonderful! Well sure, honey. We're not busy right now. You gwon over there, but you'd best bring that boy 'a yours over here, too, and let me meet him or I'll be all tore up."

Tess hesitated at the door of the diner, forcing a smile as she went inside. Jack and Nicholas were in Jack's usual booth, and she spoke to Clive and Earl as she hurried past. Her stomach did a flip-flop when she saw Jack, and she couldn't stop the huge smile from lighting up her face, as he stood up as she neared the table. Nicholas looked over his shoulder and then stood also.

"Hey, Mom."

"I see you've finished eating." She eyed their empty plates.

"Tess, how come you never told me you have a published children's book?"

"Hello to you, too," she said, sliding in across from him. "I suppose because one children's book doesn't stack up to nine mystery novels."

"I want to see it, and I want an autographed copy." Jack sounded like a petulant child.

"Oh, Jack, you don't have to do that . . . " She shot Nick a look.

"Sorry, Mom. I thought he knew."

Junebug arrived at the table. "Hidee, Tess. This boy 'a yours is the spittin' image of his mama. And he's got a good appetite, too."

"Yes, all his life, people have said he looks like me, haven't they Nick? One time, when he was ten or eleven and had begun wanting to be manly, someone said, 'You look just like your mama' and he said, 'Hmph. I'd rather be ugly and look like my dad!'"

"Ooh, law, that's funny! I wouldn't trade him for a farm in Georgia." Junebug slapped Nick on the back. "I thought it was just gonna be the fellas taday. Jaeet yet?"

Jack looked at Tess's and Nick's blank faces, so he quickly interjected. "Did you eat yet. You haven't, have you? Do you have time to order somethin'?"

"Oh! No, I haven't eaten. What's good today, Junebug?"

"I highly recommend the bacon, lettuce, and fried green tomato sandwich. It's so good tastin' it'll make your tongue slap your brains out!"

"How can I resist that? I'll have one B-L . . . uh . . . F-G-T and a sweet tea, please."

"Comin' right up."

"Okay, Tess, what do you have to show us?"

Tess pulled the letter from her purse, and showed it first to Jack, who read it, and then passed it to Nick.

"Mother!" Nick exclaimed once he saw the note. "Are you *serious*!"

"This came to the bookstore?" Jack asked with a frown.

"Yes. I thought that was strange, too, since I don't have regular hours there, per se. You didn't get one, Jack?"

"No, but the postman hadn't been to my house when I left to pick up Nick. I can go check."

"No, it can wait. You know, this person is trying to scare me off, but the more stunts they pull, the more I want to get to the bottom of this."

"I don't like it, Mom. This idiot sounds serious."

"We need to find out about relatives of the other two bank robbers." Tess ignored Nick's remark. "Jack, do you think you could ask Clive and Earl?"

Junebug came back with Tess's order, and Jack said, "Junebug, you and yours have lived here forever and a day . . . " Junebug shot him a look over her reading glasses and he backtracked. "I don't mean you, yourself, have lived here forever, I mean your family goes way back."

"Mmm hmm," Junebug smirked. "You best watch yerself, Jackson! I prepare way too much a your food!"

"Aw, Junie, you know you're prettier than a field of daisies. What I meant was, you know a lot of folks in town. Do you know anything about a Rod Pierce, or a Junior Wells, I b'lieve his name was, or anything about their families?"

"Hmm. You talkin' 'bout the boys who robbed the First National back in the thirties?"

"The one and the same."

Junebug looked at Jack, hands on her hips. "Rod Pierce was Clive's brother, ya know."

WELL PICK MY PEAS

nopie: adverb \nohp-ee\ nope or no
Nopie, not that I know of.

[July 2010]

"CLIVE?" Tess and Jack said in unison. She had just taken a bite of sandwich and bits of lettuce and bacon sprayed out with her outburst. She clamped her hand over her mouth as they all looked toward Clive, who was busy arguing with Earl.

"Don't worry, he's hard a hearin'." Junebug pulled a bobby pin out of her hair, securing the bun tighter to the back of her head.

Speaking almost in a whisper, Tess said, "Clive is *Rod's brother?*"

"Well, yeah . . . Clive Pierce. Hellooo. Y'all didn't know that?" Junebug propped her hand on her hip and continued. "Course Rod's been gone forever and a day, but Clive's still kickin'. He's a good man. Far's I know the worst thing about him is he squeezes a quarter until the eagle screams." She arched her hand on the side of her mouth, and stage whispered, "That's code for he don't tip well." She dropped her hand. "He'll figure out ten percent down ta the penny. Twelve percent on a good day. But he's good people. He don't like ta talk 'bout his brother, though."

"Does Rod have any children in town?" Jack asked.

"Nopie, not that I know of. Y'ont me ta ask Clive 'bout it fer ya?" Junebug hitched her head in Clive's direction.

"Sure. If you don't mind," Jack said. Junebug headed for the counter.

Tess was facing away from Clive, but Jack watched as Junebug sidled up to him, refilled his coffee, and began talking.

"Uh oh. Clive's neck and face just flushed a bright red and a 'Huh?' came out of his open mouth," Jack told Tess and Nick.

"Junebug's talking gently to him and patting his hand. Now she's saying somethin' else to him. Clive looks irritated." Tess took another bite of sandwich.

They heard Junebug say, "Now, now . . . " and then her voice got lower as she wiped off the counter, continuing to talk softly.

"It sounds like she's cajoling him," Tess whispered.

"Uh oh," Jack said, "Clive's face just turned beet red, and he said somethin' to Junebug. Now she's getting a piece of coconut meringue pie out of the domed plate and giving it to him."

Jack said Junebug was headed back to their booth, and Tess looked over her shoulder and saw her checking on a few customers along the way.

"Well, live and learn, die and know it all," Junebug said as she got to their table. "I just found out that Clive is the baby of seventeen children. He was still knee-high to a duck, of course, when the robbery occurred and doesn't really know that much about his older brother Rod, but he does know that he don't have any offspring. He says Rod was the black sheep of the family, who besmirched the Pierce name, and he got kind of testy with me 'bout bringin' him up. It cost me a piece of pie. So it's gonna cost you too, Jackson. Now pay up."

Junebug bent down and put her face right in front of Jack's lips, pointing to her cheek. Jack promptly complied, giving her a big kiss, and then another.

"I'm a big tipper," he told her. "You're amazing, Junie. Thanks."

"Here's a tip fer ya—never ask a barber if he thinks ya need a haircut." Junebug laughed, patting Jack on the back.

"I'll remember that, Junie, thank ya."

"Sure thing, kids. Anything else?"

"Know anything about the other man from the robbery? Junior what's-his-name?" Jack asked.

"Wells," Tess said around a bite.

"Can't say that I do."

"Do you know anything else about the robbery?"

"Jack, I'm an old woman, but not *that* old."

Jack laughed. "Okay, Junie. Thanks. You've been a big help."

Junebug went toward the kitchen, and Tess said, "Well, boys, I hate to break this up, but I need to get back to the bookstore. Anyone want the rest of this?" She pushed her plate to the middle of the table, but both men shook their heads.

Tess stood up, followed by Jack. "I'll be working a little longer this afternoon to make up for my lunch break. Hey, Nick—Lou wants to meet you. Think you can stop by the bookstore before you head home?"

"Sure, Mom."

"Tess—be careful, okay?" Jack whispered, as she walked past him.

She saw the genuine concern in his eyes and tried to sound confident. "Don't worry."

* * *

"Wull pick my peas, he's the spittin' image of you, 'cept on stilts!" Lou said to Tess, giving Nicholas a big hug.

"I know. We were just talking about that. I love it when people say that. Nicholas . . . not so much."

"Aw, Mom, that's not true."

Lou stared up at Nicholas with admiration. "Law, you're tall enough, I b'lieve you could go duck huntin' with a rake! Just how tall *are* you?"

"Six foot four, ma'am."

"I could get a crick in my neck if I had to look up at you all day. How long ya stayin' in town? I wanna have y'all over to dinner. We'll invite Jack, too. Maybe Henry Clay."

"Oh, Lou, you don't have to do that. I know how busy you are here at the store."

"Aw, busy, schmizzy. I'd rather wear out than rust out. How's tomorrow night work for y'all?"

"That would be just fine, Lou. Thank you."

"Hey, Peekal!" Lou waved as Pickle walked out of the back room. "Come on over here, and meet Tess's boy!"

As they were introduced, Nick shook Pickle's hand. "I've heard a lot about you."

Pickle looked puzzled. "Like, what?"

"Mom's told me all about your t-shirts. Sounds like you have quite a collection."

Just as serious as he could be, Pickle said, "Dude! You want a girl to talk to you? Wear a funny t-shirt. Chicks like funny."

* * *

Tess left work a little after three o'clock and found Jack waiting for her on a sidewalk bench by her car. "Hey, beautiful."

She made a show of looking all around her to see who Jack was talking about.

"Oh, come here, you," he said, reaching for her.

She sat down next to him, with his arm around her, and he handed her a sheet of paper. It looked just like the one she'd received at the bookstore.

YoU aNd yOUr
GF ShOuLD bUTt
OUT. oR ElSe.

"Well, at least he's an equal opportunity stalker."

"He called you my GF. Guess this makes it official. Now you gotta be my girlfriend." Jack looked at her, and her mouth went dry.

"I'm your girlfriend just because some lunatic says so?"

"Would that be such a bad thing?" Jack looked at her intently.

"I can think of worse," she said, shyly. "But Jack, that's what you got out of this whole message? That I'm your girlfriend? Doesn't this concern you? This sounds like a threat."

"Well, whoever it is isn't being very smart about it. They're gonna mess up. I think the more desperate he-she-it becomes, the bigger the mistake he-she-it's gonna make."

"You're probably right." Tess looked around to see if anyone was watching them. She had grown very paranoid in the last few weeks.

"Did you mention your letter to John Ed?" Jack had his arm resting behind Tess on the bench, and he moved his fingers to lightly caress her neck, under her hair.

"Of course not."

"Shouldn't we at least show these to him? He can't say you made these up. Although knowin' him, he'll accuse you or me of makin' and sendin' them."

"Oh, I guess we should. I just would rather not have to see him. He's so smug, and condescending and so . . . so wrong. The man just makes me so mad."

"Well, you just get glad in the same pants you got mad in, Missy!"

Jack had lapsed into his exaggerated drawl. She gave him a look, and he hugged her with his one arm still behind her. "Oh, I'm teasing you, Mary T. My mama used to say that to me all the time. Except for the Missy part. You want me to go by myself so you don't have to deal with him?"

"You wouldn't mind? I'd like to go home and spend some time with Nick. And I'd rather not have to talk to John Ed about this."

"On one condition." Jack smiled into her eyes.

"What's that?"

"I want an autographed copy of your book."

Tess groaned.

* * *

"So what did you two talk about today?" Tess asked Nick, as she made his favorite dinner that night.

"Mom, I'm sorry I spilled the beans about your children's book. I didn't think you cared. I just assumed he knew."

"Oh, it's okay. He was bound to find out sometime. It's just that he's a successful, nine times published author, and I have this one little children's book. It's a little embarrassing." She tasted the sauce, and then put the lasagna noodles into the boiling water.

"I don't see anything to be embarrassed about. It's a great book. Are you still working on your new one?"

"When I have time. It's slow going."

"Still not going to tell me what it's about?"

"I'd rather wait. Be careful or you just might end up in it." She shot him an amused look.

"Will you tell me the title?"

"The title is "Keep your straw out of my Kool-aid." She saw Nick's eyes go to her iced tea glass. "That's local for mind your own business."

"You're not writing porn, are you, Mom?" he teased.

"No, I'm not writing porn, Nick!" She swatted him with a tea towel. "Now, what else did you all talk about?"

"I don't know."

Tess saw Nick pick up his glass and take a sip—a tell she knew well. Then he shifted in his seat, put one leg on the other knee, and finally stood up to pour more sweet tea into a mostly full glass. Signs she'd seen too many times when he was little and trying to avoid answering her.

"What? What aren't you telling me?" She busied herself icing a chocolate cake to avoid looking straight at Nick. It was a ploy she'd used when he was a teenager, to get him to open up, and it was usually effective.

"How well do you know Jack?" He added more ice to his glass, making it almost overflow.

"What do you mean?"

"Well, it's just that you've lived here . . . what . . . two, three months? You all seem to be . . . pretty close. I see the way he looks at you." He scratched his head absentmindedly. " I don't know . . . I guess I was just surprised to see the chemistry between you two, so soon. I mean, you've talked about him a little bit, but I was just surprised . . . Maybe it's just that I've never seen you with anyone but Dad."

Nick was rambling, and she knew the subject made him uncomfortable. She didn't know what to tell him, because frankly, she didn't know herself. She thought about Jack way too much, looked forward to being with him, wanted to touch him all the time, she melted under his touch. But part of her was glad they'd been interrupted those two times. She still wasn't sure if she was ready for another relationship. At least not a serious one.

Nick's voice brought her from her thoughts. " . . . nice enough guy and all that, I guess it's just weirding me out to see you with someone besides Dad."

"I know, sweetie. I don't know what to tell you about Jack, except that I think he's a good man, and I like him a lot. We've really only been out on a few dates, although we've spent a lot of time together over this murder thing. I enjoy his company, his sense of humor, his intelligence. I feel safe with him, and he makes me feel good; it's nice to have someone to talk to again. It's nice to have someone want to be with me again." They were both quiet for a minute before she added, "Never mind that he's sexy as hell."

"Mom!"

"Oh, Nick. You're grown up. I may be almost fifty, but I'm not dead. I know it will take some getting used to. But I think the more you get to know him, the more comfortable you'll be with him. You'll see what I see. I'm not saying anything will happen, I'm just saying I like the man."

"I just want you to be happy, Mom. I'll try to deal."

* * *

After dinner, Tess and Nick talked some more and watched a movie together, while Tess scratched his back for a while, a habit they'd had since he was a little boy. When the movie was over, Nick looked at his mother and saw she'd fallen asleep. He nudged her a little and she opened her eyes.

"What?"

"You fell asleep!"

"I did not! I was just checking for holes in my eyelids."

"You know, you've gotten a lot weirder since you've been here, Mom."

Tess yawned, kissed Nick, and stood up.

"I'm sleepy. I think I'll go on up to bed. You coming?"

"No, I think I'll stay down here and watch TV for a while. Maybe Letterman or The Colbert Report. See you in the morning."

"Okay. Night, sweetie."

An hour later, Nicholas was asleep on the couch in front of the television, when he was startled awake by the sound of shattering glass. A brick came crashing through the window, landing a foot away from him, glass shattering all over the room.

He jumped up and was out the front door in a flash. He heard the slap of branches in the trees to his left and charged that way. The smell of Frasier fur filled his nose as branches hit his head and scratched his face when he ran through the clump of evergreens at the edge of his mother's driveway. He pushed them aside and kept running. He couldn't yet see anyone, but he could hear feet slapping against concrete not far away. Nick was a runner in high school and college. It had been a couple of years since he'd competed, but he was still fast.

He saw and heard a dark figure up ahead and watched as it ran right into a street lamp. The person bounced off it and staggered backward, shaking his head like a wet dog. He took off running again, but Nick got to him, reached his hand out, grabbed the back of his shirt, and tackled him to the ground. He pushed the man over, pinning his shoulders to the ground. Straining to see in the dark, Nick did a double take, not believing his eyes.

JUST SCRATCH YOUR MAD PLACE AND GET GLAD

bought air: noun \bawt air\ air conditioning
Close the door. You're lettin' out all the bought air.

[July 2010]

"PICKLE?"

Nicholas stood over Pickle, breathing hard, absolutely astonished at who he'd tackled. "You?" he managed to say as he leaned forward, resting his hands on his knees and breathing heavily. "Are you kidding me?"

"I'msorryI'msorryI'msorry . . . please forgive me! I didn't wanna do it! He made me! Oh crap, why'd I get myself into this. Why?" Pickle pounded his fist against his head.

"*Who* made you?"

In a muffled voice Pickle said, "I cain't say."

"NICHOLAS!"

Nick heard his mother's frantic call. She sounded panicked. He pulled Pickle up and shoved him toward Tess's house, holding on to him by the back of his shirt.

"I suppose you're going to tell me your imaginary friend made you do it," Nick said sarcastically, not expecting a reply. But Pickle, being Pickle, gave him one.

"Ya think they'd believe that?" he asked seriously.

"No, Pickle. I do not." They walked up the front lawn, to where Tess was waiting on the porch with the brick in her hand.

"What's going on? Who...PICKLE?" Her mouth flew open.

"Pickle." Nick's breathing was starting to return to normal. "He says somebody made him do it, but he won't say who. Don't ask him if it was his imaginary friend, he's already thought of that defense and just might go with it."

Tess was holding a note that had been wrapped around the brick. It, too, had lettering cut from a magazine.

I'LL LeARn Y*a*
Du*Rn* Y*a.*

"Why, Pickle?" Tess whispered, sounding deeply hurt.

"I needed the money," he mumbled, looking at the ground.

"Mom, go call the police, and I'll watch Mr. Shot Putter here."

"I believe the expression around here is 'call the law,'" Tess said, attempting to lighten the moment. Pickle's lip was quivering and tears threatened to overflow his eyes.

"Did you send me that note too?" she asked, referring to the one at the bookstore.

Pickle looked at the ground, shaking his head.

Tess called the police station first and then Jack. It was late, but she knew he worked late into the night most of the time. He actually got to her house before Officer Skeeter Duke. He shot a dark look at Pickle and went to Tess.

"Are you all right?" He pulled her into an embrace.

"I'm fine. Only my feelings are hurt." She smiled weakly, clearly upset at Pickle's betrayal. "I guess you were right about he-she-it slipping up soon."

Nicholas came back into the room, and Jack released Tess when he saw the look on her son's face.

"Hey, Nick."

"Hey, Jack."

"Good thing you were here. You're definitely in better shape than Ezzie or me." He went to Pickle, who was sitting on the couch, with his head in his hands, elbows propped on his knees. Jack talked softly to him, with Pickle nodding his head every now and then.

Tess let the officer in and filled him in on what had happened.

"Looks like they caught you red-handed, boy," Skeeter said, standing over Pickle. "Don't that just dill yer pickle?" He laughed at his own joke, slapping his knee, and looking around for others to join in, but no one was laughing.

It wasn't until Skeeter had loaded Pickle into the patrol car and driven off that Tess laughed.

"What are you laughing at?" Jack asked.

"Pickle's t-shirt. It just sunk in."

Jack and Nick looked at her blankly.

"Apparently in all the commotion, you didn't notice his shirt. It wasn't the invisible friend one he had on earlier today," she said. "This one said, 'High Achiever'."

* * *

John Ed walked into the Goose Pimple Junction police station bright and early the next morning. He was blissfully unaware of the events of the past evening, but Skeeter filled him in.

"He's three pickles shy of a quart," Skeeter snickered.

John Ed glared at him. "Zat supposed ta be funny?"

Skeeter cleared his throat. "No sir. Um . . . he won't talk, Chief. Just keeps sayin' he needed the money, but won't say who paid him, or why."

John Ed farted loudly as he walked away, saying over his shoulder, "That's what I think a that. Bring him to the interrogation room."

"Ya mean the break room?" Skeeter called out.

"Break room, interrogation room, powder room. Call it what ya want. Jest get his butt in there."

Escorting Pickle down the hall, Skeeter said, "Pickle, mash your hair down. It's stickin' straight up, even more than usual," he motioned to the top of his head. Pickle's eyes were red, with shadows underneath, and his clothes were wrinkled and grass stained. He flopped into a chair opposite the chief.

Chief Price looked at him for a moment and then said, "You look like somethin' the dog's been keepin' under the porch." He stared at him, waiting for Pickle to say something. Finally, the chief said, "Whattsa matta with you, boy?"

Pickle shrugged his shoulders, looking at the floor.

"You think my granddaughter's gonna wanta hang 'round with you after this stunt?"

Pickle shrugged again.

"Don't you got anything to say fer yerself?"

Again, Pickle just shrugged his shoulders.

"Okay, let's cut the crap, boy. Who told you to do this?"

Pickle shrugged his shoulders.

"You been responsible for all them other shenanigans?"

Pickle shrugged his shoulders.

John Ed glared at him.

"What's gonna happen to me, Chief Price?" a glum Pickle finally asked.

"Well, boy, that depends on yer cooperation. You cooperate, things'll go easier for ya."

"What if I say I don't know nothin'? That I just did it on my own?"

"That dog won't hunt, son. You do know somethin', and I wanta know what it is."

"Well I cain't tell ya! Stop bein' so mean to me!" screamed Pickle.

"Just scratch your mad place and get glad real quick like. I'm losin' patience. I'm gonna give you some time to think things over, but when I come back, you'd best be of a mind to spill yer guts, or I'm gonna slap you so hard, when you quit rollin' your clothes'll be outta style." He stood up and walked to the door. "But I didn't say that." He winked at Pickle and left the room to find Skeeter.

"How'd it go, Chief?"

"Like tryin' ta poke a cat out from under the porch with a rope. I want you to call his mama, get her over here."

"Will do, Chief. She's been callin' every ten minutes. Had to *make* her go home last night."

"Bring her in when she gets here."

Fifteen minutes later, Caledonia Culpepper swept into the station. She was a Southern Belle through and through, wearing a sleeveless lime green and hot pink Lily Pulitzer shift dress and white sandals with two-inch heels. A hot pink scarf held her long, blond hair back into a pony-tail. Her makeup and nails were perfect.

Bernadette, the secretary, saw her coming and said under her breath, "She's all dressed up like she's goin' to Wal-Mart or somethin'."

Skeeter appeared in the chief's doorway. "Chief, she's here."

"Send her back," John Ed growled.

The sound of Caledonia's heels clacking on the floor followed her as she walked through the police station, holding the hand of her eight-year old son, and leaving a stream of perfume in her wake. John Ed met them in the hallway telling Skeeter, "Take little . . . " the chief trailed off, waving his finger in the air, not knowing the child's name.

"Peanut," Caledonia supplied.

"...Peanut up front and keep him occupied while we *chat* with Pickle."

"What do I do with him?" Skeeter looked slightly terrified at the prospect of entertaining an eight-year-old for any amount of time.

"Play Tic-tac-toe, Tiddlywinks, or Hangman, I don't care."

"Oh, he loves Hangman," Caledonia said.

John Ed walked a few steps, sighed heavily, and turned back toward Skeeter. In a more patient voice he said, "Take him out back and show him your vehicle. Let him play with the siren once or twice."

Chief Price showed Caledonia to his office and motioned to a chair in front of the desk. "Your son's not of a mind to talk, Ms. Culpepper."

"Caledonia," she smiled sweetly, smoothing her skirt over her knees.

"He won't tell us who paid him to throw that brick into Ms. Tremaine's house, but he let it slip that *someone* did. What we're gonna do, is play good mom-bad cop with him. Understand?"

"I'm with ya, Chief."

They walked to the closed door of the interrogation-slash-break-room, and stopped. Caledonia was a true steel magnolia. She took a deep breath, worked up tears in her eyes, nodded her head, and the chief opened the door.

Pickle was sitting bent over, with his head resting on his crossed arms on the table. When he saw his mother, he jumped up. "I'm sorry, Mama. I really am."

His mother hugged him and said through tears, "If you're truly sorry, then you'll answer Chief Price's questions." She looked at him, blinking back tears for a moment and then, in a dramatic attempt to control her emotions, flapped her fingers in front of her eyes, like a butterfly on speed. She stood up a little straighter, and shook her head ever so slightly, sniffing back tears.

Bravely bringing her emotions under control she said, "I used to could always count on you to tell the truth." Then her eyes turned from sad to steely. She stood with her face an inch from her son's, and pointed a pink-painted fingernail into his chest with each word. "So let me tell you somethin', little mister. If you don't tell the truth now, I'll be all over you like stink on a skunk." Then she smiled sweetly at him, patted his cheek, and gracefully sat down at the table, crossing her legs.

Pickle and the chief joined her. Chief Price reared back in his seat, balancing the chair on its back two legs, pushing his thumbs through his belt loops, his big belly straining the buttons on his shirt. "Well Pickle? What's it gonna be, son? I need a name."

"My name's Pickle Culpepper," he said in all seriousness.

The chief made a face. "Not *your* name, ya dipstick, the name of the person who hired you."

Pickle took a deep breath and let it out. "If I have to give ya a name . . . " he looked at his mother and then at the chief. "Crate Marshall." He sat back in the chair hanging his head.

"And what did Crate Marshall tell you to do, zactly?"

"He wonted me to spy on Mizz Tess all the time. And that's all I did, up 'til last night. I swear!"

"How much did he pay you?"

"Seventy-five bucks a week," Pickle mumbled, looking at his shoes.

"Why'd he wont you to spy on Ms. Tremaine?"

"He didn't say. Just said to watch and listen and tell him what she talked about."

"Why'd he want you to go from just spyin' to throwin' bricks through her window?"

"I didn't ask. He said I had to do it, is 'all. He said if I didn't, he'd tell the law it was me who broke into her house."

"But you didn't have nothin' to do with the attack *or* the break-ins?"

"Naw sir, I wouldn't ever do somethin' like *that.*"

"But you don't mind hurlin' bricks through people's windows," the chief said matter of factly. "What if you'd hit somebody inside the house with that brick?"

"I didn't think a that," Pickle said softly.

"Dudn't sound like you thought 'bout anything." He sighed heavily. "All right, Pickle. I'ma let you go home with your mama. Mizz Tess says she won't press charges if you'll pay to have her window fixed. You just better hope she doesn't change her mind. And you stay outta trubba, now, ya hear? Or I'm gonna come after you and throw you in the paddy wagon myself, little mister."

"Yessir. I'm sorry, sir. Thank you, sir," Pickle said, jumping up.

"Not me you need to be apologizin' to."

"Oh, he's gonna do his share of apologizin'." Caledonia stood up, held her well-manicured hand out for her son to take, and led him out of the room. They found Skeeter and Peanut in the reception area.

"C'mon, Peanut, let's take yer brother home now. He'll be my indentured servant for the foreseeable future."

The chief and Skeeter stood with their arms crossed, watching the mother and two boys leave the station. Chief Price shook his head.

"Pickle . . . Peanut . . . them folks' family tree don't fork."

* * *

"Well tie me to an anthill and fill my ears with jam!" Lou was fortuitously standing in front of her chair when she heard the news about Pickle, because her knees gave out, and she dropped into it like a sack of flour. She stared into space with a look of utter disbelief.

"Lou, for what it's worth, I don't think Pickle meant to be harmful, I think he just got caught up in the money and things got carried away."

"Money? Whatta ya mean? Who was payin' him?"

"John Ed called a little while ago to tell me Pickle said it was Crate Marshall who paid him to do it."

"Of course. *Brick* Lynch's grandson told him to throw a *brick* through the window. But why on earth would *that* man pay Peekal to vandalize your home?"

Tess had hoped Jack would be at the bookstore by the time she had to get into the particulars with Lou. She didn't want to go it alone.

"Lou, do you remember that key that I found in the floor register?"

"Oh, law . . . "

"Well, one thing led to another, and . . . " Just then, they could hear the bell tinkle at the front door. Tess went to the doorway of Lou's office. "We're back here!" she said in relief when she saw Jack and Martha Maye.

"Uh oh. You brought in the cavalry, huh? Is anybody gonna tell me what's goin' on? Tess here's been beatin' 'round the bush sa long, I grew another wrinkle."

Tess and Jack told Lou about how they'd heard of her father's murder, and it led them to be curious, which they believe led to someone getting nervous, which led to all of the mayhem that had been happening to Tess and Jack, of late. Lou listened without saying a word, her eyes darting from one to the other.

"But why would y'all care about Daddy's murder?"

"Besides the fact that I love a good mystery," Jack said, "we felt, and more so once things began happening, that there was an answer to his unsolved murder. I guess it's all about truth, justice, the American way, and all that."

"What did you have to do with all of this?" she asked Martha Maye.

"I just helped them fill in some of the blanks."

"Why didn't y'all tell me 'bout this?"

"I tried Mama, but you know how you get when your daddy's name is brought up. We just wanted to spare ya the pain."

"Why would Crate Marshall do those things?"

"That's a good question. It's looking more and more like his grand-father was the killer, and for some reason, Crate didn't want that to be dredged up again."

"Ooooh! I could just wring his neck!" Lou had gotten beyond the shock and was moving on to the awe.

"I think John Ed will do that for you, Lou," Jack said in all seriousness.

* * *

The dogs were barking wildly when Crate Marshall opened the door and saw the men drive up.

"What're you doin' here?" he called out from the porch.

"Put those damn dogs in the barn and tie 'em up. Else I'll shut 'em up," the driver called from inside his car.

Tank shot the man a long, dirty look, but obliged him.

As he walked back to the house, his visitors got out of the car.

"Thought you didn't wonta be seen with the likes a me. Want me to put my Groucho glasses on?" Tank asked facetiously.

"Very funny." Tank's visitor was not smiling. "He thinks he's a comedian," he said to the other man.

They walked up the steps to the porch and Tank opened the door, but stood in the doorway, arms crossed like a bouncer.

"You gonna let us in or are you gonna let out all the bought air?"

"What're you? My daddy? I can air cond . . . well come on in," Tank said sarcastically, waving the air in front of his face, as the man pushed his way past him, reeking of Aqua Velva aftershave.

Tank made his voice soft and feminine. "There's nothing like an

Aqua Velva Man."

"Funny. A real laugh riot. Got any coffee?" the man barked.

Tank led the way to the kitchen. While the Aqua Velva man sat down at the end of the table, Tank poured coffee into mugs that said, "Bikers do it on the road." Tank put the coffee mugs on the pine farm-house table and sat down. Willy sat in between the two men.

"What brings you two way out here this time a the mornin'? Willy, I didn't think you's up this time of day."

Willy grunted and took a gulp from his mug.

"I wanted you to tell me 'bout your little visit with Miss Priss and Mr. Wonderful." Aqua Velva man slurped his coffee.

"Not much to tell. I tolt 'em enough to make 'em go away happy."

"What zactly did you tell them?" Willy asked.

Tank shot him a look. "I tolt 'em my granddaddy pulled the robbery. They asked if there was somebody else involved, I tolt 'em I wouldn't know."

Tank and Aqua Velva man talked while Willy looked on. Finally, he finished his coffee, and took the mug to the sink.

"You ever mention my granddaddy to 'em?" Aqua Velva man asked, taking a sip and slowly putting his coffee mug down.

"Hey! I ain't got grits fer . . . "

In one swift move, Willy walked to Tank's side and shot a bullet into his brain, before Tank could say 'brains' to finish his sentence. The sound of the gunshot reverberated through the silent room.

DEADER 'N A DOOR NAIL

Dog of his own trot:
adjective \dawg uhv hiz own trot\ peculiar
That boy is a dog of his own trot.

[July 2010]

"Oops." Heh heh heh, Willy laughed like a monkey. Standing over Tank, he said, "I guess I stopped a *Tank* in his tracks."

"Don't quit your day job, Willy. A comedian, you are not. Now cut the jibber jabber and clean the gun up," Aqua Velva man said.

Willy took a towel and wiped his prints from the gun. Using the towel, he raised Tank's hand, placed it on the table, and put the gun in it.

Aqua Velva man emptied the coffee into the sink, and rinsed the mugs, saying to Willy, "Smartest thing I did was set Pickle up. Worked like a charm." He dried the mugs with a towel, and put them in the cabinet. "Now quit fussin' with him and go get it out of the car."

Willy went to the car and came back into the house, whistling. After he made a trip to Tank's bedroom, he stopped in the kitchen.

"All set, Boss."

Aqua Velva man took one more look around. As he left he said with a sneer, "How's that for *strategery?*"

* * *

John Ed's police cruiser led the way up the long gravel drive to Crate Marshall's house, kicking up a cloud of dust that surrounded Officers Skeeter Duke and Hank Beanblossom's car as it followed closely. The men parked in front of the house and got out. John Ed hitched up his pants and sniffed the morning air. He and Officer Duke went to the front door, while Officer Beanblossom went to the back.

"Open up, Marshall." The chief pounded on the door. "We got a search warrant for the premises." There was no answer to John Ed's knock, except for the barking coming from the barn.

"CHIEF! BACK HERE!"

John Ed and Skeeter ran around the side of the house. Officer Beanblossom pointed to the window in the back door. John Ed looked in and saw Crate Marshall slumped over the table, a gun in his hand.

"Move along, sweet Jesus. Call it in. Get the coroner out here, too." Using his revolver, he broke the glass, unlocked the door, and let himself in. Walking over to Tank, he put two fingers on his neck. "Deader 'n a doornail."

He looked around the tidy kitchen. Nothing seemed out of the ordinary. "Check the rest of the house."

Twenty minutes later, a forensics technician took pictures of the scene while John Ed and the coroner talked.

"I don't give a damn, Leonard! It's clear as day it's a suicide," the chief said.

"Chief, who makes a pot of coffee, pours a cup, and then sits down to drink it and kill hisself? It don't add up."

"Looka here what I found, Chief." Officer Beanblossom stood in the doorway, holding up a purse. Skeeter took it from him.

"Let me guess who it b'longs to," the chief said.

Skeeter reached inside the purse, pulled out a wallet. "Tess Tremaine."

"Well, that wraps it up fer me." John Ed looked at both men, then at Tank, still slumped over the table. "He was the one who was harassin' the little lady, he hired Pickle to scare her, for whatever reason, and when Pickle got caught, he figured he would spill the beans. Nothin' left to do but die or go to jail. He chose dyin'. Case closed."

"But Chief, aren't you the least bit curious 'bout *why* he chose death over a probable fine or a few days in jail? Sumpthin' dudn't add up," Hank said.

"I don't know, nor do I care 'bout his reasons. The man's dead. *Case closed.*"

Hank and Skeeter exchanged skeptical looks. The chief walked out of the room, and Hank motioned Skeeter over to the body. Leonard followed.

"Look at this," Hank whispered, pointing to Tank's hand. "The gun is limp in his hand. He didn't shoot himself."

"Yeah . . . " Skeeter said.

"And check this out. There's no blood or blowback on his hand, or wrist," the coroner said.

"Holy smokes," Skeeter said.

"Beanblossom! Duke! I said we're done. Move it."

* * *

Nicholas drove Tess to Lou's house that night for the dinner party. Tess looked down at the bunch of flowers that she'd picked from her garden for Lou.

"What are those called?" he asked, pointing to some orange and yellow flowers, some solid colors and some with stripes on the petals.

"Marigolds."

"Why didn't you pick any blue ones?"

"There's no such thing as a blue marigold, silly. Have I taught you nothing?"

"No blue marigolds? Well, there ought to be."

They could smell fried chicken as soon as they got out of the car at Lou's house. Ezzie came around the side of Jack's house barking, running the distance to Tess, followed by Jack on her heels.

"Look at her, Mom. You've got a friend there." Nicholas bent down with Tess to lavish attention on Ezzie.

"I thought dogs were supposed to help you get attention, not take it all away," Jack grumbled.

"Aw, we're happy to see you, too. But you didn't come running, with your tail wagging like Ezzie did," Tess said, grinning up at Jack.

"How do you know what my tail—" Jack stopped and cleared his throat, as Nicholas stood up, put his hands over his ears, and said, "La la la . . . I'm just gonna go on in the house."

"Y'all comin' in or do I have to serve supper out on the lawn?" Lou called from the front door.

"Let me take the attention hog home, and I'll be right back." Jack picked Ezzie up and cradled her like a baby as he walked toward home, while everyone else went into Lou's house.

Tess looked up a few minutes later to see him coming into the house with John Ed.

"Now that wasn't a fair trade," Tess whispered to Lou.

"Sorry to interrupt the party, folks," John Ed said, "but I have some news, and Henry Clay said you'd all be together over here."

"What kinda news?" Lou asked, crossing her arms in front of her. "If it's anything like the news I got this mornin' 'bout Peekal, I don't wanna hear it."

"What's goin' on, John Ed?" Jack asked.

"I told you this mornin' that Pickle pointed the finger at Crate Marshall. Well, I went out to question him, but I didn't 'zactly get any answers."

"Why not?" Tess asked.

"'Cause he was dead. Dead'er 'n a door nail." Everyone started talking at once.

"Oh my word," Lou exclaimed, putting her hand over her mouth and sinking onto the couch.

"Well, tie me to a pig and roll me in mud," Henry Clay said.

"Dead?" Tess and Jack said at the same time.

"Dead," John Ed confirmed. "Looks like he knew he was done fer and decided to go out on his own terms. He shot hisself after he had his mornin' coffee. We found your purse in his bedroom, too, Ms. Tremaine. Looks like he was the attacker. It all makes sense. And now it's over."

"I'm not sure it all makes sense. He didn't seem to be the type to go off the deep end like that," Tess said.

"That boy was a dog of his own trot. Don't really matter no more. He's a goner, and I say good riddance. Saves me some time and work, and saves the taxpayers some money."

"John Ed, that's an awfully cold-hearted thing to say," Lou said.

"Aw, Lou, ain't nobody gonna shed a tear over that man. Facts is facts. I'll be on my way now. Just wanted to give y'all the good news myself."

* * *

"Lou, I'm so full I'm ready to pop, but this cake is delicious. I can't stop eating it. What's it called?" Tess asked.

"Better Than Sex." She blushed, and answered the quizzical stares around the table by shrugging her shoulders and adding, "That's its name."

"Is that the doorbell? Who could that be?" Martha Maye asked to no one in particular. "Buttabean, go get the door, will ya, sugar?" Butterbean ran out of the room.

"Well? Does the cake live up to its name?" Lou asked.

Tess said, "I'm not touching that one."

Nicholas said, "There's no way I'm answering that with my mother sitting next to me."

And Jack said, "It's been so long, I really couldn't say."

"Hell, at my age, fruit cake would be better than sex," Henry Clay said.

Butterbean ushered Pickle and Caledonia Culpepper into the dining room. Pickle had his hands in his pockets and was looking at his shoes. His facial expression matched the sentiment on his t-shirt: "My Imaginary Friend Kicked Me Out Of Our Imaginary Club."

Caledonia said, "Excuse the interruption, y'all. No wonder Tess didn't answer her door. We didn't know everybody was here, but that's fortuitous, since Pickle has somethin' he wants to say to Lou *and* Tess. Don't you, Pickle?" She nudged his arm.

Pickle looked at Tess and said, "I want to apologize again for my . . . "

His mother helped him out, "abominable . . . "

". . . for my amominal . . . adobin . . . abdominal behavior. I . . . " he glanced at Henry Clay, then back at his shoes.

Lou broke in. "Peekal, you're squirmin' like a worm in hot ashes. Sit yerself down and have some cake. We're not gonna boil ya in oil or nuthin'."

Pickled coughed and shuffled his feet.

"No thank you, Lou, Pickle's gonna say his peace, and we're gonna get outta your way. Go on, Pickle," Caledonia urged.

Pickle cleared his throat and looked around the room, then down at his shoes. "I'm just so ashamed of myself, Mizz Tess. You've been so nice to me, and I let the smell of money turn my head. Can you ever forgive me?"

"Pickle, are those your words or are they rehearsed?" Tess asked.

"Uh . . . both I guess."

"Well, I want to hear it straight from you," she said gently.

He was quiet for a moment, then blurted out, "Well, ma'am, I'm just flat out sorry. I don't know what got into me. But if you'll forgive me, I swear I'll do my best to stay on the straight and narrow from now on."

Caledonia piped up, "You got that right."

"What can I do to make it up to y'all?"

"You stay on the straight and narrow, Pickle, and that'll do just fine." Tess patted his arm. "I expect it's pretty hard to say no to an intimidating man like Crate Marshall, right?"

"Pickle," Henry Clay said, "did you hear what happened to Marshall?"

"Yes, thank you, we heard," Caledonia said. "Now don't you dare go makin' my boy think that was his fault. Anything happened to him was his own doin's. What do you wanna say to Mizz Louetta, Pickle?"

"Mizz Louetta, please, please, please may I keep my job? You're the best boss in town, and just like I said to Mizz Tess, I'll work my hardest to prove I'm worthy."

Lou looked at Pickle for a full ten seconds. "I'm gonna hold you to that, Peekal. But listen here, and listen good. You mess up again, and I'll slap the taste right outta your mouth! No offense, Caledonia."

"None taken, Lou," Caledonia said.

"Yes'm. I promise I'll make y'all proud of me."

"Okay, thank y'all for bein' so understandin'. We'll get outta your hair now." Caledonia pulled on Pickle's arm.

"Don't get up, Lou. I'll walk them out," Jack said, motioning ever so slightly to Tess to join him.

"I'll walk you out, too," she said, trying to cover a smile.

"Pickle, hold on a minute," Jack said, once they were all outside of the house.

"Is there somethin' more you want to say?"

Pickle looked a little puzzled, then he looked at the ground, and finally up, directly into Jack's eyes. "You can't judge the depth of a well by the handle of the pump." He turned quickly and walked away.

"Somethin's not right. He's holdin' somethin' back," Jack said, watching Pickle and his mother get in their car.

"What do you suppose he meant by the depth of the well, and the handle of the pump?"

"Beats me entirely. Sounded kinda cryptic, didn't it?"

They waved, as Pickle and his mother drove away. It was almost dark, but the sky still had some streaks of purple and red. Jack pulled Tess toward him and looked into her eyes. "Hey, beautiful."

"Hey, you," she said softly. He cupped his hand on the back of her neck and pulled her in for a kiss that started out slow, but grew hungrier. Finally, he ended the kiss with a groan, hugging her tight.

"Aw, Tess, the things you do to me."

She pulled back. "What things?" She smiled up into his eyes.

He kissed her again and then whispered, "I want you, Tess. I think about you all the time, I can't get enough of you." He stood looking into her eyes for a moment. "I think I'm falling in love with you." He kissed her again and then whispered, "I just thought you should know."

Tess pushed her hands into his thick, wavy hair and said softly, "Nick goes home tomorrow. How about you come over for dinner tomorrow night?"

WOLLERIN' IN SORRINESS

wollerin' in sorriness: verb \wahl-er-in in sawr-ee-ness\
feeling sorry for oneself
He's wollerin' in sorriness.

[July 2010]

"When did Nicholas take off this morning?" Jack asked Tess, as she cleaned up supper.

"Around nine. It was good to see him. Sometimes I wonder why I didn't move to Birmingham with him. But I wanted a small town, and Goose Pimple Junction drew me right in. Besides, what twenty-five-year-old guy wants his mama following him to town?"

"True."

"And I do like my independence. I like being able to come and go, and see whoever I want, whenever I want."

"I like that, too," he said with a grin. "But he's a great kid, Tess. You did good."

"Thanks."

"Do you mind if I give Ezzie a little treat?" Jack pointed to some of the leftover ham.

"Not at all. I'm glad you brought her tonight."

Jack put some meat on the floor for Ezzie and walked over to Tess at the sink.

"Excellent dinner, Tess." He wrapped his arms around her from behind and nuzzled her neck.

She leaned back into him for a moment. "Mmm, you always smell so good."

"How good?"

"Irresistibly good." She rubbed her cheek against his hair.

"That's what I was goin' for," he whispered.

"Let me finish these dishes, and I'll give you my undivided attention."

"What can I do to help?"

"Just stand there and look good." She flashed a smile over her shoulder.

Jack stepped back, but began rubbing her shoulders instead of walking away.

"Oh my gosh, that feels good." She closed her eyes and let the water continue to run over the already clean dish.

"Ah, ah, ah! No stopping. If you stop working, I'll have to stop massaging. We don't need the clean-up to take any longer than necessary. Unless you want to take a break and finish those later."

"You're a cruel man, Jackson Wright," she teased. "But I'm anal retentive. If I don't clean these up it will be niggling at me all night."

"Hmmm, I'd like to be niggling at you all night," Jack said in an imitation Groucho Marx voice.

"I've been thinking, Jack . . . "

"Me too. What've you been thinking about?"

"Does it make sense to you that Tank would commit suicide over a little mischief?"

"No, as a matter of fact it does not. I was thinking the same thing. He was tough as nails. And he probably would've gotten off with a slap on the wrist. Nothing major. Nothing worth dying over. And he told us about his grandfather's involvement in both crimes. So what are we missin'?"

"I don't know! It just doesn't add up." His fingers had left her shoulders and were working their way down to the small of her back. She dried her hands and put them behind her, pulling him in for a backward hug. They stood that way silently for several seconds. Then she wiped down the countertop and turned to look at him.

"So . . . what are you thinking?" she asked.

"Do you really want to know?" he asked with a mischievous grin.

"About Tank's murder, Jack." She took his hand and led him to the den.

"Well . . . I'm thinking he was murdered," Jack said simply, sitting on the sofa.

"But by whom?" She settled on the couch next to him and pulled her legs up under her.

"I haven't figured that part out yet. I've had other things on my mind." He flashed that killer smile at her.

"Hold that thought. I'll be right back." Tess was up and out of the room before Jack could stop her.

When she returned a few minutes later with a candle and matches, she found him sitting on the couch, staring at her laptop screen. He barely looked up when she came in and sat down next to him. She leaned into him, to see what he was looking at so intently and once she saw it, said, "Oh crap," while trying to take it away from him.

"Oh no you don't, Mary T!" Jack held on tight to the laptop with one hand and fended her off with the other. "You left this document open, and I innocently looked at it when I opened the computer to go online. I'm halfway into the scene. You *can't* make me stop now."

She groaned, pulled her legs up tight against her chest, and leaned forward to hide her face in her knees. *Stupid, stupid, stupid. How could I have left that chapter, of all chapters, open?* The steamy love scene she was working on rushed through her mind. She groaned in embarrassment.

Tess started to get up. Jack's arm came out to hold her in place. But she knew exactly what he was reading, and she couldn't just sit there.

"Mary T! I had no idea . . . " Jack whispered, his eyes glued to the screen.

Jack absentmindedly dropped his arm, and she sprang up and out of the room, mumbling something about getting a drink. She was pouring sweet tea into two glasses when he joined her in the kitchen. He reached around her, took the pitcher, and set it on the opposite counter. He did the same with the two glasses and then gently turned Tess around to look at him.

"Tess, you never cease to amaze me," he said, smiling down at her. "Here I thought you were this innocent, shy, genteel lady, and . . . you write erotica?"

Tess closed her eyes and dropped her head onto his chest. Her reply was muffled. "Not erotica. Romance. There's a difference. You just happened upon the one chapter that…"

Jack put his hands on her sides and lifted her onto the counter behind her, standing between her legs. "Tess, look at me."

She raised her head slightly and opened one eye.

"Come on, sweetheart, look at me," he said, laughing. "Criminy, you are so dang hot. You're a perfect mixture of beautiful lady and sexy woman." That made Tess snort with a laugh of disbelief.

"Jack, I was going to tell you about my book. I didn't want you to actually read it, though. I'm so embarrassed."

"Why? I think it's great. I think *you're* great." He dipped his head down to catch her lips. His hands ran up and down her back as he deepened the kiss. She groaned and pulled him closer.

"Come on." He led her back to the den.

"You expectin' any visitors tonight?" he asked, as they sat back on the couch. She smiled and shook her head.

"Any phone calls?"

Again her head moved side to side, her eyes locked on his.

They kissed a long, slow, deep kiss, then broke apart, resting their foreheads against each other. Jack kissed her forehead, her temple, her eyelid, her cheek, her top lip, her chin; finally his lips found hers again.

"Bar none," she whispered against his lips, not realizing she'd said it out loud.

* * *

Tess woke up the next morning to find Jack's arms around her. They had fallen asleep together on her couch, and she was wedged into the cushions. She squirmed a little, pushed her hand into his hair, and kissed his neck. His arms tightened around her.

"Oops, I slept over," he said. "Mmm…what a nice way to wake up." He moved to kiss her.

She broke the kiss and hugged him, her face resting on his shoulder. She came nose to nose with Ezzie.

"Would you like some breakfast?" she asked Jack, while looking at Ezzie, who was now trying to wedge her way to lie down between them.

"Esmerelda!" Jack scolded.

"I think she's a little jealous, " Tess said, laughing.

"Speaking of which…" Jack began. "Um . . . "

"Hmm?"

"Last night . . . did you . . . did you call me Vernon?"

"Call you, what?" she asked, snuggling into him as best she could with a dog between them.

"You know, before . . . it sounded like you called me...Vernon."

Her eyes flew open. "I did?"

"You did. Want to tell me why you were whispering another man's name? And who is Vernon?" he asked, smoothing her hair.

She looked up at him blankly. Then it dawned on her what he was talking about. She laughed and said, "Oh, Jack. I wasn't calling you Vernon." Hugging him close and resting her head on his shoulder, she explained, "I was thinking you're the best..." she trailed off.

"The best what?"

"The best, you know, kisser, and..."

"There's an and?"

"...the best everything. And I was thinking, 'bar none.' I must have said it out loud." She was quiet for a minute while Jack took that in. Then she looked up at him and added, "But maybe from now on your nickname will be Vernon."

Jack smiled as he caught her lips for another long kiss.

* * *

Later that morning, Tess and Jack sat in her kitchen eating home-made waffles. She was quiet and seemed preoccupied.

"Have I overstayed my welcome?" he asked.

"Hmm? Oh, no. Not at all. I'm sorry. I just keep thinking about Tank Marshall. Something just doesn't feel right."

"Okay, here's what we're going to do." Jack laced his fingers through hers. "Lou knows now that we've been looking into her father's murder. Tonight we'll go over to her house with that key you found, and we'll check out that trunk in the attic. How's that sound?"

"Like a plan."

* * *

Jack and Ezzie had walked to Tess's house the previous night for dinner, so they walked her to work before they headed home. When they stepped onto the curb leading to the block with the bookstore, Jack pulled Tess over to the side of the building that housed the bank. She giggled, and said, "Vernon! What are you doing?"

He backed her up against the building, blocking her in with his arms on either side of her. He stood looking down at her so closely she couldn't move. "Vernon, huh? You really think so?"

She looked into his eyes and her voice grew husky. "I really do."

Just then, movement over Jack's shoulder caught her attention, and she looked past him to find Buck staring at them from across the street. She cleared her throat and Jack stepped back, following her eyes. Buck walked over to them.

"Well knock me down and steal muh teeth!" Buck said loudly. "I had no idea y'all were so friendly."

"It's not exactly your business, now is it, Mayor?" Jack put his arm protectively around Tess. Ezzie barked her annoyance.

"Here I've been a wollerin' in sorriness, thinkin' Mizz Tess here didn't like me. It never occurred to me that she just took to somebody else. But there y'all are, big as daylight, smoochin' on Main Street."

"I guess we were just of a mind that those who know, know. Those who don't know don't need to know. And you didn't need to know. But now you know, so, is there anything else we can do for ya today?" Jack asked with an insincere smile.

"Boy, you are actin' crazier 'n a sprayed roach. I guess that's what love does to a fella. Well good for y'all. You just let me know if you get tired of him, Tess. Ya hear?" He winked at her and started off.

"Yeah, well, don't get your hopes up, Mayor," Jack yelled. "And one thing's for sure—she won't ever call you Vernon!"

AN EMPTY BUCKET
MAKES THE MOST RACKET

<u>ahr</u>: noun \ar\ hour
It's your bedtime in an ahr.

[December 1935]

Nate Hunter came out of the safe deposit box area of the bank, and came to a sudden stop. He stepped back in surprise when he saw John Hobbs standing before him. "I thought you went home," Nate said to John, with a guilty expression on his face. He hurriedly stuffed a wad of bills in his pockets.

"What are you doing, Nate?"

"It's none of your business, John." Nate brushed past him.

John followed his co-worker. "What did you just put in your pockets?"

Nate stopped and turned around. "I don't know what you're talking about."

"Nate, there's something I've been wondering about for awhile now, and I need to know." The two men looked at each other for a long moment. "Were you involved in the bank robbery?" John asked point-blank.

"You never were one for beating around the bush, were you, John?"

"Plain talk is easily understood," John said. "You were—weren't ya?"

Nate looked at John through squinted eyes and muttered through his tightly held mouth, "Say that again and you'll rue it."

"That doesn't sound like the words of an innocent man."

"John, if you love your family at all, you should keep your thoughts and questions to yourself."

"Is that a threat?"

"You betcha." Nate stood up more erect and seemed taller and bigger, as if he'd been inflated. Then he let out a tired sigh. "Look, John, how 'bout I cut you in? I can't give you much right now, but . . . " he took a wad of bills out of his pocket. "How 'bout two thousand now, and I'll get you some more from the other guys. Think about it, two thousand will buy you a lot of shoes for them kids a yours."

John thought about it. Two thousand would also be hard evidence of Nate's guilt. He decided to string him along to see how much more information he could get out of him about the bank robbery. Catching one fish wasn't as good as catching the whole school.

"Okay," he said, keeping his voice even, "two thousand now and two from each of the other fellas. And I want to know who else was involved. And I also wanna know why you did this, Nate."

"Simple. I needed the money. I'm on track to become president of the bank, John. But I gotta look the part before I become the part. I gotta look successful so they'll take notice of me."

"I see."

"Two thousand now," he counted out the bills and handed them to John, "and I'll call ya this weekend and let you know when I can get ya the rest."

John walked to his office. He stepped on a floorboard behind his desk and the board popped up. He put the money in the secret compartment in the floor, then sat down at his desk, took pen and paper out, and began to write.

[July 2010]

Pickle had shied away from Lou and Tess all morning, busying himself with unpacking boxes of books. After working a few hours, he broke the boxes down and headed out the back door, carrying them to the dumpster in the alley to throw them away. Standing at the dumpster, the faint smell of Aqua Velva filled his nose and made his stomach lurch. He didn't need to turn around to know he wasn't alone in the alley.

"You done real good, boy," Aqua Velva man said.

Pickle turned and saw the man just a few feet away, drawing on a cigarette. He looked down at his t-shirt that said, "Obey Gravity—it's the law!"

"You and the law are real tight now, huh?"

"I didn't tell 'em anything 'bout you, sir. I did just as you told me to. I swear." Pickle was wide-eyed and dry mouthed, but he managed to take a gulp, his Adam's apple bobbing in his throat.

"Yeah, I heard. That's why I'm here. You can relax. I just dropped by to give you yer money." He handed Pickle a wad of dollar bills.

Pickle shook his head. "Uh . . . sir . . . if it's all the same to you, I think I'd rather not take that this time. It just don't feel right. And I need to resign from my employ with you, too." Pickle swallowed hard again, and added, "If y . . . you don't mmm . . . mind, that is."

"Sure thing, boy. I know I put you in a tight spot. But you came through for me. I guess we can part ways as friends now. Just remember what I tolt ya." He pointed his finger in Pickle's face. "Not a word to nobody 'bout me, or you and old Tank Marshall will be pushin' up daisies side-by-side. Ya hear?"

"Ye . . . yessir." Pickle nodded his head vigorously, gulping once again. He then began to hiccup.

"I'll be watchin' you, boy." The man clasped a firm hand on Pickle's shoulder and squeezed hard. "Don't you forget that." Aqua Velva man turned and disappeared around the side of the building.

* * *

Jack saw Officers Beanblossom and Duke inside the diner as he passed, and since he had thirty minutes to spare before picking up Tess for their dinner date, he decided to stop for a chat.

He passed the old men at their usual seats at the counter, saying, "Afternoon, Clive, Earl, how are y'all today?"

"If dumb was dirt, he'd cover 'bout half an acre," Clive said, pointing to Earl.

"Ha!" snorted Earl, "An empty bucket makes the most racket."

"Aw, boys, tell ya what do," Jack clapped Earl on the shoulder as he passed by, "have some of Junebug's chocolate cream pie. It'll sweeten ya both right up."

"We's plenty sweet. What's she got that will make him smart?" Clive hitched his thumb toward Earl.

The men started arguing, and Jack started for the officers' table. He saw Henry Clay at a table with a group of men, all wearing "Price For Governor" buttons. Jack waved and Henry Clay answered with a nod of the head.

"Mind if I sit a spell?" he asked the officers, grabbing the back of a chair.

"Sure thing, Jack. What's up?" Skeeter asked.

"Y'all were over at Tank Marshall's the other day, weren't ya?"

"Yeah, we was there," Hank Beanblossom said. He and Skeeter exchanged looks.

"I was just wonderin'—how'd y'all get past the dogs?"

"The dogs?" Hank repeated.

"Yeah, you know, Foghorn and Leghorn. They always, uh . . . enthusiastically greet visitors to Tank's farm. Tank's pretty much the only one they'll mind. How'd you get past them to the house?"

"Wull . . . they were locked up in the barn that mornin'," Skeeter said.

"Locked up?"

"Yeah, that is kinda weird, now that ya mention it. I didn't think he ever locked them dogs up." Skeeter scratched his head. "Add that to the list of strange, Beano."

"What do y'all think? Do you buy the suicide theory?" Jack asked, lowering his voice.

"Off the record?" Hank whispered.

"Off the record," Jack promised. The three men leaned into the table to carry on the conversation without being overheard.

"I didn't buy it for a minute," Hank said quietly. "John Ed's the one who signed, sealed and delivered that verdict. Skeeter and I noticed some things at the scene. The coroner did, too."

"He's gonna do an autopsy," Skeeter interjected. "He says he can do an x-ray to determine the path of the bullet. Cool, huh? Then he'll be able to determine the angle of the bullet, and know if it's possible he could have shot himself. But I know it wasn't a suicide. It looked like a set-up from the get-go. The gun was limp in his hand, and there wasn't any blowback or blood. We're waitin' on a report to see if there was any gun powder residue on his hand."

"I'm glad to hear that, fellas. I don't buy the suicide theory either. Say, you guys don't like John Ed for the killer, do ya?"

"Naw, ain't no way it was him. Coroner said it happened around nine this mornin' and the chief was at the station from eight o'clock on. The only time he left was when the three of us went to Tank's. Naw, I think he's jest lazy, s'all. Dudn't want the headache of a murder investigation jest fer the likes a Tank Marshall."

"Okay, boys. Thanks a bunch."

"But mum's the word about this investigation, Jack. The chief don't know anything about it. We'd like to keep it that way."

Jack made a motion like he was zipping his lips. He winked at the officers. "Keep me posted?"

"Sure thing, Jack."

* * *

After dinner at The Silly Goose, Jack helped Tess into his truck and then got in behind the wheel, eyeing the cake on her lap. "Good thing it wasn't chocolate, or it would have melted sittin' in the truck in this heat."

"True. I'm not sure how Lou's going to react to our wanting to look at the trunk. I just thought a cake might sweeten the deal."

"That was nice of you." He leaned over to kiss her.

I think I'm falling in love with you' ran like a never-ending loop in her brain as the kiss deepened. She broke away and looked at Jack.

"I think I am, too."

"I think I know what you're saying, but I want to hear it." Jack was so close to her, their noses almost touched.

"I told Nick I like you a lot. But it's more than that, Jack." She put her hand on his cheek. "I'm in love with you."

"Aw, Tess." Jack kissed her lips, her cheek, her neck. "Do we have to go to Lou's right now?"

She giggled. "We'll make it quick."

* * *

After they'd eaten huge pieces of cake, Lou said, "Oooowwweeeee! I'm full as a tick! But y'all, I'm startin' to worry there's somethin' wrong with me. First Martha Maye volunteers to work late for me, now y'all bring me cake. I mean, it sure was mighty nice and all, but ya know you're welcome over here anytime—ya don't have to bring food, you can just bring yerselves." She looked from Jack to Tess, scrutinizing them. "There's not some bad news I don't know about, is 'ere? I'm not dyin' am I?"

Jack laughed and said, "No, Lou, you're not dying."

"But we do have something we want to discuss with you, Lou," Tess said.

"Oh. Well in that case, Buttabean, you gwon up and get yer bath now, and let the adults talk a spell," Lou told her granddaughter.

"Oh, all right," Butterbean whined, stomping out of the kitchen. "I miss out on everything good."

Once Butterbean was gone, Lou asked, "Now what's this somethin' you want to discuss? It must be a lulu to require cake beforehand." She nervously fingered the pearls around her neck as she looked at Jack and Tess.

"Lou, do you remember that key I found back when I first started redecorating the house?"

Lou swallowed hard. "Yes."

"Well, we believe it's related to your father's murder."

Lou hopped up and immediately began picking up plates to clear the table. Tess looked at Jack, and he gave her an encouraging nod. They stood up to help with the dishes, and Tess pressed on, talking while Lou washed the plates.

"Lou, I know this is hard, but don't you want to know who killed your father?"

She fiddled with the water to get the right temperature. "The report from the detective agency my mother hired said we didn't want to know."

Tess handed her a plate. "What do you mean?"

"Just what I said. After Daddy was murdered, my mama hired The Pinkerton Agency to investigate. She didn't think the police were doin' enough on their own. After a few weeks of investigatin', the PI came over't the house and said, 'You do not want to know.' That was his exact words, accordin' to Mama. I don't know what else was said, I just know that it was enough to make Mama drop it, and never talk about it again." She handed Tess a plate to dry and began washing another one.

"You mean she never talked about your father after that?" Tess dried the plate and handed it to Jack, who was stacking them on the table.

"Oh, law no, we talked about Daddy. But only the good times. We never discussed that horrible December night ever again."

"How awful. You *must* have questions."

"I believe what my mama believed: some things are just better left unknown. I'm at peace with that. Why do ya wont to go stirrin' it up now for?"

"Because someone is going to an awful lot of trouble to keep us from finding out the truth," Tess said. "And when somebody tells me I should leave well enough alone, it just makes me want to dig that much deeper. I want to know why someone's broken into my house, and called with threatening messages, and attacked us on the street. And something tells me it wasn't Tank Marshall."

"Well, whoever it is can't be the killer! Anyone old enough to kill Daddy way back then would surely be dead hisself by now."

"Which makes it all the more peculiar that someone would care. I think we need to get to the bottom of this," Tess said gently to Lou.

"H'ire y'all gonna do that?" She gave Tess another dish to dry.

"We're going to start by talking to you and seeing what you know that might fill in some blanks."

"Child, I don't know nothin'. I was just knee high to a grasshopper myself at the time. I remember feelings and emotions of that turrible time, but that's all I remember."

"You may know more than you think," Jack told her.

"Let's start with what we're sure about," Tess suggested. "We know that your father was a witness to a bank robbery three years before his death, and that could be one motive for killing him. Brick Lynch was tried, but acquitted. What about Rod Pierce?"

"He spent some years in jail. After that, I don't know what became of him."

"Why do you think the detective didn't want you to ask questions?" Tess asked.

"I s'pose it was on account of some people thinkin' Daddy committed suicide; even the insurance comp'ny thought so. They denied the double indemnity claim, and ruled it a suicide. And then there were some people who thought Daddy was in on the robbery. They thought he knew too much. And then still others thought the killer possibly was my uncle." Lou scrubbed a dish so hard Tess wondered if the paint would come off. Forcefully she said, "I will never believe it was suicide. My daddy wouldn't do that to us. And I will never believe that he stole one red nickel from that bank."

"Lou, did you just say the killer could have been your uncle?"

Lou nodded. She took the dry dishes and put them in the cabinet.

"Why would he kill his brother?" Tess asked.

Lou took a deep breath and let it out. "Because he loved my mama and wanted her for hisself. So don'tcha see? Murder, suicide, friend, foe, his own brother . . . " her voice got very soft, then she seemed to strengthen. "Whoever . . . whatever . . . it doesn't matter. My daddy's still dead. And the killer is surely dead by now, too. What does it matter anymore?" She dried her hands with a dish towel.

"It matters because it was your father. And you deserve to know who took him away from you. *He* deserves for somebody to find the truth. Can't you think of anything that might help us figure this out?"

"All right," she said, leading them to the den to continue their conversation. "The one thing I remember my mama sayin' to me was that on the night Daddy died, he had tried to tell her somethin', but he never had a chance to tell her, and she regretted that for all her days." She smoothed the wrinkles in her hot pink skirt.

"Mama said he'd tried to tell her a couple of times about somethin' in the trunk in the attic. She assumed he was talkin' about his grandmother's steamer trunk that they kept up there with old clothes and quilts in it. Mama searched it high and low but never found anything he'd left. When you said you found a key, I knew that's what it was for. It brought all those memories back." Lou's eyes got watery, but she reined her emotions in and continued talking as she fiddled with a tissue in her hand.

"At first it was an obsession with her. About once a week, she went up there to that attic and took every article out of that trunk. She unfolded and shook out each piece, examined it, only to have to fold everything back up and put it all back in the trunk. It never made sense to her. Then after the detective finished his investigation, she never went near that trunk again." Lou took a deep breath. "And then there was the insurance money . . . "

"What about it?" Tess asked.

"Mama filed a death claim suit against the insurance comp'ny, on account that her husband was shot and killed by an unknown person. I b'lieve she asked for $10,000 double indemnity benefits under a $5,000 policy he held. You know . . . it's like an accidental death benefit. But the insurance comp'ny denied the policy, alleging the death was suicide. That just about killed my Mama. I mean, how could it have been suicide? His gun hadn't been fired, and there were three bullet holes in his car windows. It just didn't add up. But sometimes life makes as much sense as bowling cleats."

"Okay, that trunk has been searched—right?"

"And searched and searched," Lou said.

"Could he have been talking about something else besides the steamer trunk? Try to think of what else was in the attic that could have been considered a trunk." Jack leaned forward in earnestness.

Lou closed her eyes and put her hands on her temples. Finally, she said, "I just don't think there was anything else up there. There were some old chairs, and some Christmas decorations in boxes, and excess stuff like that up there, but nothin' else that you'd call a trunk."

"Okay, can Tess and I see the trunk? Sometimes a new pair of eyes can see somethin' others have missed."

"Y'all are welcome to gwon up there and look at it. I hope ya won't mind if I just stay put."

"Of course you can stay here, Lou, can we get you anything before we go up?"

"No sugah, I'll just go check on Buttabean."

Thirty minutes later, Jack and Tess came back down the stairs, looking dejected.

"Well?" Lou asked.

"Here's the thing, Lou," explained Jack. "We didn't find anything, but I think it's possible that old trunk may have a secret compartment. I once wrote about an old trunk from that era in a book of mine, and I did some research on them. They *always* had secret compartments that were hard to find. It's so dark and cramped up there, would you mind if we took it to one of our houses to get a better look at it? It's getting' late, too, and it might take us awhile."

"Y'all really think somethin' could be hidden in that trunk?"

Jack and Tess both nodded, and Tess answered, "It's worth a looky-loo."

"But Mama surely knew about a secret compartment, or else why would Daddy hide somethin' there?"

"I don't know, Lou. I'd just like to go over it with a fine-tooth comb to be sure."

"Just promise me somethin'."

Jack raised his eyebrows in a question.

"If ya find out somethin' horrible, you'll keep it to yerselves and tell me y'all didn't find a thing. Deal?"

"Deal," they said in unison.

"Alrighty then, gwon. Get it outta here." She waved them off upstairs.

Tess and Jack came down the stairs with the trunk, just as Martha Maye came in the front door with Henry Clay.

"Where on earth are y'all takin' that old trunk?"

Lou came into the hallway, holding a Barbie doll. "Ah, don't mind Sherlock and Watson. They think they're hot on the trail of a mystery."

Martha Maye looked at Tess and whispered, "You got her to talk? How?"

"Long story. We'll talk later, okay?" Then louder, Tess said, "Lou, we'll pack this up in the truck and then take off. We'll let you know tomorrow what we find out, okay?"

"Why don't y'all just look at it down here? You don't have to take it to one of your houses," Henry Clay said.

"I'd rather 'em take it, Henry. No tellin' what they might find, or how long it'll take. Y'all gwon, and remember our deal. And thanks for the cake. It wasn't better 'n sex, but it was delish."

Tess and Jack went next door to his house and sprung Ezzie from lock-up. She trotted happily at their sides out to the truck.

"Let's put her in the cab with us," Tess said, looking at the sky. "It looks like it's blowing up a cloud."

As they drove away from the house, they could see Martha Maye, Henry Clay, and Lou sitting down in the living room.

"Should we have stayed to make sure she's all right with this?" Tess asked.

"Nah. She'll be fine," Jack assured her. "Henry Clay and Martha Maye will see to it."

WELL I'LL BE DIPPED IN PEANUT BUTTER

veeola: interjection \vee-oh-lah\ voila
And veeola, there it is.

[Sunday, December 15, 1935]

"Daddy, phone's for you!" Ima Jean called.

As soon as John said 'Hello,' Nate Hunter said, "Be at the old Goose Creek Bridge tonight at seven o'clock." He heard a click, and the line went dead.

John went to his bedroom, dodging his sons and their toy cars along the way. He took a folded sheet of paper from his dresser drawer, picked up the trunk key, and went up to the attic, where he went to the bracket-footed Victorian trunk.

I've got to leave it here. If the worst-case scenario plays out, people will be swarming the house. I can't chance just anybody seeing this.

John knelt down and slowly ran his fingers along the top edges of the trunk. It had a secret compartment that would open once a trigger spot was pressed. The trick was to find that one very subtle, well-disguised spot—so subtle, one couldn't find it by sight. He closed his eyes and felt for a slight fingertip-sized depression. Once the small indentation was found, he pressed his finger into it and heard the faint sound of the spring releasing.

After unlocking the trunk and raising the lid so the side panel could lift upward, he bent down at the side of the trunk, where the released spring had raised the side panel ever so slightly. Using his pocketknife to make room for his fingers to get under the panel, he slid it up, revealing tiers of small drawers, and one narrow but deep pocket at the bottom of the trunk, hidden to the eye by its feet. He pulled his revolver out of the deepest space, placed it in his suit coat pocket, and put the letter to Maye in one of the small drawers.

Pushing the drawer back in and sliding the side panel down, he loaded the spring in place. Locking the trunk back, he thought what a mistake he might have made in never telling anyone about the hidden compartments. He'd kept his secret hiding place to himself because he didn't want to chance anyone but him finding his gun. *I'll have to find a way to tell her about it now, so she'll know to look here just in case I don't return home.*

He sat there for a long time, just staring at the key.

[July 2010]

Jack and Tess carried the trunk into her house and sat it on the floor of her living room. Suddenly they could hear the roar of rain hitting the house. Tess and Ezzie went to the window.

"We got in here just in time. Look at it out there! It's really coming down in sheets."

"Good," Jack said. "It's been so hot and dry, you could blow dust out of the rain gauge."

Ezzie was restless with the storm and went running from window to window.

Tess joined Jack on the carpet in front of the trunk. "Do you really think there's a secret compartment in this trunk?"

"I do. When I researched these Victorian trunks for my book *Victory Days*, I found out they often had numerous compartments, ranging from basic to complex. A basic trunk was usually comprised of a hatbox, a shirt compartment, a coin box, and a document box. A complex trunk, however, could have several hat and shirt compartments, a coin box, several document boxes *and* a secret compartment. The trunks were strategically designed so that no one would know of a hidden compartment's existence except for the owner. It made it safer when traveling."

Jack studied the trunk for several minutes in silence. He looked it over top to bottom. They'd taken everything out of it except for some tissue paper on a shelf and left the contents at Lou's. He took the shelf and paper out, laying them on the floor. Ezzie inched over, took the tissue paper and began shredding it.

He studied the inside of the trunk, looking for a false bottom, then he sat back, momentarily perplexed.

"What's wrong?" Tess asked.

He reached for her and lay back on the floor, pulling her on top of him as he went. "I just need some fortification," he said, kissing her.

She looked at him in a shocked and strange way.

"ForTification," he said quickly. "Although the other could be arranged." He flicked an imaginary cigar in the air and wagged his brows.

After several minutes of kissing, laughing and rolling around on the floor, Jack suddenly froze.

"What is it?" Tess asked.

"I just remembered somethin'. Hidden compartments often have trigger spots that can't easily be detected."

He sat up, closed and locked the trunk, and began running his fingers over the top of it. Tess sat up, watching intently.

"I can't believe I didn't think of this before. Damn if you aren't some kind of distraction." His smile told her he wasn't entirely kidding.

"Well, seeing how you just remembered something vital after kissing me, I'd say I'm a good distraction."

"That you are, Mary T. That you are." His eyes sparkled at her.

Jack shut his eyes. "I remember reading the Braille method is the best way to find the hidden trigger point. It's often so subtle it isn't any bigger than an almost invisible depression. He continued slowly running his fingers over the surface of the trunk. At last, he stopped and looked up at Tess with excitement.

"I see something in your eyes. You found it, didn't you?"

He nodded. "The most intricate designs have an end that slides up, revealing drawers concealed in the false bottom. Because of the shallowness of the secret drawers, the hidden compartment could easily pass unnoticed. Once you find the trigger point," he took Tess's fingertip, placed it on the trunk, and pushed down, hearing a soft click, "you can pull the side panel up."

Jack put the tip of his pocketknife under the small crack in the side of the trunk. "And voila." Pulling the wooden side panel straight up, he proudly announced, "Behold, the secret compartment." He slid three long, shallow drawers out, revealing a single sheet of paper in one of them.

Pulling the letter out of the drawer, and with awe in his eyes and voice, he said, "Well, I'll be dipped in peanut butter! Would you looka here."

Tess squealed, then scurried around behind him so she could read the letter over his shoulder. Mid-way through, she gasped, and splayed her hand over her mouth. The room was silent except for the sound of a hard rain, the rumble of thunder, and the tearing of tissue paper.

My beloved Maye,

If you are reading this, I must be dead. I'm so sorry darlin', I didn't want to hurt you and the children, I just wanted to find the truth and have justice reign. Please take this letter to Bug, and do not show or discuss it with anyone else. As you are now sadly all too aware, this is serious business.

I have had thoughts of Nate Hunter's involvement in the bank robbery for some time now, because of these reasons:

1) He lowered the window shade on the day of the robbery about two minutes before the bandits entered the bank, although it didn't register with me until later. This was strange, because not only has that shade never been raised or lowered in the twelve years of my employment at the bank, there also was no cause to lower it. The sun was not shining into that window. I believe Hunter was signaling his cohorts that the time was right for them to begin the robbery.

2) The robbers' choice to take Nate hostage instead of Tallulah was a peculiar one. Why take a big man, when you could take a small woman?

3) Nate didn't seem to be shaken up when he came back to the bank after the robbers let him go. He also couldn't provide any details about the robbers, their car, or which way they were headed. Or was it that he <u>wouldn't</u> provide those details?

5) At first he was wishy-washy about identifying the robbers.

*6) He's made some peculiar purchases since the robbery that seem
out of bounds on his salary.*

*And then tonight after closing time, everyone had gone home except
for Nate and me. As he closed the vault to the safe deposit area,
I saw him stuffing a wad of bills into his pocket. I questioned him,
and he threatened me. Then he offered me a cut of the bank robbery
money to keep quiet. I went along with him, and told him I needed
more—some from each of the bandits. Once I find out who they all
are, I'll take the money and the information to Bug. For now, the
money Nate gave me is in the floorboard behind my desk at the
bank. If something should happen to me, tell Bug to look there,
and show him this letter.*

*I felt the need to leave this account of my suspicions. I can't tell
anyone else, for fear I'll put them in danger. I pray to God this all
ends peacefully and you will never have to read this letter.*

Your loving husband,
John

"Holy cow," Tess said, after she'd finished reading. She shook Jack's
shoulder with excitement. "It was Nate Hunter. Jack! We've found it! It
was Nate Hunter!"

They both looked at the letter again, and reread the entire page.

Suddenly, the room went dark. They both froze. Ezzie whined and
moved in between them. Tess reached for Jack.

"Jack . . . "

"It's okay, Boo. It's just the storm." As he finished his sentence, the
lights came back on.

"Whew. I've been watching too many movies." Tess laughed
nervously.

"There's one problem now, Mary T."

"I know. Ezzie made a mess with the tissue paper." She looked
across the room to the carpet littered with shreds of tissue paper. "She

had quite a fun time though, didn't she?"

"Yes, but that's not what I meant. Our big problem is we don't know who's related to Nate Hunter." Jack looked at his watch. "Twelve thirty. It's too late to call Martha Maye or Lou, isn't it?"

"I'd say so. Let me get my lap top, though. We can look online and see if we can find anything on one of the genealogy sites."

Tess opened her laptop, and tried to log on to the Internet. "Hmm . . . that's weird. My Internet is down."

"I'll bet it's the rain. It's happened before. When the lights tripped a minute ago, somethin' probably happened with the phone lines, too." He went to the cordless phone across the room. "Yep. It's dead."

"Well, there's no reason why this can't wait until tomorrow morning. Everyone assumes the culprit was Tank Marshall. With him out of the way, whoever's responsible for all of this probably thinks we're satisfied the case has been solved. Tomorrow morning we'll talk to Martha Maye and Lou. If they don't know who's related to Nate Hunter, we'll find somebody in town who does know."

Jack went back to the trunk, looking one more time for anything else that might be hidden. Then he put the letter back in the compartment and closed it and the trunk lid, putting the key on top. Tess got up and walked to him, wrapping her arms around him.

"Tess, I can't believe you're not itching to clean up that mess." His eyes pointed to Ezzie's tissue paper mess.

"Well, I've never had a Vernon in my life."

He smiled and kissed her. Ezzie wagged her tail, her whole bottom moving along with it.

* * *

The next morning, Tess had just finished getting dressed when her doorbell rang. Jack had said he'd be by to pick her up around nine o'clock, so she assumed he was at the door.

"You're earl—" she stopped when she saw the intimidating men at her door and immediately tried to close it, but Willy and his burly friend were too fast for her. They pushed their way in, and shut the door behind them.

HE PUT THE 'E' IN IG-NERNT

ignernt: adjective \ig-ner-uhnt\ ignorant
He put the 'e' in ignernt.

[July 2010]

"Go close the curtains," Willy ordered the other man, pushing Tess into the den.

"Willy, what do you think you're doing?" Tess demanded.

"Tying up loose ends." He looked at the trunk sitting on her living room floor. He took the key off the top and opened it.

"Looka here, Joe Bob," Willy said. "Look at this nice big trunk. Are you thinkin' what I'm thinkin'?"

"Uh . . . what are you thinkin'?"

"Joe Bob, I swear you put the 'e' in ig-nernt." Willy threw him some rope. "Tie her up," he barked. "She's goin' in the trunk."

"You? You're not serious." Tess snickered. "You can't be the one who's been behind all the shenanigans." She began laughing. He moved toward her while tearing off a piece of duct tape with his teeth.

"Hold her still," he told Joe Bob. He roughly plastered the tape over her mouth. He was standing so close to her, she could smell coffee and cigarettes on his breath. He smoothed the tape over her cheek and let his hand linger on her face. He let it trail down her neck, leering at her, as she struggled to get free.

"Mmm, mmm, Doll. You and me coulda had us a *good* time. Might still have time for that." His smile made her shiver.

Joe Bob finished tying her hands together. "C'mon, Willy, we gotta move it. The boss said get her PDQ."

Willy looked confused. "Huh?"

Tess let out a muffled laugh. *Even I know that one.*

Willy looked blankly from Joe Bob to Tess. In a tone that suggested he couldn't be any more stupid, Joe Bob said, "Pretty Dern Quick. Get it?"

"Yeah, yeah. I knew that." He cleared his throat. "You got her hands tied good and tight?"

Joe Bob tugged on the rope around her hands tied in the back. "Yep."

"Head or tail?" Willy sneered.

"Huh?" It was Joe Bob's turn to be confused.

"Aw, crap. Nemmine. *I'll* get her head *and* her tail." With that, Willy picked up Tess, fireman-style, and carried her to the trunk. Tess kicked and squirmed, but he just laughed as he held on tighter. She kicked harder, and Joe Bob took hold of her legs; together they put her into the trunk and tried to shut the lid.

"Gad night a livin'," Willy cursed. "We're gonna have to undo her hands. We can't close the lid unless we can get her to curl up into a little ball. She won't be goin' anywhere anyway, once the lid is shut and locked. Gwon, untie her."

Joe Bob untied Tess's hands and pushed her head down into the trunk. It was a tight fit, but she was small enough and the trunk was big enough for it to just work out. As soon as they closed the lid, she pulled the tape off of her mouth.

She could feel the trunk being picked up and could hear the men talking.

BUMP. *They must've run into a wall or something. Bunch of bumbling idiots.*

She felt a jiggling sensation, and she could tell they were walking. Then she felt herself being lowered and dropped, and then seconds later being picked back up. *What are they going to do to me?* She could see daylight through a small crack in the trunk. *Who's behind this?* She felt a sliding motion and figured they were loading her into a vehicle of some kind. *Where are they taking me?* Her mind was racing. *What will they do to me?* Her breathing was heavy. *Will Jack find me in time?* It was so hot inside the trunk she had to breathe through her mouth, but exhaling made it hotter.

She heard Willy say, "Damnation." Then she heard a car door and someone else's voice.

"Willy? What in tarnation are you doin' here?" a woman's voice said.

Tess tried to slow her breathing and strained to hear what was being said.

"And where you goin' with my mama's trunk?"

"Help!" Tess screamed.

"What's that noise? What are you—" She heard Martha Maye scream, then heard movement, like a scuffle.

Martha Maye! Oh no.

"Hey!" she screamed.

The tailgate creaked. A heavy thud landed right next to her. Then there was darkness. Doors slammed shut. The truck started and began moving.

* * *

When Jack arrived at the police station, neither Skeeter nor Hank were there.

"Do you know if they got any information back on the little matter they were looking into?" he asked Bernadette.

"Hey, Jack." She sidled up to him. "They said if you came by to tell you, um . . . " She leaned over her desk and picked up a Post-It note. "They said to tell you the test was pos'tive, whatever that means, and they've gone back out to try to gather more evidence. That answer your question, sugar britches?"

"It sure does, thanks." He headed toward the door.

"You're not pregnant, are ya?" Burnadette laughed.

"Don't think so," he said over his shoulder, running toward the parking lot.

Jack hurried to his truck. "The donuts will have to wait, Ezzie. We need to get to Tess's house. This is getting curiouser and curiouser." He pushed his foot on the accelerator. She stuck her head out the window, nose high in the air, ears flapping like a flag in a stiff breeze. "We gotta go and pick up Tess. I want to talk to Lou as soon as we can. And I don't want Tess outta my sight until we find out who's behind this. Although, I reckon even then I won't want her outta my sight."

He pulled into Tess's driveway, and Ezzie trotted beside him to the door. He knocked and tried the knob, but it was locked. He waited. He knocked again. "Where is she, girl?" She cocked her head at him. He stepped off the front porch and walked toward the side of the house. And then he noticed it.

"Oh no." Dread enveloped him. "The drapes are closed."

WOUND UP
LIKE A CHEAP ALARM CLOCK

<u>kin</u>: noun \kin\ family
You got any kin around these parts?
<u>kin</u>: noun \kin\ can
Kin I go up to the store for a spell?

[July 2010]

Jack broke the glass of a windowpane in Tess's kitchen door, reached through and unlocked it, racing through the house, searching and calling for her. "Tess!"

She was nowhere to be found. He glanced into the den on his way back down the stairs and saw the trunk was missing. *Oh no. There's no way she could move that herself.*

Racing back out the door, he yelled, "Ezzie, stay put. And don't eat anything."

He checked the garage. "Damn. Still there. This isn't good."

After a frantic drive through town, which yielded nothing suspicious, Jack stopped at the bookstore to talk to Lou. He'd called John Ed to report Tess missing, and John Ed promised to get the whole police force looking for her. Even the chief sounded alarmed.

Pickle was outside the store sweeping the sidewalk as Jack stalked toward him. "You!" Jack said, grabbing his shirt and pulling him inside the store, "Get your butt in here."

"LOU! Lou where are you?"

She came running from the back of the store.

"Good Lord, Jack. You're wound up like a cheap alarm clock. What in the world's the matter with you?"

"Lou. Let me ask the questions. This is serious. Tess is missing . . . "

"Tess is missin'?"

"Yes. Listen to me. She's missin' and so is the trunk. Tell me somethin'. Nate Hunter. He have any kin around here?"

Pickle knocked a stack of books off a table behind Jack.

"Nate Hunter? Why?" Lou stammered.

"Lou!"

"Okay, okay, you're askin' the questions." She looked at Pickle who just stood there, bug-eyed, with his mouth wide-open.

"Lou!" Jack said again, louder than he'd intended.

She put her attention back on him. "Well, yeah, hon. John Ed's wife was Nate's daughter. Why?"

A crushing, cold feeling of panic rose up in Jack.

"John Ed?" he repeated, in disbelief.

"Wull . . . yeah . . . what's all this about, Jack? You're scarin' me."

Out of the corner of his eye, he noticed Pickle quietly backing away. Jack stepped backward three steps and grabbed him by his t-shirt, stopping him. He spun Pickle around and glanced at his shirt, which said, "I Make Stuff Up."

Pointing to Pickle's chest, he said, "That certainly is appropriate for you, boy. Start talkin'. *NOW.*"

"I don't know nothin' 'bout John Ed."

Jack squinted at him. "What *do* you know about? Spill it." He was inches from Pickle's face.

The kid started talking a blue streak, his sentences running together. "Okay I lied I'm so sorry but I was afraid of him you see nobody knows the real dude he's meaner than a sack of snakes he threatened me, and I didn't know what to do the whole thing started out 'cause I wanted to get in good with him on a count a Charlotte and well . . . the pay was good but it got outta hand, and I didn't know what to do and he—" He was talking a mile a minute, not even stopping to take a breath.

"Pickle!" Jack interrupted. "Slow down. Slow down. We can't understand a word you're sayin'. Who are you talkin' about? Are you sayin' *John Ed* hired you?"

Pickle took a deep breath, pacing back and forth, holding his hands on the sides of his head, as if it was going to fall off. "No. Henry Clay."

"Henry Clay?" Jack's knees felt wobbly.

"Yeah. At first he told me to spy on Mizz Tess, which seemed harmless enough, on account of her workin' here. It was easy for me to listen in on conversations and then just report back to HC." He looked quickly at Lou and added, "He told me to call him HC. And now you know why my straw was always in your Kool-Aid. I ain't naturally nosey."

"Go on, Pickle," Jack said impatiently.

"Well, that's all, until the thing with the brick. I didn't want to do it, but that's when he got mean. Said I'd do it, or he'd make it look like I was the one who attacked y'all, and I promise, that wadn't me!"

"Okay, Pickle, I believe you, now go on."

"He told me to throw the brick. He said if I got caught I should tell 'em it was Tank Marshall who hired me. Said if I didn't, he'd see to it I'd never see his daughter again, plus he'd hang me out to dry to boot. Said I'd end up with jail time, or worse. Said he could make it happen on account of John Ed bein' his daddy. I didn't know he was gonna kill anybody. Then, after Tank died, HC said I'd end up as worm food alongside Tank if I squealed. So see? I had no choice but to do what he said! Oh Lord, I'm so sorry. But Jack, that's what I was tryin' to tell y'all when I said that 'bout the well and the handle. He ain't what he seems."

"Henry Clay. Unbelievable." Jack shook his head, pacing back and forth. "Unbefreakinglievable." He stopped in front of Pickle. "Who else is involved in this little scheme? Henry Clay isn't the one who attacked us, is he?"

"Naw, I don't reckon. I don't know who else, though. That's all I know. *I swear.*"

Lou was white as a sheet as she listened to Pickle's confession. Suddenly, she blurted out, "Martha Maye. I gotta call and warn her." She picked up the phone, started to dial, but hung up. Panicked, she said, "Oh no. I forgot the phones are dead."

"Cell phone?" Jack asked.

"Neither of us is that fancy, Jack." She stood up. "I gotta find her."

She stopped, turning to Jack. "Jackson, do you mean to tell me Nate Hunter killed my daddy, and Henry Clay killed Tank Marshall?"

"That's what I'm saying, Lou. And now Tess and the proof is missing. We found a letter from your daddy in the trunk last night. It's pretty much proof of Hunter bein' the killer. Of course it was written before the fact, but your daddy was afraid, and he'd spelled it out for your mama. I'll bet if we were to go over to the bank and look in one of the floorboards in his old office, we'd find confirmation, but I'll tell you about that later. We gotta find Henry Clay . . . and Tess, first." He ran his hands through his hair and walked to the window, as if the answer was out on the sidewalk.

Lou followed him, wringing her hands. "But why would the detective say we didn't want to know what happened to Daddy, if it was Nate who killed him?"

"Lou, I suspect the private detective was paid off. Nate probably spread the gossip about your daddy bein' involved in the bank heist, too."

"Well I'll be battered and fried," Lou said, staring into space.

YOU CAN PUT A PORCUPINE
IN A WOOD CHIPPER,
BUT YOU WILL NOT MAKE
MAPLE SYRUP

<u>gotcherself</u>: verb \gotch-yohr-self\ got yourself
You gotcherself in a heap a trouble.

[July 2010]

The truck slowed and came to a stop. Tess heard the hum of a small motor and gears working somewhere. The truck moved forward, then stopped, and the engine died. She heard the sound of the motor again and a *clunk* that sounded like a garage door hitting the ground. The trunk rocked as the two men got out of the vehicle and slammed the doors shut. Tess heard Willy barking orders.

"Cut the 'lectricity on them doors, Joe Bob, while I call the boss. We don't want nobody comin' along and tryin' to get in."

"Yeah, Boss—calm down," Willy said. "I know that wadn't part of the plan—"

Silence.

"We couldn't hep it—"

Silence.

"What choice did we have?" His voice grew more faint until a door slammed shut, and the only thing Tess could hear was a sniffling sound beside her, and Joe Bob whistling "When The Saints Go Marching In."

She waited until she heard Joe Bob's footsteps disappear too, and then putting her mouth as close to the crack in the trunk as she could, she said, "Martha Maye? Is that you?" She heard a gasp.

"Tessie? Oh my gosh! It *is* you in that trunk," Martha Maye whispered. "I tried to tell myself it wasn't you I heard in your driveway, but it sounded like you, and—"

"Yes, it's me," Tess interrupted. "Are you okay?" She strained to talk through the crack in the wood.

"I'm okay, but that trunk ain't big enough to cuss the cat in. How'd they get you in there? You do still got all your body parts, don't ya?"

"Of course I do, but it's a tight squeeze. I can't feel my left foot, and my neck's killing me, but I'm all in one piece…Martha Maye, I can't see anything. Where are we? What's happening?"

"I don't know what's goin' on. One minute I was talkin' to Willy in your driveway, the next I was trussed up like a chicken and thrown into the truck bed. They put a big blue tarp over us and now, goin' by the smells, and the sound of that garage door, I'd say we're in old man Crowley's fillin' station, which is not indicative of anything good, 'cause I heard he closed it down and went on vacation for the week." She stopped talking for a moment, and Tess heard a rustling sound. Martha Maye said, "Yep. I just peeked out of the tarp. We're in one of the bays. What do you think they're gonna do with us?"

"I don't know, Martha Maye."

"Tess . . . "

"Yes?"

"I'm scareder than a porcupine in a nudist colony."

"Don't worry, we'll get out of here. Somehow."

Tess heard more rustling and felt movement in the truck bed, and then she heard a scratching sound on the trunk.

"What are you doing?" Tess asked.

"Tryin' to pick the lock with my bobby pin. Fortunately, I decided to wear my hair up today. Just hold on, I'll get you out in a jiffy."

"Where are they? They won't see you, will they?"

"Naw, I think they're in the office, and there's a car in between us and them."

It took a few minutes, but she managed to pick the lock and open the trunk lid.

"Martha Maye—I thought they tied you up," Tess said, sitting up and rubbing her neck.

"They did." Martha Maye helped Tess out of the trunk. "But

apparently neither one of 'em was a boy scout. They can't tie knots worth a lick. I got outta them in no time. But I didn't want them to see me movin' back here, so I stayed still."

"That was good thinking."

As Tess looked around at the surroundings, she sat in the truck bed stretching her legs and feet, rotating her head in a circle to work the pain out of her neck, and shaking her arms to get the blood circulating. A car was up on hydraulics between them and the door to the office, where she figured the men were. The garage doors had windows, but there was nothing and nobody outside.

"What in the world is goin' on, Tessie? Why did they grab you and put you in the trunk?"

"Martha Maye, do you know that co-worker of your grandfather's? Nate Hunter?"

"Yeah, sure . . . "

"Does he have any family still living in Goose Pimple Junction?"

"Wull, a course he does. Nate Hunter was a friend of my grandfather's. He was so nice to us after the murder; he kinda took us under his wing—"

"Martha Maye!" Tess interrupted impatiently. "Are any of his relatives still living here?"

"Well, yeah, you see John Ed married Medora, Nate's daughter. John Ed, Medora, and Mama grew up together, just as Henry Clay and I did . . . "

Tess couldn't believe her ears. She felt like someone had punched her in the stomach. "You're kidding . . . J . . . John Ed?" Tess stammered.

" . . . was Nate's son-in-law. Yeah. Tessie, what's goin' on?"

"John Ed? I knew he was a good for nothing so-and-so, but I didn't think he was capable of all this . . . "

"What are you talkin' about, sugar?"

"Well, the short version is Jack and I found a letter in the old trunk last night. It's from your grandfather, written right before he was killed, and he points the finger at Nate Hunter."

Martha Maye went still as a statue. The color drained from her face. "You mean to say that John Ed's behind all this? No, I can't believe it. It can't be."

"I'll bet there's proof in the floorboards at the bank. Willy must be workin' for him, but what I don't know is how they knew that *we* knew."

Martha Maye blinked back tears. "I know how they knew."

"How?"

"After y'all left with the trunk last night, I thought Henry Clay acted kinda strange. He was real antsy, ya know? And then, all of a sudden he had to go home and check on somethin'."

"You mean you think Henry Clay was in on it?"

"I don't know, I'm just tellin' ya what happened last night," Martha Maye said.

"So you think one of them was at my house last night, watching us?" She thought of Jack and her rolling around on the floor and blushed. "Oh my . . . "

The ladies heard a car drive up outside, and they looked up to see Henry Clay getting out of his car.

"Well, shave my legs and call me smoothy," Martha Maye whispered, bug-eyed. She stared out the window at Henry Clay like she was in a trance. "I heard Willy say he was callin' the boss. Now Henry Clay shows up here. Tessie, you don't think . . . "

"Yes, I do think, Martha Maye. I think Henry Clay's in this up to his eyeballs. Quick—get back under the tarp, and try to make it look like you're still tied up. I'm going to grab a crowbar and hide on the side of the truck. Hopefully, they'll think I'm still in the trunk. If we get the chance to get Henry Clay alone, I think we can take him. If you can, try to distract him and get him to turn his back to me. Just say . . . oh I don't know...*trunk*. When I hear you say that I'll fly out and, whomp," Tess made a practice hit into her palm, "I'll hit him over the head. Hurry up, he's coming. Oh, and don't act like you know anything. Act like you think he's here to save us."

Martha Maye lay back down, while Tess closed the trunk lid, covered her back up with the tarp, then climbed over the side of the truck and crouched down.

Loud voices came from the office, but Tess couldn't hear what was being said. Suddenly, the voices got louder, and Tess heard Henry Clay say, "Stay here. I wanna talk to 'em first."

First? She heard footsteps coming toward the truck.

He peeled back the tarp, and Tess could hear rustling and then, "Oh Henry Clay! I'm so glad you're here! You gotta save us! Those men . . ." she began crying.

"Shh . . . shush now, Mart. It's gonna be okay. Tell me what happened."

Martha Maye quickly relayed the events of the past thirty minutes, leaving out the fact that she knew Tess had been in the trunk, or that she was no longer in there.

"So . . . what's in the trunk?"

"I don't know. Why would they want it? Why'd they grab me and truss me up like a chicken?"

"Martha Maye. I've known you all my life and been in love with you for over half of it. I think there's something you're not tellin' me. Spill it."

Martha Maye sniffed, and her voice grew hard. "Why don't *you* spill it, Henry Clay? Tell the truth, and shame the devil. Your granddaddy killed mine, didn't he?"

Tess heard feet shuffling. He let out a heavy sigh. "Yeah, Mart," he said softly. "Well, he and Brick Lynch. I don't rightly know who actually pulled the trigger. But my granddaddy had aspirations of becomin' president of the bank, and your granddaddy was goin' to ruin that for him. He had to do it."

"Oh no he didn't, Henry Clay. Just like you don't have to do this. Have you taken leave of your senses?"

"Martha Maye, I promised him. I promised him I wouldn't let the world find out it was him. I wanted to stop all this from gettin' out, to save my family's reputation, and because I love you."

"And I suppose you wantin' to be governor dudn't have anything to do with it."

"A scandal woulda ruined any chance of that, it's true. I wanted to be somebody you'd be proud of. Things just got outta hand, is all. I'm sorry. I'm so, so sorry."

"You can stuff your sorries in a sack, mister! You ain't right in the head. But even so, I know you don't wanna hurt either of us. You gotta come clean and end this nonsense."

"Either of you? I thought you said you didn't know what was in that trunk."

"Henry, stop your jibber-jabberin'. You can put a porcupine in a wood chipper, but you will not make maple syrup."

"What's that supposed to mean?"

"Means you are who you are. You gotcherself into a heap of poop, and you ain't gonna come out smellin' like a magnolia. What are you gonna do? Kill Tess *and* me? And then what? You'll have to kill Jack, and then Mama, and then—" she broke off and whispered, "Butterbean." She took in a shaky breath. "It's time to stop all this, Henry."

Tess peeked around the truck.

"All right. If that's how you feel." Henry Clay stood with his hands on his hips and barked, "Willy!"

"Huh?"

"You cut the electricity off to these bay doors?"

"Duh."

"Don't you sass me, boy. Didja lock 'em?"

"Well, no, you didn't say to do that."

"Do I have to tell you everything? Come out here, lock the doors, and throw me the key. Then you go find Jack. And Pickle. Bring 'em on back here. Take my car." Tess heard the sound of keys being caught in a hand.

Her legs, back, and neck were hurting from being locked up in the trunk and from squatting behind the truck, so she knelt on her hands and knees, craning her neck around the back of the truck to see what was going on. She saw Henry Clay swipe his hand over his face, and she ducked back behind the side of the truck. Hearing squeaking and feeling the truck rock a bit, she figured he'd sat down on the tailgate. She thought about trying to strike him from that position, but decided against it.

Willy locked both garage doors, and said, "Heads up, boss."

Tess heard a key fall on the concrete floor. Looking under the truck, she saw it had landed at Henry Clay's feet, and Martha Maye got to it before he could.

"Let me have it, Martha Maye." The truck rocked as Henry Clay stood up.

"Why? So you can kill us?"

Crouching on her hands and knees, Tess watched under the truck as Martha Maye's feet moved backward toward the front of the bay.

"Who says I'm gonna kill you?" He stepped toward her. She took another step back, and he followed, as did Tess, duck walking.

"Well, what *are* you gonna do?" Martha Maye asked, continuing to back up toward the front of the truck.

"I haven't quite figured that out," he said, following her.

"While you're figurin', can we let Tess outta that TRUNK?"

Tess had slowly worked her way around the back of the truck, holding the crowbar, as they were moving toward the front. At the word, "trunk," she leapt up and with all her might, hit Henry Clay over the head with the crowbar. He fell like a sack of potatoes.

The office door sprang open, and Joe Bob called out, "HC? Everythin' okay out here?"

Tess stepped over Henry Clay, putting her finger to her lips and motioning to Martha Maye to keep moving toward the front of the truck. As Joe Bob came out to check on Henry Clay, they tiptoed to the front of the car that was up on hydraulics.

"HC! Buzzard on a buzzsaw! What'd they do to you?"

When Joe Bob bent down to check on Henry Clay, the women made a dash for the office. They pushed the big metal desk in front of the door, just as he reached it and started pounding. Tess pulled Martha Maye down in front of the desk two seconds before bullets started pelting the door.

IT'S SO HOT YOU CAN PULL
A BAKED POTATO
RIGHT OUT OF THE GROUND

<u>Idjit</u>: noun \ idj-it\ idiot
He was acting like an idjit.

[July 2010]

"Cut the light off, Jack," Lou said, as she walked ahead of Jack and Pickle out of the bookstore.

"Lou, I'm sure you won't have any trouble finding Martha Maye," Jack said to reassure her.

"She'd best be at home." Lou locked the bookstore door. Without another word she took off to find Martha Maye as fast as her Easy Spirit Oxfords would allow.

"I need you to think, Pickle. Where do you think Henry Clay might have taken Tess?"

"I don't know, sir. I really don't. But if I had to guess, I'd say Willy's in on it. I seen 'em together, and here he comes." He pointed down the street to Willy, who had parked and was walking toward them.

He walked the half block to his prey, calling, "Mr. Wright!"

Wearing a black denim jacket and black jeans, he walked up to Jack and said in an overly friendly tone, "Just the man I was lookin' for. And if it idn't his trusty sidekick, Boy Wonder. I'd say it's very fortuitence . . . fortuit . . . lucky I found you, too."

"It's a hundred and forty-six degrees out here, Willy. Why're you wearin' a jacket?" Jack looked at him with a mixture of annoyance and suspicion.

Willy's smile turned from friendly to threatening. He pulled a gun, keeping it partially hidden beneath his jacket, and said, "*Gotta keep this little piece of metal outta sight, Jack.* Now come on, let's go." Willy motioned with the gun for them to walk toward Henry Clay's car.

"Forget it, Willy. I'm not goin' anywhere with you. And Pickle's goin' home."

"I don't think that would be in the best interest of y'all's health. Pickle, don't you make a move, except over to that there car," Willy snarled.

"Uh, Jack, idn't that Henry Clay's car he's drivin'?" Pickle pointed toward the Cadillac.

Jack's head whipped around from Pickle to Willy. "What in tarnation have you done with Tess?" Jack narrowed his eyes, still not budging.

"Ah, the lovely Mizz Tess. That's one fine woman, let me tell you. Had she chosen me over you, things might have turned out different. But she didn't, and here we are—"

Jack lunged for Willy, but the gun came up between them. "GUN trumps fists every time, Ratchetfoot."

Jack backed up slightly, glaring at Willy. "If you've so much as touched one hair on her head . . . "

Willy laughed. "Ha! It don't look to me like you're in much of a position to be threatenin' me, mister. Looka who's got the gun and looka who don't."

Jack started at Willy again, but the little man poked the gun into Jack's stomach and said, "Ah, ah, ah! Mind your manners! I already killed one idjit this week. I don't mind a'tall makin' it two . . ." he glanced at Pickle, "...or three," he said with a menacing grin.

"Leave Pickle out of this," Jack said through gritted teeth.

"No can-do, buckaroo. Kid knows too much."

"Is John Ed in on this, too?"

"Aw, hell no. That old coot's a gutless wonder. Naw, he probably suspected who it was but didn't want to find out he was right."

"So who did the mugging? You or Henry Clay?" Jack asked. "I mean, I need to thank whoever it was for the bump they put on the back of my head."

"Well you can thank me for that bump, Jack. Want another one? How about two this time? One, if you don't stop askin' so many questions and another one if you don't start movin' toward that car." Again, he motioned with the gun, but this time he jerked his head toward the car too.

"Where is she, Willy? What have you done with her?" Jack hissed.

"Well if you'll get in the car you can see for your galderned self." Willy was getting exasperated.

"Buddy, I will come back from the grave to personally take you apart piece by piece if you've so much as touched Tess with your pinky."

"Yeah, yeah, yeah. Talk's cheap. Get movin', pretty boy. You don't wanna be late for your appointment with your maker."

"I told you I'm not goin' anywhere with you," Jack snarled. "What're you gonna do? Shoot me right here on the sidewalk in the middle of town in broad daylight?"

Willy pulled out a cell phone from his pocket. "Well then, I'll hafta make me a little call, and see if we can listen in while Joe Bob persuades the fine Mizz Tess to persuade *you*."

Jack looked around the empty town square. It was so hot out, even at ten in the morning no one was lingering outdoors. The humidity hung in the air like a sauna, making people want to go straight from air-conditioned car to air-conditioned store as quickly as possible. Jack began moving slowly, hoping for a chance to catch the eye of someone coming out of a store.

"Where are we going? What's your brilliant plan once you have us all in one place?" he taunted as they began walking, Jack and Pickle side-by-side, and Willy behind them, the gun pointed at their backs.

"First we're gonna go get that nosey girlfriend of yours, and then we're all gonna take a long drive out to the country. It's so sad that Goose Pimple Junction's about to have itself a bona fide tragedy. I can see the newspaper headlines now, *'Four die in fiery crash. Willy Clayton hailed as a hero for his rescue attempts.'*" Willy made a fake crying sound.

"Four? Whaddaya mean four? I'da thought even a dunderhead like you could count Tess, Pickle and me equals three."

"Har har har. You think you're so smart, but you ain't because you don't know all there is to know."

"Huh?" Jack and Pickle said, gaping at each other.

Looking smug, Willy said, "We got Martha Maye too, smarty britches. That woman has one big mouth. And she was in the wrong place at the wrong time. Just like you two are gonna be in just a little short while."

They were getting closer to Henry Clay's car. Out of the corner of his eye, Jack noticed Pickle slowly put a finger over the lettering on his t-shirt that said, "I Make Stuff Up." Jack turned his head slightly to look at Pickle, who tapped his finger and raised one eyebrow. Jack gave an almost imperceptible nod.

Pickle said, "Say, Silly—I mean, Willy, did you know Skeeter Duke's a sharpshooter?"

"No, I did not. But it don't matter. He ain't gonna find y'all in time to sharp shoot anything. Now keep movin' and stop whinin'."

"Uh...Wull...lookie there." Pickle motioned with his head to across the street. "Speak of the devil. There's Officer Duke now, with his shot-gun pointed right smack dab at your ugly head. Hello there, Officer!" Pickle called out, waving, and looking to his right. It was just enough of a distraction to make Willy look away briefly and lower his gun slightly. Pickle jumped to his right, and Jack jumped to his left.

The gun fired.

THAT BOY'S CHEESE DONE SLID OFF
HIS CRACKER

<u>sitcheeation</u>: noun \ sich-ee-ey-shuhn\ situation
Let me tell you the sitcheeation.

[July 2010]

The left front tire of Henry Clay's car hissed and deflated when the bullet hit it. Jack charged at Willy, grinding and stomping on his foot, grabbing his hand with the gun, and twisting it behind his back. The revolver fell to the ground and Pickle scurried to pick it up. Once he had the gun and the real danger was over, his legs gave out and he sat down on the curb, chanting, "Oh crap, oh crap, oh crap oh crap."

Both Jack and Willy got punches in at each other before Skeeter and Hank came running from the diner with guns drawn.

The three of them wrestled Willy to the ground, and Jack began pounding his face with fist after fist. Skeeter pulled Jack away and Hank jumped between them asking, "What on God's green earth is goin' on?"

"This birdbrain has Tess and Martha Maye," Jack screamed. "He was tryin' to kidnap Pickle and me and take us all somewhere and kill us, make it look like an accident." Jack kicked Willy in the ribs, hard.

Willy moaned. "No, no, no. He attacked *me*! Right here in broad daylight!"

"You lyin' piece of vermin . . . " Hank struggled to hold Jack back.

"I heard a shot. Are y'all all right?" Skeeter asked.

"The bullet hit the tire over there." Jack pointed toward the Cadillac and the deflated tire. "We need some handcuffs and a jail cell for this big bad-wannabe man." He waited a beat and added, "Oh, and some clean shorts for Pickle." Jack winked at him. "You okay?"

Pickle nodded.

Hank took the gun from Pickle, while Skeeter handcuffed Willy, pulled him up, threw him against the building, kicked his legs apart with his foot, and patted him down.

"What'd he want with you two? And you said he has Tess and Martha Maye? Has 'em where?"

Jack walked over to Willy, grabbed his hair, pulling his head back so he could look him in the eye. He yelled, "Where are they, bonehead?"

Willy smirked silently.

Suddenly a long, shrill whistle pierced the air followed by two short bursts.

Jack let go of Willy's head with a push, broke into a huge smile, and said, "That's my girl!" He turned to the officers. "I'll fill y'all in later. Come on! They're at the fillin' station!"

Jack, Hank, and Pickle took off running, while Skeeter took Willy to the squad car.

As they ran almost two blocks to the filling station, Hank spotted a state police cruiser and waved him down, hollering and pointing, "The fillin' station! Head over there!"

He called to Jack as they ran, "Thank the good Lord above! We called the staties a while ago, on account of the coroner's findings. We knew we couldn't trust John Ed."

They were nearing the back of the station when Hank pulled on Jack's shirt. "Jack! Hold up. We need a plan. You can't just go runnin' up to the door. We don't know what's goin' on in there."

They stopped at the side of the building just as John Ed's cruiser screeched to a halt in front of the station, and the state trooper pulled in at the back of the building.

"'Bout time you got here!" Hank called out to the trooper. "All hell's done broke loose since I called ya."

A huge man in a state trooper's uniform got out of the vehicle and walked toward the group, putting his hat on his head. His size, dark hair, and even darker eyes gave him an intimidating appearance. He was the type who could either be your real good friend or your worst enemy.

"Holy cannoli," Pickle said in awe. "Talk about yer redwoods." Pickle stood, gawking up at the well-built trooper who must've stood six-feet-five and was all muscle.

"Folks call him Paul Bunyan," Hank whispered out of the side of his mouth, then introduced the officer as Trooper Johnny Butterfield.

Buck came running down the sidewalk from City Hall and joined Jack's group, which had congregated on the side of the building. Shortly after Buck's arrival, Skeeter rolled up in his police car, with Willy hand-cuffed in the back seat. The officer got out and jogged toward the group.

"I did some old fashioned persuadin' with old Willy," Skeeter said. "Henry Clay and Joe Bob are in there, sure 'nough, with Tess and Martha Maye."

"Oh, Lord," Lou cried, overhearing him as she rushed up to the group. She grabbed Pickle and hugged him tight. "What's goin' on?" Her hands were shaking, and her eyes were filled with tears.

Suddenly a shot rang out from the garage bays, hitting the police chief's car. John Ed ducked back behind it.

"Hey now! You knock that nonsense off right now, ya hear?" John Ed called out.

Jack said, "I'm not waiting another second. I'm going around front for a look-see." He disappeared around the front of the building before anyone could stop him. The garage bays jutted out farther than the office did, and the brick wall obstructed the garage's view of the office door.

He tried the office doorknob, but it was locked. The door had six paned windows on the top half, and he looked through the window and locked eyes with Tess who was crouched in front of the metal desk. When she saw Jack, she ran to the door.

Jack said, "Oh thank you, Lord." Then to Tess he hollered, "Are you all right?"

Tess shouted, "We're locked in here. It's a keyed deadbolt lock on both sides of the door. Can you spring us?" Just then, a shot splintered through the thick office door, joining half a dozen other bullet marks that Joe Bob had made just a few minutes earlier. Tess hit the deck. A bullet hit the Coca Cola machine that had been in that same spot for over fifty years. One of the mini Coke bottles shattered as a bullet hit it.

Hank and the statie came up behind Jack. Butterfield nudged Jack aside and called out, "Stand aside, ma'am." Tess and Martha Maye duck walked to the left of the door where they crouched and locked arms, holding on to one another.

Butterfield kicked once, twice, and the third time it busted open. Tess came flying out and into Jack's arms, running to him with such force she almost knocked him down. Martha Maye ran out, flapping her hands like a chicken, and straight into the arms of the surprised state trooper.

"Nice to meetcha," he sputtered.

"Sweet mother of all that is Good and Holy!" Jack grabbed Tess, enveloping her with his arms. "Are you sure you're all right?"

Tess nodded against his chest, holding him tight. "It was Henry Clay, Jack! Henry Clay's Nate's grandson."

"I know darlin', I figured it out. Sorry it took me so long." He hugged her close to him and she held on.

Buck rounded the corner with Lou, who looked at Tess and said, "That grip looks like she might not ever let go."

Lou ran to Martha Maye. "Heavens t' Betsy! My precious girl. Let me look at you. Are y'all all right?" Lou took the trooper's place, and alternated between squeezing Martha Maye's face so tight she looked like a fish, to hugging her with fervor. A shot rang out again, this one hitting the police cruiser.

"If you want to fight me, you better pack a lunch and bring a flashlight," John Ed hollered to Joe Bob. Another shot rang out.

Butterfield corralled everyone back to the side of the building, telling Skeeter to go tell John Ed his son and Joe Bob were in the garage bay. He started toward the chief, as Joe Bob yelled out, "Once I get my hands on you, I'ma whip you like cornbread."

Martha Maye began talking a blue streak, telling everyone what had happened as she held on tight to her mother.

"Henry Clay's out cold, but Joe Bob has a gun, and we moved the desk in front of the door, to keep him at bay—" she broke off laughing, "...at bay, in the bays . . . " She was close to hysteria over her ordeal, and her unintentional pun nearly pushed her over the edge. "We have the key to the garage doors," she handed them to the trooper, "but we couldn't get out of the office on account of the door bein' deadbolted and we didn't have the key for *it* and—"

"Hold it, hold it!" Jack made a T with his hands. "Henry Clay's out cold? How?"

"Tessie here packs a mean wallop, 'specially with a tire iron." Martha Maye patted Tess's back.

Hank turned to the state trooper. "Here's the sitcheeation. The dude doin' the shootin' is so dumb he couldn't pour rain out of a boot, with a hole in the toe, and directions on the heel. So while he's distracted with John Ed out front there, I say we sneak in through the back and surprise him."

"Why don't you just go through the office door?" Lou asked.

"No, no! The noise of the desk being moved will draw his attention. We can sneak up on him through the back way. If Henry Clay's unconscious, and he's distracted with John Ed, it'll be a piece of cake," Hank said.

"Sounds like a plan." The trooper and Hank started for the back of the building.

Another shot rang out, and as the two men walked around back, Jack heard the trooper say, "I think that boy's cheese done slid off his cracker."

"None of the three ain't got any walkin' around sense, that's for sure," Jack said. "And to think I was gonna vote for Henry Clay."

Jack herded everyone to the back of the building, while officers Butterfield and Beanblossom went for Joe Bob.

"Joe Bob, zat you? You dang fool, quit them shenanigans, and get yourself on out here," John Ed called out. "You got a hurt man in there who needs medical attention."

"I won't, Chief! You'll have to shoot me dead!"

"Son, it's time to paint your butt white and run with the antelope," the chief hollered out.

Tess, still holding onto Jack, raised her head to look at him.

"He means to . . . "

Tess interrupted and answered for him, "He means to quit fussin' and do the right thing."

Jack used his exaggerated twang, "Very good, Mary T. I b'lieve you've done gradjeeated in southern speak!" He hugged her tightly, rocking her gently side to side.

Moments later, one of the garage doors opened, and Hank escorted Joe Bob out of the building and toward the trooper's patrol car. Butterfield went for John Ed, who had already surrendered his weapon to the mayor.

"I wanna see my son," John Ed yelled.

They'd handcuffed Henry Clay, and he was coming-to when Lou

marched into the garage behind the trooper and John Ed. Before anyone could say a word, Lou walked up to him and with hands on her ample hips said, "Henry Clay, you are rude, crude, grossly unattractive, your feet stink, your mother makes your clothes, and you don't love your Jesus."

Then she turned and stalked off while everyone stared after her.

* * *

Hours later, sitting around Lou's big pine kitchen table, Martha Maye served cake. "You mean this whole thing was over a reputation?"

"Greed, reputation, love. All powerful motivators," Jack said.

"But yeah, it does all boil down to reputation," Tess said. "John Hobb was killed because Nate Hunter didn't want his reputation hurt; Henry Clay was protecting his and his grandfather's reputation; while John Ed was protecting his own, and Henry Clay's. He looked the other way because he suspected his son was involved."

"I still can't believe the hurtin' Tessie put on old Henry Clay!" Martha Maye said, shaking her head. "Lands sakes, you sure did a number on him! Y'all shoulda seen her in action. When they loaded him in that ambulance, it looked like you'd beat him with an ugly stick, Tess."

"Ugly stick, hell, he looked like he fell out of an ugly tree and hit every branch on the way down," Lou said.

"Well, I'm relieved he's going to be okay," Tess said. "I wanted him out of commission, but I didn't want him dead."

"I 'spect he'll have one mighty fine headache for at least a week," Jack said. "And a ringing sound in his head for even longer." Everyone laughed.

The doorbell rang, and Butterbean yelled, "I'll get it."

Moments later, the state trooper walked into the kitchen. "Evenin' folks, pardon the interruption. I just wanted to tell y'all that sure enough, just like you predicted," he looked at Tess and Jack, "two thousand dollars was found under the floorboard in an office at the First National Bank." He chuckled and shook his head. "Poor old Henry Clay was walkin' around it all that time, and his grandfather did the same. They never knew it." He shook his head. "How's that for irony? Uh . . . " he cleared his throat, "I also wanted to make sure everyone's all right." He looked at Martha Maye, who lit up like a red pepper.

"Well, isn't that the sweetest thing! In all the commotion over at the fillin' station I don't think we were properly introduced. I'm Martha Maye . . . " she got up to shake his hand.

Johnny blushed and stuck his hand out. "Yes ma'am. We've howdied, and . . . uh . . . hugged, but we ain't shook yet. I'm Johnny Butterfield." He wiped the sweat off his brow.

"Have a seat, Trooper Butterfield, how 'bout I cut you a nice big slice of chocolate cake?" Martha Maye smiled up at him.

"Just Johnny will be fine. And thank ya, ma'am. Thank ya ver' much."

Johnny pulled his eyes from Martha Maye and said, "I also wanted to tell y'all that John Ed has resigned his position as police chief. He's under review for hinderin' an investigation."

"Who's gonna be police chief?" Lou asked.

"Well . . . the position's open. And they're takin' applications," he added, darting a glance at Martha Maye.

Tess said, "What I don't understand is why John Ed overlooked all the mayhem? If he wasn't in on it with Henry Clay—"

Johnny broke in, "Hank asked him that, actually. He won't admit it, but I think after the first break in, Henry Clay told him not to look into anything at the old Hobb house. After that, I think he just assumed Henry Clay was involved."

There was another knock at the front door, and Lou craned her neck around the edge of the kitchen door. "Shh . . . y'all be quiet now. Charlotte's here. Not another word 'bout her daddy and granddaddy, ya hear?"

Butterbean ushered in Charlotte and Pickle, who was carrying two suitcases.

"There's the man of the hour," Jack said. "That was some quick thinkin' you did under pressure, Pickle. I'm proud of ya. And grateful." He clapped Pickle on the back and everyone cheered. Pickle blushed.

"Thank you, Mizz Louetta, for lettin' me stay here," Charlotte said softly.

"Oh law, child. I wouldn't have it any other way. Now come on, I'll take you up and get you settled. This way, Charlotte . . . you too, Pickle."

"That was really nice of you all to take Charlotte in like you're doin'," Tess said to Martha Maye after the three had gone upstairs.

"Well, it kinda seems we're bound by the same tragedy. She's prob'ly the one hurt most out of all this. Her mother ran off a few years ago and never looked back. Now she's lost her daddy and granddaddy, too, in one fell swoop. Henry Clay for sure will do time, and John Ed prob'ly will. She didn't have anywhere else to go, and we're glad to take her in. She's gonna need some TLC. Mama's good at that. And b'sides, we'll have a built-in babysitter."

"Or two. It looks like Pickle might be around here a lot now, too," Lou said, coming back into the room.

Jack stood and said, "Well, we'd better be on our way, folks. It's been a long day."

Lou hugged Tess. "Honey, you take tomorrow off, now, ya hear? You rest up."

"If you insist," she said, as Jack grabbed her hand and pulled her toward the door.

"She insists," he said firmly. "Trooper Butterfield, thank you for all you did today. We 'preshade it more than we can say."

"Just doin' my duty, and call me Johnny," Butterfield said.

"Thank you, Johnny," Tess said.

"Goodnight, y'all!" Jack and Tess said together, leaving the kitchen. Jack looked at her with a smile in his eyes and whispered, "You're turning into a Southern Belle already."

"Night, you two," Martha Maye said almost as an afterthought. She was preoccupied watching Johnny.

Lou followed them to the door. "I swan, y'all are cuter 'n a sack of puppies. Jackson, you haven't let go of her hand for one second today. Just be sure you let her go tinkle by herself now, ya hear?"

"Yes, ma'am. And thanks for dinner, Lou. Goodnight." They both waved and stepped out onto the porch.

Outside, he put his arm around Tess. "Hey pretty lady, wanna come to my house and eat green M&M's?"

Tess smiled, put her head on his shoulder, and answered, "Absolutely, Vernon. Absolutely."

The End

ABOUT THE AUTHOR

Amy Metz is the mother of two sons and is a former first grade teacher. When not actively engaged in writing, enjoying her family, or spoiling her dog Cooper, and granddogs Gage and Arlo, Amy can usually be found with a mixing spoon, camera, or book in her hands. She lives in Louisville, Kentucky and can be reached at:

amymetz.com.

CPSIA information can be obtained at www.ICGtesting.com
Printed in the USA
LVOW120532130912

298625LV00002B/1/P